The Bride Wore Red Boots

The Bride Wore Red Boots

A Seven Brides for Seven Cowboys Novel

LIZBETH SELVIG

AVONIMPULSE
An Imprint of HarperCollinsPublishers

Excerpt from *The Bride Wore Denim* copyright © 2015 by Lizbeth Selvig.
Excerpt from *Right Wrong Guy* copyright © 2015 by Lia Riley.
Excerpt from *Desire Me More* copyright © 2015 by Tiffany Clare.
Excerpt from *Make Me* copyright © 2015 by Tessa Bailey.

EPub Edition SEPTEMBER 2015 ISBN: 9780062413949

Print Edition ISBN: 9780062413956

AM 10 9 8 7 6 5 4 3 2 1

To Evie,
for someday.
When it comes time to choose your destiny,
no matter how old or young you are,
I hope you take the path that leads toward your heart.
—Nana

Acknowledgments

AS ALWAYS, THE biggest thanks go to my family. My husband, Jan, who is the inspiration for every romance hero I ever write. My adult kids, who wish they had a nickel for every time I say "I don't know how this is going to get finished" and then act proud when I actually get it done. My parents, who passed down their creative genes and then encouraged me to use them. My sister-in-law Robin, who is a most wonderful groupie (everyone needs a groupie). And all my sibs, aunts, and uncles who are the best PR team I could have!

I couldn't do this without my critique partners, Ellen Lindseth, Nancy Holland, and Naomi Stone, who are so talented in their own "writes," and who are my biggest inspirations.

My agent, Elizabeth Winick Rubinstein, is my driving force and never lets me go very long without checking in and taking my pulse to make sure I'm still acting like a healthy writer. My books are where they are because of her.

My Avon Impulse editor Tessa Woodward is also brilliant. Do you know what she called this book? "Pure Lizbeth magic." There is NO higher compliment from a boss, and I'm honored she is mine.

Thank you to Dr. Benjamin VanVranken, an internal medicine specialist at the VA Medical Center in Minneapolis, Minnesota (a.k.a. my son-in-law), who was my medical expert for this book. He answered questions anytime, often during work hours, and gave me all the numbers I needed for authenticity. Any mistakes in the medical information in this book are solely mine.

Thank you to Velma B. Johnston (1912–1977), a.k.a. Wild Horse Annie, who brought the mustang to life for me when I was very young. She fought to end mistreatment of wild mustangs in the '50s, and pushed for laws that protected America's mustangs for the future.

Author's Note

THE ROCK SPRINGS Mustang Holding Facility in Rock Springs, Wyoming, is a real place. Although there is no "Claire" as in my book, there is definitely a caring staff for the 700 wild mustangs that are rounded up in annual Bureau of Land Management (BLM) Horse Management Area gatherings. These animals are available on a first-come first-served basis for adoption by qualified individuals.

For more information visit http://www.blm.gov/wy/st/en/programs/Wild_Horses/rs-wh-facility.html

Also, BLM Extreme Mustang Makeover competitions are real events, and every year professional and amateur trainers show what amazing and versatile animals the hardy mustangs are. Competitions and challenges are held across the US.

For information visit: http://extrememustangmakeover.com/

DR. AMELIA CROCKETT adored the kids. She just hated clowns. Standing resignedly beside Bitsy Blueberry, Amelia scanned the group of twenty or so young patients gathered for a Halloween party in the pediatric playroom at NYC General Hospital. She didn't see the one child she was looking for, however.

Some children wore super-hero-themed hospital gowns and colorful robes that served as costumes. Others dressed up more traditionally—including three fairies, two princesses, a Harry Potter, and a Darth Vader. Gauze bandage helmets had been decorated like everything from a baseball to a mummy's head. More than one bald scalp was adorned with alien-green paint or a yellow smiley face. Mixed in with casts, wheelchairs, and IV poles on castors, there were also miles of smiles. The kids didn't hate the clown.

Amelia adjusted the stethoscope around her neck, more a prop than a necessary item at this event, and glared—her sisters would call it the hairy eyeball—at Bitsy Blueberry's wild blue wig. Bitsy thrust one hand forward, aimed one of those obnoxious, old-fashioned, bicycle horns-with-a-bulb that were as requisite to clowning as giant shoes and red noses, at Amelia's face and honked at her rudely. Three times.

Amelia smiled and whispered at Bitsy through gritted teeth. "I detest impertinent clowns, you know. I can have you fired."

She wasn't *afraid* of clowns. She simply found them unnecessary and a waste of talent, and Bitsy Blueberry was a perfect example. Beneath the white grease paint, red nose, hideous blue wig, and pinafore-and-pantaloons costume that looked like Raggedy Ann on psychedelic drugs was one of the smartest, most dedicated pediatric nurses in the world—Amelia's best friend, Brooke Squires.

"Look who's here, boys and girls." Bitsy grabbed her by the elbow and pulled her unceremoniously to the front of the room, honking in time with Amelia's steps all the way. "It's Dr. Mia Crockett!"

She might as well have said Justin Bieber or One Direction for the cheer that went up from the kids. It was the effect Bitsy's squeaky falsetto voice had on them. Then again, they'd cheer a stinky skunk wrangler if it meant forgetting, for even a short time, the real reasons they were in the hospital. That understanding was all that kept Amelia from cuffing her friend upside the head to knock some sense into it. She waved—a tiny rocking motion of her wrist—at the assemblage of sick children.

"Dr. Mia doesn't look very party ready, do you think?" Bitsy/Brooke asked. "Isn't that sad?"

"Not funny," Amelia said through the side of her mouth, her smile plastered in place.

Bitsy pulled a black balloon from her pinafore pocket and blew it into a long tube. Great. Balloon animals.

"I know a secret about Dr. Mia," Bitsy said. "Would you like to know what it is?"

Unsurprisingly, a chorus of yesses filled the room.

"She…" Bitsy dragged the word out suggestively, "is related to Davy Crockett. Do you know who Davy Crockett was?"

The relationship was true thanks to a backwoods ninth cousin somewhere in the 1800s, but Mia rolled her eyes again while a cacophony of shouts followed the question. As Bitsy explained about Davy and hunting and the Alamo, she tied off the black balloon and blew up a brown one. She twisted them intricately until she had a braided circle with a tail.

"You're kidding me," Mia said when she saw the finished product.

"That's pretty cool about Davy Crockett, right?" Bitsy asked. "But what isn't cool is that Dr. Mia has no costume. So I made her something. What did I tell you Davy Crockett wore?"

"Coonskin cap!" One little boy shouted the answer from his seat on the floor at the front of the group.

Mia smiled at him, one of a handful of nonsurgical patients she knew from her rounds here on the pediatric floor. Most of her time these days was spent in surgery and following up on those patients. Her work toward fulfilling the requirements needed to take her pediatric surgical boards left little time for meeting all the patients on the floor, but a few kids you only had to meet once, and they wormed their ways into your heart. She looked around again for Rory.

"That's right," Bitsy was saying. "And this is a ball*oon* skin cap!"

She set it on Mia's head, where it perched like a bird on a treetop. The children clapped and squealed. Bitsy did a chicken flap and waggled one foot in the air before bowing to her audience.

"I want a boon-skin cap!"

A tiny girl, perhaps four, shuffled forward with the aid of the smallest walker possibly in existence. She managed it deftly for one so little, even though her knees knocked together, her feet turned inward, and the patch over one eye obscured half her vision. She wore a hot-pink tutu over frosting-pink footie pajamas, and a tiara atop her black curls. To her own surprise, Mia's throat tightened.

"But, Megan, you have a beautiful crown already," Bitsy said gently.

Megan pulled the little tiara off her head and held it out. "I can twade."

Mia lost it, and she never lost it. She squatted and pulled the balloon cap off her head then held it out, her eyes hot. "I would love to trade with you," she said.

Megan beamed. Mia placed the crazy black-and-brown balloon concoction on the child, where it slipped over her hair and settled to her eyebrows.

"Here," Megan said, pronouncing it "hee-oh." "I put it on you."

She reached over the top of her walker and pressed on Mia's nose to tilt her face downward. She placed the tiara in Mia's hair and patted her head gently. It might as well have been a coronation by the Archduke of Canterbury. Megan had spina bifida and had come through surgery just four days earlier. No child this happy and tender and tough should have such a poor prognosis and uncertain future.

"You can be Davy Cwockett's pincess." Megan smiled, clearly pleased with herself.

"I think you gave me the best costume ever," Mia replied. "Could I have a hug?"

Megan opened her arms wide and squeezed Mia's neck with all her might. She smelled of chocolate bars, apple-cinnamon, and a whiff of the strawberry body lotion they used in this department. A delicious little waif.

She let the child go and stood. A young woman with the same black hair as Megan, arrived at her side. It could only be Megan's mom. She bent and whispered something in her daughter's ear. The child nodded enthusiastically. "Thank you, Doc-toh Mia."

"You're welcome. And thank *you*."

The young mother's eyes met Mia's, gratitude shining in their depths. "Thanks from me, too. This is a wonderful party. So much effort by the whole staff."

"I wish I'd had more to do with it."

"You just did a great deal."

Megan had already started on her way back to the audience. Mia watched her slow progress, forgetting about the crowd until a powerful shove against her upper arm nearly knocked her off her feet. She turned to Bitsy and saw Brooke—grinning through the white make-up.

"What the heck? Clown attack. Go away you maniac."

A few kids in the front row twittered. *Bitsy* honked at her, but it was *Brooke* who leaned close to her ear. "That was awesome, Crockett," she whispered. "It's the kind of thing they need to see you do more of around here."

"They" referred to the medical staff. It was true she didn't have the most warm-hearted reputation—but that was by design. She grabbed Bitsy's ugly horn.

"*They* can kiss my—" Honk. Honk.

All the kids heard and saw was Davy Cwockett's Princess stealing a clown's horn. Bitsy capitalized, placing her hands on her knees and exaggerating an enormous laugh.

"Hey! I think I have a new apprentice clown. What do you all say?"

Bitsy pulled off her red nose and popped it on Mia's. The kids screeched their approval.

"I'm going to murder you." Mia's tone belied her pleasant smile.

"Our newest clown needs a name. Any ideas?"

Princess! Clowny! Clown Doctor! Sillypants! Stefo-scope!

Names flew from the young mouths like hailstones, pelting Mia with ridiculousness.

"Stethoscope the Clown, I like it." Bitsy laughed. "How about Mercy?"

"Princess Goodheart." That came quietly from Megan's mother, standing against the side wall, certainty in her demeanor.

"Oh, don't you dare." Mia practically hissed the words at her friend the clown.

"Perfect!" Bitsy called, her falsetto ringing through the room. "Now, how about we get Princess Goodheart to help with a magic trick?"

Mia's sentimentality of moments before dissipated fully. This was why she couldn't afford such soppy silliness, even over children. If she was going to turn to syrup at the first sign of a child with a walker and a patched eye, perhaps pediatrics wasn't the place for her.

On the other hand, Megan represented the very reason Mia wanted to move from general to pediatric surgery. She had skill—a special gift according to teachers and some colleagues—and she could use it to help patients like Megan. They needed her.

"Pick a card, Princess Goodheart." Bitsy nudged her arm.

Mia sighed. She'd have thought a party featuring simple games, fine motor skill-building, and prizes would have been more worthwhile. The mindlessness of magicians and the potential for scaring children with clowns seemed riskier. Indeed there were a few uncomplicated, arcade-type games at little stations around the room, but the magic and clown aficionados had prevailed. Mia grunted and picked a six of clubs.

"Don't show me," said Bitsy.

"I wouldn't dream of it."

"Now, put the card back in the deck. Who wants to wave their hand over the deck and say the magic words?" Bitsy asked.

"Oh, God, help! Oh, help, help please. Something's happening to him!"

Bitsy dropped the card deck. In the back of the room, next to a table full of food and treats, a woman stood over the crumpled body of a boy, twitching and flailing his arms. Mia heard his gasps for breath, ripped the ridiculous nose off her face, and pressed into the crowd of kids.

"Keep them all back," she ordered Brooke, right beside her and already shushing children in a calm Bitsy voice.

The fact that she continued acting like a clown in the face of an emergency made Mia angry, but there was no time now to call her out for unprofessionalism. In the minute it took Mia to reach the child on the floor, five nurses had surrounded him, and the woman who'd called for help stood by, her face ashen.

"Are you the boy's mother?" Mia asked.

"No. I was just standing here when he started choking."

"Out of the way, please." Mia shouldered her way between two nurses, spreading her arms to clear space. They'd turned the child on his side. "Is he actually choking?"

"He's not. It looks like he's reacting to something he ate," a male nurse replied.

She knelt, rolled the child to his back, and froze. "Rory?"

"A patient of yours?" the nurse asked.

"The son of a friend." Mia hadn't seen him arrive. She forced back her shock and set a mental wall around her sudden emotions. "Is there anything on his chart?"

She'd known Rory Beltane and his mother for three years and didn't remember ever hearing about an allergy this life-threatening.

"I don't believe there were any allergies listed," the nurse said. "We're checking his information now. He's a foster kid."

"Yes, I know," she replied with defensive sharpness. "His mother is incapacitated and temporarily can't care for him. Is the foster mother here?"

"No. At work." The nurse said. "Poor kid. He was just starting to feel better after having his appendix out. This isn't fair."

She had no time to tell him exactly how unfair Rory Beltane's life had been recently. "I need a blood pressure cuff stat. Get him on IV epinephrine, methylpred and Benadryl, plus IV fluids wide open."

"Right away, Doctor." Nurses scattered.

The male nurse calmly read from a chart, and Mia's temper flared.

"Excuse me, nurse, are you getting me that cuff?"

"It's on the way," he said, and smiled. "Just checking his chart for you. No notations about allergies. I'll go get the gurney."

Mia blew out her breath. She couldn't fault him for being cool under pressure. Another nurse, this one an older woman with a tone as curt as Mia's, knelt on Rory's far side holding his wrist. "Heart rate is one-forty."

Mia held her stethoscope to the boy's chest. His lips looked slightly swollen. His breathing labored from his tiny chest.

"Here, Dr. Crockett. They're bringing a gurney and the electronic monitor, but this was at the nurse's station if you'd like to start with it."

Mia grabbed the pediatric-sized cuff, its bulb pump reminding her of Brooke's obnoxious horn. With efficient speed, she wrapped the gray cuff around Rory's arm, placed her stethoscope beneath it, and took the reading.

She'd always been struck by what a stunning child he was. His mother was black and his father white, and his skin was the perfect blend, like the color of a beautiful sand beach after a rain. A thick shock of dark curly hair adorned his head, and when they were open, his eyes were a laughing, precocious liquid brown.

"Seventy-five over fifty. Don't like that," she said.

The male nurse appeared with a gurney bed. "I can lift him if you're ready. We have the IV catheter and epineph-rine ready."

"Go," Mia ordered.

Moments later Rory had been placed gently on the gurney, and three nurses, like choreographed dancers, had the IV in place, all the meds Mia had ordered running, and were rolling him to his private room.

"We've called Dr. Wilson, the pediatric hospitalist on duty this week who's seen Rory a couple of times. He'll be here in a few minutes," said the male nurse, who'd just begun to be her favorite.

She frowned. "It wasn't necessary to bring him in yet. I think we have this well in hand. We need fewer bodies, not more."

"I'll let him know."

The epinephrine began to work slowly but surely, and most of the staff, at Mia's instruction, returned to the party to help the remaining kids. The older nurse and the male nurse remained.

Ten minutes after he'd first passed out, Rory opened his eyes, gasping as the adrenaline coursed through him and staring wild-eyed as if he didn't believe air was reaching his lungs.

"Slow breaths, Rory." Mia placed her hand on his. "Don't be afraid. You have plenty of air now, I promise. Lots of medicine is helping it get better and better. Breathe out, nice and slow. I'm going to listen to your heart again, okay?"

Mia listened and found his heart rate slowing. A new automatic blood pressure cuff buzzed, and Rory winced as the cuff squeezed. Tears beaded in his eyes. Mia stared at the monitor, while the nurse calmed the boy again.

"That's a little better," Mia said. "But, I think we need to keep you away from the party for a while. That was scary, huh?"

"Dr. Mia?" He finally recognized her.

"Hi," she said. "This is a surprise, isn't it?"

"You saved me," he whispered in a thick, hoarse rasp. "Nobody ever saves me."

For the first time Mia truly looked at the two nurses who stood with her. Their eyes reflected the stunned surprise she felt.

"Of course I saved you," she said. "Anybody would save you, Rory. You probably haven't needed saving very often, that's all."

"Once. I ate some peanut butter when my mom wasn't at home. I couldn't breathe, but Mrs. Anderson next door didn't believe me. " His voice strengthened as he spoke. "I can't eat peanut butter."

"What did you eat today? Do you remember? Right before you couldn't breathe?"

He shook his head vehemently. "A cupcake. A chocolate one. I can eat chocolate."

"Anything else?"

"I had one little Three Musketeer. Bitsy gave it to me. She said the nurses said it was okay to have one because my stomach feels better."

Bitsy again. Rory looked solely at Mia and avoided the nurses' eyes, as if he feared they'd contradict his story.

"And you don't remember any other food?" Mia asked.

"I didn't eat nothing else. I swear."

"It's all right. It really is. All I care about is finding what made you sick. Look, I'm going to go out and talk to some more nurses—"

"No! Stay here." He stretched out his arm, his fingers spread beseechingly.

"All right." She let him grab her hand and looked at him quizzically. "But you're fine now."

"No."

He was so certain of his answer. Mia couldn't bear to ignore his wishes, although it made no logical sense. At that moment a white-coated man with a Lincoln-esque figure appeared in the doorway.

"My, my, what's going on here? Is that you Rory?"

Rory clung to Mia's hand and didn't answer. Mia looked over the newcomer, not recognizing him, although his badge identified him as Frederick Wilson, MD.

His eyes brushed over Mia, and he dismissed her with a quick "Good afternoon." No questions, no request for an update from her, the medical expert already on the case. She bristled but stayed quietly beside Rory, squeezing his hand.

"How's our man?" Dr. Wilson asked. You doing okay, Champ?" He oozed the schmoozy bedside manner she found obsequious, and the child who'd been talkative up to now merely stared at the ceiling.

Dr. Wilson chuckled. "That's our Rory. Not great talk show material, but he plays a mean game of chess from what I hear. A silent, brilliant kind of man. I'm Fred Wilson." He held out a hand. "You must be one of the techs or NAs?"

She stared at him in disbelief. A nursing assistant? Who was this idiot? She looked down and remembered her badge was in her pocket. She fished it out and shoved it at him. "I'm *Dr.* Amelia Crockett, and I've been handling Rory's case since the incident about fifteen minutes ago.

"Crockett. Crockett." He stared off as if accessing information in space somewhere. "The young general surgeon who's working now toward a second certification in pediatric surgery. Sorry, I've been here two weeks and have tried to brush up on all the staff resumes. I'm the new chief of staff here in peds. Up from Johns Hopkins."

She had heard his name and that he was a mover and shaker.

"Dr. Wilson," she acknowledged.

"So, since you're a surgeon and not familiar with Rory's whole case, maybe I'll trouble you to get me up to speed on the anaphylaxis, and then I'll take over so you can get back to what I'm sure is a busy schedule." Dr. Wilson crossed his arms and smiled.

She glared at him again. He may as well have called her *just* a surgeon. And to presume she hadn't familiarized herself with Rory's case before prescribing any course of action…

"I'm sorry, Dr. Wilson," she said. "But with all due respect, I happen to know this child, and I'm also well aware of the details of his case. I, too, can read a patient history. I believe I can follow up on this episode and make the report in his chart for you, his regular pediatrician, and the other docs on staff who will treat him."

"It really isn't necessary," he replied, and his smile left his eyes.

Unprofessional as it was, she disliked him on the spot, as if she'd met him somewhere else and hadn't liked him then either.

"I was here to help with the Halloween party," she said. "My afternoon is free and clear."

"That explains much. So that isn't your normal, every-day head ornamentation?"

For a moment she met his gaze, perplexed. *Oh, crap.* Her hand flew to her head, and in mortification she pulled off the tiara still stuck there with its little side combs.

"I didn't mean you needed to take it off. It was fetching." Dr. Wilson said. He winked with a condescending kind of flirtatiousness—as if he were testing her.

She flicked an unobtrusive glance at his left hand. No band, but a bulky gold ring with a sizeable onyx set in the middle. She got the impression he was old school all the way, a little annoyed with female practitioners, and extremely cocky about his own abilities.

"Rory is improving rapidly since the administration of Benadryl and epinephrine. We are uncertain of the allergen. From what he's told us he has a suspected sensitivity to peanut butter, but as far as we know he hasn't eaten any nuts."

Dr. Wilson nodded, patting Rory periodically on the shoulder. Rory continued his silence.

"Rory, do you mind if I do a little exam on your tummy?" Dr. Wilson asked.

"Dr. Mia already did it." He turned his head just enough to look at her.

Again he smiled, ignoring Mia. "I'm sure she did, but I'm a different kind of doctor, and I'd like to help her make sure you're okay. Maybe if everyone left the room except you and me and Miss Arlene, it won't be so embarrassing if I check you out? Dr. Crockett and Darren can go and make sure there's nothing out at the party that will hurt you again."

Arlene and Darren, she noted absently. She hadn't taken the time to look at their nametags.

Rory shook his head and squeezed Mia's hand again.

"As you can see," she said, curtly, "the child is still fearful and a little traumatized. Perhaps in this case you and I could switch roles? I'll stay with my patient, and you'll make a better sleuth with Darren?"

Dr. Wilson's mouth tightened, and he drew his shoulders back as if prepping for a confrontation. In that instant, the sense of recognition—the confrontation if not the chauvinism—she'd had earlier flashed into unexpected clarity.

Gabriel Harrison.

Her stomach flipped crazily. Fiftyish Dr. Fred Wilson didn't look a bit like the arrogant, self-important, patient advocate she'd met six weeks before at the VA medical center in her old home city of Jackson, Wyoming. In truth, nobody who wasn't making seven figures as a big-screen heartthrob looked like Gabriel Harrison. The trouble was, just as Dr. Wilson knew he was good, Lieutenant—retired Lieutenant—Harrison knew he was gorgeous. Both men believed they had the only handle on expertise and information.

She'd met Harrison after a car accident in the middle of September had left her mother and one of her sisters seriously injured, and he'd been assigned as a liaison between them, their families, and the hospital. He'd made himself charming—like a medicine show snake oil salesman—and her sisters, all five of them, now adored him. Her mother considered him her personal guardian angel.

However, he'd treated Mia like she'd gotten her degree from a Cracker Jack box, and he continued doing so in all their correspondence—which was frequent considering how he loved ignoring her requests for information.

Mia was glad that at her planned trip home for Christmas, her mother and sister would be home and Gabriel Harrison, patient advocate, would be long gone from their lives. Unfortunately, it wouldn't work quite so easily with Fred Wilson. She was stuck more-or-less permanently with him.

"I want Dr. Mia to stay."

Rory's fingers tightened on her hand, and the last vestiges of memories from Wyoming slipped away.

"That settles it in my opinion," she said. "At my patient's request, I'll stay with him. Darren, would you be willing to accompany Dr. Wilson to the lounge and ask some questions about the food? Arlene, would you please get Mr. Beltane here a glass of juice and maybe some ice?"

"Yes," Darren said. "Sure."

"Of course," Arlene replied, with the first smile Mia had seen from her.

Fred Wilson, on the other hand, looked as if he might need the Heimlich maneuver. "If I might have a word with you outside, Dr. Crockett."

She met his gaze coolly. "Rory, I need to help Dr. Wilson with some things, but I'll be right back. I promise."

"No."

"I promise, honey." She smoothed the child's hair back and he nodded, his eyes shining.

Dr. Wilson patted Rory on the shoulder a final time. "I'll see you tomorrow, young man. You may even get to go home. Bet you'd like that."

Rory gave an anemic shrug.

She slipped out of the room with Fred Wilson behind her, took several steps away from the door, and spun to face him.

"Would you care to explain what this is about?" she demanded.

"Dr. Crockett, I have heard your reputation as the wonder child of this medical community," Wilson said. "But in this department you have no seniority, and a fast track to the top is not impressive. No matter how good you are technically, nothing can take the place of years of experience. And just because you wear a stethoscope and have been in this physical location longer than I have, doesn't mean you possess anywhere near the experience I do. You were insubordinate in front of the patient and my staff. I won't have that."

She didn't blink or raise her voice. She put her hands in her lab coat pockets to keep from showing her flexing fingers. "In point of fact, Dr. Wilson, you treated *me* like a first-year intern in there, even though I am the lead medical staff member in this matter. I also have the trust of the patient, and you ignored that along with his wishes. I treated you with the respect you commanded. It's not my style to kiss up to anyone or brown nose a superior to make my way. Good medicine is all I care about. You or one of your hospital staff docs will handle his care in regard to his recent appendectomy, but at the moment, because he is still in a little bit of shock, that is secondary to aftercare from the anaphylaxis. I didn't appreciate you not bowing to my expertise or asking me to debrief you—even if I didn't just come from Johns Hopkins."

"You take a pretty surly tone."

"I apologize."

For a long moment he assessed her, and finally he shook his head. "I don't like your style, Doctor. But the staff thinks highly of your skill. We'll let this slide because the child did request your presence."

"I don't love your style either." She smiled. "But I've heard the staff thinks highly of your bedside manner. I hope we can grow to understand each other better as we are required to work together."

"I hope that's so." He nodded curtly and left.

Why were older doctors so prejudiced when it came to believing surgeons knew their stuff? Mia was tired of dealing with the game playing and politics of staff. What was wrong with just being a damn-good physician?

She let herself back into Rory's room, and he smiled with relief. "How are you, kiddo?" she asked. "Do your stitches or anything inside your tummy hurt?"

"No."

"You didn't want Dr. Wilson to stay and examine you. Do you not like him?"

"He's nice."

That stymied her. "Then why—?"

"He didn't have nothin' to do with making me better." Rory interrupted. "Only you and Dr. Thomas who took out my appendix. And…you…" His huge, dark eyes brimmed with tears that clung to his lashes like diamonds but didn't spill.

"I what, Rory?"

"You saved me. And I want you to save Jack."

"Jack?" A slice of new panic dove through her stomach. She knew Jack. "Your cat?"

"Yeah."

"Why does Jack need saving?"

"Buster has him," he said. "But Mrs. Murray, the foster lady, she said I couldn't bring him with me 'cause she's allergic to cats. And Buster said he'd keep him for a while, but he can't keep him forever because mostly the shelters won't let him have a cat neither."

A slight dizziness started her head spinning. "Who's Buster?"

"I lived with him awhile after my mama got taken away."

"Where does Buster live?"

"Everywhere," he said, and Mia's stomach slowly started to sink. "He's my best friend. Sometimes he goes to the shelter by the church in Brownsville. Sometimes he lives under the bridge by the East River. Sometimes he stays in the camp with his friends."

"Rory? Is Buster a homeless man?"

"Buster says he doesn't want a normal house. He says he owns the whole city of New York, and he should 'cause he fought for it. But Jack does need a house 'cause it's going to snow pretty soon, and he'll freeze. So…will you save him like you saved me?"

"Oh, I don't know if…"

She thought about all the animals she'd had growing up on one of the biggest cattle ranches in Wyoming. Until leaving for college she'd never imagined that some kids might not have pets. No dogs, no cats, no horses.

"Please? Jack's the only one left who really loves me."

"That's so not true, Rory. I know it's not true." She sighed and sat next to him on the mattress. "I love you. I'm your friend, right? And your mom loves you so much."

"Mrs. Murray, the foster lady, said Mom was too sick to be a good mother. 'Cause she's in the hospital, too."

"Again?" Mia stared at him, heartbroken. "Rory, since when? What happened?"

"I don't know when. Before I came here. I tried to call her to tell her I was sick, but she wasn't at the jail."

For the past three months, Monique Beltane had resided in a women's prison in upstate New York where she was serving one year for theft and illegal possession of a narcotic. She was also living through treatment for breast cancer.

"That's not true, Rory. Your mom will never be too sick to love you. And she's a good mom, too. She's just been sick for such a long time.

Mia knew Monique's story well. She'd become addicted to prescription opioids after botched shoulder surgery. One year after that operation, Mia had been the one to operate again and managed to relieve some of Monique's permanent pain. During the three years that had followed, she'd kept in touch with Monique and her son, Rory. She liked the woman, plain and simple. Monique wanted to get well. She was just weak when it came to pain. Still, she'd gotten herself clean, and Mia believed she might have made a success of it. Then, six months ago, she'd been diagnosed with the cancer.

She'd managed the chemo, but the mastectomy and the oxycodone to which she was so highly addicted had pushed her back over the edge. Three months ago, she'd purchased oxycodone from an undercover agent, and that had been the end.

But she was back in the hospital. Mia didn't know what was wrong, but her intuition left her worried. At this stage in her recovery, no illness boded well. She made a mental note to track down Monique's physician.

And now here was Rory.

You couldn't make crap like this up.

"But even if Mom gets better, she's in jail for a long time. All I got is Jack."

"But if Jack can't stay with you at the Murrays, where would he go if we find him?"

He shrugged, and his eyes filled with water. Mia sighed. This was so *not* in her job description. How did one even begin to try looking for a homeless cat in New York City?

"Please, Dr. Mia."

She smoothed his thick curls. She'd never find one cat in a city that must have a billion. "All right, listen to me, okay? I will see what I can find out, but you're practically a young man and you're smart. You know I might not have any luck. You promise you won't be angry with me if I don't find him?"

He smiled a watery-but-genuine true, toothy, ten-year-old's grin. "You will."

Chapter Two

MIA MET BITSY transforming back into Brooke in the staff locker room two hours later, after the party ended. Mia had missed the grand finale—an appearance by the Teenage Mutant Ninja Turtles, aka four custodial staff members. She didn't regret missing the performance. While the Mutant Ninja Janitors had fake-saved the world, she'd followed up on two pressing questions—and had gotten answers.

"You should have come back to the party, you know. Everyone wanted to congratulate you." Brooke set her blue wig on the bench in front of her locker and kicked off the Converse tennis shoes she wore in lieu of giant clown shoes.

"There wasn't any reason for people to thank me. I wasn't a hero. It was an easy diagnosis."

"I never said you were a hero. But you did get the win."

"I won't win until I find out what the allergen was. I need to talk to his foster mom, but she hasn't shown up yet—can't get off work."

"I'm not too sure about her." Brooke removed her pinafore and dress of clashing stripes, polka-dots, and checks. Mia made a show of shuddering.

"You do know that standing there in tights with a face the color of a skull, you're now a hideously frightening clown?"

"You need to get over yourself." Brook huffed out a breath. "Clowning is a noble art."

"It's an obsession. Case in point: you're in a hospital, a kid stops breathing, and you don't even break character for that."

She hadn't really meant to bring it up, but Brooke was defending it as a noble art. Her friend, however, quickly became a very annoyed hideous clown. The stars painted over her eyes shrank as she lowered her lids.

"Okay, hang on a dang minute. It scares kids if a clown breaks character when in make-up. You actually find me scary now because I'm not talking like Bitsy." She crossed her arms. "For your information, it was very difficult to stay in character and pretend it was Bitsy helping. But it was worth it, which you didn't hang around to see. Learn a little about people why don't you, Amelia?"

Mia rubbed her eyes. She had to concede. She could see how a child would find it freaky if a clown with a high, squeaky voice suddenly began talking like a normal person.

"All right. I apologize," she said. "I'm still trying to deal with the whole Rory situation and I'm touchy. I react to adrenaline a little differently than most."

"You *over*react. Like Rocky Balboa to a fight bell." Brooke smiled kindly. "You just need to relax and be a little more of a team player with your coworkers. Trust us to know what we're doing, too. But, hey, why am I telling you this for the millionth time?" She grinned.

Mia stuck out her tongue. "Face it, I'm your challenge. Everyone has to have one."

"Except you, right?"

"Sure. I'm perfect. No challenges." She sighed.

She could say such things to Brooke, who'd always understood Mia's sarcasm and even her sometimes-gruff personality. Brooke was one of the nicest people on the planet and had proved it many times during their seven-year friendship.

"Speaking of perfect, I heard you had a dustup with our new Freddie Wilson today."

"I don't know that I'd call it a dustup. He was irritating Rory, so we had a little disagreement."

"That right?" Brooke grabbed a towel and make-up bag and headed toward the nearest sink. "Well, from what I hear, you might want to consider apologizing."

"What you hear? Good grief, it wasn't that big a deal, and I've already apologized."

"All right. Just remember, he is one of the people you need on your side right now. When do they decide on the head resident's position? You really don't mind going back to being the equivalent of a student?"

"No. It's what I have to do. They announce the choice the beginning of next week—November sixth or seventh. The job starts in early December."

"And if you get it, you can take your certification exam next fall."

"I need that one year back in a lower-level position of authority to be eligible for the exam, yes. And then Sidney March over at Mount Sinai retires, and his spot as associate chief of pediatric surgery will be vacant. I've got a solid reputation there, and they've all but promised me a good shot at the job if my certification is complete. You know that's been my dream job since the beginning."

"And, you deserve it; you've worked your butt off. Everyone knows there's not a better surgeon in New York."

"You and I know that." She scoffed and shook her head. "No, I know full well I'm hardly the best, but there'd be no better way to keep climbing toward it than getting that job. I only wish the timing weren't so tight."

It was one of the few things that got Mia's stomach into knots—the fact that she'd been kept so busy with her general surgery duties she hadn't been available to apply for the chief resident's job before now. She could juggle a lot of balls, and she was capable of advancing through required tasks and performance reviews faster than any other candidate, but she couldn't make the AMA change policy for her. The cert tests were given once a year, and she had to have the leadership component of her training completed in order to qualify to take the exam.

"You and your life plan." Brooke smiled fondly. "I sure don't know anyone with more talent and drive than you have. But if you're nervous, I advise you to kiss and make up with Doc Freddie. You do need to play the game to win the prize."

Mia approached the sink adjacent to Brooke's and watched her friend smear make-up remover over her white face. "I don't kiss up."

"Don't I know it? It wouldn't hurt you to learn how, sooner rather than later, so you can nail this job and quit whining."

"I don't whine either." She didn't. Whining was always counterproductive.

"Look." Brooke turned, her makeup puckered from the remover, looking like a clown whose skin was melting off. "Just be nice."

"Too late for that," Mia replied flippantly. "I'm now planning to hold my tiny reserves of sweetness and light safe for Samantha down in the community outreach clinic. If I'm lucky, she's going to find me a cat."

Brooke sputtered into the washcloth that was finally starting to remove Bitsy's face. "Forget sucking up to Fred. You need to start making friends with the staff up on eight."

The psych department.

"You're not far from right. Rory asked me to rescue his cat from a homeless man."

"And you listened to him?"

"I—"

Her phone rang from the open locker, and Mia cut herself off, since she was waiting for a call from Samantha Evans. Sam, a social worker with endless connections, had been another good friend and valued ally since Mia had begun her quest for this second specialty field. She grabbed the phone from her purse. The number was completely unfamiliar. She didn't answer unknown calls on her private phone. The person could leave a voice mail.

"Anybody important?" Brooke asked.

"No. Look, I know how freakily attached to this cat Rory is, so I'm going to see what I can dig up."

"Just watch young Mr. Beltane. He's a cocky little guy. Cute as a fox kit but smart as the daddy fox."

"He's precocious—has been ever since I first met him. Now, though, he's mostly scared. His mom is in pretty bad shape."

"Addicted to prescription opioids, if I read the history right."

"And a very recent cancer survivor. Monique and I have developed a trust over the years, maybe even a friendship. I owe her to look after her son as best I can."

"Okay, you've made your case. As for Rory, I said it before. I'm not entirely sure about his foster family. The mom is nice enough, but she's kind of a ditz. Sorry, shouldn't say that."

"Hey, all I know is they haven't even gotten her to come in yet because she's at work. Hell's bells, I'd have been here two seconds after he'd gone down."

Brooke gave her face a last long swipe with the washcloth. "And this is what I'm saying. Turn some of that empathy you have for the kids on the grown-ups, and you'll be unstoppable."

"Why do you think I'm a *surgeon*? Like my dad always said, 'I don't have time for the extra bull crap.' I don't either."

"Your dad didn't say bull crap." Brooke laughed.

"No, he didn't. But I'm a genteel young professional woman."

"Bullshit."

Finally laughing, Mia said good-bye to her friend and made her way back to the pediatrics floor, quiet now that the afternoon party was over. Naps were in progress, and preparations were underway for the dinner hour.

"Dr. Crockett. Great! You're still here. I was about to page you."

Darren met her as she approached the nurse's station, his face as friendly and open as a big kid's, and surprisingly welcoming considering there'd been precious few fuzzy moments between them in their short acquaintance.

"Looks like I saved you the trouble. What did you need?"

"Shawna Murray, Rory's foster mom, is here. We thought you should be the one to see her."

The conspiratorial look he gave her forced a smile from her lips. "Even though I'm not the department head?"

"You know, I can't seem to find him right now, Dr. Crockett."

Darren's unspoken vote of respect only proved the point that straightforward talk, along with curbing extraneous emotions, made for efficient and effective patient treatment. *Take that, Brooke, you old mother hen. He likes me even though I don't know how to play nice.*

"Well that's certainly a shame. But, since he seems to be unavailable, I'll be happy to talk to Mrs. Murray."

"Mrs. Murray?" Mia entered the room to find Rory half-asleep and his foster mother watching the TV, one ankle crossed over the opposite knee, her foot jiggling so hard the chair beneath her squeaked. "I'm Dr. Crockett. I took care of Rory this afternoon."

Mia had met many foster parents throughout her medical career. They came in all shapes, sizes, and colors, but Shawna Murray was unique. Dressed in brightly patterned Lycra workout pants, equally blinding neon-yellow tennis shoes, and a white, Nike zippered jacket, its collar flipped preppily up against her ears, she looked like she was headed for a high school gym class. She even had her blonde hair gathered into a bouncy, beach-worthy ponytail.

"I'm so glad to meet you." The woman jumped to a stand as if grateful to do so. She shook hands like The Flash would shake: in triple time and with power she didn't realize she possessed. "Thank you for everything you did. I'm so sorry I was slow in coming, I was in the middle of teaching a Zumba class."

That explained the high-end workout clothing. But a three-hour Zumba class?

"I see."

"I tried to get my boyfriend to come, but he had the two other kids to watch, and then he had a get-together with friends, so I waited for my mother to get off work and finally here I am. I'm so relieved Rory is all right. Do you think there's any chance of a relapse?" She spoke like The Flash, too, barely taking a breath between long sentences.

No more caffeine for you, Mrs. Murray.

"A spontaneous recurrence can happen on occasion, although it's rare. Rory's regular doctor and surgeon can decide how long they'd like him monitored." Mia indicated Mrs. Murray should sit, and she did, her knee immediately taking up a frenetic bobbing.

"He was supposed to come home tomorrow or Thursday. Do you think that will still happen?"

"I'm not familiar with the details of his surgical case, so I can't tell you for sure. The nursing staff will make sure Rory's doctor speaks with you."

A stirring from the bed pulled Mia's attention from Shawna Murray to Rory, who opened his eyes and squirmed in an attempt to sit. Mia smiled. "Hang on there," she said. "Let me raise the head of the bed—that's way cooler."

"You're my doctor," the boy said as his bed transported him to a sitting position.

"I was your doctor for this accident, kiddo," she said. "But Dr. Thomas knows what's best for taking care of you after your operation. And all we want is what's best for you."

"You can look at my chart. Then you can be who decides."

Mia squelched the laughter threatening to spill out. Rory's fear and the fog from his meds had lifted. Here was the feisty Rory she knew: much more self-aware than the average ten-year-old.

"I'm glad you have so much confidence in me." She patted his leg. "But we're friends, remember? A doctor isn't supposed to treat her friends."

"But you saved me even though we're friends."

As flattering as his unswerving belief was, Mia shook her head. "Lots of people who work in a hospital know about the kind of thing that happened to you. I think anyone would have saved you, honey."

"Nope. Anybody didn't save me. You did."

His findings were final and absolute. Mia sighed. "Well, I'd do it again because you're kind of cool, you know that? A little crazy maybe…"

He laughed. Mia turned back to Mrs. Murray, who was watching the exchange with a blank expression. "You sound like you know Rory," she said.

"I do. I met his mother several years ago and we became friends. This is a strange coincidence."

"Everyone says it's a small world," she said.

"Yes. But the most important thing is that we learn what caused this reaction and make sure to keep Rory away from the allergens that trigger it. His reaction was life-threatening. You need to be aware of that and be vigilant at all times."

"I can't imagine what it was," she replied. "I made him chocolate cupcakes out of a mix and brought them up to the hospital this morning so he could have them for the party, but nobody ever said he was allergic to chocolate. Just peanut butter."

"You didn't report that to the staff," Mia said. "There's no notation of his allergy in his chart."

"I didn't? Oh, dear. I guess it slipped my mind in the panic."

Mia sighed. "Regardless. There were no nuts in the recipe at all? Even the frosting?"

"No. None of the kids like nuts."

"No nut oils? Peanut oil or even olive oil—"

"Peanut oil?"

"Yes…"

"My boyfriend, Matt, bought peanut oil last night because the gas station convenience store was out of regular cooking oil. I know, who bakes with peanut oil? But I had no time to get anything else. Besides, it's oil. I never even thought about that being an issue."

Are you serious?

"You didn't know peanut oil was made from peanuts?"

"It's processed."

"Ma'am, are you aware that people with severe allergies to nuts *can* react just by kissing someone who's eaten them? Any nut product is dangerous."

"I…Kissing? For real?"

That was her reaction? "Yes. Something you maybe should have known or looked up when you knew you had a child with allergies in your home."

"I am sorry. I've fostered lots of kids over the past few years and never dealt with this. We have a busy household, and somebody from the state should have warned me how dangerous this could be. Matt didn't know about the oil either."

Her contrition would have been more palatable if not for the web of defensiveness she wound around the apology.

"I'm not sure if Matt is part of the original application for approval as a foster care home or not," Mia said. "If not, then it isn't his responsibility, it's yours. Regardless, you made the food. Mothers are responsible for their children, whether they're biological or fostered."

Shawna Murray looked like she might haul back and slug her. Mia stood her ground. She had dealt with social services enough to know the dire responsibility fostering children in crisis situations entailed. In her opinion, this woman's clueless attitude was entirely too flippant and self-centered. Not that Mia expected hysterics or tears, but some regret might have been appropriate. Maybe a hug for the boy?

"You can rest assured there will be no more peanut oil in any food in the house," Shawna said at last, her voice tight. "And you'll know what to look for now, too, right Rory?"

"I guess."

"And we'll train Matt." She smiled.

Rory frowned and turned his head slowly away. One little fist clenched against the white sheets. "Don't think that'll help."

"He and Matt are still getting to know each other," Shawna said.

"How long has your Matt been in the picture?" Mia asked.

"Oh? Six months."

"And you're sure he's safe with the children?"

Shawna stood again. "Excuse me? What are you insinuating?"

"I'm only asking questions any county inspection worker would ask. I'm not insinuating anything."

"For your information, he's a great guy who loves people. He's a body builder and personal trainer at the gym where we both work. He's in great shape and can do all kinds of great healthy, physical fitness things with the kids."

Sounded like Matt was simply a *great* person all around. Awesome. Two gym rats caring for kids. Thinking of them as such was unfair and a gross generalization, Mia knew, but with every sentence, Shawna Murray sounded more and more like Workout Barbie.

"Big deal. He can bench press Lisa." Rory still didn't look at them.

"Bench press?"

"Lisa is my daughter. She's six. She thinks it's funny that Matt can lift her up like a barbell. It's very cute."

It probably was. What had Brooke said? Loving and nice, but ditzy? So far, so accurate.

"Ms. Murray," she said, calming her voice, trying to follow Brooke's earlier advice and channel some of the patience she had with Rory. "Now that we know the source of Rory's trouble today, you can probably use some information. I think if you go out to the nurse's station and tell them I sent you, they'll have pamphlets you can take home that will help you know how to prevent this from occurring again in the future. I have a couple of questions for Rory about how he's feeling, so I can stay with him until you come back. Is that all right?"

She deserved a medal for that sweet performance.

Shawna relaxed in place, seemingly accepting the apology at face value. "That's a good idea. I'd like the information to read over. Who knew allergies could cause such issues?"

Mia shook her head and turned back to Rory when his foster mom had gone. "Okay, you. How *are* you feeling?"

"I'm all right."

"It's good Mrs. Murray finally came, isn't it?"

"Yeah. Whatever."

"Rory, listen. You don't have to tell me anything, but I'm a friend and if you want to talk, I won't repeat anything you don't want me to. How is life with the Murrays?"

"It's okay. It's boring. Mrs. Murray, Shawna, she's mostly in love with her kids. She's nice to me, but I think I'm there because she gets extra money from the county when I am. Lisa is six, and she talks a lot just like her mom. Cameron is only one. He don't talk at all."

"Who takes care of them when she works?"

"Matt. I don't like Matt."

"Can you tell me why?" She braced for an answer she really didn't want to hear.

"He's loud and he doesn't do much. Like, he hates to change diapers, so he makes me do it."

"Makes you?"

"Sometimes he gives me a quarter. But that ain't worth it. If I say that, though, he says he'll tell Shawna I was mouthy, and I'll have to do even more work."

"So, he threatens you?"

"He never does nothin', but he's kinda loud and scares the other kids when he yells. He says it's one of my jobs around there, but nobody told me that before. And it's a gross job. But I just think, before I was there did Cam sit around in poopy diapers all day? So I do it."

Mia wasn't sure what to think. She'd never really seen forced diaper changing listed as a charge for child abuse.

"Do you feel safe when Matt's there alone?"

He shrugged. "Yeah. He spanks Lisa once in a while, but not hard or anything. And sometimes he plays catch with me. Mostly he watches TV and waits for Shawna to come home. Then he goes to work."

"And how is it then?"

"Fine. I go to school, so I'm not there most of the time. It's just kinda like eating vanilla ice cream. It's not very exciting."

Mia laughed at the adult-sounding comparison. "How'd you learn a smart thing like that to say?"

"Buster used to say it all the time when he got bored."

"Ahhh. So, how old was Buster?"

"I asked him once. He's the same age as my mom, twenty-nine."

That stopped her questions momentarily. She'd been expecting to hear he was an older man, wise and grandfatherly. What was a young man like that doing homeless?

She chastised herself. This was New York. There was no single demographic for the homeless population, she knew that.

"He's a young man," she said at last. "How did you meet him?"

"He used to come and help Mom with little jobs, like washing a window or scrubbing a floor, and she'd pay him with lunch. He's funny. He said it was a kind of justice having a poor white man work for a black lady. But Mama said that was silly, and anyway it was just people helping one another."

Mia listened, rapt, to his animated storytelling. The child was a wonder—he had true gifts of personality and understanding, and yet he seemed so vulnerable, as if he knew his situation but didn't really think beyond passing through it.

"And you ended up with Buster? How did that happen?"

His story tightened up then. "Mama got sick, and Buster tried to tell her to get help. But she went and found more medicines she wasn't supposed to have instead. When they took her to the police station, Buster told everyone he was my dad, so they wouldn't take me away, too. My mama ended up in jail, and when they tried to take me away, me and Buster just ran off."

"But they found you."

"After one month! We were doin' fine, but they wouldn't let me stay with him."

It had been several months since Mia had visited with Monique. She hadn't heard these details.

They both looked up to see Shawna standing in the doorway. Her shiny figure suddenly made Mia feel like a dusty ranch hand—which she had been once upon a time.

Rory halted in his story, which told Mia he'd chosen her to be his only confidant and wasn't going to waver.

"Look, Rory," Shawna said. "I got all kinds of information about allergies. How about when I go home tonight, I leave some of it with you, and we can both learn?"

Rory shot his foster mother a pained look.

"Tell you what," Mia said. "I'll round him up a set of his own. I might even be able to find some that are geared toward his age. You go ahead and take those with you."

She was rewarded with a smile from Rory, who pulled up his blanket to cover his mouth. She was about to tease him when her cell phone rang from her lab coat pocket. She pulled it out, and saw the same unknown number as earlier. This time her stomach twisted in concern.

"I hope you'll excuse me," she said. "I need to take this and then finish work. But I'll stop by again in the morning, okay? Maybe I'll hear that you get to go home."

She gave Rory a little wink, and he tugged at her sleeve as she turned. "You're still going to look for Jack?"

"I'm going to ask some questions about him," she said evasively.

"Now, Rory, we've discussed this," Shawna said. "Jack is better off finding a different home…"

Mia edged out of the room feeling vaguely guilty. Both she and Shawna had dismissed Rory's feelings. And yet, it really was just a cat. She answered her phone, hoping to catch the caller before he hung up.

"Amelia Crockett."

"Hello, Mia?" A deep male voice took her by surprise.

For a moment she didn't reply while she tried to place the person on the other end of the phone who knew her familiar name—

And then she knew. Her heart beat straight up into her throat. "Lieutenant Harrison?"

An indecipherable grunt—annoyance? humor?—rumbled across the connection. "Good memory, Doc. But, please, call me Gabriel. I'm a civilian these days."

She hadn't corresponded with the man in two weeks, and today he'd not only crossed her mind, but he was now inescapably live on her phone.

"My goodness, *Mr.* Harrison." She amended her greeting pleasantly, ignoring his request for first names. "I have to go with the cliché here and say, this is certainly unexpected."

"And a pleasure? That would finish off the cliché if I'm not mistaken."

Oh, it was Gabriel Harrison, all right. He not only thought he was handsome but funny as well. "How could it possibly be anything other than a pleasure? Is there a problem?"

"Am I catching you at a bad time?"

"I assume the nonanswer means you aren't calling with an emergency."

"Your sister took a minor fall in her room today trying to get up by herself. She's absolutely fine so, no, not an emergency. Just some news."

"A fall? How did they let that happen?"

"She decided on her own to get up. She's not restrained, of course, and they took her for an immediate MRI. She's asleep and asked me to call you if she hadn't heard from you by now. She left a message for you about forty-five minutes ago, but she expected you'd be busy."

Mia grimaced. "I'm so sorry. I didn't recognize this number and was heading for a patient, so I let it go to voice mail. It's been a crazy day, and I'm afraid I haven't checked the messages even yet."

"Hey, it's not a problem. She called from a clinic phone and I'm doing the same—you probably saw the general clinic-wide number."

Mia lowered her prickly guard slightly. He was less abrasive on the phone than in person or curt e-mails. So far, she didn't even want to choke him. "So what's going on now? She's really all right?"

"After the MRI, Joely met with an orthopedic surgeon specializing in spinal cord injuries. The upshot is that there's some experimental surgery he'd like her to consider. It's somewhat risky and it would, as you know, be Joely's third surgery since the accident, so I think the idea of this one makes her nervous. She'd like to see if there's any way for you to be here at the next consultation with this doctor. In other words, she wants a second opinion, and she very much wants it to be yours."

A hundred questions blossomed after Harrison finished. What was the surgery? Why were they discussing it? What were the alternatives? What had they said that would make stubborn-minded Joely nervous? What did their other sisters think?

The question that came out was none of those. "Why did she have you call and not one of the family?" She rubbed her eyes and immediately blew out an apologetic sigh. "Sorry, that has no bearing on anything medical."

"It's all right. Kelly went back to Denver; Harper is in Chicago for three days. Grace is taking your mother shopping, I understand. Your grandmother is at home. I'm the only one left."

He'd definitely listed all her normally available sisters, and her mother.

"All right, so you're the messenger. Can you tell me any more of the details?"

"I was only authorized to tell you about the appointment and pass on her question so you could call her. I can't discuss anything else."

Of *course* he couldn't. Mia's irritation with him surfaced again. Mr. Harrison's sense of what was appropriate to share seemed to have been formed in his ancient basic training days—where only the drill sergeant could tell others what to do.

"Now listen here," Mia said, honestly angry. "Don't you dare call me up and relay a message that basically says 'get home, your sister needs you,' and then pick and choose what information you give me. We've been through this before. If I'm to help, I need all the facts."

"And *there's* the Amelia Crockett I grew so fond of during our many meetings in September." The underlying hint of condescending amusement in his words finally brought up the desire in Mia to throttle him, but he continued, oblivious.

"The fondness is not mutual, Mr. Harrison, but that's beside the point. You're supposed to advocate for and with the entire family."

"And here I am on the phone doing exactly that. Fulfilling my client's wishes to the letter."

"Oh, for the love…Don't use your smug semantics on me, Buster—" She stopped short, realizing she'd just used the name of the man she'd promised to locate on Rory's behalf. Her anger deflated. Why was she wasting her energy on this stubborn man when she had things to do? "Look, tell me what exactly Joely needs, and I will do it if I can."

"Her next appointment is in two weeks—Tuesday, the fourteenth of November. If it's not possible for you to be here, she'd like to know if you would be willing to Skype during the appointment."

Mia's mind scanned mentally through her calendar. She'd taken some time off in August for her father's funeral and then again in September for Joely's accident, but vacation wasn't her problem; she had time to spare. She did, however, have surgeries scheduled in two departments through Thanksgiving. And, in one week she fully expected to have a new job as chief resident. That would put a vise grip to her ability to travel.

"Amelia?"

She refocused. "I may not know until next week if I can get any time off, but of course I'll be happy to speak with her specialist. What's his name?"

"Perry Landon, with twenty-five letters after his name. Look him up. He's one of the best spinal surgeons in the country."

"Good friend of yours, I presume?" She smirked.

"Never met him before today."

"Odd. I thought you knew everybody in the VA personally."

"I don't. But they all know me." A confident smile in his words turned his voice whiskey smooth.

"Well, then. Thank God for you."

The laugh he returned, easy and smoky, did something to transform her annoyance into a flutter in her chest. Siccing her anger on the quivery sensation, she snapped at him again. "Is there anything else, Mr. Harrison?"

"There is. And seriously. Call me Gabe."

Chapter Three

Fifteen minutes after that delightful conversation, Mia received two pages from social workers: one she expected from a woman she'd contacted about trying to find Buster. The other call was from her friend Samantha, who specialized in children's issues. Both worked for New York County social services, but both kept hours twice a week in the hospital's Outreach Clinic.

She dreaded what Sam might have to say, knowing the meeting with Shawna Murray hadn't exactly led to a new BFF, so she sat first in front of Hannah White, watching her scribble on a yellow legal pad.

"I had a little bit of luck, believe it or not," Hannah said. "I made calls to three different shelters in the area you said your little patient mentioned. The woman I spoke to at one of them, St. Sebastian's Shelter in Brownsville, knows a man everybody calls Buster. His real name is Aaron Sanderson. They didn't know anything about a cat or remember that he ever had a child with him, but he fits the description. The downside is he doesn't show up on any kind of regular schedule."

"But someone there might be able to find him?"

"I assume you know what that area of Brooklyn is like, Dr. Crockett. If I were you, I'd do my best to handle this by phone." Hannah tore the piece of paper she'd been writing on from the pad and handed it to Mia. "Here are the name and number of the woman I spoke with. What you might do is ask them to pass on a message to your guy the next time he shows up. Sometimes, if it's an unusual situation, they'll let the shelter guests make a phone call. Buster could get in touch with you."

"This is very helpful. Thank you so much."

"This must be pretty important to you."

Mia wanted to say that it was more an accidental promise than important, but Rory's heartfelt pleas wouldn't leave her mind. He might be sharp as a fox, but his missing cat might be the only family he had for a while.

"Yeah," she said. "It kind of is."

She stood to leave and Hannah smiled. "I'll let you know if I get any information from other calls I put out."

"I can't thank you enough. By the way, do you have any information on animal foster homes or institutions? The boy's foster mother has said he can't keep the cat with him. I'll talk to her, but…"

"I have a few place names, but no real contacts. I'll let you know."

Mia nodded and headed for Sam's office where, she had a feeling, the news wasn't going to be nearly as positive.

Sam's space was small and tucked into a corner across the hall from Hannah's, but it was a relatively cheerful office, with a large desk and three file cabinets, bright yellow walls and a handful of inspirational posters. Sam grinned when Mia entered.

"Hey you, thanks for taking time to come in before you leave for the day."

"Anything for you," Mia said. "I hear you're the goddess of children."

"I wish. Sit down. I heard you've had a long day."

"Certainly an eventful one." Mia rubbed her aching temples.

"You saw Rory. Small world, huh?"

"I was shocked to hear about Monique. I'm worried about her. And about Rory ending up in the system after all this."

"I know. Which brings me to the point. There's been a complaint filed, and I'd like to ask a couple of questions. You had a chance to meet Shawna Murray today, didn't you?"

Here it comes.

"I did. I'm sorry, Sam. I admit to being astounded by Mrs. Murray's cavalier attitude about some issues related to her foster son. I said some things in haste—"

"Wait, Mia, no. The complaint wasn't against you. It was against Mrs. Murray by another member of our staff."

For a moment Mia sat stunned. She'd been told several times today that she needed a less brusque way of dealing with adults. She'd simply assumed Shawna Murray had joined the Dr.-Crockett-had-no-bedside-manner Club.

"Oh! What was the complaint?"

"That while she might be well-intentioned as a foster parent, she doesn't seem to be providing the safest environment. Evidently Rory spent four or five days severely ill at home before he was brought into emergency with a ruptured appendix. Rather than have his symptoms checked, Mrs. Murray relied on the opinion of her live-in boyfriend, a man who wasn't in her life when she was approved as a foster parent."

"I just learned that this afternoon," Mia said.

Sam nodded. "The second complaint is that Mrs. Murray used peanut oil in cooking for the child even with full knowledge that he has a severe peanut allergy."

"I did speak with her about that. She was not deliberately negligent, according to her story. I do believe she didn't have any idea what she'd done was dangerous. I'll be honest, though, Sam. I did criticize her actions—perhaps a bit strongly."

Mia wasn't sure what, exactly, made her defend the woman, but as much as she wasn't Shawna Murray's biggest fan, it *was* her job to be as objective and honest as she could.

"The complaint definitely says that Mrs. Murray's motives are not being questioned, nor are there allegations of any abuse. There was simply concern expressed that this home might not be the best fit for this child."

"I hadn't heard the appendectomy part of the story."

"I was wondering if you could add anything to this issue from your perspective."

"I have a few opinions," Mia said slowly. "A lot of them are subjective, though. I don't believe the woman has an uncaring heart."

"Caring and safety aren't necessarily the same thing," Sam said. "My concern is whether the child is safe."

"I can tell you what Rory told me. He doesn't like the boyfriend, but it doesn't seem to be because he feels unsafe. He made the boyfriend seem like a mere presence, not any kind of hands-on parent."

She related the rest of her interactions with Rory and Shawna as factually as she could, but she didn't really feel as if she'd contributed much damning evidence. She allowed one personal opinion, however, at the end of the conversation.

"I know a situation like Rory's is stressful for a parent, especially a foster parent. My worry is that I didn't think Mrs. Murray showed the right amount of concern for what happened. She treated it like an unlucky accident. A 'stuff happens' kind of thing. I may be off base, but if it were my decision, I'd at least make another home visit."

Sam nodded. "That's actually helpful."

"Is there a chance Rory will be moved to a different home?"

"A chance. Sometimes we just have to try several places in order to find a good match."

"Can you keep me in the loop? I'd like to be able to find him."

"Of course. Goes without saying."

THE AFTERNOON'S EVENTS should have elated her. Buster semilocated. Social services looking into Rory's well-being. Instead, her head pounded with concerns she really didn't want on her plate. Hunting down a homeless cat. Monique's health. Half-worrying about Brooke's prediction that she'd overstepped her bounds with Dr. Wilson. Finding time to help her sister. Knowing she'd have to speak again with the annoying Gabriel Harrison...

Wondering why her stomach insisted on flipping cartwheels every time his name and the memory of his low, smoky voice ran through her brain.

She reached her office and gratefully closed the door. She had no more rounds today and no more meetings. More than ready to leave, she gathered her coat, her purse, and her laptop. And yet, a weird, internal nagging feeling that she needed to follow up on Buster wouldn't let her walk out. With a sigh, she sat at her desk and unfolded the yellow sheet of paper from Hannah White. Picking up her office landline phone, she dialed the number for St. Sebastian's Shelter.

The woman she spoke to remembered the earlier call about Buster. Mia identified herself and her reason for wanting to find the homeless man.

"I'm not looking for him as such," she said. "I am only after any information he has about my patient's cat. Even if he can tell me no such animal exists."

"I will be glad to have Aaron—Buster—contact you if I see him again," the woman said. "I haven't seen him in nearly two weeks, however, so I can't promise you when that might be."

"That's all I can I ask," Mia said. "Thank you for your help."

"I wish you good luck," the woman said. "I hate hearing about lost pets and sick kids. I hope you can reunite the boy with the cat."

Her attitude sent the first warmth in four hours through Mia's body. She wouldn't do the woman's job on a dare. Surgery was a snap compared to figuring out how to shelter and feed the homeless and hungry.

By the time she reached her building in the Upper East Side an hour later, her headache had peaked into the kind of pounding pain that made climbing the steps to her third floor apartment excruciating. Not that the pain was unfamiliar. Lately headaches had become all too commonplace—so much so, she had a routine to deal with them.

She flipped her low-heeled pumps straight from her feet into their corner of her bedroom and stripped every stitch of clothing, from her red-and-white pinstriped blouse to her navy pencil skirt, bra, and underpants, off her body and set them into the laundry hamper. Gratefully and gloriously, she replaced them with her loosest, ugliest gray sweatpants and a fairly hideous multicolor striped, polar fleece pullover that, strictly by virtue of its coziness against her skin, eased her impending migraine by a fraction.

One glass of ice-cold water and the full adult dose of eight hundred powerful milligrams of ibuprofen later, she shuffled into the kitchen, popped a K-Cup of hot chocolate into her trendy new single-serve coffee maker and slipped her favorite mug into place. *Surgeons Do It on the Table*, it said.

"If only," she said out loud.

While the chocolate brewed she opened the refrigerator and searched fruitlessly for anything that sounded or looked good. This, too, was part of the headache routine, and as usual she closed the fridge door without choosing anything. There wasn't even a lack of choice—she kept a well-stocked kitchen—but cooking sounded far too painful, and fresh anything sounded far too healthy. Finally, when her cocoa was ready, she grabbed a package of graham crackers from the cupboard and carried the nonnutritious comfort food into the living room.

She loved her condo. It truly was her one haven away from the world of relative insanity she inhabited eighty percent of the time. She'd chosen that chaotic, high-pressure world, and she loved it, too, but here—headache or no—she could leave the hospital behind if she chose.

She retrieved her laptop from her briefcase in the foyer and flipped on her gas fireplace on her way back to the couch. On the mantle her array of family photos smiled out from various rustic frames collected at flea markets and antique shops over the years. A group picture of her and her five sisters from twenty years before always made her smile. She'd been twelve, Harper ten and Joely seven. Each had held one of the triplets, not quite four, and each was dressed in jean shorts, a western-yoked shirt, and her favorite pair of cowboy boots. Mia's had been red. Back then she'd never let any of her sisters copy her red boots—they were her symbol, her favorite thing even now. The triplets could wear pink; that was as close as she allowed. The others were at the mercy of brown, black, or blue.

They still teased her even though she'd lifted the ban long ago. The sisters had recreated the picture just two months ago at their father's funeral. Now six grown women smiled out from that image—*successful* women all. They still looked darn good in cut-offs and cowboy boots. Mia's boots were still red. But they weren't any of them nearly as carefree as they'd been in the original photo.

She touched the picture of her father, the pang of loss always stronger after a tough day. Sam Crockett, tough, proud, handsome—a Wyoming cattleman to the depths of his heart. He'd inherited, expanded, and run one of the largest, wealthiest ranches in the state. And he'd died at age sixty-eight leaving Paradise Ranch to his wife and six daughters. None of whom had possessed the slightest interest in running it.

Mia had been the only one groomed for the job, and her father had expected to take over until the day she'd left for college.

She turned away, settled into the deep, heavenly cushions of her burgundy leather sofa and pulled a thick afghan, knitted by her beloved Grandmother Sadie back in Wyoming, over her legs. She'd broken her father's heart the day she'd turned her back on the ranch. Or so he'd claimed—if not in those exact un-masculine words. It had been more like, "This isn't what I hoped for, darlin'. I've got nobody who can take my place. You were it."

She'd never understood how, out of six children, he'd only picked one to groom. But it had been true. The burden had been hers, and she'd never quite lived up to the task of carrying it. No matter how many As in school, or awards in science fairs or Future Farmers of America competitions or letters in chess she'd received, there was always improvement to be made.

She looked again at the mantle and picked out the picture of her sister Harper with her soon-to-be husband. Harper wouldn't have been second or even third choice as heir, stuck as her head had always been in painting rather than cattle and the management of fifty thousand acres. And Cole standing beside her had once been Mia's beau. She should be bitter, but she was grateful. She and Cole had never belonged together, for so many reasons. And they'd never been as deliriously happy as he and Harper were today.

And she'd never in ten lifetimes have agreed to run Paradise Ranch with him the way Harper had.

"Daddy, I hope you see how right it is that I'm still here and your crazy little artist is running the place," she said to the picture, and flushed at the sound of her voice in the quiet room. She glanced around the serene space with its neutral color scheme—rich browns and taupes with touches of burgundy and sage green.

Her unusual contemplation unnerved her slightly. It had to be the headache, and the silence after the insanity of this day—surrounded by children and parents and all their current worries not so much different from the ones she'd grown up with. Now more concerns about Joely back home made being alone throb like an old, aching wound.

She rubbed her temples, broke open the crackers, and dunked one resolutely in the steaming mug of cocoa. She bit into the softened graham-y heaven and closed her eyes. This had been her favorite snack since childhood. Another slice of her headache slipped away.

After three crackers, she opened her computer and brought up her work schedule for the next month. What had Gabriel said? The fourteenth. That was Joely's appointment. Wait, Gabriel?

"Please, call me Gabriel. I'm a civilian." He'd been making that request since the day they'd met. She mimicked him out loud in a ridiculous voice that didn't do him justice—or fairness. But he was an arrogant know-it-all. Well, sometimes.

A movie-star handsome, arrogant know-it-all.

Oh, for crying out loud.

She pushed him out of her thoughts and studied her appointments and scheduled surgeries. Every day through the tenth was filled. And she had two routine tonsillectomies scheduled for, crap, Tuesday morning the fourteenth. That was going to make it pretty much impossible to get to Wyoming during the day.

Disappointment rose bitterly, although she didn't know why. Joely's situation was something she could discuss perfectly easily over Skype. Her schedule was always filled.

She really was exhausted.

She closed her laptop and set it aside, pulling the afghan close around her chin and fluffing a throw pillow behind her. With little care as to what appeared in front of her, she turned on the television set. Six o'clock evening news. Perfect.

Gabriel Harrison appeared on the screen. A large Garfield-colored cat lay draped in his arms, and he stroked it slowly, with pinky raised, like Dr. Evil in an old Austin Powers movie.

"Dr. Crockett, I'm sorry but you cannot speak to this cat. He's my client, and he does not want to go into foster care."

"He has no place else to go. It's not safe to wander the streets."

"You'll have to take it up with the Supreme Court. I'm only doing my job."

"I know my rights, Lieutenant. I demand to know where you intend to put him." She stomped her foot to make her point.

"He's going to a group home for indigent cats. He has no way to pay for a nice foster mother."

"The veterans' administration can't just kick him out. He has eight more lives, but they'll be wasted overnight if he goes to a group home."

"I'm just doing my job." Somewhere next to him a phone began to ring. "Excuse me," he said. "This is the director of the home now."

"You have the same phone ring I do," she said, confused.

Her eyes flew open. Beside her on the coffee table, her phone buzzed, and her ring tone blared through the empty room. The news was just ending. Bolting upright, she pressed four fingers of her right hand against one temple, but the headache had lessened substantially. Afraid she'd miss the call, she answered without looking at the caller ID.

"Hello, Amelia Crockett."

"Dr. Crockett? Hello. This is Aaron Sanderson. You might have heard my name as Buster. I think you're the answer to a prayer."

Chapter Four

GABRIEL HARRISON RAN a hand over his eyes and stared
at the mayhem spread out before him like a buffet of frat-
boy pranks. He hadn't believed over the phone that the
aftermath of this practical joke was so widespread. Now
he knew he was probably flirting with losing his job by
laughing.

His men didn't do things by half.

The Honda Civic belonging to the head of Wyoming
VA's Department of Veterans' Benefits stood at the front
of a line of three cars right outside the veteran's service
building. It was plastered bumper to sunroof to trunk
with colorful sticky notes. Not a sliver of paint showed,
not a glint of window could be seen. One door was pink,
another green, and the windows were all like checker-
boards, with blue and white squares. Spelled out along
one side in purple notes was the phrase "Send a memo,
Dick." A reference to the car's owner, Dick Granville.

The third car in the lineup, a green Ford Escape, belonged to the deputy director of the whole medical center, and it was swaddled front to back in who-knew-how-many layers of clear plastic cling wrap. Gabriel winced and rubbed his eyes.

The real mess, however, came at the expense of the middle car, a brand-new black Lexus owned by the executive director, Frank Simms. Someone had rigged a mini-bomb with a payload of whipped cream to trigger by opening the car door. A partially demolished box about eighteen inches square sat on the ground beside a back tire, and every spot in its wrecked vicinity was covered in dripping white goo. This included the car's interior, the bases of three flag poles in a center island of the driveway, and six people, one of whom was Frank Simms himself.

Gabriel knew exactly who'd done the deeds, as well as why. No matter. He and the eight men participating in his experimental PTSD project were in serious effing doo-doo here. But, damn, this was a seriously skilled prank job by his guys, who'd clearly paid way too much detailed attention to his stories about the college hacks he'd taken part in back in the day. An unconscionable flare of pride in his group got tamped down quickly. What Gabriel saw as a nonviolent outlet for serious frustration by a group of angry-but-healing, mentally wounded men, who could just as easily have taken a far more dangerous tack, would be viewed as vandalism by the higher-ups.

"Harrison!"

He swallowed the last urge to burst into laughter and faced Pete Oswald. For all intents and purposes he and

Pete did the same job, but because he'd been at the job six months longer, Pete was de facto leader of their patient advocacy staff. A humorless man at the best of times, he now wore the crazed mask of someone looking for live bodies to hang.

"Pete. This is…" The traitorous urge to laugh assailed him again, and he coughed into his hand. "This is a mess. I'm sorry."

"You have every reason to be. Your band of crazies has been racking up confrontations with the director and the benefits office for three months now. I think it's fairly obvious they targeted the top three people at this facility on the exact day they had an all-hands meeting." He shook a limp piece of paper in front of Gabriel. "Besides, they left this."

The paper had clearly been a victim of the cream, but the writing was still legible.

"To the leaders of our esteemed Veterans Administration. Over the past several months, many attempts to get the attention of anyone who can help us have failed. We're forced to conclude that you haven't received our e-mails, letters, or phone calls. We hope that once you've received these messages, you'll finally consider our requests. We are in need of help with the following servicemen's records. Once our requests have been acknowledged, we'll appear in person and discuss discipline for our actions."

There followed the names, service identification numbers, and case numbers from all eight of the men Gabriel was working with.

"Well, this seems pretty straightforward to me," Gabe said.

"It's straightforward, all right. You get these guys into my office by eight hundred hours tomorrow, or I'll have them up on charges." He started to turn away.

"C'mon, Pete." Gabriel touched the man's upper arm to stop him. "You don't have the power to do that."

"They are under our auspices, and you're the one who put them there. The nail goes into our coffin, so in this fight they're our dogs. Your dogs."

"Look. They all live in the same building and they talk. They're frustrated, and they don't have faith I can help anymore because the benefits jokers don't listen to me, either."

"Beside the point. If they act like a gang of street thugs, talking each other into shit they'd never think of on their own, somebody has to act like a parent." Pete grinned humorlessly. "Hello, Daddy."

"They won't come. Unless it's for us to listen to them."

"Oh, I think they will." Pete's voice was threatening, like a rattlesnake emerging from under a rock.

"Or what? You can't court martial them. Are you going to threaten to halt their benefits? Half of them are already waiting for decisions on money or services they should have received months ago. Have you ever considered helping me side with them?"

"The United States doesn't negotiate with terrorists."

Gabriel had to laugh. "Right. Terrorists should all be this benign. Look. Help me get them heard. We'll make them pay for damages, and if the director wants to press charges, so be it."

Pete deflated slightly. Gabe looked over his shoulder at the whipped cream-covered director who was speaking with several police officers. To Gabriel's surprise and relief, Director Simms was wiping his shirt with a towel and smiling.

"Why these guys, Gabe?" Pete sighed. "Eight of the most cracked men in the West, and you put them together."

"Because we're the ones who cracked them. We sent them to hell, and now we expect them to come back and behave like nothing's different in their worlds. I know from personal experience that isn't close to true. And this 'shit' they pulled tonight is nothing remotely like the shit they were asked to pull in that Sandbox. So cut 'em some slack, give them some time. Let me explain to—" Gabe was cut off by the electronic warble of his cell phone.

He pulled it out and saw the private number for one of his favorite clients, a severely injured auto accident victim named Joely Crockett. It was nearly seven thirty—awfully late to be calling him. His brows drew together.

"I have to take this, Pete."

Pete waved him away. "I'll deal with this now. I'd rather be the one to do it anyhow."

Gabriel nodded and answered his phone. "Joely?"

"Gabe?" Her voice shook with tightly coiled anxiety. "I'm so, so sorry to call you this late."

"Hey, it's perfectly all right. Is something wrong?"

"The doctor came up tonight and said they'd taken a more thorough look at the MRI from this afternoon. They found something they want to double check—a…a cyst that's formed unexpectedly. They want to do another MRI right now because, if it's where and what they think it is, they want to do surgery first thing in the morning. But, it's risky; they'd be working right on the spinal cord. I don't know much else."

"I'm sorry, Joely. What can I do?"

She was a fragile patient physically, recovering more slowly than anyone liked. She'd lost the use of one leg, and nobody seemed to know if the injury could or would be reversed. Joely normally didn't panic but tended to turn somber and fatalistic. She did suffer from depression, however, so the fear in her voice worried him.

"I know it's probably ridiculous, but I really want to talk to Mia, and I can't reach her."

Mia. His pulse hiccupped and then sped forward like a Ferrari hitting a speed bump. Dr. Amelia Crockett, Joely's sister, was a general and pediatric surgeon in New York. The woman was pretty much everything Joely was not: demanding, abrasive, pushy. She didn't take no for an answer ever, and when she'd been here in Wyoming the first two weeks after Joely's accident, she'd gone over his head to Pete multiple times, and over Pete's head at least once. And yet, Amelia was brilliant, devoted to her sister and, at age thirty-two, a prodigy of a surgeon from what he'd been able to research about her—not that he'd admit Googling her to anyone. She was also stunning—a satisfyingly sexist observation—and the rich, warm, musical laugh that had accompanied her rare smiles came to mind every time he heard her name.

"And you need me to call her again," he said.

"Everyone at home is still out somewhere. I've left all of them messages but…" Her voice cracked and halted.

"I'm sure everything is fine," Gabriel said.

To his surprise, she laughed weakly. "I'm so sorry. This is what self-absorbed panic sounds like. I wasn't worried about them, isn't that awful?"

"Of course not. I'm glad you weren't. You should be thinking about yourself."

"You're a nice person," she said. "So it's your own fault you got this call. It's just that I'd feel so much better if Mia could talk to the doctors here—even on the phone. I know she would ask the questions none of us here know to ask. They're so grave about everything. I don't know what to be worried about most."

"I will call your sister. And I'll be at the hospital in five minutes. I'm just across the campus at the administration building."

"I left her a message, but they're coming to get me any moment and I won't be able to take my phone."

"I'll find her. And I'll find you. Okay? We have all night to figure this out."

He heard a slight sniff. "You rock. I did get the best patient advocate. This isn't in your job description."

"For you, Miss Joely, there's no job description. Happy to make it up as we go along. I'll see you in a few minutes."

"Thank you, Gabe. So much."

He hung up and sighed. He'd already talked to Amelia once today. It hadn't gone that badly. She'd only called him Buster, vain, and a user of smug semantics.

Whatever. He could handle a battle of nouns and adjectives with a *girl*. He smiled and checked his watch. It would be nine thirty in New York. She could be dealing with her own emergency patient. He found her in his address book and hit call. He'd leave her a message now and figure out later why his nerves vibrated with anticipation as he waited for her voice mail.

SHE WAS CERTIFIABLE. Nobody would disagree with her.

Mia had felt safe enough in the subway, but once she surfaced she knew she never should have agreed to Buster's request no matter how heartfelt it had been. He'd promised to meet her at the top of the subway exit stairs and walk her the two blocks to St. Sebastian's, and she'd confirmed with Gwen, the shelter director, that Buster/Aaron was legit. Despite her precautions, she looked around the dark, grimy street after emerging from the station and saw nobody who looked like he was waiting for a foolish doctor far from her comfort zone.

Not that she was alone. Although the nicest term she could use to describe this neighborhood was sleazy, a couple walked the sidewalk across the street from where she stood; one wiry black man leaned in a doorway, eyeing her blandly while he exhaled cigarette smoke; and at least two pairs of feet in tattered shoes stuck out from a dilapidated storefront three doors down.

Mia had lived in New York for eight years, and she'd spent plenty of time volunteering in mobile and free clinics. She wasn't put off by poverty, nor was she squeamish about bodies sleeping outdoors—sorrowful, yes, but not shocked. She'd never, however, made a habit of walking tough neighborhood streets alone. And this was one of the toughest.

She drew a breath and nodded to the man in the doorway. Just past the subway surround, she nearly stumbled into another body, seated against the upright iron posts of the green fencing. He held out a small plastic container containing a measly few coins and a couple of crumpled bills.

"Spare a dollar, Mother?" he asked.

She stopped and stared down at him. She knew handing out money to a panhandler was usually counterproductive. This man might want a fast food meal or sandwich at a local grocer, or he might head for the nearest cheap bottle of wine. She had no way of knowing which. "I'm heading two blocks to St. Sebastian's. Will you walk with me? There's warm food and a bed there."

"I don't need no place to stay." He stared at her, affronted. "I'm lookin' to he'p my little child. No more than that."

"Now, Arthur, just because you don't recognize this lady as being from around here, that doesn't mean it's all right to tell her your old fake little child story."

Mia sagged with relief and looked into the kind face of the woman whose voice she recognized from two phone calls. She was maybe in her fifties, more mature than her voice had given away. Behind her stood a thin, bearded, white man of medium height wearing a green army jacket, brown knit cap, and tweed gray fingerless gloves. He carried a large cardboard box, covered in animal designs, by a handle.

"Gwen? Buster?"

"I'm so sorry we're late," she answered. "We had a rush at the shelter all of a sudden. I think the weather forecast changed slightly, so everyone came in. We're headed for a cold rain tonight."

Mia couldn't help but turn in her spot and peer down the street at the worn shoes sticking onto the sidewalk.

Gwen nodded. "We'll get to them and try to convince them to join us. But there are a few who have such fear of crowds that they'll huddle under trash before coming inside." She waved to the man in the door. "Francis," she said.

"Miss Gwendolyn," he replied.

"I'm sorry." She turned back to Mia. "I'm Gwen Robertson. Dr. Crockett, it's so good of you to come. This is Aaron."

"Hi, Aaron."

"I prefer Buster," he said pleasantly, and held out one hand. The glove was stained but not completely filthy.

"Buster, then. And Gwen. I'm Mia."

"Please, won't you come with us? Buster can tell you his whole story in the shelter where it's warm. When my replacement arrives, I'll be happy to take you back home as I promised."

That had been a selling point—she didn't have to ride the subway back home with a cat. Everything else connected to this trip was insanity. "That was very kind of you."

"Come on, Arthur," Gwen called. "Bring your earnings and put them in safekeeping for the night."

Arthur rose from his seat on the concrete, a lanky grasshopper unfolding angled legs. He was all knees and height when he stood, and not much older than Buster, perhaps thirty-five or forty. He tipped a worn baseball cap at Mia. "Sorry 'bout sayin' I had a child."

"Well, you fooled me once," she said lightly. "Won't happen again."

"No, ma'am."

They headed down the sidewalk and turned at the corner, a nippy breeze greeting them with a quick little blast.

"How is my little dude Rory?" Buster asked, switching his hold on the box to two hands and pulling it close to his chest. "I miss him."

"He's going to be all right," Mia said. "He talks a lot about you. You two must have had quite an adventure."

"He's a smart kid. We lived pretty good out here, but I knew he couldn't stay. I just had to convince him it was better to go live in a house where it was safe."

"Glad you did. Is that Jack there?"

"Ha, man, dat's Jack in the Box!" Arthur hooted at his own joke.

"It is," Buster acknowledged. "I didn't want to leave him alone. Everybody loves Jack. Someone would take him."

"Do a lot of your friends have pets out here?" Mia asked.

"Some. A couple have dogs. Not too many have cats; they get too wild living out here. Jack is different."

"I remember him as a kitten. As I recall, he's a gorgeous cat."

"That he is. Rory grabbed him from the house when his mom got in trouble, but then he wasn't allowed to bring him to the foster home. I never saw a little kid work so hard not to cry. That's when I said I'd keep Jack safe until Rory could have him."

"And now you can't keep him either," Mia finished.

"It would be hard."

They reached the front of St. Sebastian's; a red sandstone building next to a church, it was caked in the dust and grime of a dilapidated Brooklyn neighborhood but nonetheless wore a dignified air. The instant Gwen opened the door, warmth, light, music, and the lingering aroma of warm bread banished the cold unfriendliness of the street.

"Welcome to St. Sebastian's Shelter," said Gwen. "We serve over two hundred meals a day and up to a thousand on holidays. In the winter we can bunk up to a hundred people easily and up to two hundred in an emergency. We have few real amenities aside from cots, sleeping mats, heat, and food. We have toilets and very minimal showering facilities. Our most prized possession is a fairly new jukebox, which visitors can use until ten thirty every day. It's quite popular, as you can hear."

Mia didn't recognize the rap song playing. It was far out of her limited repertoire of favorite artists.

"We try to keep current music for them. There are all genres. You could very well hear Miranda Lambert next and Green Day after that. Nothing offensive, but otherwise we don't discriminate." She smiled. "We sneak a few hymns in there too. They get played on occasion. Come on in. We can talk in the small office off the kitchen. Arthur, why don't you go register your money with Susie and pick a bed? Have you eaten anything today?"

"Yes, ma'am. I had lunch."

"There are some cookies and sandwiches left."

The man left them with a wave, walking away like a gangly marionette. Gwen shrugged. "He's a rare type. He has some learning disabilities, and he can't keep a job, but he takes his begging as seriously as any career. He's nice as the day's long despite making up all those stories."

The room they moved through was thirty feet square, half filled with tables and benches, the other half with people sitting on the floor in front of the bright jukebox. Gwen pointed at two archways off the room that led to four more open rooms, those filled with cots, sleeping mats, and a handful of cribs. The simple complexity of the operation amazed Mia.

The kitchen was large and utilitarian, with an institutional-sized stainless steel stove, two ovens, a refrigerator, and a dishwasher. Sturdy cafeteria-style plates, bowls, and mugs were stacked in columns on heavy duty shelving.

"Here's our office." Gwen opened a door off a small corridor into a room painted a cheerful, robin's egg blue. Two desks, two armchairs, and a small round table filled the space, along with three full-sized file cabinets. "Have a seat."

"I've never been back here," Buster said. "I feel special. Can I let Jack out?"

"Of course. We want Dr. Crockett to meet him."

When Buster opened the box, Mia stared, stunned, at one of the most beautiful cats she'd ever seen. It emerged like a prince, calm and curious, its long, silken coat a muted, creamy buff, its ears, tail, paws, and face all a rich, beautiful black. Most startling of all were its bright blue eyes—sharp, assessing, missing nothing.

"Hey, Jack-man," Buster crooned. "Come and meet Miss Amelia."

"I knew he was pretty. I didn't remember how beautiful. And huge."

"The vet told us he's a gray seal point ragdoll cat. He weighs about eighteen pounds, but they're the biggest cat breed, so that's not even all that large."

Without prompting, Jack walked regally to Mia's feet, wound his way in a figure eight around her ankles and then sprang into her lap. He sat fully upright, facing her like an Egyptian cat god, and waited for her to pet him. His fur was velvety and rabbit-like, and the instant she touched it, Jack's purr filled the room. He rubbed his cheek to hers twice, turned around neatly, and curled into her lap.

She'd known myriad barn cats in her life, but she'd always been a dog person. None of that mattered as she swiftly, thoroughly, and pathetically fell in love.

"You can see why he's a favorite wherever Buster goes," Gwen said.

"I can," she agreed. "But you really can't keep him?"

"Buster is one of our success stories," Gwen answered, pride obvious in her voice.

"I've got a job." Buster took over his tale. He was a unique man, slender, nice-looking in a sandy-haired way, slightly clichéd with his army surplus look. Yet he was obviously erudite and well-educated. Likeable. "I don't want to own a house again or have any of the trappings. But I would like to be able to buy my own clothing and food and pay for my time here at the shelter."

"We're working on the no-home part," Gwen said.

"I won't be here every day to watch over Jack, and I don't trust anyone else with him. People move around too much, and they'd take him. I was going to bring him to the animal shelter tomorrow and beg them to not adopt him out until we could get him to Rory. But the lady I talked to said they don't board animals—they find homes, and if they can't…" He shook his head. "I couldn't have that. I didn't know what to do, so I came here tonight to ask for advice. It's the craziest thing that Gwen had your number."

She couldn't help it; she was moved. Here was a man pulling himself up out of utter poverty who was worried more about an animal than himself. It reminded her of the ranch hands in Wyoming who'd go without food for two days to ride out and find a missing cow and calf.

"I have to be perfectly honest," she began. "I don't have any place for a cat to be outside if that's what he's used to. I live in an apartment."

"He used to live inside at Rory's," Buster said, without any urgency.

"Oh, Buster, I'm not sure why I came. Maybe to try and talk you into keeping him, I don't know. But I promised Rory—"

Her phone rang out, and she saw Joely's number again. Minor panic filled her.

"I'm so sorry," she said. "This is a family call. I have a sister who's ill, so I should take it."

Buster stood and pulled Jack from her lap. Mia popped out of the office and answered the phone. "Joely?"

"Hello," replied the voice that turned her throat to sand and her pulse to useless fizz in her veins. "Déjà vu."

Chapter Five

"GABRIEL HARRISON?" SHE stared around the shelter's kitchen, surprised and lost for more words.

"At last. I've graduated from Lieutenant."

"Look," she said, worry snapping her out of her surprise. "I know that's the most important issue for you, but I need to know right now everything is all right."

"Everything is all right."

Tension that had twisted up her spine like a steel snake relaxed its grip. Her breath released in a long sigh. "So, why are you using my sister's phone?"

"I wanted to make sure you answered. I thought you might not if it was me." She sensed he was telling the truth even though his words were bright with humor.

"Hah, you're probably right. What's going on?" she asked.

"There has been a new development with Joely. After a closer look at her MRI, the doctors found a suspicious spot in her spinal cord. It's not a tumor," he added quickly. "They've taken her down for another image, and this one has her a lot more upset. She missed you when she tried to call and nominated me to try again."

"Is she in immediate danger?"

"No. I wouldn't have purposely lied about everything being all right."

"I'm sorry. It seems Joely is lucky to have you. You're becoming her private secretary."

"Hardly. Your sisters and mother do all the work. This just happens to be an unusual day."

"So is there something I can do?" She brushed past his conversational chat.

"Yes. Joely would like you to talk with her doctor because surgery could get moved up to as soon as tomorrow. She wants your opinion before that happens. Even a phone call between you and Dr. Landon would ease her mind."

"The need for surgery will obviously depend on what they decide this object or injury is. Some things *would* have to be dealt with quickly. Others could wait or be treated with physical therapy and/or drugs."

"You have a very calm, professional voice."

She wasn't sure whether that was a compliment or his passive-aggressive way of saying she was unfeeling. He at least made it *sound* like the former, and she softened, relieved at the less confrontational vibe they'd struck. "I think most doctors have The Voice," she said. "It's like putting on protective armor. At any rate, tell Joely of course. I'll talk to whomever she wants."

"It's getting late there now," he said. "But is there a chance we could set up a call for tonight?"

"Yes, but unfortunately I'm not even home at the moment. I'll be back in my apartment within an hour, and then I'll have access to my computer and some privacy."

"I'm sorry if I interrupted something."

"No apologies needed. I'm glad you did."

"Hot date?" His voice was teasing.

Just like that, the easy atmosphere they'd built evaporated. "I hardly think that's any of your business, Lieutenant."

"Fair enough. Although I wasn't really being serious…"

Oh, don't actually apologize, she fumed to herself, more embarrassed that he'd caught her being hypersensitive about dating than she was truly angry. "Why am I not surprised? We aren't talking about anything serious about after all."

A low, nerve-strumming chuckle floated through the phone. "Sorry, Doc. I have a lot to learn about being serious. So I've been told all my life."

She ignored the late, insincere apology. The self-satisfied, arrogant man.

"Look," she said. "Can I do anything else for Joely right now? Which would make more sense, for me to call him or vice versa?"

"He's an amiable guy. I'll have him give you a call if that's all right. What's a good time?"

"Let's say ten o'clock my time. If I don't answer, have him leave me his contact number."

"Will do. Well, I've done my job, Dr. Amelia Crockett." Her name rolled off his tongue like poetry. "So, are we okay before I say good-bye this time? We don't want to go to bed angry."

Her breath caught in her throat. Go to bed angry? The man was, without question, challenged in the professionalism department. "Good night, *Mr.* Gabriel Harrison. I promise I won't go to sleep angry. It simply wouldn't be worth the time."

"That's the spirit. All right, good night. And you know, if you need anything from me, you have my number. I answer anytime, too."

"I think I have all I need, not that we have the best track record with exchanging information, as I recall. Good-bye."

"Bye now."

He was gone. Like a recurring dream—not frightening but definitely disconcerting. She stood in one place until her head cleared, and she focused for a moment on Joely, sifting through possibilities of things they might find on a new MRI. A blood clot—fairly easy to identify; a prolapsed disc—they would have recognized that; a hematoma—very rare in a spinal cord and highly unlikely. Giving the back of her neck a rub, she went back through St. Sebastian's office door. Buster looked up from where he'd sat on the floor, his eyes concerned.

"Everything is all right?"

Mia allowed a reassuring smile. "It's been an interesting day, but yes. All's well."

"That's good. I've been thinking," he said. "If you can't keep a cat for the long term, is it possible you could just take care of Jack for a week until I can find a foster home for him?"

Jack meowed at the sight of Mia and strolled toward her. Without thinking, she sank onto the floor beside Buster and gathered Jack into her lap. "I'm sorry I left in the middle of my answer. There's no need to look for a foster home, Buster. I'll take Jack. You're right, we have to keep him safe until Rory can have him. In fact, I'll talk to his foster mom again myself."

Buster's face lit like a child's. "You have no idea how happy that makes me."

A thousand memories from her childhood flooded her in that instant: The light in her heart and the joy on the faces of her five sisters whenever a new litter of kittens was discovered or a calf happened to be born close in rather than out in the summer pastures; the unconditional love a dog could give; the comfort of stroking a horse. It had been so long since she'd had animals in her life. She'd forgotten.

Or maybe that's exactly why she'd taken the subway to Brooklyn.

"I know a little about pets," she said, basking in unfamiliar delight. "Will you tell me exactly how you take care of him, so I can do things as close to the same way as possible?"

"I'll be honored to show you."

AN HOUR LATER, as she surveyed the drastic change a few cat accoutrements could affect in a small New York apartment, Mia's enthusiasm had faded to something more realistic. The cat was still beautiful. He'd seemed unperturbed by his journey in the car, wandered around the apartment with unruffled curiosity, noted where she put his litter box and food dishes, and now swatted experimentally at the mini-blind cords in her living room. But it suddenly felt like her ordered, busy-but-quiet life was bursting with too many things she couldn't control.

The litter box took up space in a back hall closet area. A handful of toys decorated the carpet. An oval, stuffed bed sat on her bedroom floor. She had to figure out how and where to stop for more cat litter and food. She worried about leaving Jack for a whole day tomorrow.

Then there was Joely. And Rory. And Shawna Murray. And her concern over the new job. And it was too late now to reach Monique Beltane's physicians to find out how she was doing. After staring almost catatonically for fifteen minutes, sorting mentally through her rearranged life, she got up to pour a glass of wine. She'd taken her first sip when her phone rang. This time she recognized the Wyoming area code and the VA Medical Center's exchange.

"Hello?"

"Is this Dr. Amelia Crockett?"

"Yes."

"This is Perry Landon. I'm an orthopedic surgeon working with your sister in Jackson, Wyoming."

She settled deeply into the corner of her couch and set her wine glass beside her, relieved to have something on which to focus. "It's good to hear from you." Jack sprang into her lap. She stroked him, surprised but comforted.

"I promised Joely I'd call you as soon as I got the results of her latest MRI. Hers is an unusual case, but I'm glad to report I think we have some answers."

"That's good to hear. So you've identified the spot or mass on her spine? Mr. Harrison said you weren't sure what it was."

"We have. It's a spinal epidural hematoma, probably caused by the little fall she took."

"Oh, it *is*." Professional curiosity warred with personal concern. "I admit, that was at the bottom of my list of possibilities."

"It's definitely unusual."

"So is more surgery required to drain the hematoma? I've never done one, but I know quick intervention is key—especially if Joely's neurologic symptoms are worsening."

"In my opinion, they had been. She lost bladder and bowel control and some feeling in her previously unaffected leg. In addition, her pain had increased."

She couldn't stop the small sound of concern that escaped.

"I'm sorry," Perry said, genuine warmth in his voice. "I went about this in a poor order. You're family, too, not just a surgeon. I should have begun by explaining that we've chosen to treat immediately and aggressively with steroids, and she's already begun to improve. Those new neurologic signs have almost all disappeared. We'll take one more image in the morning to see if the hematoma is shrinking. The good news, I guess it's good news, is that because of this I found a hidden injury I think it's important to repair."

"Oh?" She was grateful for his sensitivity. The kind, she knew, people were always telling her to develop. She supposed she should take notes on this conversation.

"Three small bone fragments are pressing into the spinal dura just below the T-four level. I can send you the image if you'd like."

"That would be great." She gave him her e-mail address.

When he repeated it back with not a single hesitation or question, the strangest revelation hit. Perry Landon hadn't irritated her once. Her guard was down; he spoke her language; she wasn't rolling her eyeballs. It was the first ordinary, calm thing that had happened all day.

"I'd recommend surgery once her strength from this is recovered," he said. "I know Joely is very worried, however. You'll see when you look at the image—there, I just sent it—that this won't be routine surgery. The fragments are so close to the spinal cord itself that, while the hope is Joely would notice improvement, there could also be further damage to the nerves."

"There's a reason you guys are the experts at this. It's crazy delicate work. I'll be happy to talk to Joely about the surgery. I'm sure she's just exhausted from this whole ordeal."

"She thinks the sun rises and sets on you, and rightfully so judging from your resume. Youngest board certified general surgeon at New York City General. Three research grants accepted. Half a dozen JAMA articles."

Wow. This man knew how to play to a woman's vanities. No innuendo. No cockiness. She pictured Gabriel Harrison, prepared to throw mental darts at his smug image, but for some reason all she could recall were images of a million megawatt smile. *Are we okay before I say good-bye? We don't want to go to bed angry.*

Oh for pity's sake.

"That's very kind," she said into the phone. "I've been lucky to have time to pursue my interests."

She moved Jack gently from her lap to a spot right next to her thigh, then picked up her laptop and opened her e-mail. She smiled when she saw Perry Landon's va.gov e-mail and pushed Gabriel Harrison out of her mind as professional curiosity took over.

"Got your e-mail," she said. "Hang on."

The three images were remarkable. Mia studied them silently, and Dr. Landon allowed her the time. "Oh my," she said at last. "Impressive job spotting the hematoma. And it's amazing that the steroids seem to be working."

"And you see the fragments. Looks like they came off that left T-six transverse process."

"I do." She studied more closely the little wing on the vertebra he'd indicated. "I can see why you want to operate, but man, I also see why you have no clue whether it will work."

"I guess my question is whether you'd concur that it's worth the risk."

She hadn't thought about it before, but she wondered how much experience this man actually had. Exiting her e-mail, she quickly brought up the Wyoming VA's site.

"I truly have to defer to you on this," she said. "I am not a spine expert."

She searched on his name, and his picture popped up. She grinned in spite of herself. He looked like a mature version of Cary Elwes in *The Princess Bride*, complete with pencil-thin mustache, straight blond hair, and high cheekbones. Unlike the character Westley, however, Perry wore glasses and his face was broader and a little more handsome, with a professorial attractiveness about him.

"No, but you understand surgical risks. My question is just one colleague to another."

"All right. Then I'd counsel my sister to have the surgery."

He was silent a moment. "I appreciate that," he said at last.

"It helped to speak with you. I appreciate you sharing all this information." *Unlike a certain retired lieutenant I could name.* "I hope at some point when I'm in Wyoming to visit, we can discuss the positive outcome to Joely's surgery in person."

"I hope so, too. I know your sister would be extremely relieved if you were here when and if we choose to go ahead. Is there a chance of that?"

The tiniest spark of guilt flickered to life in her chest. Gabriel had called that morning to ask this precise question, and she'd promised to make every effort. But if Joely's surgery were to take place within the next ten days…When she got the new position, she'd have a lot of prep work to do if she was to start December first. It might even put her Christmas visit home in jeopardy.

"I'm not sure there is, I'm afraid," she said. "I expect to start a new job within the next month, and that's going to require my staying here. A lot depends on when surgery would take place. I'll definitely try."

"Then I'll hope for it to work out. It was good to meet you if just by phone."

"I look forward to updates as we go along. Thank you for taking such good care of my sister."

"My pleasure. Have a good night, Amelia."

"Good night," she replied.

The instant she set her phone down beside her computer on the coffee table, Jack nudged his way back onto her lap. She closed her eyes and stroked him, basking in the decadence of his incredibly soft, pelt-like hair. She pictured Perry Landon's photo, but the image blurred and morphed into the dark-haired, square-jawed visage of Gabriel Harrison.

Immediately every relaxed muscle in her body went rigid with tension. Why the man invaded every potential peaceful moment from her dreams to cat-cuddling she didn't know. He'd annoyed her so much she couldn't get rid of him. She growled and grabbed Jack around his substantial middle, hauling him to a stand in her arms.

"Come on, you," she said, nuzzling him between the ears. "It's only our first night together, but how would you like to come to bed with me?"

We don't want to go to bed angry.

"Arghh," she said again and looked up at the ceiling. "Get away from me, you boorish man. It's too late—I'm plenty mad at you."

But she really had no idea why.

SOMETHING WALKING ON her face woke her up. She cracked one eye, because the second was sealed shut with pressure from a creature's soft paw, and groaned at the clock.

"Seriously? You couldn't wait ten more minutes?"

She rolled to her side, pushing Jack off her cheeks, and curled an arm around his thick body. He settled in, shoving his head into her hand and purring. The rolling motor hum soothed her, and a vague memory returned of falling asleep to the same comforting drone. Not a dream had spoiled the night.

"Aren't you the big, surprising wonder cat?" she murmured.

For all of the turmoil from the day before, once she grudgingly got out of a very comfortable bed to feed her new roommate and shower, she faced the new morning with surprising optimism. It wasn't because of the cat. That would be too syrupy and sweet-animal clichéd. Nevertheless, the cheeriness that followed her right up to the pediatric floor and Rory's door had everything to do with the child she'd so unceremoniously walked out on the day before.

Rory sat fully upright in his bed, eyes glued to the television set mounted on the wall ahead of him. Although it was only 7:45 a.m. the remains of breakfast sat on his bed tray.

"Hey, buddy, what are you watching?"

He turned his head with a welcoming grin. "Sponge Bob."

"Did you know that show goes right over ninety percent of grown-ups' heads?" She approached his bed. "We don't get it."

"It's dumb, but it makes me laugh."

"Laughing is very good. But, hey, would you be mad if I interrupted you? I have something I'd like to show you."

He shrugged. "Naw, I ain't mad. I gotta go home today."

"What do you mean, you *have* to go home? I'd be excited."

"You might. But I'm not."

"Rory." Mia sat on the mattress at the foot of the bed, facing him. She picked up his remote and turned down the TV. "You do know that when the social workers come for their home visits you can tell them you'd like to go to a different place. If you're uncomfortable at the Murrays'."

"No social workers listen to what I say. Else I wouldn't be there at all."

"They'll listen if there's a problem."

"There's no problem. I just don't like it."

"You don't like Shawna's boyfriend, Matt?"

He nodded. "I don't like watching him drink his dumb power shakes all day. Or changing Cameron's pants."

"Rory, we can make a list of all the things you won't be allowed to do for quite a long time because of your appendix surgery—like change a one-year-old's diaper."

"Really?"

"Really. No lifting or holding down a squirming baby. That's for grown-ups to do."

"Why can't you just be my foster mom? My mom said you should if anything happened to her."

She stared at him, alarmed. She didn't like at all the casual way he'd brought up the subject or so easily that his mother had said something. It had to be little-boy wishful thinking. Transference or some other psycho-babble term.

"Rory, nothing's going to happen to your mom. And I wouldn't be a good foster mother."

"Uh-huh. You don't make kids feel stupid. You're like Buster."

He was right about that. Now that she'd met Buster, she could see he probably would be a good foster father.

"Hey, sometimes kids are much more fun to be around than adults that's all. But here's the thing. It's a pretty tough job, and it's very important. There's a lot of responsibility."

"You'd be the best."

"That's really sweet of you, kiddo, but I wouldn't be a great mom. I work way too many hours and stay away from home too much."

His features fell so far she almost believed he'd been honestly hoping it would happen. She sat on the bed and ruffled his hair. "Hey. Don't be sad. I have some cool news, and something to show you."

"Yeah? What?" Full enthusiasm didn't return to his voice, but he lifted his gaze.

With a little flourish she pulled her phone from her lab coat pocket and brought up a video of Jack eating and then nosing the camera phone in curiosity.

"Last night I met someone I believe you know."

He took the phone, and the suspicion in his eyes lasted only for the half-second it took to hit the play arrow.

Chapter Six

FIRST RORY YELPED. Then he let out a yowl of joy that was sure to bring every nurse on the ward running. The next thing Mia knew, he'd leaped out of the bed and was pumping his little legs in place like a football player's running exercise. Before she could catch him, he'd taken off, zooming around the bed while watching the phone screen. When he turned to come back, she grabbed him.

"Hey, hey!" She laughed. "You can't go jumping around like that, you just had surgery."

He threw his arms around her waist and hugged her for all he was worth. "Jack! Jack, Jack!" he chanted. "You found him! You saved him."

She squeezed him back, her eyes stinging slightly. "I got lucky. Maybe the angels were watching out for him."

"Where is he? Where…" He grimaced slightly and put a hand to his side.

"Come on, young man. Into that bed." She helped him climb back in, and once she'd inspected his surgical site and determined he hadn't popped anything, she tucked him in. "Jack is at my apartment. I went and got him from Buster last night."

"Buster!"

"He's a very nice man. You were lucky he's the one who helped you when your mom got sick."

"I would live with him if I could."

She stroked his cheek. The child obviously craved anyone and anyplace where he could get attention. "I can see why. But you know you can't live on the street, even if Buster does. And there's good news for him, too. He got a job. That's why I took Jack home with me. Buster can't watch him during the days anymore."

"Good morning!"

Shawna Murray interrupted the celebration over Jack, entering with a small suitcase and a back pack. Today her workout pants were hot pink and purple, and her shoes a brilliant shade of chartreuse. She'd covered it all with a purple-and-aqua Columbia jacket.

"I have clothes for you to go home in," she said. "When I get done with my classes this morning, I'll come back and get you. Matt is waiting and he's—"

"Look!" Rory forgot to be apathetic and interrupted her by holding out Mia's phone. "It's Jack! Dr. Mia found Jack!"

Shawna shot Mia a confused and unhappy look. "The cat he's always talking about?"

"His cat, yes," Mia replied.

Shawna watched about ten seconds of the video and handed the phone back. "Rory, you know we talked about this. I won't have cats in the house. Not with the baby and with Matt's allergies. He has to find a better home."

"Mrs. Murray." Mia stepped closer to the woman. "As a physician, I can tell you how good medically and psychologically this would be for him. He's in a difficult place, and having someone from his family with him would ease his way. Especially since his activities will be limited over the next few weeks."

The woman who turned on her—after one of Mia's better efforts at a pleasant bedside manner if she did say so—was someone she hadn't seen before. Shawna's brows pinched into arched arrows, and her pupils narrowed to pinpoints.

"Excuse me, but this is really none of your concern. You aren't Rory's doctor, and you don't know the dynamics of our busy household. You lectured me about the dangers of allergic reactions yesterday. Well how would it be to have a mangy animal come in and set off allergies in the rest of the family? The cat is not welcome in the house, and I made that abundantly clear to the case worker who set Rory up with us."

On the bed, Rory, whose face had been so euphoric moments earlier, clutched at his blanket and stared at his foster mother, his lip quivering.

"Mrs. Murray, sit down," Mia countered, her voice calm but unmistakably firm. "There's a chair right here. You need to stop before you upset Rory further."

"I am sorry to upset him; that's not my intention," she said. "But he knows the rules and knew them from the start. I won't have you telling Rory he can have that cat," she said. "What gave you the right to go find it for him anyway?"

"The right one friend has to another," she said. "Now if you need to calm down so Rory sees everything is all right, I have no problem asking you to leave for a few moments. If you'll recall, I never insisted you take the cat, nor will I. I merely observed something that could help Rory. Since that won't work, we'll find another way."

"You're right, we will."

"Let me help you put this in the closet."

Mia reached for the backpack, and Shawna whirled it from her, smacking her knuckles on the edge of table. With a cry she finally sank into the chair. "I insist you leave." She hissed out a breath. "What are you trying to do?"

"No!" Rory was full on crying now. "I don't want her to leave. She's the only one who cares about me or my cat."

At that Shawna seemed to gather her wits. She set Rory's suitcase on the floor and leaned forward in her chair, blowing on her hand. "I am sorry, Rory. I had a very hard morning with the kids, and I'm taking my crabbies out on you."

Unkindly, Mia wondered how often that happened. But she kept her mouth shut.

"I just want to see Jack." Rory held his hands out toward Mia. "I want to be where he is."

"You can't be with Jack," Shawna said, straightening back up in the chair. "I'm sorry, but that all changed when your mother got sick.

"Good morning, troops! How's my patient this morning?" The room got even more crowded as Fred Wilson entered. "Dr. Crockett. Surprised to see you here."

"She shouldn't be here."

"She found my cat."

Shawna and Rory spoke simultaneously.

"Do we have a problem?" Dr. Wilson looked directly at Mia.

"Not at all," she replied. "Rory is correct. I located his cat last night. I came in this morning to say hi and to tell him Jack is fine."

"I want to take him home," Rory said, almost sobbing now.

"I have an idea, Mrs. Murray," Mia said. "I have to leave because I have surgery scheduled in an hour. But perhaps you'd bring Rory to visit Jack? If he could see him once or twice, perhaps he'd feel better."

"I want to visit. Please?" Rory tugged on Shawna's jacket sleeve.

"Rory." Shawna sighed, as if exhausted by the subject. "You know how busy nights and weekends are. We'll see."

Mia reached into her breast pocket and pulled out two of her business cards. She handed one to Shawna and the other directly to Rory, who stared in awe, as if she'd given him Willy Wonka's golden ticket.

"I'll be happy to get him back and forth from your home to mine," Mia said. "Please give me a call to set something up."

Shawna nodded curtly, stuffed the card in her pocket, and turned to Dr. Wilson. "So Rory can still come home today, right?"

Mia sighed. She had little hope Shawna would follow through on her end with the cat.

"Oh, I think we can let him leave." Wilson chuckled. "Sound good to you, Rory, my man? I'd like to take a listen to your heart and tummy, and if everything sounds good we'll set you up with an appointment in two weeks and spring you."

Rory shook his head adamantly. "Dr. Mia can listen. And I want to go see Jack."

"You can't go see Jack today," Shawna said. "And you have to let Dr. Wilson check you out, or you can't go home."

Mia brushed past Wilson, garnering a glare, and reached the far side of Rory's bed. She took his hand. "Since Dr. Wilson is the one who's in charge of deciding when you're well enough to go home, he has to be the one who listens. I know it sounds silly, but the hospital has rules. You let him do that, and I'll stay right here. When he's done, we'll talk some more about Jack."

"Don't get his hopes—" Shawna began. Mia held up her hand and cut her off.

Rory gripped her fingers tightly and nodded, so she motioned to Wilson.

Once the exam was completed, Mia patted Rory's shoulder. "I'm proud of you. Now, here's what I'm going to do. In my office I have a way to print the pictures off my phone. I'll do that and make sure you get them before you leave."

"Will you come and say good-bye?"

"I will try, but I won't promise, okay? Because I don't know if the surgery I have to do now will be finished before you go, and I don't want to tell you something that turns out to be a lie. But I'll find you soon and show you more pictures of Jack."

"I'll come and see him." His bravado crumbled a little, and he looked toward Shawna who spoke with Dr. Wilson.

Mia leaned in close to whisper. "We'll keep working on it."

She patted his arm again and stood, excusing herself. She was pushing the button on the staff elevator for the first floor when Wilson caught her.

"Dr. Crockett. *May* I have a word with you please?" His clipped words were not a request.

"Anytime," she said coolly.

"I find your attitude toward that mother in there—and, frankly, toward me—highly offensive and inappropriate."

"I'm sorry to hear that." She held her tongue, again, with a great deal of trouble.

"You may be some sort of wunderkind in your general surgery group, but up here you do not rule."

"I don't rule anywhere, Doctor. My job is to care for the patients, and that's precisely what I did in this case. I also made it possible for you to examine *your* patient without a meltdown on his part. I'm not precisely sure what your problem with me is."

"You're a surgeon, not a pediatrician or even an internal med doc. You didn't belong in that room."

She spun on him. "Have you forgotten I'm a longtime friend of the child's? I was the only one in that room he wanted to speak with. If I were you, I'd be *thanking* me." The elevator beeped and the doors rolled open with well-oiled precision. "Now if you'll excuse me, I have a three-year-old's hernia to repair."

He didn't follow her onto the elevator, and she breathed a sigh of relief when the doors closed on his unyielding features. She never intended for words come out as stridently as they did, but she hated having to placate people. The way she saw it, all she wanted was for Rory to be safe and happy. All Fred Wilson wanted was to be in charge.

The elevator doors slid open again, and she made for her office. One voice mail message awaited her, from the suddenly omnipresent Gabriel Harrison. She almost expected the array of emotions, from anticipation to mild exasperation to the thrumming heartbeat that took over her entire body.

"Good morning, Dr. Crockett." His voice, with its hint of teasing, made her smile in spite of herself. "I'm playing secretary one last time to let you know Joely went for two more follow-up tests early this morning, and if you want to reach her she'll be back in her room by noon. Also, your sister Harper is back in town, and she'll be able to take over communications, so I won't be clogging up your voice mails." He hesitated slightly and chuckled. "Not that

I mind—there's really nobody else I'd rather cross swords with. So. You have a great day. And call if you have a question. Or need a good argument."

She covered her mouth with one hand and tried not to laugh. What should have irritated her only made her regret he wouldn't be Joely's messenger any longer. The man was aggravation and immaturity, salted with minor helpfulness, and what would have made her rejoice yesterday—the thought of not having to speak with him anymore—today made her slightly sad. Maybe, as her hippie sister Harper would say, Mercury was in retrograde.

She cleaned out her e-mail inbox and gathered what she needed to take with her for surgery. The phone rang while she was reaching to turn out her light. Only Gabriel's message that Joely was having more tests made her decide to answer.

"Amelia Crockett."

"Dr. Crockett, I am Justin McNeil, an attorney representing Monique Beltane. I have some news that directly affects you concerning Ms. Beltane's estate. Do you have a moment to speak with me?"

She had no more than a moment, but there wasn't any way she was going to let that hook hang unaddressed for two hours. "Of course, Mr. McNeil, what can I do for you?"

"You're no doubt aware that Ms. Beltane is undergoing treatment for breast cancer."

"Yes."

"Before her recent hospitalization, she made some alterations to her will. You consider yourself to be good friends with Ms. Beltane and her ten-year-old son, is that right?"

"Yes I do, although I have only seen her once since she's been in prison. May I ask before we go on what currently has her hospitalized?"

"I'm not allowed to divulge medical details, as you know well, but I can tell you that cancer was detected in the breast that had been unaffected, and she underwent a partial mastectomy."

Mia's stomach dropped in dismay. "I'm so sorry," she said.

"I do know the prognosis is not hopeless, so she'll continue with chemotherapy. Nevertheless, she has wanted for some time to make arrangements for her son. To that end, she has named you as Rory's legal guardian should anything happen to her.

"I'm sorry? Guardian? Legal? What does that mean?" Shell-shock was not too strong a word for the panic clawing through her chest.

"Should anything happen to Ms. Beltane, custody of Rory would be yours unless a relative makes a protest, or there are questions about your fitness as a parent."

That was the most ludicrous thing she'd ever heard. Parent?

"Mr. McNeil, I don't think I want to accept this."

"I know it's a shock." For the first time he didn't sound like an automaton. "The will is signed and witnessed, so it's legal. What I would suggest is you have a conversation with Ms. Beltane."

"I will definitely be doing exactly that."

"I don't have any more details for you, Dr. Crockett. The will was signed and notarized yesterday. I wanted to give you a chance to handle the information as you see fit. You could, of course, refuse, but Ms. Beltane hopes you will accept."

The room spun slightly and Mia hit her desk chair like a ragdoll tossed by a child. Even when the spinning stopped she couldn't make herself believe.

"Can I answer any questions for you?" McNeil asked.

"Could I have your contact information?" Mia rubbed her eyes. "I'm sure I do have questions, but I can't think of a single one at the moment. May I call you?"

"Of course. I'll send you my contact information in an e-mail. Feel free to talk to Monique. I can get you access to her despite the fact that she's in a secure wing of the hospital."

"Thank you for calling."

She should have been more cordial or chatty, but her brain seemed to have frozen. When the line went dead she had to sit for ten long minutes before she had enough strength to compartmentalize her emotions and head for surgery. There were often surprises in the OR, too, but at least she had a modicum of control over that world. It was more than she could say for what had gone on outside the OR these past two days.

It was only November second, but the Wyoming air had turned into stinging needles of cold. Despite the arrival of wintery weather Gabe walked the two blocks from Pete's office to the hospital, barely turning up his jacket's fleece collar and lifting his head periodically to peer at the mountains visible from the front of the VA complex. This had to be one of the most beautiful hospital campuses in the country. He'd grown up in central Nebraska, which had its charm, but he'd fallen hard for the Rockies after returning from Iraq six years before and landing the job here. He could no longer imagine leaving. Even on his lowest days the Tetons could awe him.

It was a pretty low morning.

He'd met with Pete to discuss the conduct of his group, and although the guillotine hadn't come down, there were hands poised on the lever waiting to drop the blade.

"If the only thing these guys are going to do is run around covering cars with paper and condiments, they can do that without being under a program we're funding." Pete was clearly done with their escapades. "The deal for them is this: yesterday's incident will be forgiven and forgotten so long as there's not another. And I mean nothing—no getting fired from a job, no drunk and disorderlies, no plastic wrap under a toilet seat, no college-level protest pranks. One more episode and the plug gets pulled."

It was too harsh a reaction in Gabe's mind, but he did understand. The program was under scrutiny, and to survive it needed to be clean. The men needed to behave. "Fair enough," he replied. "They'll get the message."

"Gabe," Pete had said. "Be realistic about this. Don't get so invested you can't see what's going on. You can't save everyone."

Gabe entered the hospital cold and far from calmed. He punched the button for the elevator and knew he had to get a grip before seeing his patients, but it was difficult this morning. He detested it when anybody told him he couldn't save everyone. The trouble with people who spent all their time bean counting was they forgot that everyone *deserved* to be saved.

Everyone who got sent to wage war at their country's behest and who managed to get back still breathing was changed forever. They didn't all have PTSD, not everyone came back with missing limbs or even recurring nightmares. But everyone was changed. And those who did return with the most serious problems deserved every program and experimental program and not-yet-funded-or-conceived-of program that could possibly heal him or her.

Of course he could not literally save everyone. But by heaven he was going to his grave having tried. He owed it to his buddies who hadn't come back, and Jibril and his family, too.

He took the elevator to the fifth floor where Joely Crockett had been in residence for two weeks. For nearly a month before that, she'd been in the intensive care unit. And now it sounded like she might have even more hospital time ahead of her.

He forced the morning's bad energy from his thoughts and rapped on Joely's open door. "Good morning," he called. "I see you're back from the torture that is physical therapy, and it's not noon yet. Pretty good."

She smiled, no longer shy with him about the scar traversing the length of her right jawline and across her chin.

With other visitors, even her sisters, she tended to draw her hair forward to cover those most visible signs of her accident. Today she had the television on, a rarity, as well as magazine open in her lap.

"Multitasking, I see," he teased.

"I'm supposed to be giving myself motivation but, really, I'm only depressing myself." Despite her words, she smiled again. "I shouldn't be watching things about horses."

"I'm sorry. But maybe it's good you're starting to think about them again."

Her shrug was that of a sad, weary person. "I miss my girl. I'm working on not feeling guilty."

"Because?" She didn't answer his prompt so he urged her with his voice. "It wasn't your fault."

"I know. I know."

She might never be convinced the accident in which her horse had died truly hadn't been her fault, but he wouldn't give up telling her. "What did they say after your tests this morning?"

"Surgery one week from today. One more week of close monitoring to make sure the hematoma doesn't return. They doubt removing the bone fragments they found will solve the nerve issues in the bad leg, but there's always a slim chance. There's also a chance something could go wrong, and I'll end up with more damage."

"That's not going to happen. I'd trust Perry Landon with my own spinal cord."

"I'm not worried."

"You're lying. Because if you truly aren't worried, you aren't normal."

She put down the magazine and lowered her eyes. "I really hate that you make me be honest. Can't you take off your therapist's hat once in a while?"

"It just comes right back on."

"No wonder my sister finds you so annoying."

His stomach gave a cheerful flip. The sister she referred to did indeed find him annoying, and he'd likely ticked her off as usual this morning with the flippant voice message he'd left, but he couldn't help it. Getting a rise out of Amelia Crockett was solid fun. She always gave him a spirited run for his money, and he'd grown to appreciate the firecracker in her personality.

"I'm happy to annoy any of you Crockett sisters, anytime. Now tell me why you're depressing yourself with horses."

She gestured toward the television. "This is a special about the Wyoming Mustang Makeover. It's a competition where trainers take an untrained, adopted mustang and work with it for three months. Then they're all judged against each other. My sisters and I did it three times, and I'd always planned on doing it again. Now…?"

"You're all horse trainers, too?"

"In the amateur division. It takes a lot of time and commitment, but it taught us a ton of patience."

He gave a rueful laugh. "Sounds like something I could use. I have eight men who are definitely testing my patience."

"Yes, your big experiment. Well, give the guys in your program mustangs—they won't have time to test anyone's patience."

He laughed. "Eight retired veterans with wild horses. I'd fear for the mustangs—they'd wind up painted like zebras and sent to mill around in someone's office."

"Or the mustangs would kick the guys' butts and teach them to respect animals and people."

"Tell you what, Miss Joely. Let's work on tossing off that depression of yours. I prescribe that you get good and riled up about this program and use the energy to heal fast. I think I'd like to see you train a mustang."

"You know who made a surprisingly good trainer was Amelia. She's great with animals. It's like she sees straight into their hearts, even though she doesn't take any guff."

No, he thought. I'll bet she doesn't. "I think I'd like to see that, too."

Chapter Seven

SAMANTHA EVANS BUZZED Mia's security intercom Friday evening, and Mia's stomach danced in anticipation as it had been doing since that morning when she'd learned Rory was leaving Shawna Murray's foster home.

"Good evening, Dr. Mia," Sam said through the speaker. "I have the world's biggest cat lover with me, and he needs a place to chill for the weekend. Is it true you have an actual cat up there? "

"It's true, indeed. A very lonely cat. Come on up."

The process of finding Rory a new foster family had begun. Meanwhile Mia had been allowed to take him for the weekend, and she felt as if she'd been prepping for a date. She had no illusions, however, that for Rory the date was with Jack. After two months of separation from his cat, he didn't care two hoots about Dr. Mia.

Sure enough, when she opened her apartment door to a smiling Sam, Rory made no pretense of a cordial greeting. He said hello and his eyes darted around the room. When they lit on his pet he yelped just as he had in the hospital.

"Jack!"

He pounced on the cat the way it would have done to a mouse, and if Mia had doubted for a moment the two were bonded, her doubts vanished. The cat rolled over like a small dog and meowed in answer to the boy's cry. Mia swore, as Rory scooped Jack up and buried his face in the long buff hair, that she saw a glistening in his eyes. After watching that one minute of reunion, she knew the weekend was already a success.

"Thank you for letting me take him." Mia turned to Sam, who set a huge box and a suitcase on the floor next to the door.

"Hey, you followed up to find the cat. That's above and beyond."

"No. It was just me getting mad and stubborn as usual. I went to see Buster as much to tick Shawna Murray off as anything."

"Keep telling yourself that. You wear such a tough shell, but you can't fool me. This was all about the kid." She held up a hand to stop Mia's protest. "I'm sorry this first foster family was a bad match for Rory. When that happens, it gives the child a bad taste for the system and makes it harder to place him in the future."

"I think you did right by him, though. He'll remember that people listened when he said he was unhappy. A child getting his concerns met immediately doesn't happen often."

"Sadly, you're right. Options are limited, and great foster homes aren't plentiful enough."

"So, do I have to watch my back with Mrs. Murray now? Is she furious?"

"I think the appropriate word would be relieved. This was not a legal action per se. We told her a complaint had been lodged and asked if she felt maybe her match with Rory wasn't the best for either of them. She jumped at the chance to let us find him a new foster family."

"Maybe she's not as crazy as I thought." Mia laughed. "I'm so happy Rory didn't have to go back. The rest will fall into place one way or another."

IT TOOK RORY until the next morning to stop treating Jack as if he were about to disappear without warning or break like glass. Mia had straightened up her second bedroom and ensconced Rory in his own space. He slept the whole night without a peep and with his cat curled beside him. It was Mia who couldn't sleep. She awoke twice and tiptoed through the dark to check on him. Both times Jack raised his head and meowed as if to say thank you.

She finally fell asleep for the last time at 4:00 a.m. and didn't awaken until she felt the now-familiar kneading of paws on her head at seven. Bleary-eyed, she removed the cat from her face and tried to tuck him under her arm.

"I think he's hungry."

She started at the voice and sat up, then grinned at Rory who stood in her doorway, clad in Iron Man pajamas. "Good morning," she said. "I'm sure you're right about Jack, but he's pretty easy to feed. It's you I'm worried about. I'm not sure I have the right kind of breakfast for a young human. You might have to eat cat food, too."

"What do *you* eat?"

"Grown-up food. Like waffles or muffins."

"Waffles?"

"Sometimes. Have you ever tried them? They're a pretty acquired taste."

"A what? A choir taste?"

She giggled. "Acquired. It means it takes time to get used to something."

"I don't have to get used to waffles. Everybody likes waffles."

"That can't be true."

"It is."

"Just for that I'll have to make them. I'm pretty sure you won't like them."

"I will."

He helped her, and although he was unskilled in most kitchen tasks, he was a willing pupil. When he poured the first scoop of batter into the waffle iron, he beamed as if he'd spun straw into gold. When she set the first round, golden Belgian waffle in front of him, he stared as if he'd frame it if he could.

"I don't have the kind of syrup you probably like, either," she said. "I have real maple syrup."

"I'll like it." He insisted again.

After he'd inhaled two waffles, Mia sat beside him at the small kitchen table and shook her head. "You must be half grown-up," she said. "I really didn't think you'd like them."

"I've never had waffles like these. I've had really flat ones. These are the best."

"That is a great compliment. Thank you, Master Beltane."

Since Rory was only six days out from his appendectomy, Mia had planned to spend most of the weekend at home, but she did give him a choice of several easygoing outings for that afternoon. They all made him bug-eyed with disbelief and anticipation. It shouldn't have surprised her that he'd seen very little of New York. He'd never seen the Statue of Liberty. He'd never been to Central Park.

They ended up at the Central Park Zoo and taking a carriage ride through the park itself. She tried to make sure he rode more than walked, but the child was a dynamo. Keeping him still was like containing a squirrel. When they arrived home at eight o'clock that night, far later than Mia had ever intended, Rory went straight for his cat, only allowing him out of his hold to take a bath. He chattered about the animals they'd seen at the zoo and the black horse named Sheila who'd pulled their carriage. When he finally talked himself out, Mia left him in front of a movie and went to prepare the hot cocoa she'd promised him as a treat before bed.

"So maybe we'll have a quieter day tomor—" She stopped next to the couch with two steaming mugs and smiled down at the scene. Rory had collapsed onto his back, his head lolled backward, his mouth open, and his pretty features completely relaxed. Jack lay on his young master's stomach, equally relaxed, but he lifted his head and meowed at Mia.

She set Rory's cocoa on the coffee table and took a seat on the end of the sofa nearest his feet. Pulling her grandmother's afghan from the sofa back, she spread it over the boy's legs. A moment later, Jack stepped across it and eased into her lap. Purring loudly he curled up like a little husky, and she buried one hand in his soft, thick hair. For the first time since Rory's arrival she allowed the subject of Monique's will to surface and remain in her conscious mind. It was the only cloud in a rare weekend of fun.

She rarely thought about the future beyond her career goals. She'd always imagined having children one day. Her biological clock functioned as well as any woman's did, and she loved family. However, she'd never quite been able to reconcile her insane schedule and work plans with a home, a marriage, a husband. There wasn't much future in the field of domestic bliss for a surgeon with goals like hers. She'd never let herself love anyone enough to change those goals.

But this…She stroked Rory's leg through the blanket. This was nice. If disaster struck could she make it as the parent of a half-grown child?

She hadn't told anyone about the lawyer's call. She wouldn't. She put all her energy into praying she'd never need to think about it. Monique would recover.

She and Rory got through Sunday with movies, grilled cheese sandwiches, and multiple games of Go Fish, War, and poker, which Mia wasn't sure she should teach a ten-year-old but did anyway. She enjoyed the process of showing Rory how to bid matchsticks and watching him rake in winnings as he grew more proficient. She talked to

Joely and managed to convince her that the surgery was worth the risk. Even though it wasn't possible to get back to Wyoming for it, Mia promised to follow it every step of the way. The day passed too quickly in a blur of fantasy and reality.

Monday morning came with depressing inevitability. Sam arrived early to pick Rory up. Since he had to take one more week off of school, arrangements had been made for a temporary foster home, but with luck, social services would have a permanent foster family by that evening.

Mia surprised herself with how sad she was to let him go.

"Can't I just stay with you?" he asked. For the first time all weekend, he gave her a hug. Small, short, but meaningful.

"You know I'd like that," she replied. "But it would be really hard because I work so much, and couldn't be here with you. Plus, you never know, they might not want me to keep you. I could be a bad guy in disguise."

"You're not a bad guy." His little brows formed a disgusted line. "Who should I tell?"

Mia and Sam laughed. "He's like that," Mia said. "Ten going on thirty."

"Didn't I call it?" Sam tousled Rory's hair. "Clever as a fox."

He put his jacket on and found Jack for one last hug. "Be good," he said.

He followed Sam out the door into the bright hallway and turned back. "Good luck with your job today."

That nearly undid her. When they'd had a discussion about what he wanted to be someday, she'd told him briefly about the job she was planning to get. He'd remembered.

"Thanks, you," she replied. "I'll let you know."

TWO SURGERIES THAT morning, the announcement of the job decision, two surgeries in the afternoon, and hospital rounds awaited her at work. Mondays were notoriously full. Today, however, she entered the hospital with as near a bounce in her step as she ever did. Despite the secret of Monique's will, the weekend had rejuvenated her.

Her first surgery, a digestive tract blockage in a five-year-old, went smoothly. Her second, a simple tonsillectomy, went equally well. She finished talking to the parents of the child and was back stripping from her scrubs when she got the page from Dr. Thomas, the hospital's chief of surgery, to meet in his office half an hour later. Suddenly her fingers didn't work, her breath came too quickly, and her professionalism deserted her completely in her excitement. She didn't have any reason to worry—she got what she went after, and she'd covered all her bases for this job. Still, this was the culmination of a lot of work, and excitement climbed quickly into nervousness.

She finished dressing, made sure her make-up was perfect but subtle, and took the elevator to Dr. Thomas's office on the sixth floor. With a deep breath she knocked, found his secretary waiting, and was ushered immediately in to see her mentor. Mason Thomas had taken her under his wing and given her pediatric experience she might have never received without his help. He'd encouraged her in this pursuit and believed in her skill. His warm smile as she sat in front of his desk calmed her and brought perspective back to her jitters.

"Thanks for coming so quickly, Amelia," he said. "I know you just got out of surgery."

"It's my pleasure," she replied. "I've been looking forward to today, and the surgeries went well so I had no trouble getting here."

"You've been logging a lot of hours." He smiled. "I understand you've made yourself available for extra on-call shifts, and you're the go-to girl for anyone with a schedule conflict."

"I took time off in August and September for my father's funeral and my sister's accident. I'd like to make up for some of the help I got during that time."

"You haven't come close to using up your vacation time. And you know you aren't required to make sacrifices all the time. We do have residents for that." He winked.

"I know. I simply wanted to make it clear I consider myself worthy of this position and will do all it takes."

At that Mason leaned back and studied her with unreadable eyes. Finally he smiled.

"I'm not going to prolong this," he said. "Amelia, you know you're an asset to this hospital, one of whom we're inordinately proud. The youngest board certified general surgeon in our history, three grant proposals accepted, four studies published in JAMA. That's an amazing resume."

"Thank you. I've been very lucky with my opportunities. I try to make the most of all of them."

He released a long breath. "Amelia, we did not award you the chief resident's position this time."

The words made no sense at first. They tumbled into a void of buzzing white noise and she stared at him almost as if he were static on a radio that needed tuning to the right frequency.

"A leadership position like this requires more than extraordinary surgical skills. It's about managing your team of colleagues. In all honesty, that's an area you need some more time to develop."

"I…I don't understand."

"You haven't gotten high marks on getting along with your fellow docs. I know that's blunt, and I'm sorry. Interactions with other physicians are so important when it comes to scheduling, to department morale, to case discussions. If your staff doesn't trust and respect you, you start behind the eight ball. As recently as last week—"

"Is this coming from Fred Wilson? He and I had a small run-in over a patient, but it wasn't anything major."

"It's not just Fred. And this is not permanent, Amelia. This is just a postponement so you can perfect your skills. You are phenomenal with the young patients. Let's put some of that into practice with your colleagues."

The rest of the conversation passed in a fog. She barely heard the condolences or the further explanations. She recoiled inside at the name of the candidate who *had* been given the job, an actual resident working on his first certification. An obsequious man five years her junior who was a good surgeon but a better manager. Is that really what they wanted? When Mason asked her for the second time what she'd like to do in the next year, she had to shake herself out of a fog.

"I don't know," she replied dully. "I'm blindsided."

"I understand."

She pressed her fingers against her eye sockets, ashamed that behind the pressure tears were forming. Mason stood and moved to stand in front of her, grabbing a tissue along the way and handing it to her.

"I'm sorry, Amelia. I know you were hoping to finish your certification in time to be considered for the opening at Sinai next fall. It's a dream job, you say, but you'll be a much stronger candidate for a similar position later. Meanwhile, I have a recommendation. You need to take some of that vacation you've accumulated and relax from the ungodly hours you've been keeping. You can come to terms with this decision and decide how you want to structure the next year."

"You've been behind me and this plan all along; could you just tell me who suddenly changed your mind about me?"

"I've never changed my mind about you," he said. "I know you'll be a superstar in this field just as you are in everything else you do."

She stood, a surge of anger washing over her. "Don't patronize. Did you or did you not recommend me for the job?"

"I did. But I also agreed with the rest of the committee that it wouldn't hurt for you to take one more year."

"Well, I thank you for that honesty anyway. If I'd known that what you and the committee really wanted was a wet nurse for the staff and not the best doctor for this hospital's patients, I'd certainly have played the game a little differently. As it was, I simply did the best medical job I'm capable of doing. Clearly I made the wrong call."

"I'm sure you feel that way."

"Oh, I do. Thank you for your time."

"Amelia. This is what I mean. You need to learn not to say the first things that come into your head."

"Dr. Thomas, I expect no less of myself than I do of everyone else I work with."

She didn't say anymore, just turned and left the office, her heart a confused and battered lump in her chest.

Chapter Eight

"GABRIEL! DARLING BOY. Thank you so much for coming!"

Gabe accepted a huge hug from Bella Crockett, the girls' still-beautiful mother, and let her lead him toward a square of couches in a private corner of the VA hospital's surgery waiting area. He'd learned early on that when the Crockett women got together at the hospital, some sort of a party broke out. It could be they smuggled in a bottle of contraband Scotch to celebrate a milestone—like Joely getting staples out of a surgical incision—or started an all-day poker tournament to stave off boredom. And, from the day he'd become Joely's patient advocate, he'd been dragged into the family's dynamic circle, despite all attempts over the weeks to stay neutral and aloof.

"Bella. You're looking more perfect every time I see you," he said. The girls' mother had been in the automobile accident with Joely but had been released from the hospital two weeks ago. Only a slight limp and a cast on one arm remained from her ordeal.

"A result of you getting us the best of care," she replied, her smile genuinely warm. "I'm so glad you're here. You've been such a help in all this. It feels like you're one of the family."

"A result of you being the best of families. Now—I see Joely's surgery is spawning a Crockett party. What do we have this time?" He lifted a bottle of pinot grigio and then a bottle of petite sirah and checked the labels as if he knew what he was doing. "Very nice," he said. "Never too early in the day for a good wine?"

"It's *almost* lunchtime." Harper, the second-oldest Crockett sister, grinned and pointed at a tray on the table in front of them. "So we have sandwiches to start off with. The wine will get opened as nerves set in. They said it could take a while."

"It could," he agreed. "But Joely will be fine. The wine will be in preparation for celebrating, I promise."

Before he sat, he smiled at the three remaining women in the little circle. Raquel and Grace, indistinguishable from each other until he spoke to them, represented two-thirds of the Crockett triplets, the youngest of the sisters. They sat on either side of the most amazing of all the Crockett women, their grandmother, ninety-four-year-old Sadie. He squatted in front of the delightful senior and took her hand.

"It's officially a celebration since you're here. How are you, Sadie?"

"Happier than an old woman has a right to be now that I have your handsome face to look upon," she said.

"You're a be*guiling* woman." He laughed and kissed the back of her hand.

"Well, I used to be." She laughed, an infectious and hearty sound for a nonagenarian.

He winked at the triplet to Sadie's right. "You know I'm horrible at getting you right on sight alone. You three switch places between here and Denver so often that I can't keep you straight. But let me try." He took in her tweedy dress pants and polished boots, compared them to her sister's faded-leg jeans, and his memory kicked in. "Grace," he said.

"Awesome," she replied.

She was the sedate, sweet, polished sister who fit her name. Raquel the tomboy would never have bothered to polish her boots. "And Raquel."

They each stood and offered a quick hug, and he left them impressed without giving away his tactics. At least they hadn't all three been here.

"I just stopped by for a little while to see if there was anything you needed," he said. "They just wheeled her in."

A cell phone buzzed. Harper drew hers out of a purse pocket and checked the screen. "It's Cole," she said, referring to her new fiancé, Cole Wainwright. Together they'd just taken over the reins of the family's empire—Paradise Ranch. One of the largest spreads in Wyoming. "He texted that he's sending up lots of prayers for Joely." She looked at Gabe. "They're setting winter fencing, and he couldn't be here," she said. "He made me promise to keep the updates coming."

Even thought they'd recently lost their father, the man who'd run Paradise with an iron will, the girls had struggled but were clearly pulling together now. Gabe smiled at Harper. "Cole's a good man."

"Yeah." Harper smiled back. "He is. I got lucky."

Her text got Gabe to pull out his own phone, hoping to see anything from one of his motley band of eight. It was nearly eleven. This time of the morning they all should have been out job hunting with cell phones at the ready. But there was nothing. For the third time, he brought up Jason Brewster's number and excused himself while he slammed down a text. "Brewster, you know I don't trust you as far as I can throw you today. Call me so I know your dumb ass isn't going to get me and the rest of you into hot water."

It wasn't an idle fear. Brewster and two of the other men had finally received letters from VA Benefits, only to be told they weren't eligible for full coverage on their psych benefits, but their cases were being reviewed and they would hear back again shortly. Gabe completely understood their anger and utter frustration. But based on their reactions to the letters, he didn't trust them to stick to harmless pranks any longer.

"I'm serious, call—"A full-fledged screech cut him off before he finished the text. He pushed send anyway, his alarm at full strength. "What's wrong? What happened?"

All the Crockett women, except Sadie, were on their feet. He followed their line of sight, and a wrecking ball hit him in the chest. Dr. Amelia Crockett strode from the doors of the OR suites toward their corner, a small rolling suitcase behind her. A baby blue sweater and colorful scarf hugged her upper body, nicely worn, soft-looking jeans encased her long—long—legs, and the most stand-out, classy pair of red cowboy boots he'd ever seen popped out from beneath the hems of the jeans as she walked.

"Mia!" Raquel shot down the hall and threw her arms around her sister. "Oh my gosh! This is fantastic. I thought you couldn't make it."

"I didn't think I could either," she replied, and Gabe's mouth went a little dry when her eyes met his over Raquel's shoulder.

Their view was blocked when Grace enveloped Amelia in a second hug. By the time the threesome made its way to the couches, Harper and Bella were holding out their arms.

"Hey, hey, it's all right." Amelia's voice soothed from the middle of the pack of sisters. "I got the chance to come, so I came. It's no big deal."

"But you just missed her!" Raquel said.

"Girls, let your sister put her things down," Sadie said, and when Amelia had parked her suitcase and set an over-coat on an empty chair, she bent to embrace her grand-mother in a long, hard hug.

Gabriel looked away from the reunion and let his pulse slow. He was more than surprised himself, since she'd made it pretty clear the last time they'd spoken that she wasn't able to leave New York.

"Well, well. Good morning, Lieutenant."

He looked back to find her just feet from him, her brown eyes flecked with fiery gold sparks, her soft brown hair piled in a sexily dilapidated, bun-like array that looked as if she'd slept on it in a plane, and her lips curved in a provocative smile.

"Well, well. Good morning, Dr. Crockett. Imagine meeting you in a place like this."

"I know, right? They'll let just about anyone into a hospital these days." Her smile met his, shaded with barely discernable teasing.

His heart warmed into the game that had grown familiar over the course of their recent conversations, but before he could retort again Bella tugged on Amelia's arm.

"Now, you two, don't you start." She chided them both. "Mia, sweetheart, how did you get here?"

"You didn't really just ask that, did you, Mommy?" Amelia turned and wrapped her mother in a teasing hug. "It might have been on an airplane, but I started long enough ago I'm not entirely sure."

"That's exactly what I asked," her mother said, patting Mia's cheek. "It's not easy to get into Jackson before eleven in the morning."

Amelia released Bella and rubbed her eyes. "LaGuardia to Atlanta. Atlanta to Salt Lake. Commuter to here. There was a three-hour layover somewhere."

"Honey," Bella said. "You didn't have to put yourself through that."

"I did if I wanted a shot at talking to the surgeon before he started." She sighed but seemed to regather her self-assurance. "I made it. Barely. I'm sorry I didn't let you know I was here, but I went right to pre-op and found Perry, uh, Dr. Landon. I talked to Joely, too. I think

I've got the lay of the land, and I think she's in very good hands. He knows his stuff."

Perry, was he? Gabe scowled at the hint of resentment that settled in his gut. He was still a sardonic "Lieutenant Harrison," but the surgeon he'd put her in touch with was already "He Knows His Stuff" Perry?

His resentment faded when she turned back to him. "Thanks for hooking me up with him. It's been helpful."

She'd read his mind?

Lord, he hoped not.

"It's what I do," he said. "I'm glad you could get here. Something must have changed in your schedule."

Nothing changed in her features but everything changed in her face. He wondered if everyone else saw it, too, and it took him a moment to decipher the transformation. It was her eyes. The illusion of hot, golden flecks in them had disappeared. Although she still held onto her pleasant smile, some fire within had gone out. He studied the muddy brown of her irises, and she didn't turn, not at first. Deeply he searched for any sign of the previous heat, and for the briefest moment he caught a repeat of the yearning he'd imagined in her voice earlier, only this time it was visible. Buried in the dullness of her captured gaze was something painful. He recognized it because he'd seen much stronger variations of it in hundreds of service men and women coming through the VA's doors. Amelia's wasn't the same kind of trauma, but it was… something. He fought a startling urge to pull her into his arms the way her mother had done.

And then it was gone. As if someone had found the extinguished pilot light and held a match to it, her eyes flared back to life, this time fueled by annoyance and anger. So familiar—the Amelia Crockett he'd grown to know so well right after the accident two months earlier.

"I rearranged my schedule, that's all." She snapped at him. "I decided my sister was more important than kids I didn't know."

He guessed that was true to a certain extent, and yet her words didn't ring with conviction—simply with anger.

"I know that meant a lot to her," he replied.

Her troubles were her own, he counseled himself. And yet something touched him and made him want to delve behind her anger. That had never happened the million other times she'd snapped at him. He'd seen her as the hard-assed, know-it-all Crockett sister and left her to herself whenever possible. During their spate of phone calls over the past two weeks, however, he'd more than once heard a softer side of Amelia Crockett. He'd hoped her distaste for him might have softened, too.

Apparently he was still little more than a bureaucrat who existed only for the purpose of throwing road blocks in her way.

Everyone shifted and made room in the circle of seats, and Bella guided Amelia to an empty sofa cushion next to Gabe. They smiled tightly like two awkward teenagers forced together at a mixer. She laced her fingers in her lap. A scent of perfume rose around her, so light he barely noticed it, yet beckoning until he had to fight himself to keep from leaning in. He rarely paid attention to a woman's fragrance unless it was strong and overwhelming. This was feminine and subtle like walking unforced through a spring garden of flowers and spice.

He shook himself free of the mini spell and looked away. Holy crap, what alien had just invaded his brain? He sat back, slightly shaken, and decided on the spot he liked talking to Amelia Crockett on the phone much better than in person.

"Tell us what Dr. Landon had to say," Bella asked. "Maybe he could explain things to you in more detail than he could to us."

Gabe sat back and listened to Amelia describe the injury and the surgery. She had a straightforward but gentle style of explanation, and he was thoroughly impressed with how clear she was without resorting to condescension. Where had this doctor been back when he'd first met her? Nearly every time he'd been with the family while she'd been around, she'd done nothing but take him to task for each decision made, any information he wasn't allowed to divulge, and whatever explanation he'd tried to give. This doctor was a gifted teacher.

"So you think her chances are good?" Grace asked.

"I have every confidence she'll come through well. Nobody knows if removing those fragments will make a difference to the movement in her damaged leg. That's the long shot. And Joely knows that, too. She wasn't given any false hope. At the very least, I do think this will eliminate some of the pain she's been having and make her rehab easier. If we're very lucky, she'll get a bonus."

Nobody spoke. In the contemplative silence Gabe studied each woman in turn and was struck by the serenity underpinning each one's concern. When he slid his gaze to Amelia's face, he was startled to find her watching him back.

He grinned irreverently. "I like your boots."

She stared for a moment and then broke into laughter. It spilled from her reluctantly with hiccups and hitches until she shook her head. "You're just a little off-kilter, aren't you, Lieutenant?"

"Gabe." He leaned toward her and half-whispered his name slowly, in an even, pleasant voice. Touching the lapel of his sport coat and then lifting the collar tip of his casual, button-down shirt, he leaned a notch closer and caught another intoxicating whiff of her perfume. "Cheap civilian jacket. No bars. It's just Gabe, Amelia. And your boots are worthy of comment. I meant it as a compliment."

"Then thank you," she replied, also in a near-whisper. "Gabe."

"You also did a great job explaining the surgery to all of us. You're a good teacher. That should have been the first compliment, but I stumbled over the boots."

"That's because they're lucky. I'll never get on a plane without them."

She caught her lower lip in her teeth and flicked her eyes away as if hiding embarrassment...or a smile.

"It's been that way since she was four." Bella leaned in from Amelia's other side.

"Mother!"

"Oh, it's a great story," Bella countered despite Amelia's warning tone.

Amelia actually sought Gabe's eyes for camaraderie, rolling hers helplessly.

He grinned. "I'll tell her I don't want to hear if that's what you'd like me to do."

"As if that would do any good." She sat back, her arms crossed, her face resigned.

"It started at her very first barrel race at age four," Bella said.

"Four?" He raised a brow.

"You ain't a ranch boy, are you?" Amelia asked, putting on a hokey accent. "We start young. Any two-year-old cain't rope and tie a calf is sent to remedial school. They start babies on barrels soon as their first teeth show through the gums."

The girls all snorted in laughter and answered with a chorus of "amens" and "preach it, sisters."

"Mia had a brand new pair of little red cowboy boots she'd picked out for the occasion," Bella continued. "They were a titch big, but she wore them loud and proud. Well, around the second barrel, her pony, Chloe, went left, Mia went right, and her right foot slipped all the way through the stirrup. That's never supposed to happen with boots, but her foot was so little the heel of the boot didn't stop it. In her regular boots she might have been stuck, but since she'd insisted on the new ones that were a little too big, her foot came out of the boot, she popped out of that saddle, and landed flat on her feet. Her daddy told her so earnestly that red sure was her lucky color in boots—"

"That she's believed ever since red boots are her good luck charm," Grace finished, and wrinkled her nose at Amelia.

"All right, all right." Amelia had never looked so unlike her perfect, professional self, hunched forward on the edge of the cushion, hands playing with the blue-and-red patterned scarf she wore around her neck. "So I'm a big baby when it comes to flying."

"And trail riding, and driving any kind of machinery," Raquel teased.

"And I haven't died doing any of those things, have I?" Mia countered her sister's claim with a sneer, but she smiled and Gabe sat back, unsure what to make of this freer, far more sister-like Amelia. He liked her. A lot. He wasn't sure she was real.

"Which is why we *all* wear red boots for dangerous missions," Raquel said, catching Gabe's eye with a nod and then a wink. "Not."

Amelia shook her head, unfazed. "I'll be happy to give up each of your good luck charms. The only one who never believed me was you." She turned to Harper. "You were always your own person."

"Stubborn," Harper agreed.

"She's right," Raquel said. "I have a four-leaf clover Grandma Sadie had encased in a pendant for me. I won't leave home without it. Kelly has the ugliest teddy bear you've ever seen. Seriously, the thing was designed by gargoyle carvers in the caves of Creeplandia. She's terrified TSA agents with it."

"Aw," Harper started to laugh. "How can you say that about Mr. Beenie?"

"Because I have to live with him," Raquel replied. "He's banned from any community spaces in our apartment."

"He is," Grace agreed.

Gabe chuckled at the growing silliness. "And what's yours, Grace?" he asked.

"Yes, Gracie." Amelia crossed her arms again. "What *is* your lucky charm?"

"Praying for everyone else's lucky charm," she said.

"I know you do actually do that, Mini Mother Theresa, but I happen to know—"

"That I only wear blue underpants when I fly?" Grace grinned directly at Gabe. "It's true."

"Do you pray for them, too?" Raquel asked, and the whole group rocked back into their chairs, holding their bellies and gasping in laughter. Even Sadie covered her mouth and let her shoulders shake.

"Oh, cripes," Harper said. "They're gonna confiscate our wine before it's even open. Man, I hope you pray for us, too, Gracie. We're certifiable."

"Every day." Grace choked on her laugher.

Gabe settled back into the sofa, taking in the rare sight. The mirth between the sisters was more genuine and relaxed than he'd ever seen before. He'd always sensed nothing but tension between Amelia and Harper. He'd never seen the three older girls treat the twenty-four-year-old triplets with as much equal standing as in this moment—they were usually the babies.

He had no moral authority or deep enough knowledge of the girls to speculate on why this moment galvanized them, but something had changed when Amelia had arrived. Whatever she'd brought from New York made her just what they all needed.

She'd changed something inside of him, too. In the short half hour since she'd appeared, he'd gone from shock over her presence to desiring a way to figure out all her layers—layers she'd kept tightly out of sight until now.

It was time to take a break and clear his head.

"Ladies," he said when the laughter had calmed and they all started reaching for food. "I have some appointments, but I will check back in a couple of hours. If you need anything at all, please, you know how to page me." He faced Amelia and found it easy to shoot her a friendly smile. "You, too. You have my direct number. Although I think you'll have all the access you need. I'm very glad you're here for everybody."

"That's…nice of you to say." She let one corner of her mouth quirk back into a half-smile of acquiescence. "Gabe."

"Come sit down and tell us about yourself now. I want to hear all about that new job. Didn't you say it was all happening a couple of days ago?"

It happened again. Immediately and without question. Amelia's eyes blanked into an opaque shade of dull brown. She spun her gaze from his and pressed her lips together, swallowing as if to gain time.

"Oh, yes, my news," she said. "I made a few changes to my plans," she said. "It's all good. I'd just rather pursue a different path than I thought. Things weren't going to be quite as they'd advertised with the potential new job."

For all the closeness and connectivity of moments before, the rest of the family caught nothing of what Amelia was really saying.

"Well it sounds exciting as usual," Bella said. "But come and tell us what changed your mind. It's got to be something pretty big."

Oh, it was, Gabriel thought as he studied Amelia's stoic shoulders and slow attempt to arrange her body into nonchalance. They might not have seen it, but he knew. This was it. This was her secret. She would not have willingly veered from her goal. That much he knew.

"See you in a bit," she said, giving him one last carefully placed smile. "Thanks for your kindness to my family."

He had no plausible reason to reverse his decision to leave. She would know in an instant that he only wanted in on her explanation. She'd spoken adamantly enough on the phone about her new job as chief resident in the pediatric department for him to know it was a means to a big end for her.

"Sure," he said reluctantly, that tug toward her filling him again. He forced himself to turn, but then he spun back and touched her upper arm as lightly as he could. "Hey."

The familiar defensive anger returned to her eyes. "What?"

"Whatever brought you here?"

She placed a palm against his chest and pushed him three steps farther from the group. Pressing forward until her mouth was just inches from his, she shocked him with the anger in her words. "Don't you dare say it happened for a reason."

"I…wouldn't say that because I don't know what 'it' is. I was going to say that I just saw a perfect example of why family is so powerful. They will support you."

She dropped her hand, and her mouth relaxed enough to appear troubled instead of angry. "You might think so. But you have no idea what a person has to live up to in this family."

With no further explanation she walked back to her family with the air of a condemned woman.

Chapter Nine

MIA FILED OUT of Joely's quiet room with her sisters, stopping to give her mother a kiss as they passed. "She's doing really well, I promise. She's almost asleep again, but you can talk to her for a minute."

"I'm so grateful you're here," her mother replied, and the gratitude helped keep the desolation in the pit of Mia's stomach at bay, as it had all day. The catch was, eventually she'd have to tell her grateful, proud family the truth about why she'd returned.

She shuffled into the ICU family lounge, which had grown far too familiar over the past two months, and tried to stave off the insidious tentacles of exhaustion slithering through her body, searching out every cell. Grandma Sadie looked up from a chair and smiled, and Gabriel was back, sitting beside Sadie, waiting. Relief soothed her inner turmoil. She was too tired to think about why he created that effect.

"Hi," he said, and she offered a weak smile. "You look kind of done in."

"Most of the time it's much easier on the other side of the OR doors," she replied. "Waiting helplessly is draining."

"As is flying across country for twelve hours."

She had no idea where this solicitous and mind-reading male had come from. He'd been nothing but pig-headed and self-important whenever she'd tried to get information from him early on. She liked "Gabe." But she was definitely more comfortable sparring with Lt. Gabriel Harrison.

"Raquel and I are going to take Grandma home," Grace said. "It's nearly six thirty and we'll get something started for dinner."

"I'll wait for Mom," Mia said. "She wants to stay a little while. That's fine. She was a patient for so long herself that she wants to put in her time as caretaker."

"Don't let her stay too long." Grandma Sadie stood, resting one hand lightly on her distinctive cane—black lacquered wood decorated handle to tip with elegant red primroses and sweet lavender violets.

"I won't, Gran," Mia promised. "You've been amazing today. Thanks for the fun."

Her grandmother patted her cheek and nodded. "Come home soon."

Once she'd shepherded her family to the elevators, Mia returned to find Gabriel engrossed in his cell phone. He'd spent most of the day away, since he did have an actual job to perform, but he'd stopped to check in multiple times during the five-plus hour surgery. Each time he'd brought treats or fresh reading material. Once he'd handed out warm, wet face cloths. He'd taken it upon himself to be their private butler, and despite all her efforts to remain unaffected, Mia had been won over. The man had gone far above and beyond his job description.

She had noticed one quirk, however, an obsession with his phone. He checked it often, lost himself texting in what looked like sheer, angry frustration, and only came back to himself once the phone was back in his pocket. Somehow the answer to the minor mystery didn't interest her. Instead she felt connected to him knowing he had secrets just as she did.

She sat without him noticing her return, and weariness engulfed her like ocean waves. She let her head fall back against the armchair's back cushion and tried to sink beneath the surf of beckoning sleep. For a few moments nothing disturbed the peacefulness.

"Son of a biscuitwhacker!" His noncurse carried across the empty space with all the invective of an actual profanity, and Mia startled upright in her chair.

"Gabriel? What's wrong?"

He spun in place and stared at her. "Oh, damn. I'm sorry. I had no idea you were back yet."

She almost laughed at the incongruity of his swearing. Why "biscuitwhacker" if you were just going to damn it seconds later?

"You were so engrossed I didn't want to interrupt you."

"Engrossed." He scoffed. "More like incensed."

"I can kind of see that." She smiled, but he was back at his keyboard. "Do you need anything? Shall I leave you alone? Can I help?"

Genuine surprise crossed his features. "Amelia, you must be even more exhausted than you look. Help me?" His mouth relaxed into an easygoing smile, one that evoked genuine warmth. "Don't you remember? That isn't how it works. I antagonize you, you get mad at me, and then we just annoy each other."

"Yeah, but I thought just this once I'd ask. Since I am so tired and all..." She shrugged and studied him studying his phone once again. "Do I really annoy you?"

"Sure," he said without hesitation and looked up. "But I kind of like it. I was thinking at the end of last week that I missed our recent phone chats."

She was going to say something snarky—but despite their topic of conversation it didn't feel quite right. She shrugged again. "Yeah. What's that all about?"

"Don't ask. Better not to delve."

"Agreed."

His phone buzzed, and he looked down. Seconds later his mouth tensed, and hard furrows sank into the skin at its corners. "Idiots." He whispered, but she heard him anyway.

"All right," she said, "either spill the beans or take this little lover's quarrel to another part of the lobby."

He snapped his gaze back to hers, honestly incredulous.

"I'm kidding. I'm kidding." She held up her hands. "You're just making it impossible not to eavesdrop. At first I honestly didn't care, but I'm starting to change my mind."

"You know? Now that I think about it, you might be just the person who could help me. At least since you're a doctor, you could tell me what I should do."

"Seriously? Be still my heart."

"Knock it off." He grinned, and she grinned back. Weariness was starting ever-so-slightly to sluice away. "I'm serious. I have a group of pea-brained, infantile vets who can't seem to get their heads out of their you-know-whats, and I'm at a loss."

"That needs explaining all right."

HE PERCHED ON the edge of the chair at right angles to hers, and their knees brushed as he adjusted his seat. "Sorry," he said, but he wasn't. There was nothing electric or sensual about the touch, but the proximity to her was reassuring.

"A dumb thing to be sorry about but, but okay, thanks."

He wondered for a moment where to start and finally plunged in. It wasn't like he should bother trying to impress her—their relationship had already forged its trajectory.

"A year ago, after working with a number of veterans who were not just stymied by the VA's paperwork and frustrated with quality of benefit distribution, but who were also suffering from emotional injuries that literally took away their ability to cope with the stress, I came up with a program idea. It took some fast talking to get my bosses in the benefits department to agree and go after funding, but they did."

"You got the government to give you money for something important?"

He laughed at her incredulity. "Truth is stranger than fiction. Thank you for assuming it's important just on faith."

"I'm a patient woman."

"You are not."

She bit on a thumbnail and hid a smile. "No. I'm not. But I have nowhere else to go. Keep talking."

"I gathered together eight men from three branches of the services, ranging in age from twenty-three to twenty-eight. Three have officially diagnosed PTSD, four have blast-induced TBI, and one lost an ear and his hearing in one side in an IED explosion—he's pretty messed up."

"Wow," she said, clearly sobered.

"They're all great guys. I hand-chose them because they have brains and potential. I also wanted men who'd originally refused psychiatric treatment, who claimed to have no problems they couldn't handle, and yet who weren't antisocial. I'm afraid I did too well on that last criteria."

She laughed. "Okay put this into context for me. What's the program? What's the plan?"

He told her about the early weeks of the project, officially called "The Brother to Brother Small Group Community," but which the guys called "Cluster Foxtrot House," after the VA had found them individual, bare-bones apartments all in the same building where Gabe lived. They'd been given a small monthly stipend to cover food and necessities contingent on them all starting counseling and finding jobs within six months.

"They were told their task was to support each other through the job hunting process, through therapy, through hard times," Gabe said. "For the first month they ate all dinners together, had weekends to themselves until Sunday nights, and were required to attend a group counseling session in addition to their individual therapy programs."

"And?"

"It worked." He rubbed the back of his neck. "Once they believed that tough, brave guys from all branches of the service were not turned into blubbering fools or ostracized by their peers because they talked about their issues, they started to heal. It's a slow process, I admit, and what I didn't foresee was the streak of lunacy we'd all share. I meet with them Sunday nights, and we discuss our goals for the week. I told them humor had been the only way I could get a foothold once I got home was with humor."

"You?" Her eyes shot their gold sparks again, and he scowled.

"You wound me." His hand went theatrically to his heart. "I'll have you know I used to be very funny, according to my ancient year book. True, I'm old now and that was a long time ago. But still."

"You're not so old. I've checked you out—you're only two years older than I am, and I'm a freaking thirty-two-year-old prodigy. Snort."

Pure self-denigration spilled into her tone. Gabe considered for a fraction of a second but decided not to pursue it and ruin their easy conversation. Later...

"Seriously? You checked me out?"

"It's not flattery, I didn't stalk you."

"That's too bad."

Her mouth pursed into a cute little scowl that went along with an eye roll. He laughed.

"My guys are making great strides, but they aren't turning into the outwardly perfect specimens my bosses would like to see. They're learning to channel their anger but…" He opened the picture gallery on his phone and found snaps of the three sabotaged cars. "These are their versions of letters of complaint. The director, deputy director, and head of the Department of VA Benefits were not amused."

Amelia took the phone and slowly covered her mouth with one hand. "Oh my gosh."

"Yeah."

"Long story short, this wasn't their first prank, and they've run out of chances. The program ends with the next incident. On the other hand, if they can keep their noses clean, they'll have eight more months to settle in and integrate into a more normal civilian life with ongoing access to mental health services and job searches help as long as they need it."

"So the phone messages." She nodded as his hands. "They're in trouble."

His heart lightened simply with her words. No censure, no criticism—she got it, and he suddenly wasn't alone.

"At least this time it was only three of them. They went to some acquaintance's farm between Jackson and Wolf Paw Pass with a stock trailer, and attempted to load a Guernsey cow with the intent of tying her in the lobby of the administration building. Something about a note around her neck to the effect of 'the Veteran's Administration refuses to moo-ve.' "

Saying it out loud made it all the more ridiculous.

"Did they make it?" She pressed her lips together and rubbed on her cheeks. He swore she was trying not to laugh.

"No. The ringleader got himself nailed in the thigh with a back hoof."

"Oh crap." Her laughter burst free. "Is he all right? Are they bringing him here?"

"No, although I told them in no uncertain terms they should. They're bringing him home. He says 'upon reflection' it would be better if nobody knew they'd had something planned."

"But a cow kick is extremely powerful. I know. I grew up around them. He could have a broken femur."

"He says no. Says it's only bruised. And if he's right, it's true a hospital report would reach my bosses."

"He could make up any number of stories about trading a…" She lost it and laughter choked her words. "c… cow, for magic b…beans." She dragged a deep, steadying breath. "Or that it ran…away, and he was returning it!"

"Dr. Crockett! I'm appalled. I didn't know you had a side like this."

It took a minute more for her to control her paroxysms. "Whew!" she said at last. "This makes me think of the idiotic things my dorm mates did in medical school. Granted these guys are older and should know better, but still." She wiped her eyes. "Is this for real? Or are you trying to keep me awake?"

"You have no idea how I wish I were making it up. I feel like the foster father to a group of octuplets from Jupiter."

Her face grew thoughtful. "Foster father, huh?" she asked slowly. "It's kind of what you are, actually."

"Whatever. I need to get back and see to Brewster."

"That's his name?"

"Jason Brewster."

"Well, Jason Brewster needs to see a doctor."

His brain churned with a sudden, insane idea, and he spit it out before rational thought could temper it. "Like a doctor willing to think this a great joke, and tell him he should get to an ER?"

"What? Wait, me? Oh, no."

She didn't look as horrified as she should have.

"Twenty minutes. I could have you back here to take your mother home in a flash, and I wouldn't have to have an argument with Jason."

"Oh, good Lord." She wiped her hands across her face again and took another deep breath. "You know, everything today has been so surreal, and your story is so completely nuts, I might just have to come and see this."

He let himself savor the stunned, happy sensation her answer created. Surreal didn't begin to describe this day, and finding this side to Amelia Crockett that wasn't uptight and, even better, was slightly subversive, only made it more so. If someone had asked him to choose an accomplice for this ridiculousness, she would have come after everyone else on the planet who didn't have a rap sheet. Not for one second had he expected his silly request to lead to this.

SHE'D ONLY HAD one glass of wine all day, but she still had to be drunk. Why else would she be in a stranger's car on her way to a stranger's house to see a stranger who should be in a hospital ER after being kicked by a stolen cow?

Anyone who knew Mia would describe her as logical—to a fault—and someone who followed the rules of common sense if not every social constraint. She knew this about herself. She counted those traits among her strengths. And yet the familiar landscape of western Wyoming passed in a blur, carrying her in the opposite direction of Paradise Ranch where she so badly wanted to go. Home, to sleep.

There was the exhaustion of course. Some formula equating sleeplessness to high blood alcohol levels was clearly exacerbated by adding one glass of wine—

"I really can't thank you enough for this." Gabriel broke into her tipsy-like musings.

She waved a hand at him. "Paying you back for the hot towel treatment today. That was pretty epic."

He laughed and they settled into silence. Oddly enough, it was the first truly quiet moment she'd had since arriving. It had been frantic races to reach Joely and Dr. Landon before surgery, then the adoring welcome from her family, and then constant conversation for five hours. And through it all, there'd been the persistent tension caused by the man beside her. Instead of their teasing banter annoying her, she found it…stimulating. In more than one way.

She rubbed her eyes. Yeah. She really did have to be intoxicated.

Rory's sad-hopeful face drifted into her mind, and she closed her eyes. She'd only been able to talk to him before leaving New York. He was living temporarily with a foster family of five kids where he was the youngest, and he didn't like it either. She'd had to disappoint him with the news that they couldn't visit this weekend. Jack still couldn't stay with him, since the new foster house had two large dogs, who were very friendly to people but very lethal to cats. Jack would be staying with her friend Brooke.

"She'll help you visit him, and I'll be back soon." she'd promised. "And we can text if you want."

Some perceptiveness in his character had heard her sadness. He'd wheedled the truth from her about her job interview and had become one of very few people who knew. Instead of telling her he was sorry, he'd sent her a hug over the phone.

"I'm glad you won't be the boss," he'd said. "You'd be too busy to be a good doctor."

If any of her adult friends had said such a thing, she'd have considered it condescension. Out of Rory's mouth it felt like a compliment from the angels.

"Almost there." Gabriel broke into her thoughts again, before she could sink into gloom over the job failure. She didn't do failure well.

"So you're right in Wolf Paw Pass then," she said, swiveling her head to take in the main street of the oldest small town in the area.

In a way, coming into town was as good as reaching the ranch. Her great-grandfather and uncles had helped found Wolf Paw Pass. There were a couple of Crockett-era buildings left, and Mia and her sisters had haunted the ice cream shop, the local diner, and the homes of their "city" friends their whole lives.

"Couple of blocks from here," Gabriel said. "It's an apartment building from the seventies. Four floors of eight apartments, a little retro, but nicely renovated. I was already living there, and the VA negotiated fantastic rents for eight more apartments."

"The more I think about it, the more unlikely it seems that you pulled this project off."

"I know. It *was* unlikely. There's a reason they called me Slick in school."

"I am riding to the scene of a crime with a comedian named Slick?"

"I was not the upstanding citizen in high school that I am now," he agreed. "But I promise I'm completely reformed. Makes me such a great parent for those alien octuplets."

"I have no choice but to take your word for it."

"That and wait for me to prove myself." He grinned without looking at her. "So, this project is set up for one year only. If I have success with these guys, the concept will continue but probably not the physical parts of this pilot program. My goal is for it to be a specialized service

Eglinton Square 416-396-8920

Toronto Public Library

User ID: 2 ********** 3204

Date Format: DD/MM/YYYY

Number of Items: 1

Item ID:37131173138397
  Title:The bride wore red boots
  Date due:11/07/2016

. . .

vets will apply to get into. I'd like to have had three years, but I took what I could get."

She watched the tight, precise motion of his jaw as he spoke, saw his knuckles whiten and relax on the steering wheel as his passion flowed and ebbed through his words. He was every bit as Hollywood gorgeous as she'd remembered, but that wasn't what drew her. His intensity reminded her of herself, but the fact that he could exude such fervor without sounding angry both impressed and intimidated her. She knew she didn't possess his kind of quiet self-control.

He turned his head unexpectedly and caught her staring. The resulting smile in the dim light of the car drove through her like a million little sparks.

"What?" he asked.

"Absolutely nothing." She snapped at him and then looked away, her skin hot. She hadn't meant to sound so harsh, but this was why he irritated her so easily. He bested her emotions without even trying, and it was usually an ability to control the emotions around her that was *her* stock in trade.

She couldn't control anything about him. She'd never been able to, not without going over his head. The realization made the sparks of attraction turning into agitated quivers in her stomach all the harder to take.

He pulled into the parking lot of a nondescript, but tidy, rectangular two-story wooden building. She noticed immediately the abundance of lighting around the doors, and could see as they passed the main entrance, a full-fledged security system. She wondered why, in this town where she remembered people leaving bank drafts in their unlocked cars without fear, there was such a big precaution.

"Okay," he said after pulling into a spot and turning off the engine. "Brewster lives in apartment fourteen, which is sadly notorious for its tasteless décor. I apologize ahead of time for the indefensible amount of thinly clad skin portrayed on the walls."

"I've seen plenty of body skin," she said curtly as the door opened and the car flooded with light. "I don't have time to worry about whether the person under the skin is sexist or not."

"Very liberated of you. Or, wait, *is* that liberated? If you're a female?"

She shook her head, softening at his discomfiture. This was a ridiculous way to best *his* emotions, but it was strangely satisfying, even a little flattering. "Stop trying so hard. He's a single guy, and I've seen naked girl pictures. Don't worry about it. They don't turn me on."

A flush crept over his ears, and his eyes locked with hers. "I sure wish you hadn't put that image in my head."

"And that, ladies and gentlemen, is how to torture a US Army lieutenant, retired."

He curled his lip. "I liked you better when you were just annoying and didn't think you were funny."

"Really?" His teasing warmed her. She was getting used to this brand of it. "I didn't like *you* better when you were just annoying."

"I never was."

"Oh, right. I forgot."

He gave a quick laugh and stepped out of the car.

They entered the building and climbed the stairs to the second floor. The hallway was brightly lit, glowing off of cool, blue carpeting. Four doors lined each side of the hall, and each door was fitted with its own mini-version of the security system outside. Again it struck her as overkill.

"Big on security here for this little town, aren't you?"

He walked silently a moment, serious again as if planning his answer. "There are lots of what you might call boogie men threatening these doorways. The locks keep away some of them."

His words held no chastisement, only a tinge of wistful regret, but Mia felt the sting of embarrassment. She should have connected the dots herself. Even she wasn't so insensitive she didn't understand emotional injury to some war veterans. Gabe had told her himself he'd handpicked these eight for their severe traumas.

"Of course," she said quietly. "Sorry. I wasn't thinking."

They reached apartment fourteen and Gabriel's mood changed. He made no pretense of knocking politely but pounded on the door with a clenched fist. "Open up you pile of crap idiots."

So much for sympathy over the boogeymen. Still, she loved the evil scowl on his face as he pummeled away.

A moment later a door opened, but not the one in front of them.

"Gabe. Down here."

They turned to the right, and Gabriel's features hardened into disbelief. "What the hell are you doing there?"

"Damn cow musta kicked the keys out of Brewster's pocket. He's locked out. We used your emergency key."

"You couldn't have used your own, Hauser? Or hacked in seeing as you're the electronic genius."

"Nah. I got no food in my place."

"Care to explain?" Mia asked, far more amused by the exchanges than she should have been.

"That's my place," he scowled. "Freeloading jackidiots."

"Aw," she soothed. "C'mon. It'll be fun to see where you live."

"And let you see all the whips and toys in my playroom? Hell no."

For a moment, the bizarre reply struck her dumb. He turned toward his open apartment without a single wink, grin, or giggle to indicate he'd been kidding. Of course, he was. On the other hand, the response had been awfully glib.

"Man," she said, turning with him. "I sure wish you hadn't put that image in my head."

Chapter Ten

AT FIRST GLANCE Gabriel's apartment looked like the set of a bad movie about human sacrifice. Four figures—two in hoodies, one in a tight-fitting wife-beater that showed off a colorful tattoo sleeve, and one actually holding a knife—stood around a body on its back in a leather recliner. The only light came from one lamp in the corner of the room, the overhead fixture in a room around a corner, and a flickering flat-screen television.

The bluish glow, the macabre tableau, the weird get-ups—it had to be a set up. Or there really was a scary playroom somewhere around a corner. Mia shot Gabe a skeptical look and got rolled eyeballs in response.

"What are you doing to my chair?" he bellowed.

"They're killin' me here, Gabe," came a moan from the body.

"Quit your bellyaching, Brewster." The figure with the knife bent forward and stabbed the implement downward into the chair. Mia choked.

"Hey, G." The tattooed man approached, a Tom Cruise smile spreading across his face. "Brewster dropped two Tylenol down the cushion. Hauser is fishing 'em out with a dinner knife."

Mia covered her mouth to hold in a sputter and leaned closer to Gabriel. "You weren't worried about any playroom," she accused in a strangled whisper. "You didn't want me to know you lived in a psych ward."

"Oh, good, you figured that out." He moved toward the group. "Hauser, get that knife away from my leather chair; it's four flippin' days old. Brewster, if you got blood on it, I'm charging you."

"I'm not bleeding. And, hey, love you, too, man."

"Oh, quit your whining. If you aren't dead I've got no sympathy. What were you thinking?"

"I wasn't," the man said easily. "I was just cracking myself up with the picture of a cow crapping on the floor of the VA—kind of like they're crapping on us."

Mia followed Gabe, closing in on the men with fascination. The kid in the chair, Brewster, was muscular but wiry with a long patrician face and short, mussed blond hair. The recliner footrest was extended, and on top of that, his right leg was propped on a pillow. A bag of frozen vegetables lay limp across his midthigh.

"You know this is the bullet that kills us all, right?" Gabriel said. "When did that occur to you?"

"About the time Madeline wouldn't get on the trailer," Hauser replied.

"Madeline?" Gabe asked.

"That's what they told us the cow's name was."

"Oh, for the love…" Gabe placed his hand gently between Mia's shoulder blades. "I brought you a doctor even though I should let you suffer. I'll let her help you under one condition. You will do whatever, and I mean what*ever*, she tells you to do. No argument."

The room went perfectly still. Five pairs of eyes raked her up and down in astonishment. Mia couldn't have cared less and wouldn't have under any circumstances. She'd held her own against gang members from South Bronx. But in this case, it wasn't the men but Gabriel's fingers against her spine that stole her focus and sent delight shimmering across her body.

"This is Dr. Amelia Crockett," he said. "She's a highly skilled surgeon from New York. So behave yourselves or I'll let her practice on you all."

He dropped his hand from her back, and the distracting fog over her world cleared. Every man greeted her at once, vying for her response like prep school boys who hadn't seen a girl all semester. She shook their hands, processing each name but knowing she'd need more passes through the introductions to remember them—Rick Hauser, Dan Holt, Damien Finney, Pat MacDougal. When she finally reached the leader and instigator, he was waiting for her with arm outstretched.

"Hell-ooo, Doc. I am very glad to see you."

"I suppose you are. And you must be the famous Jason Brewster."

He looked around to all the others, smiling. "Hear that? I'm famous."

"You're probably about to be famous in the hospital," she said.

"Oh, I don't think I need to go there," he said with an exaggerated wink. "A little something for the dull ache, and I'll be good to go."

"That right?" Mia smiled. "Glad to know I'm your second opinion. Well, maybe you're right. Can I take a look?"

"Sure." Jason picked the bag of frozen carrots off his leg and tossed it to Finney. Beneath it, however, he wore gray sweatpants. Mia crossed her arms.

"Sorry," she said. "Those need to come off."

The room erupted in hoots and whistles, all aimed this time at Brewster. "Come again, Doc?" he said and looked around at the repeat of the snickers.

"Okay." She smiled sweetly and squatted next to the arm of the chair. "The sweatpants need to come off." She repeated in a sing-song voice. "So you need to tell me whether you can stand up and remove them yourself or if you need *moi* to sacrifice them by cutting them up the front."

"Oooh, not my favorite sweats, Doc." He grinned at her again, but from this close, she could see the pain shimmering in his eyes. The tough soldier was doing his job.

"Okay, Mister Brewster. Then get your buddies to help you up and strip to the boxers. Or tighty whities. Whichever form of undergarment you prefer won't be a secret much longer. And one more thing. If I *don't* see a pair of boxers, briefs, or that weird boxer-brief combination thing some guys like, then you won't be coming tonight or any other for a while. You'll be on a fast track to the ER."

She stood and kept his eye with a smile. He smiled back, but something else had joined the emotion in his eyes—respect. Snark didn't always work on narcissistic guys—especially if they were truly that into themselves. But when it did work, she rarely had problems afterward with sexist and sometimes even threatening sarcasm.

With surprising gentleness, two of his friends helped Brewster out of the recliner. Once he was upright, Mia held up her hand.

"Can you put weight on the leg?" she asked.

He rocked his weight onto the injured side and winced mightily, but he stood steady. "Yeah," he said. "Once I'm on it it's not so bad."

"Point to where the kick site is," she asked, and he placed four fingers over the spot.

"Let me feel first," she said and purposely looked him in the eye. He opened his mouth and then shut it over a grin. She pointed at him and winked. "Very intelligent man. I like that."

"Haven't I always said?" He looked around for approval again.

Mia made her exam quickly and had him take just the one leg out of his sweats. The injured thigh was not bruised yet, but it was red and quite swollen. In the end she didn't really think it was broken, but she had no way of knowing for certain without imaging equipment.

"I can't make you go to the hospital," she said, when Brewster was dressed again and back in the chair. "I don't think it's broken, I think she—Madeline—kept it to the muscle. But that doesn't mean there isn't a crack or a chip. I really would feel a lot better if you got it X-rayed."

"Nothing is a secret around here, Doc," Dan Holt told her. "We go in, we get nailed by more than a hoof."

"Nobody really wants them to pull the plug on our little experiment here," MacDougal added. "Jason's sorry. Aren't you, honey?" He made kissing sounds.

"Oh shut up," he retorted. "I shouldn't have considered the cow. I knew that before we went after it. But we have no recourse about anything, do we?"

"We'll find one," Gabriel said quietly from the side. "But for what it's worth, I understand."

Mia studied him. Two months ago she'd found the man an arrogant, self-serving, by-the-book stick-in-the-mud. How many times had she asked him for access to Joely's insurance information, her eligibility for services, about the information he'd gotten in conversations with others, and he'd refused? Now here he was herding these damaged men like the foster father he'd compared himself to, helping them get out of hot water they almost deserved to face, and making it clear he understood why grown men broke rules in certain cases.

She tried to break rules, too, with the colleagues on her teams, but clearly none of them—as her failed job interview proved—would follow her to trouble and back like this group followed Gabe Harrison. She was just the bitchy female doctor. Not tough. Not focused. Just bitchy.

And bitchy didn't win jobs.

The weariness that had left her temporarily during the distracting examination settled back over her as the men broke away for their respective homes. She prescribed ibuprofen for Brewster's pain, told him in no uncertain terms what signs and symptoms should send him to the emergency room, and accepted his now-heartfelt thanks without hesitation.

"Lie if you feel you need to, but don't stay away from the hospital if something changes." She issued the warning with more gentleness now.

"You found a cool one, G," he said as he hobbled out the door flanked by Gabriel and Finney.

"I guess I did." Gabe winked at her. "I'll be right back."

Alone in his apartment, Mia took her first chance to really look around. With the lights up and the men gone, the living room no longer looked dark or macabre. It was, in fact, nicely appointed with rich leather furniture, pale blue walls, thick beige carpeting and plenty of pictures and books. She wandered to an open-shelved bookcase and studied the framed snapshots on each shelf. She could surmise that some contained family members and others army buddies, but one image stood out. A boy with Middle-Eastern features and two piercing brown eyes, smiled from four or five photos. In one he wore an Arizona Diamondbacks baseball cap and held a flat length of wood on his shoulder like a bat.

"I'm back."

She turned in place and met the genuine warmth of Gabe's smile. For the first time she let the phenomenal good looks he bore so effortlessly sink in. She'd never let anything, from his thick brown hair to his classically angled cheeks to his sexy beard stubble, penetrate more than surface deep. But once she gave herself permission to ogle, his hot, hot…oh-so-hot face, voice, hands, and body, her exhausted female hormones thanked her with liquid hot sluices of pleasure that dove for all her feminine places.

"Everything okay?" he asked.

"No," she said, dreamily. "I'm so tired I could be standing on an empty corner hallucinating you. But I've decided it's okay. I don't think we dislike each other for the moment."

His laughter rolled, easy and comforting. "You are tired."

"Why, am I wrong? You dislike me?"

"Lord, no. You saved my ass, Dr. Crockett. I am so in like with you. For the moment, of course."

"For reasons I will not bore you with, it seems I totally needed weird tonight. And believe me, this fit the bill. I don't normally do weird."

"You do it well."

"I—" She frowned and tried to dissect the compliment, but it didn't make any sense. "How can I do it well if I don't do it?" She giggled.

"It's time to get you back," he said. "I think jetlag has hijacked you."

"Wait. One thing." She turned back to the shelves and pointed to the picture of the boy. "Who is this?"

He couldn't have shuttered up faster if he'd been planning for a hurricane. Immediately the warm roll to his deep voice cooled and tightened. "Why?"

"He's cute." And he made her homesick—his deep brown skin reminding her of Rory. "And he's here five times. I just wondered."

"He's nobody. A kid who lived near the Green Zone in Baghdad. He reminded me while I was there that the war was always about people. That's all."

It wasn't all. Nobody got that upset over a random child. But she was too tired to pursue the question. "Ahh. Well, I'm sure he's a great kid. Reminds me of a boy I know."

"Kids remind us of kids," he said. "Nothing magical about that."

"That's a little jaded."

"Yup."

He offered no more, but when she moved away from the shelf and the pictures he relaxed, and once they left the apartment, his humor slowly returned.

"I can't believe how well you handled Brewster," he said, as they settled into his car for the drive back to the hospital. "He's a good man, but he never lets anyone see it. It was like you spoke his language."

"The language of no BS. Most people don't like that about me," she admitted. "I'm supposed to learn to blow smoke up peoples' butts even when they're being idiotic."

"In the medical world, especially, there's a fine art to smoke-blowing. It's not easy to give people bad news and make them think they're happy about it."

"Games." She sighed. "I thought I'd learned very early on in life that if I had something to get done or a goal I wanted to meet, there was no time for game-playing and no substitute for honesty and hard work. What good does it do to cater to egos or lie?"

"Like I said. A fine art."

When they'd pulled onto the highway that connected Wolf Paw Pass with Jackson to the north and the VA Hospital and Paradise Ranch to the south, Mia took out her phone and checked it for the first time since leaving the hospital ninety minutes earlier.

"Ach, I missed a message from my mother."

"I'm so sorry. Everything okay?"

She dialed the voice mail number and listened with trepidation until the reason for the call became clear.

"Everything's fine," she said. "Joely's awake and a little restless, so Mom wants to stay at the hospital. I'm supposed to pick up the car and take it home. Cole will come get her when she's ready to leave.

"It's silly to strand her," Gabriel replied. "Tell her I'll take you home, and she'll have her car whenever she wants it."

"I can't ask you…"

"You do remember the huge favor you just performed for me, right? This is nothing."

"Are you sure? It adds half an hour each way." And yet, she thought, she'd get to spend an extra half hour with him.

"Don't ask again." He admonished her. "Do you need to stop by the hospital first?"

"I'd like to pick up my suitcase from the car. But that adds another—"

He stopped her with a tsking sound favored by grandmothers around the world. "What did I tell you? Close your eyes, put your head back, and enjoy the ride. I'll have you and your suitcase home in no time."

She hesitated only a moment then did exactly as she'd been told. For a few blissful moments she was in a fairy tale, being whisked ever further from the person she really was. She didn't recognize this woman who wasn't annoyed by being ordered around, however kindly the orders were intended. She tried to figure out if Gabe was acting differently this visit, or if she was just so numb from the long, long day that she could ignore him.

Her body relaxed into the Jeep's comfortable bucket seat but then, rather than drift further into the sweet dream, her real-life memories returned. Slowly they grew and expanded, gobbling up the pleasant fantasy existence. By the time they reached her mother's car in the hospital parking lot, she moved like a robot and retrieved her suitcase in silence.

Gabriel didn't fill that silence with questions or even concerns. He let her stay quiet and uncommunicative. For the first time since her dreadful failure of a conversation with Mason Thomas she allowed his words to play through her head. "A leadership position requires more than superior surgical skills…You haven't gotten high marks on getting along with your fellow docs…This is just a postponement so you can take some more time to work on the floor and perfect your skills…It's an area you need some more time to develop."

For the first time since Mason had handed her a tissue in his office, tears stung behind her closed eyes. She hadn't failed at anything she'd put her mind to doing since she'd lost the spelling bee to Meg McPherson in seventh grade. It was like her father had always told her—"Your brain wasn't built for failure, Amelia. You come from stock that knows how to make success happen."

She did know how to make it happen—her resume was proof positive. And the rub was, this failure wasn't her failure—it was based on a difference of philosophy: What was more important, patient care or managing inflated, and therefore fragile, egos? Inflated egos needed to be deflated—she still believed that. And yet, she was the one who'd had her dream skewered with back-stabbing scalpels.

"Hey. You okay?"

Gabriel's voice finally interrupted the silence, and as she surfaced from her trance, she heard the little squeak of unhappiness she'd let slip. Hastily she straightened in the seat and blinked her eyes to clear them.

"I'm fine," she said, too quickly. "I'm awfully tired. Must be half-dreaming."

"You never said what changed in your schedule to allow your trip. You must have had to do some fancy scrambling."

She supposed she had, since she'd taken only eighteen hours to set everything in order. Mason had casually reassigned and rescheduled her surgeries and smoothed the way for four weeks off. It was another prick to her ego that he'd accomplished it so easily. She hadn't told a soul.

"A change in the schedule," she said, dismissing his query.

"Lucky for us."

Her emotions finally cycled around to annoyance. What she wanted to do was tell him to drive, go back to saying nothing, and stop trying to schmooze her. Instead she was the one who said nothing as they continued toward Paradise Ranch.

The scenery would normally have been obscured by the dark, but tonight the landscape, almost as far as she could see into the rolling hills that led toward the Teton mountain range, shone with silver-edged shadows and the blue-white light of a full moon. Harper, the painter, would have been able to capture the light perfectly on a canvas, but Mia could only stare mesmerized as the moonlight turned rugged Wyoming hills into ethereal beauties.

The movement in the distance happened so subtly Mia dismissed it at first as just more distant shadows. But then, yards and yards away, several animal shapes broke from a single dark mass, and Mia caught her breath.

"It can't be," she whispered.

"What?"

"Pull over! At the overlook just ahead. Would you? Please?"

She had to be making it up. She craned her neck as Gabriel swung the yellow Jeep off the road and aimed its nose out over the rolling valley.

"What are we looking at?"

"Turn your lights off," she said, still whispering, although even if she was right, whispering didn't make a bit of difference. "Straight ahead. Past that knoll."

She pointed, leaning left and peering through the windshield. Gabe leaned right so he could follow the line of her finger. His head bumped softly against hers.

"Sorry."

"S'okay." She watched a moment more and then the shapes defined themselves. One, two three, four…she counted to nine. "There!"

"Are those?"

"Mustangs!"

Every dour, angry thought fled as the equine shapes fanned out. Running! Her heart thrummed like rain on a rooftop, and her breath quickened until she officially grew light-headed. She hadn't seen mustangs in fifteen years. She'd been gone, of course, but in addition, nowadays the horses stayed north nearer the Montana border or south in the Buttes. Cattle ranchers had made sure they'd been driven off of grazing lands, her own father chief among the mustang detractors. The sight of this small band was like a gift of miraculous healing—to the land, to her sore heart.

"I've never seen wild horses," he said.

"So rare around here." Her voice continued to emerge in a reverent whisper. Tears formed again, but this time they had nothing to do with failure. This welcome home was simply overwhelming.

"This is the damnedest thing."

"I know."

"No. I mean, weird. I've never thought about mustangs in my life, and it was just the other day I happened upon your sister Joely watching a documentary about something she called a Mustang Makeover. She was almost depressed about these horses, but this time, with you, it might as well be a heard of unicorns."

She turned to find his nose just inches from hers. The stubble of his beard was so close she could count the stiff, sexy hairs even in the dim interior of the Jeep. She swallowed, forgetting the horses for a long, dry-mouthed second. He smiled. "You didn't strike me as a unicorns and rainbows kind of girl," he said.

His breath was sweet and hot, and he smelled of warm skin and his wool coat. She forced a slow breath and turned to look back out the window. "Every girl turns into a unicorns and rainbow believer when wild mustangs show up."

The herd had stopped running and now stood about two hundred yards distant, some grazing, some with heads up like statues gazing in their direction.

"What does it mean that they're here?"

"They've wandered from their sanctuary and nobody has rounded them up yet."

"Someone will round them up?"

"Ranchers don't like them. They compete for grazing space with cattle."

"Really? There are, what, a dozen of them? How can that hurt?"

His words elicited a smile. "In my opinion, exactly. Especially nowadays. A few generations ago there were a lot more horses and the land was more stressed. It's an old fight."

"Aren't they protected?"

"To a certain extent. The herds are culled and their numbers controlled with yearly roundups and drives. You can adopt a mustang from the Bureau of Land Management. That's how a lot of people get horses to train for the makeovers. My sisters and I used to get one or two and turn them into cow ponies."

"Joely said you were a good horse trainer."

"I guess I was." She thought back to the days when she'd been the one to guide Joely, the bleeding heart, into toughness and Harper, the dreamer into focus. "I was the practical one. I didn't care how pretty the horse was or how big. I watched its gaits and its heart."

"Ever sensible."

"We never won a makeover competition, but we came close every year. Consistency—that's what my dad said we were after."

"Could you still do it?"

She dared to turn back to him. His eyes twinkled, but his question was sincere.

"Other than the fact that I don't have a hundred days in a row to work on a horse, yeah. I think I could."

"Cool."

The simple word unattached to any expectation or questions, suffused with warmth. It *was* cool. She'd once had a life *filled* with strange, cool things.

"Can we just watch them a little while?" She leaned forward and crossed her arms on the dashboard. "They'll disappear tonight and chances of seeing them again are small. I'm sure it's just a transient band." She looked at him again. "I mean, if you can. I'm keeping you, sorry."

"No. You're not. It's fine. Hang on."

He left the Jeep and went to the back of the vehicle. A moment later he opened her door, two large, plaid wool blankets in his arms. "This Jeep has a tough old hood," he said "Let's get up off the ground and lose the reflections of the windshield."

She wasn't quite sure how to react. He'd switched gears so many times tonight, this was just one of many quick changes in attitude, aspect, and activity he'd performed. She exited the car and followed two steps to stand beside the front wheel.

"Step on the running board and then on top of the tire. Let me know if you need a boost."

"I've got it," she said in a low voice, and looked over her shoulder at him as she climbed the side of his Jeep.

He grinned. "I'm gonna hand it to you, Doc. You've been a pretty great sport tonight. Considering how tired you must be, another little adventure like this is a fun surprise. Meet you up top."

She blinked and he was gone. Mere seconds later he was kneeling on the hood and extending his hand. "Oh my gosh," she said. "Did you just fly up there?"

"Yup. C'mon."

Their palms met, and his thumb hooked around hers, solidifying his grasp. With smooth, easy power, he helped her over the fender, and she sat nimbly, letting him release her hand only after he sat as well. Deftly he folded one of his blankets lengthwise and laid it against the junction of the windshield and the hood, covering the wipers. The second one he shook out and spread across their legs.

"This'll give us a few extra minutes out here in the cold," he said.

"So prepared," she teased.

"You grew up in these mountains. You know what the weather is like around here. I've learned the hard way over six years to be prepared."

She was glad for her heavy jacket, which, although not a full-fledged parka, had kept her plenty warm through the past two New York City winters. The Wyoming night was still, but a bite in the November air nipped her cheeks and had her pulling the edge of the blanket up to her chin. The hood beneath her seat radiated warmth from the engine. When she leaned gingerly back against the windshield Gabriel did the same, and his arm aligned with her as they snuggled, accidentally but pleasurably, together adding more warmth to the chilly night.

"They're still watching us," he whispered.

She focused into the platinum-etched night and found the herd. Five or six horses still faced the Jeep and its humans, and the others grazed peacefully. Somehow, climbing around and clattering on the car hadn't spooked the little band.

"I needed this so badly," she said with a sigh, but the moment the words were out she regretted the dejection she'd hadn't filtered from her voice. Purposefully, she brightened. "But, then, who doesn't? Everyone should see this."

"Everyone," he agreed. "Some of those guys you helped tonight—they should see this. The one who most recently got home left Afghanistan nearly ten months ago, and I still don't think he believes there are truly peaceful places left in the world. Everything is a fight to him."

"Which one?" she asked.

"Brewster, the injured one."

"The angry one."

"Yes. But I don't think even he could be angry in a spot like this. Look at those beauties—they don't know an IED from an Iraqi school boy—all they care about is pure life and living."

"I don't know. They struggle to survive, too." Something prickled through the night air, something electric between her, Gabriel, and the wild horses that made her as bold as the stallion allowing his band to stand so bravely close to potential enemies. "Iraqi school boy," she said. "The boy in the pictures at your house is more important than you let on."

He stiffened, and she didn't try to coax him out of the reaction. The worst thing he could do would be to get angry or ignore her, and there wouldn't be much new in that. But he did neither. Instead he inclined his head slightly toward hers. "This trip. You didn't just decide to change your schedule for your sister."

The prickling in the air increased until it felt as if it came from her face, heating everything around her with embarrassment. She'd dreaded telling anyone how badly she'd blown her much-touted master plan. Now here she was, faced with lying to save face or telling the truth to the only person in Wyoming she'd fantasized would one day acknowledge her success and expertise.

"I lost the job," she said in a rush.

The words only stung a moment before a strange new sensation flowed through her veins from the touch of his hand taking hers. He wrapped his fingers around her hers and squeezed.

"That's okay," he said quietly. "I lost the boy."

Chapter Eleven

LOST THE BOY?

Gabe could not believe he'd uttered those words to
anyone, let alone Amelia Crockett. She had gone over his
head like a tattling kindergartner when she'd been unim-
pressed with his actions in the past. How much of a disaster would his reputation be once she wheedled this whole
story out of him? And she would.

And yet…His pulse slowed and his immediate panic
dissipated. This was the woman who'd just counseled
one of his men to lie if he had to—the Amelia Crockett
he didn't yet have figured out. Somewhere in the midst
of their mutual admissions to one another he'd taken her
hand, and she hadn't pulled it away. Out in the distance
stood some of the most amazing creatures he'd ever seen.
The combination of all that had pulled a confession out
of him as easily as a dose of sodium pentothal. Or a uni-
corn's spell.

Damn.

He tried to free his hand, but she gripped it in both of hers with sudden, surprising tenacity. "Tell me," she said. "It's okay. The story will never leave this spot. Tell me about losing a boy."

Hearing the words come back at him, he winced. It wasn't as if he'd never told the story—he'd gone through his own months of denying that he'd needed help all those years ago after returning from Iraq, just as his guys were going through it now. He'd finally submitted to counseling, finally learned to accept that the incident wasn't his fault, finally allowed himself to move ahead with his life. But his out-of-the-blue declaration that he'd lost Jibril, and his reaction to Amelia's request now, proved he'd never truly let himself off the hook.

"Jibril al Raahim," he said, "the boy you saw in the pictures, was exactly who I said he was—a kid who lived just outside the Green Zone in Baghdad where I was stationed for three tours. He was also a kind of self-appointed side-kick the last eighteen months I was there. I," he hesitated only a moment and forged ahead. "I stretched more than a few rules when it came to Jib."

"Did he have a family? Or was he the equivalent of homeless? What was his story?" Amelia's questions held all the intensity of a digging journalist and yet carried a note of genuine interest.

"He had a large family: seven siblings, uncles and aunts, a loving mother, and a very strict father who was a good man. I met them all. But Jibril had a fascination for all things American, and I showed him everything he wanted to see. By the time I figured out he was a little parasite, he'd gotten his pincers into me, and I'd taken a liking to him."

"What's wrong with that?" Amelia asked.

"We were supposed to be friendly and helpful and 'make friends' with the locals, but we weren't supposed to adopt them. Jibril, though...do you know what his name means in Arabic?" She shook her head. "Archangel of Allah. The Angel Gabriel. He had my name and vice versa. He believed that meant we were brothers."

"I find that heartwarming." She smiled.

"Yeah. Well, in the end, his family didn't. First he begged me to teach him English. Then he wanted to know about baseball and baseball cards. Pretty soon it was the music the soldiers listened to. I didn't take all of this seriously enough. To me it was harmless fun, a few hours here and there. Until the last day I saw him."

A familiar squeeze started in his chest, the one that made it a little harder to breathe. He'd learned not to fight it.

"I'm sorry." Amelia's apology surprised him. "I shouldn't have made you tell this story. It sounds like it has a bad ending."

"That's just it." He gave a helpless shrug. "I don't know. One morning he brought ten friends, brothers, and cousins to a sandy old neighborhood park so I could teach them all how to play baseball. We never knew when IEDs would turn up, and we certainly didn't know about the one an insurgent had placed in a trash can in the park. It went off right behind our makeshift third base while I and one of my squad buddies were chasing after a well-hit ball."

"Oh, God, the kids." Amelia squeezed his hand more tightly.

"Four children were killed—that's what we knew for certain. None of the ones we saw were in the group playing with us. They were just watching. As best we could tell, our group scattered. In the chaos, the smoke, the fires, we searched but when we couldn't find them, we assumed they were all right. Our job at that point was to secure the scene, so we had to finish working. Hours later, I went looking for Jibril but he was nowhere to be found, nor was his family. Their house was abandoned."

"How is that possible?"

"It's a question that's haunted me for eight years. According to neighbors, Jibril and a cousin died, and their grieving families snatched them from the scene so the evil Americans couldn't touch them. They buried the boys, shunned the town because the military was based there, and they left within hours.

"According to others, though, Jibril didn't die, but his parents were angry, specifically with me, because I'd seduced him. They spirited him away so I couldn't find him. I looked for him and his family for months but never found a trace. I had to believe he was alive because nobody was angry enough to tell my superior officers that he wasn't. Iraqi parents mourn their children very hard, and they will lay blame on the murderer of their sons."

"But you don't truly know to this day if he lived or died?"

"That's right. I lost him."

"I'm sure you're right, Gabe. You'd have known if he'd died."

"The thing is, even if he didn't it was my fault his family moved away—left their life and everything they knew. All because I insisted on getting too close."

"You could look for him now. Have you ever tried?"

"I think about it all the time, but why would I do that? I caused him enough trouble."

"Or, maybe you gave him some culture and understanding he's never forgotten."

He turned his head against the windshield and looked at her. She'd done the same and was staring back at him, her eyes sincere gray pools in the moonlit darkness. She still clasped his hand, and what amazed him was how secure it made him feel. He'd forgotten about tingles or first touches or the weird madness/magic of the night. He'd never considered that he might have done the kid any favors. He didn't consider it now. But she was a hell of a woman for suggesting it.

"Believe me, over the years I've learned that I got a lot more from him than I ever could have given. I thought he was clinging to me, but it was really me trying to turn him into a piece of home."

"Come on," she chided him gently. "That sounds wrong on the face of it. There's a lot more to your story than what you've told me."

"Of course—eighteen months of complicated story. But you've got the gist of it."

He turned his head forward again and placed his right hand behind his head. A quick glance assured him the mustangs still grazed within sight.

"Enough about me," he said. "Your turn. Spill it about the job."

He tried to make light of the heavy atmosphere, and she gave a smile that made a better grimace.

"There's not much to tell. I fully expected to get the job. Everyone who pointed me to it, helped me prepare for it, and had anything to do with hiring for it, knew exactly what my goals and plans were. I was the best qualified and the only logical choice. And they gave it to a second-year resident."

The matter-of-factness that seeped slowly into her voice as she spoke turned her tone into the one he remembered from months before—harder, more defensive, perhaps slightly entitled. But he knew her better now, and although it was no more than a guess, he believed something other than ego and self-importance fueled these bouts.

"I'm really sorry, Amelia. That sucks. What reason did they give?"

She seemed surprised by his sympathy. One hollow laugh filled the space between them.

"I'm bad with people," she said.

The blunt answer honestly took him by surprise. "Well, that's a load of bull crap."

"Or not."

"Look what you just did for me—for my guys. That's not the act of someone who's bad with people."

"I'm fine with patients." Her voice only wound tighter.

"Weren't you fine with Perry Landon? I know you were. He's done nothing but sing your praises. He's not a patient. Who told you this pile of nonsense?"

"No nonsense, Gabriel. No couched words or euphemisms. You know it's true—I don't have time for hospital politics or kissing up to people. You know I can be difficult. I don't make excuses, though, and I don't happen to think it was a valid reason to keep me from the job. Nonetheless, I didn't get it and, further, it was suggested I needed to use a month of built-up vacation time. Me being here isn't heroic. It's my equivalent to being sent to the corner to think about what I've done."

"What you've *done* is be very heroic to your people in Wyoming over the last twelve hours. Maybe you just don't like New Yorkers."

"After eight years? They're practically my people."

"I don't know. I think your people are right here."

They both settled back again, explanations as complete as they were going to be for the moment, secrets safe in the dark. They unclasped hands, the need for immediate comfort past, and for the next fifteen minutes they watched the mustangs wander as they grazed, moving farther away, ever in search of fresh forage. The Jeep's hood had long since cooled beneath them, and the air chilled as the time crept toward ten o'clock. Amelia pulled the blanket more tightly to her chin. Gabe expected to feel her shiver next. Instead, a small, delicate stomach rumble emanated from beneath the plaid wool. She giggled.

"Sorry."

"Man!" Understanding dawned. "We never ate dinner."

"I haven't been remotely hungry, but I've kept you from eating as well."

"Believe me, if I'd thought of it nothing would have stopped me. I'm not one to miss meals voluntarily."

"Proof of what a weird day this has been." At last the shiver he'd awaited sent a quiver through her body. "I guess it's time to head on," she said. "I'm not on my own here—there are people actually waiting for me."

"You need dinner first?"

"If I know anything about home, there'll be food all over the place. You're welcome to come in and scrounge with me."

"Oh, I couldn't impose on your family."

"You couldn't impose if you tried—I hear them talking about you, St. Gabriel. C'mon. I am hungry now, but I don't want to head back the other direction just to find a restaurant."

Gabriel had never been to Paradise Ranch. He'd heard tales of the enormous, fifty-thousand-acre spread and the influence its owners had once had in the area—like the fictitious Ponderosa spread of the old *Bonanza* television show. Today it was still one of the largest ranches in Wyoming, but modern ranching techniques now available to any rancher and an economy that favored nobody, made Paradise less of a powerhouse and more a revered old dynasty.

Gabe had done his homework when he'd become a patient advocate for the two injured Crockett women. Since Samuel Crockett, the last male heir to the ranch, had died just the past August, his six daughters shared ownership of Paradise. But only Harper and her fiancé had agreed to stay and make a go of the operation. Rumor had it that Sam had left the ranch in shaky financial condition and the future was still iffy.

Of course, he knew better than to base anything on rumor. And knowing the Crocketts as he was beginning to, he didn't think he'd bet against any of them.

He leaned forward over the steering wheel and peered curiously out the windshield as he turned into the Paradise driveway and approached the main house. The massive log home they came upon definitely did justice to the ranch's reputation, and it did its best to intimidate him. A massive porch, the full length of the house, stretched across the front. To the left of an imposing oak door were three full-sized picture windows, to the right was another. Two large gables jutted from the roof, and a massive addition grew from the left side of the main house. To a kid from a small city in Nebraska, this was a full-fledged mansion.

"Impressive," he said quietly.

"Yeah." Her voice had a muted quality to it, as if the sight of the house intimidated her, too, which made no sense, of course.

"You okay?"

"I usually feel zero nostalgia coming here. It's not actually the house I grew up in—except for the last couple of years of high school. It feels warmer tonight, though. Based on how this day and night have gone, that shouldn't surprise me, should it?"

"You're tired."

"I am that."

Windows glowed like a Terry Redlin painting as Amelia led him up the front porch steps and to the huge door. She reached for the handle, and the door sprang open before she touched it.

"Mia!" In seconds she was enveloped in a huge hug from one of the triplets. Gabe looked past them and met Harper's eyes. Behind her stood her fiancé, Cole Wainwright, much more relaxed and comfortable than he appeared when visiting the hospital. "We wondered where you'd gone. I'm so glad you're back safely."

"I was in good hands." Amelia pulled free and smiled back at Gabriel.

His pulse hiccupped like a school boy's.

"Gabe?" Grace noticed him and danced forward to offer the same warm hug. "This is a great surprise."

"Come in," Harper said. "Close the door and get warm. It's nice to see you, Gabe. How'd you get taxi duty all the way out here?"

"It seemed silly to make anyone run back to get your mother in the middle of the night. I already had Amelia in the car, and this pays her back for the favor she did for me."

"Trading favors. How modern. And awfully quick, you two." Another triplet appeared and raised her eyebrows. From the innuendo, he assumed it was Raquel. Grace wasn't one to leave the straight and narrow.

"Welcome to Paradise." Cole held out his hand and scanned the women as Gabe shook. "Nice to have a little male reinforcement."

"You're a braver man than I am." Gabe chuckled.

More hugs went around, including one between Cole and Amelia. There was supposedly a history between them, but Gabe didn't know the details. He couldn't imagine needing to know them, and yet curiosity made him study the embrace surreptitiously. It seemed easy and uncomplicated, even fond. As fond as the one between Amelia and Harper.

"You two look pretty comfortable already," Amelia said. "I don't ever remember an atmosphere like this when I've come home before. The place actually looks…lived in."

"We love it here," Harper said. "We've moved some things around, hung a few different paintings. Mom's letting us leave unfinished books and magazines around." She laughed. "I don't stand on the ceremony Dad did."

"God bless him," Amelia said. "I know there's a hole without him, but I do notice the difference."

"Good," Harper said simply.

Gabe's introduction to Paradise couldn't have been warmer or more impressive. Raquel and Grace sat him down with Amelia at a huge table in a dining room large enough to accommodate the entire Crockett family. Moments later, homemade potato soup and crusty slices of sourdough bread sat before them, the soup steamy, the bread warm and aromatic. Amelia sipped a glass of bright Chablis with her dinner. Gabriel was offered choices from beer to water. He took an IPA Cole recommended and didn't think about the drive home. He was hungry enough now that the combo might as well have been the mythical ambrosia of the gods.

The rest of the family didn't ignore them—they dragged chairs around the table and sat, gleaning stories from him and, less easily, from Amelia. He explained his project with the men, their penchant for sophomoric practical jokes, and Amelia's examination of the cow hoof imprint in Brewster's thigh.

The jovial atmosphere didn't change until Harper innocently asked about Amelia's time off.

"I never even asked how long you could stay this time," she said. "I'm assuming you need to be back sooner rather than later?"

"I'm staying at least through Thanksgiving," Amelia replied dully.

The sight of her sitting at the table, a forlorn pup instead of a tough alpha she-wolf, tugged at something in Gabe's center. He shouldn't feel sorry for her. She was fine—most people had to struggle now and then on the way to their goals, and from what he knew about Amelia Crockett from her sisters and mother, she hadn't struggled with much, ever. But her sadness was real tonight. It might have been over a first world problem—but this admission was clearly hard for her.

"Thanksgiving?" Harper set down her glass of wine and caught her with a confused eye. "What changed? I mean, that's fantastic, but I never hoped you'd stay that long."

"Well, you know that job I was so sure about?"

"You didn't get it?" Grace's mouth dropped open like a guppy's.

"I didn't. Apparently I—"

"Have too many credentials." Gabe couldn't stop himself from interrupting her confession. She'd been painfully honest with him, and he didn't see any reason she had to self-deprecate herself in front of her family when she was already this tired. "Didn't you say they gave it to a kid just going for his first specialty?"

"I…yes, that's what they told me." She stared him down, but surprised flecks of gratitude softened her eyes.

"Honey, I'm so sorry." Harper reached from her seat beside Amelia and took her hands. "I know you really wanted that job so you could take your certification next year. Are you okay?"

Amelia looked genuinely surprised at the heartfelt reaction.

"I'm…disappointed. But it's not the end of the world."

"Bet it felt like it, though." Harper frowned.

Amelia only shrugged, her face the slightest tinge of pink. Gabe wondered why she remained slightly aloof from the warm sympathy. She reminded him of a new pet overwhelmed by too much sudden, loving attention.

"Well their stupid decision is our gain, at least for now," Grace said. "It doesn't make up for it, but we were all saying how glad we are to have you here. None of us understands at all what's going on with Joely. She just doesn't seem to be getting any better."

"I…" Amelia looked around the table, still uncertain. "I want to spend a little time tomorrow discussing her case thoroughly with Dr. Landon. I'll have a better understanding after that. Remember, her injuries were very severe. The kind that don't heal quickly. And Joely is pretty depressed at the moment. It's going to take a lot of time. But, this is not abnormal."

"See?" Grace smiled. "You have the background to make us all feel better."

"Believe me. That's about all I can do." Amelia sighed. "I wish I were more of an expert in spinal injuries, but it's very specialized."

"You're here—that's all we care about," Grace said. "Thank you for coming home."

Once again Amelia didn't say anything, but she smiled for the first time.

Gabriel pushed his chair back from the table and smiled, too. He could see the exhaustion starting to flood her eyes and slump her posture. Poor kid had to be dead on her feet.

"I need to get back. I have an early meeting tomorrow morning. You can tell them about our sighting and head for bed yourself."

A ridiculous dart of attraction shot from his gut to his groin. He imagined crawling into bed with Dr. Amelia Crockett and easing the exhaustion from her shoulders, from her back, from her eyes. It seemed sexist and clichéd to imagine anything more, but he did anyway. She suddenly seemed like a woman made not of ice and confrontation, but of sensitivity and vulnerability—one who'd always give as good as she got in all the best ways. The intrigue was sexy as hell.

And he must be exhausted, too.

She walked him to the door after everyone else had reiterated their thanks and said good-bye. She stood in the doorway, and he turned on the porch to face her. Sometime during the evening she'd pulled every comb, pin, and holder out of her hair, and it swung in dark waves past her shoulders. He jammed his hands in his pockets to keep from finding out what it felt like.

"I just…wanted to say thank you," she said. "You saved face for me in front of them, and you did not have to do that."

"I figured one full confession a night is all anyone needs to suffer through." He laughed. "You didn't tell on me either, so I'd say we had each other's back. You can tell them the truth later, or don't. There's nothing to be gained by putting yourself down in front of them. They think you walk on water."

"I hope that's not true." She rubbed her eyes. "Oh, how I hope they think no such thing."

"Why? We all need to feel powerful sometimes."

"Because—" She stopped herself and set her mouth firmly. "This is silly. I don't want to discuss deep philosophical human nature. Let them worship me—it's their problem."

He thought she was kidding—but Amelia's joking wasn't always easy to spot. "Go get some rest."

"Fine. But thank you again. You went above and beyond for us today."

He started to turn away and then spun back. "Would you like to repay me?"

"Excuse me?" Her dark eyes now held smoky flecks of amusement. "Didn't know this was a quid pro quo."

"I'm just a mercenary at heart."

"That's so comforting."

"But I'm serious. I'd never been here before, and now my interest about the famous Paradise Ranch is piqued. Would you show me around the place sometime? Give me a personalized guided tour? I'd like to see what kind of land and operation attracts a band of wild horses."

"Really?"

"Yeah." He shook his head, suddenly fully enamored with the idea. "You pick the time and tour format. I'll take care of food—pay you back for being just as big a help to me today."

"Gosh, Lieutenant Gabriel Harrison, are you actually proposing a more serious truce?"

"Think we could handle it?"

"I can't imagine."

He laughed and her cute, tired giggle mingled with it. Another lance of attraction nailed him. "Let's try anyway."

"It's Thursday, how about this weekend? Meet here Saturday or Sunday, wear your iron britches—when's the last time you spent a day on a horse?"

"Horse? I was thinking maybe my Jeep…"

"Hah, city boy. You can't see the landscape in a Jeep. You *have* ridden?"

"Like a pro," he scoffed, hoping the lie was transparent.

"Saturday, then." Her eyes sparkled beneath tired, half-mast eyelids.

He fought with himself a moment, the urge to bend and kiss her almost overwhelming. But that would be an idiot's move. He held out his hand instead, and she took it without hesitation. With her fingers curled around his palm, he forced down the urge one more time and gave a firm shake.

"To the start of a beautiful truce," he said.

Chapter Twelve

"AND THAT'S IT. From what I can see, we definitely cleared away those bone fragments and left the spinal cord untouched." Perry looked up from a paper printout of Joely's latest MRI and handed it to Mia. "Only time will tell if it makes any difference to your sister's prognosis."

"Amazing work." Mia had seen the images straight from the imaging lab, but she still nodded with appreciation at the photo in her hands. "Thanks for taking such care."

It was awkward to be on the family side of a surgical consultation and rare to be the one giving praise rather than receiving it. She hoped her gratitude sounded as sincere as she intended.

He shook his head to ward off the compliment. Again, something she wouldn't do. He deserved the praise—he should take it.

"What's next?" she asked. "I'd love to hear how you think Joely should go forward with rehab and your private thoughts on the medical aspects of her case. You must have some body of experience you're drawing from."

He grinned. "I can't think of anything more stimulating than discussing a case with another brilliant doctor. Joely has given verbal and written permission to share all aspects of her care with you, so what would you think of taking our discussion to lunch? The Basecamp Grill in Wolf Paw Pass has a pretty good lunch menu."

She considered his eager invitation, which matched his eager eyes, and wasn't sure what to think. Did the idea of lunch with a new doctor simply stir his professional juices? Or was he actually asking her—Amelia, not Dr. Crockett—out to lunch under the guise of work?

Vestiges of jet lag still made it too hard to analyze his hopeful demeanor.

In the interest of expediency she decided she didn't care what his motivations were. "Sure, I'd like that."

"I'm ready anytime." He stood.

"Let's go."

Perry chatted easily all the way to the lobby, telling her without being prompted about his move to the Jackson Hole area three years before. How he'd come to love the area after growing up in Cincinnati, and how satisfying he found the work at the VA. He'd never served in the military, but he wanted to give back to his country and the service men and women somehow. This seemed like the best way he could contribute.

She listened with amused interest. He was an unusually talkative man, answering questions more than willingly, sometimes before they were asked. In some ways she didn't mind—it kept him from digging too much information from her. In other ways, however, she couldn't help but compare him to—

"Why, Dr. Crockett, as I live and breathe."

She looked up as they reached the middle of the lobby. "Gabriel!"

He strode toward her from the direction of the hospital clinic hallway, grinning irrepressibly, wearing dress pants and a crisp white shirt under a gray wool coat with a classy red-and-black tartan lining. A hyper swoosh of oxygen left her brain, and the world bobbled a little.

Not fair. It should be illegal for you to sneak up on people.

She'd definitely have to add "distinguished" to his list of physical attributes, a list topped by "killer handsomeness."

Then she noticed Brewster behind him, swinging awkwardly on a pair of crutches.

"Jason?" she asked.

"Hey, Doc. Surprise." He looked like a petulant boy ready to pick up a rock and throw it at someone.

"What happened? Is everything all right?"

He softened slightly. "A spot in the middle of where I got nailed turned black last night. Gabe forced me to take your advice."

"And thank God he did. Have you already seen somebody?"

"Yeah. Just coming from urgent care." Sheepishness didn't play kindly with the tough-guy persona he wanted to project. "They dug out some dead muscle, and I've got an ass-ugly, see-through bandage on it."

"Right," she said. "To promote the granulation of new tissue. I'm so sorry."

"Don't be sorry." Gabriel shot Brewster a quelling look. "The jig is up on this one. Part of the deal with this project is that all medical consultations get recorded and evaluated. He's already been called to the boss's office."

"Boss?" She turned the question on Brewster.

"He's more like a damn warden." Resolute hardness returned to his face.

"He's a zookeeper." Gabe's dimmed smile barely registered, but she saw his concern. "Aw, hell. We'll figure something out; we always do."

"Where are you headed now?"

"To the pharmacy and then to my boss's office."

"For The Meeting? About this incident?" she asked.

"The very one." Gabe nodded.

"What did you tell the doctor today?"

"That I needed to get the cow from point A to point B, and she didn't want to go."

"And that was good enough?"

"Hell no. But I told them the 'why' wasn't anyone's business."

Mia couldn't stop a laugh, even though she knew how painful Brewster's injury would be for the next few days. "Personally, I salute you. I guess I'll wait to hear what the boss says."

She met Gabriel's eyes hoping to share the camaraderie of the moment and found him studying Perry with suspicion.

"Heading out?" he asked. "Sorry we're keeping you."

"Lunch date," Perry agreed. "To discuss Joely's case."

"Have a great time." Gabriel raised his eyebrows at her.

She scowled, not understanding. He stared almost like a jealous suitor, and it made no sense. She and Gabriel might have a truce, but their relationship went no further.

"Let me know what happens," she said.

"Of course." He fired up his smile again. "Our best hope is if Brewster the Mouth here can keep from making the powers that be angry."

Mia leaned toward Jason Brewster. "I'm the last one to talk because I tick people off all the time, and I hate BS," she said. "So my only advice is, seriously, don't act like I do. Nod and smile."

Brewster looked at Gabriel and knocked him lightly with an elbow. "Why can't she be my doctor? We'd be done and outta here."

"Good question," Gabriel replied. "See if you can get her to work on that."

"I'm not that kind of doctor," she replied. "I could crack you open and fix your insides, but I'm no good in a clinic."

"Bummer." Brewster shrugged.

"Holler if you need anything," Gabriel added, as Mia and Perry turned. "I'm at your service."

"I'm sure we've got this part," Perry replied. "But thanks."

Amelia couldn't help the smile that crept onto her lips. She thought of the little band of mustangs she and Gabriel had watched last night. She'd picked out the stallion with no problem—he'd been the one slowly circling the herd, popping his head up at the slightest disturbance, snorting out warnings and directions that had carried across the still night air. Here she had two would-be leaders—their slight wariness equal to a stallion's warning snorts. The brand-new attempts at posturing quite humorous.

They probably didn't have a clue they were doing it, but it was crystal clear to her. And even though neither had a single claim to dominance, her ego, which New York had so thoroughly wounded, loved every minute of the silly display.

FOUR HOURS LATER, still stuffed from a delicious steak salad at lunch, Mia presided over Joely's slow efforts at eating her dinner. The food at this hospital was better than most, but Joely insisted, nonetheless, that she didn't want a single drop of soup or the smallest spoonful of pudding.

"It's only been a day since the surgery," Mia said in her best bedside voice. "You need to take a few bites just to keep your system working, but I know you aren't hungry."

"At least you aren't harping on me like Mom does. She's turned into an old grandma over all this."

"She's a mother. You might as well just nod and smile because you'll never stop the fussing."

Mia gave a little inward snort at the words she'd used to advise Jason earlier. Nod and smile—in fact, she'd done a fair amount of that at lunch today with Perry. The man was fascinating and had stories enough for a book. He was also as nice as the food was delicious. But he could talk like three women in a coffee shop—truly an unusual male.

"Yeah," Joely sighed. "But it's still irritating."

Mia smiled. "Eat, Joely, eat. You're wasting away to skin and bones."

"Aaaack."

"So, I should tell you what Gabriel and I saw when he brought me home last night. Actually on Paradise land, live and beautiful. A little band of eight or ten mustangs."

For the first time, Joely drew out of her funk like an uncertain kitten being enticed out to play. "Really?"

Mia described the scene with as much romance as she could—not her strong suit. Joely listened, rapt.

"Gabriel said it was a funny coincidence," Mia said. "That he'd just had a conversation about mustangs with you. Kind of cool, don't you think?"

"It sounds beautiful," Joely said. "And it is weird. I've had them on my mind for a week now. Deadlines for the Mustang Makeovers around the country are hitting everywhere. It's hard, because even though I don't want to ride, I hate thinking I can never do that again."

"First of all, I don't know why you'd say that. You're a long way from being done with your healing. Second, if the loss of movement in your leg happened to be permanent, think how impressive training a mustang would be. Forget it, sis. No sympathy. You fight for your next chance at this."

"Sometimes I think you're just a little too optimistic." Joely's voice crossed a sulk with depression. "You don't have to have a fake happy bedside manner with me."

"Take it while you can get it."

Mia's cell rang from a side pocket of her purse, and she pulled it out. Her stomach flopped at the name and she held up a finger to Joely as she answered.

"Gabriel?"

"Hi, Amelia." He sounded sluggish, heavy, as if his words weighed a ton each.

"Everything okay?" She knew it wasn't.

"Just wondering if you still happen to be with Joely."

"I am."

"Do you by any chance have time to stop by my office sometime?" He hesitated—an unusual phenomenon from him. "I'm looking for a completely unprofessional brainstorming session. And I need you to bring self-righteous, kick-ass, warrior Dr. Crockett with you."

If she'd been truly vain, she'd have thought he was getting back at Perry for lunch. But too much resignation and weariness came through the phone for her to believe he was thinking of such things. This was, as they said, not a drill.

"When?"

"I'm here a good while yet. Anytime."

"Well, I'm kind of sick of watching my sister chow down her food like a big pig." She kissed two of her fingers, flicked the kiss at Joely, and grinned. "How about in fifteen minutes?"

She almost heard his sigh of gratitude. "That would be great."

"See you in a few."

When Mia hung up, Joely met her eyes with impish accusation. "I sense a pretty big change in the air around you and my patient advocate."

"I know," Mia said. "It's disturbing."

"He's adorable, you know. I say grab him."

"That's totally absurd. We live and work more than two thousand miles apart and have nothing in common. He's just turned out to be not quite as big an ass as I originally thought."

"You always were slow when it came to anything but facts and figures. Of course he's not an ass. Any more than you are."

"Thank you. I think."

"Go. I don't know what he wanted. I don't want to know. Just go see him."

"Fine."

"I want details when you're done, though."

"Forget it. No dessert for little girls who don't eat their supper." Mia pointed to her sister's dinner tray.

"Maybe you are an ass."

Mia bent over and kissed her forehead. "We already knew that."

IT HAD TO be something about the Brother to Brother program. She'd seen Brewster today, seen the concern in Gabriel's eyes although he'd brushed it off. Even when they'd first met, when she'd barely been able to tolerate his constant cheeriness, he'd never been without that jaunty, bright personality. The near-depression she'd heard in his voice could only mean something dire had happened.

But why call *her*?

She made her way from the hospital to the administration building a block away and took the elevator to the fourth floor and the Department of Patient Advocacy. One lone secretary still sat at her desk in the small lobby, and she smiled when Amelia approached.

"I'm looking for Gabriel Harrison's office," she said.

"You must be Dr. Crockett," the woman, middle-aged and efficiently friendly, replied. "He's waiting for you. Take the hallway to my left, and his is the second door on the right."

"Thank you."

The lobby was fairly spartan, with just a few upholstered chairs and the requisite odd assortment of magazines. A couple of generic scenery pictures hung on the walls, alongside several signs explaining how and what to present when requesting assistance. Mia didn't read any of them, instead she entered the hallway, even plainer than the lobby, with attractive slate blue carpeting but plain beige walls and no ornamentation. Nothing intimidating but nothing inspiring either. She reached the second office and found the door open, a simple plaque affixed to its pale wooden surface. *Gabriel Harrison, Patient Advocate, Behavioral Health.*

Behavioral Health? That usually meant psychology or social work credentials of some kind. He'd never mentioned any kind of expertise in dealing with mental health issues. She stepped into the doorway and knocked lightly. His head popped up.

Her heart gave a happy extra thump, and she fought for calm.

"Hi," he said. "Thank you so much."

"Don't thank me yet. Kick-ass Dr. Crockett doesn't have the best track record with you, remember?" She smiled.

"For some reason, tonight I'm not the least bit worried about that. Come on in."

The office was as big as a good-sized bedroom, with plenty of room for Gabriel's desk and three comfortable, modern chairs with red upholstered cushions and wooden arms. The walls contained several random posters—a giant Denver Broncos logo; a portrait of five servicemen, one from each branch of the military; and incongruously, a poster of a woman wearing a headset with the caption "Customer Service: Giving you precisely correct and totally useless information when you need it the most."

Mia snorted her laughter and then scanned the shelves lining two walls. Most were filled with books, but others held random items that would probably reveal a lot about Gabriel if she had time to study them. She recognized a set of juggling pins, and wondered over a black box about a foot square covered in stars and moons, with what looked like a magician's magic wand lying across its top.

"So," she said, eyeing the box. "This is the place where all the *magic* happens. Tell me about the wand there and about that sign on your door saying you're into 'Behavioral Health.' "

His color deepened slightly. "I used to do magic tricks at local restaurants when I was in college to earn extra money. A distant but fond memory. I also finished the last year of a bachelor's degree in clinical social work after I got back from Iraq. I'm a very poor man's counselor."

A pang of surprise turned swiftly into admiration. "No wonder helping your experimental men is so important to you. That's impressive."

"I don't know. I'm beginning to wonder if even an actual psychiatrist could handle this."

"So—we come to the crux of the matter. What happened?" She sat in one of the chairs and leaned across his desk surface. "I get the impression it's nothing good. Did they pull the plug on your project?"

He smiled with a touch of wistfulness. "No, they didn't pull the plug—but Brewster is on probation along with Damien Finney. They have two weeks to find jobs or something that occupies work hours, or they're out. The top brass does not seem to find their frat boy pranks as charming as I do."

" 'Charming' you say? Not sure I blame the brass." She smiled, hoping he knew she was joking.

"Of course they aren't charming. But I've told you before that I find their antics hopeful, and I see them as letting off steam. But it's true, a person can't bring a cow into the Veteran's Administration. Nor can he blow up a can of whipping cream in and on the director's car. A flashing sign across from an office or a fake can of peanuts with a spring-loaded snake maybe. I'm out of ideas for incentivizing these guys. It's like telling them to behave when the people in charge don't have to do the same."

"Might it *be* time to let them go?" she asked. "Maybe they can't be helped."

He stood, his face a thundercloud. "*Everyone* can be helped. I absolutely will not let them go. Not when they're making such great strides everywhere else."

"Okay," she replied calmly. "That answers that."

"Sorry."

"No need to be. I can see your passion."

"You're not the first one to suggest I'm a little too obsessed. But it's no different here than it is in the field. You don't leave anyone behind."

"So why did you call *me* here?"

"What's the toughest thing I can do to them? Where can I send them? You must see a lot of crap working where you do—worse than this."

"I'm not an ER doc."

He sighed and nodded. "I know. In truth, I'm not sure why I'm asking you. Wit's end, I guess."

"You probably thought of me because I can be mean and rude." She offered a curled-lip smile.

"Those are not the words I'd use."

"Really?" One brow arched upward. "What would you use?"

"Tenacious. Smart. Clever." He sat back in his chair.

"Smart and clever are redundant."

"No they aren't. Smart is figuring out what the problem is. Clever is knowing how to solve it."

Once again she found herself staring at him in wonder. He had ways of phrasing things that made the most mundane words twist into compliments. Compliments that weren't false praise.

"I wish I was worthy of that," she said, finally. "I don't know anything about veterans and their issues. I think it takes more than a casual doctor or a doctor who's really a specialized surgeon."

He sat back in his chair and smiled. "I can't believe I ever thought you were self-centered."

"Oh, I am. I admit to being pretty career focused. And knowing how to get done what I need to do."

"Obviously. You wouldn't be where you are at your age if that wasn't true. But I'm beginning to think that's a façade."

"And so the therapist comes out." She folded her arms and fixed him with a knowing look.

"Nah. Just trying to say thanks in a very awkward way. I appreciate you bothering to come. I never think out loud—I'm not one for hashing things out over coffee. Make a decision and see it through, that's my motto. So, it's hard to admit I'm lost, but I am."

"Then you're a very evolved male."

"Nope. Just a desperate Neanderthal."

She uncrossed her arms and leaned on one elbow, thinking. "Is it possible to find Brewster a job? Or Finney? What do they do?"

"They all have different interests. None of them is a professional as such. Finney was a truck driver. Brewster's family owns a small chain of grocery stores. I've had them in the apartments for four months, and four of the men have permanent jobs. Two have part-time gigs that don't pay much. Brewster and Finney have each started and quit two positions. Every one of these guys have been through severe traumas. They've seen death, and they've pulled their triggers and killed, quote, the enemy. They're having a hard time coming to grips with that. These are not your Chris Kyles. These are guys who just wanted to grow up and live normal, boring lives."

"I'm so sorry." The idea of young men living through such hell made her ill. "It sounds like they need to see some normal life. Be around some living things."

"Living things," he repeated. "Seems so simple. But everywhere they turn they only hit dead ends. Pun sort of intended."

Her mind raced through a hundred different possibilities for jobs. Greenhouses, animal shelters, dog walking, landscaping. Anything but an office job—

"The ranch," she said, almost as shocked as Gabriel looked. "There isn't much more in-your-face living than at a ranch. Cows, calves, horses, hard work, cold weather. I have no idea if there's anything they could do, but I'd be willing to ask Harper and Cole if they could use any help."

Gabriel's eyes shone like he'd been given a stay of execution. "Would you really?"

"I'll be completely honest. My dad, when he died, didn't leave Paradise in the best financial shape. Harper and Cole have their work cut out for them. I'm not sure there's anything they can do. But it can't hurt to try. Even just some seasonal work—this is a busy time of year repairing things, setting up for winter. Heck, the horses move inside during the day. A little stall mucking is about as real as it gets."

He laughed—a relieved sound she hoped wasn't thoroughly misplaced. "Maybe I'll wait before I tell them I found work picking up shit."

"Wise," she agreed. "They'd bolt the program on their own."

A short silence enveloped them. Gabriel stared at his desk, deep in thought. Mia tried to guess what could possibly be going through his mind. Her guesses weren't remotely close to what finally came out.

"You don't have any mustangs hanging around in that barn you mentioned?"

"Mustangs?" She laughed. "Hardly. What made you ask that—other than the obvious?"

"That was pretty cool last night," he said, allowing himself a moment of distraction to smile and elevate her pulse with the slight dimple in his left cheek. "But it was really something Joely said. About how those horses humble you really quickly. We both joked about how retired vets with too much time on their hands might benefit from being bossed around by a horse."

"They don't nickname the national Mustang Makeover contests 'challenges' for nothing." Mia sent her mind back to the three times she, Harper, and Joely had entered Makeovers. Six horses all together. Four had been straightforward to train—not easy, but not mean. One, humorously named Angel Baby, had turned out to be the horse that had nearly killed them all. In the end she'd come around, but Mia shuddered, envisioning a couple of non-horsemen ending up with a project like Angel.

Still...

"You know," she began, and hesitated again.

"What?"

"Your guys wouldn't be chosen to participate in a real makeover challenge. They don't have any experience or credentials. And, the makeovers take place all through the summer, so it's far too early to even apply. But. There's both a privately owned wild horse preserve and a Bureau of Land Management mustang holding facility within half a day's drive. You can adopt mustangs any time. What if Paradise did its own little mustang makeover?"

"I keep asking this. Are you serious?"

"I don't know. Am I?"

Her brain raced again, but this time with an actual idea—insane and unlikely to happen as it probably was.

"What's going through that clever brain now?" he asked.

Her heart pumped and her adrenaline made her jumpy in the seat, and it wasn't even all Gabriel this time. This was beyond a doubt the craziest notion she'd had since she'd been a teenager.

"I am certifiable," she said, and gave him a goofy grin she hadn't used in years. "But if I get the right answers to my questions after I leave here, how do you think Brewster and Finney would feel about a trip to visit some wild horsies?"

Chapter Thirteen

"I WISH I thought this was a really stupid idea." Harper looked at Mia over the kitchen table and ran her index finger over the handle of her coffee mug.

Mia nodded. "I know. I do, too. But I can't shake it. I'm not this frivolous."

"No, you're not." Harper didn't smile. "And that's one of the reasons I'm so taken with this. If your brain is working out the logistics, there must be something to it."

"Oh, no. Don't go by that. My brain has checked out completely this trip."

"Hah. Your brain never checks out. We'd all kill for your brain."

"Please don't say that." Mia tamped down the slightest bit of resentment.

It was half a miracle to be sitting here with Harper having a fairly normal conversation. They'd been polar opposites and mostly adversarial all their lives. Until their father had died and Harper had taken Mia's old boy-friend—a fact that made Mia happier than anyone would ever understand, since Harper and Cole were perfect for each other. Mia didn't want this moment spoiled by any reference to the things that had once torn the sisters apart—her "amazing" brain being one of the biggest. Mia had always hated being set apart.

"It's a compliment, dork." Harper finally smiled.

"It's never been a compliment."

"Mia!"

"Forget it." Mia returned the smile. "My brain is a topic for another day. And anyway, I'm not so smart, asking you and Cole to think about a program like this when you're struggling to get this place back on its feet. You've only had a couple of months to take stock."

"We did all right selling the cattle this year. Prices were up from the last five years, so the projections were a little more dire than reality has turned out to be. And we have a lot of plans and ideas. Not that it won't take several years to implement them. The thing is—this place belongs to all of us. I want us all to have ideas."

"This isn't a money maker."

"It doesn't seem like it on the surface."

Mia sighed. "They're good men, just a little damaged."

"It sucks," Harper said. "Nobody should have to go through such trauma."

The back door opened, and Cole entered, filling the space with his height and breadth. He looked good—windblown and healthy. Downright happy. He kicked off his shoes and padded stocking footed into the kitchen, winking at Mia but heading straight for Harper.

"Miss me?" he asked, and bent to kiss her.

"Oh, believe me, I was a wreck. I didn't know how I'd make it through those two hours." She made a face and kissed him back. "Pathetic."

"And proud of it."

"Hey, Mia."

"Hey, Cowman. You're starting to look the part."

"Like riding a bike," he said. "All the lessons my daddy taught me are coming back."

He'd grown up on the neighboring ranch, now a part of Paradise, since Cole's father had sold to the Crocketts years before.

"Seriously," Mia asked, "is it all going okay? You guys took on a lot."

"It is," he said. "We aren't going to live like kings for a good long while, if ever, but I think we can pull Paradise out of the doldrums eventually. It's going to take a combination of things, a little diversifying, and some creative thinking."

"Like what?"

"We don't know for sure yet. Kelly thinks we should raise organic beef. Skylar wants alpacas—says the fiber, hair, wool, whatever the heck they grow, is worth a fortune."

"Skylar." Mia laughed. She was the spitfire, fourteen-year-old daughter of the ranch's foreman Bjorn Thorson. "How is she?"

"Fine. Still whining about homeschooling. Still riding that horse of hers off for days at a time and worrying her parents to death. But she's really a good kid."

Skylar's horse. Mia remembered the flashy paint named Bungu with a flash of hopefulness. Skylar had trained him herself with guidance from her grandfather Leif, the ranch's longest-lived employee, and it was an amazing animal. Maybe she could be another resource? "Speaking of horses," she said.

"Yeah," Cole replied. "I've been giving that plan you talked about last night some thought."

"You have? I was just telling Harper I'm a little embarrassed I brought up such an ambitious idea when you guys are barely getting going."

"Well, now, here's the thing." Cole pulled a Coke out of the refrigerator and joined the women at the table. "I just went and took a good, long look at the horse barn, the pastures, and the fencing. There's still that five-acre fenced area with the six-foot fences from back in the day when you guys did the makeovers. It's in rough shape, but we probably have repair materials already here if the men were willing to fix it."

"I haven't been out to that pasture in ages," Mia said. "I figured it would have to be built from scratch."

"You can take a look at it. I think it could work. The other thing I talked to Leif about was the idea of having these men do some work for us. We've been talking about how soon we could reasonably hire more hands. Come spring, when it's time to take the cattle back out for the summer, we'll need a couple of men for sure. Right now it sure would be nice to have at least one extra body to take care of some fencing, to do some building maintenance, and a few other things, but we'd decided we have to slog through ourselves. We just can't afford to hire anyone right now—not in the winter. But—if someone wanted to work in exchange for keeping the horses, we could talk about a very small—really, really small—additional wage. For a couple of people."

Mia didn't know if having the men work without pay was even feasible. She had no idea what kind of financial shape they were in. Obviously they'd lasted four months on something—but, all she could do was ask.

"This is so generous, Cole. I have to ask a whole lot of questions on your behalf, of course. But it's a start. The two mitigating factors are that I'm not going to be around to see this project through. At least not permanently. The second is, the men themselves might think this is an idea akin to consorting with folks who try to contact aliens with tin foil hats and short-wave radios. If they don't want to do it—we're all off the hook."

"Well, it wouldn't be the worst thing either way. I kind of got the impression Harper here is itching to see some mustangs around here again." He kissed her again, this time on the top of the head. "But I had another idea. What if I ride along with you and Gabe for the first half hour or so on Saturday?"

"You know about that?" Mia hadn't told anyone that Gabriel had invited himself on a date. No. A tour.

"Nothing is a secret in a small town."

"This is not a small town."

"It's a big ranch. You grew up here. You know it's its own small town."

"Big mouth Bjorn." She smiled. "I asked him who the gentlest horse was. Someone for a relatively new rider. He extrapolated."

"And I baited you, and you confirmed." Cole grinned. "It's great that Gabe is coming. He's a good man. Glad you're finally seeing that."

"Everybody stop picking on me!" She groused to hide the bubbling excitement in the pit of her stomach. "He's dedicated. I admit it fully."

"And he's really, really cute," Harper said, garnering a scowl from Cole.

"Is he?" Mia raised her brows. "I know he can be as annoying as I am."

"You are a lot alike." Harper grinned.

Mia furrowed her brow. "Hey. I think you were supposed to disagree with me there. Thanks a lot."

Harper laughed. "Sis, we're all annoying. Heaven only knows why this one is still around." She flipped a thumb at Cole.

"You're all also addicting, that's why," Cole said. "Now. I have to ride out and check two of the trapper cabins Saturday. What's the verdict on horning in on your date?"

"Oh, for crying out loud, it's not a date! Come along. Harper, too."

"I wish I could." She sighed. "I have a group coming to paint at the Double Diamond. Gotta go get them settled and do an orientation."

Harper had recently started a new enterprise that was already bearing fruit—a retreat for artists and writers based at Cole's old homestead, where they could hide away or paint in solitude. And she'd set up a schedule of community classes for the coming year to be taught by visiting artists and talented locals. She'd had her first paying guests a month ago and was booked through New Year's. What had seemed a long-shot, esoteric idea had proven to be irresistibly popular.

"That's wonderful," Mia said, meaning it. "You've done a fantastic job already."

"Amazingly, it sells itself," she said. "To more kinds of people than I ever thought would care. Some folks will pay stupid amounts for a nature experience. Anyhow, beside the point. Go, have fun on Saturday. See what Gabe thinks of this mustang thing. I meant it that I think it's a great idea, too."

The praise warmed Mia. It truly felt like she'd been waiting for this kind of closeness with her sisters for a lifetime. For one instant an unfamiliar sense of intimacy gripped her.

"Thank you. And, fine. I am looking forward to Saturday."

She braced for teasing, or a knowing wink between Cole and Harper, but her sister only nodded.

"I know."

"YOU'RE NOT DOING too badly for a newb, Newb." Mia waited at the top of a long rocky path and called down the hill where Gabriel allowed his gelding, Mitch, to pick his way up the trail. The pair reached her, Gabriel puffing a little, as if he'd physically helped the horse up the steep grade.

"Thanks, but I'm permanently bowlegged already," he said.

"It's been a few weeks since I've ridden, too," she said. "I'll be sore as well."

"Glad to be in good company at least."

"This is the picnic spot." Mia turned her mare, Penny, in a circle and glanced around the hilltop clearing. "Sounds like you're ready to dismount and stretch anyhow. Good timing."

"You really do have some beautiful country. I had no idea there was so much diversity."

"Biodiversity. Raquel loves to wax philosophical on the virtues of all the biomes and ecosystems the ranch contains. She says it's aptly named because we have everything here you could want in Paradise except desert. And I can only show you such a small sliver. It takes weeks to ride the entire property."

"Have you ever done it?"

"Once. Rode the perimeter with my dad and a crew when I was thirteen or fourteen." We all had to do it with him at least once. I think maybe Joely's done it a few times. It's pretty eye-opening. This is quite a kingdom my great-grandfather Eli started."

She dismounted and led her mount, Chevy, to a sturdy tree. Gabriel copied her example and landed ungracefully but upright on the ground after his dismount. He exaggerated a rolling, bowlegged walk and led Mitch to stand beside Chevy. Mia showed him how to tie the horses with quick-release slip knots.

"All there is to it," she said, when he'd mastered the knot. "They'll munch a few leaves and be fine. Let's unpack the saddlebags."

"I'm with you, Doc."

Lunch looked as good as a celebration feast for royalty, simple though it was. Mia didn't remember being so hungry in years. They'd been riding three hours, but the clean, bracing air and the crispness, like a perfect fall apple, in the breeze, had filled her with an eagerness for exploration and a deep satisfaction with what she was rediscovering. Cole had shown off the first of a half dozen small cabins on the property, used in the past for hunting overnights or cattle round-ups, to an impressed Gabriel, then headed off on his own to check another for vandalism and needed repairs.

Sharing the ranch's diverse landscape had added a dash of excitement and pride to the outing she hadn't expected. It had been a long time since Paradise had brought her this much contentment. The morning had left her stomach growling. For the picnic she'd dug out some chicken cranberry pasta salad Raquel had made, found a new loaf of an artisan bread crusted with rosemary, and a round of smoked Gouda cheese. In one of her saddle bags was a thermos of homemade chicken soup. Best of all, she'd spent time the night before with her mother, baking the thick, gooey brownies she remembered from her childhood.

She untied a roll of woolen blankets from behind the cantle of her saddle and spread one over the flattest area of ground she could find. Gabe pulled the food containers from his bags and met her at the blanket table.

"You definitely know how to stuff a saddle bag."

"Years of misspent youth wandering the landscape with leftovers from dinner the night before."

"I'd have been happy with PB and J."

"Nothing so pedestrian." She laughed. "It was soup and hot cocoa for us. Lemonade in the summer."

"Cocoa would have been good." Gabriel rubbed his hands together.

Mia pulled a second thermos out of her bag. "A step ahead of you."

"I am in heaven. No." He corrected himself. "Paradise."

She laughed and beckoned him to the blanket, handing him a small, stacked set of camping utensils as he sat. It didn't take long to open the various containers, pour steaming cocoa and soup into their metal bowls, and breathe in the first aromatic scents of the nontraditional lunch.

"Wow," Gabriel said. "Who'd have thought you could get to a gourmet restaurant on the back of a horse, ten miles from civilization. This is fantastic, Amelia. Thanks."

"It's nothing fancy really, but you're welcome. I haven't had a chance to show off my childhood home for a long time. It's been fun."

"It has. I admit I have a hard time imagining fifty thousand acres." Gabe dunked a piece of bread into the chicken broth. "Don't take this the wrong way, but is so much land necessary for one family to own these days?"

"Of course not. Not the way we're running it. We don't have that much livestock. The acreage certainly isn't all fenced. And I admit full out that right after my father died last August, I was the first to counsel that we sell this place. Part of me still wonders the same thing you just asked."

"But it doesn't sound like Harper and Cole would consider selling."

"No. They never wanted to from the start. And do you know what? Today, the thought of selling it makes me so sad. I'm grateful Paradise Ranch was here for me to come back to."

"You seem…relaxed?"

"Maybe. Oblivious may be more accurate. I suddenly seem to be able to get lost in my thoughts. I try to be upset about the job, and I am, really, if I can think about it. But I haven't had to think about it here."

"Let's see." Gabriel held up a hand and ticked off on his fingers. "Surgery consulting, clandestine cow kick injuries, wild horses, rescue missions, playing tour guide."

"Rescue missions?"

"Crazy guys calling you for help."

"Oh, that." She smiled. "Yeah, that was a huge time suck."

She pulled out the container of brownies and waved it under his nose. "Here's the penalty."

"Oh, jeez, how am I supposed to get back on a horse if I eat any more?"

"He won't notice."

"Oh, but I will." Gabriel took a thick brownie square and bit a solid third of it off without fanfare. "Man." He mumbled through the mouthful.

"So what did you really think about Cole's ideas for the mustangs?" Her question came out equally garbled through her own mouthful of brownie.

"I've been spending a lot of time the last hour and a half trying to form my proposal to the guys so they can't refuse."

"It's not for everyone," Mia admitted. "It's also not without risks. And they won't make much money."

"Half of them are living on disability for the moment. They'll continue to get their paychecks, but if they get paid anything, it will fulfill their requirement to find meaningful employment. Ranch work? Doesn't get much more meaningful, and I mean in the hard labor sense of the word."

"I hope a couple of them will want to try it. I won't even be here to watch them progress. But I could plan a trip or two back…"

"Why, Dr. Crockett. It almost sounds like you care."

"I didn't think I did, but the whole idea is very addicting." She shrugged. "Maybe I'm changing my mind."

"What's the deal with the tough act you put on sometimes?" He licked the last of the chocolate off his fingers and leaned back, bracing on his elbows, crossing his long, long legs at the ankles. "Not that I've seen much of it this trip."

"It went the way of your arrogant act. You've controlled that pretty well yourself."

"Arrogant?"

"You'll tell me anything I want to know this trip. I couldn't get Joely's room number out of you when we first met."

He studied her as if assessing how blunt he could be. With a wry little lift of his lip he closed his eyes and lay all the way back onto the blanket, hands behind his head. "Honestly? You were just so much fun to get a rise out of. You'd turn all hot under the collar, like you couldn't figure out how anyone could dare counter you—the big-city doc coming to Hicksville with the answers."

The teasing tone of his voice was clear, but the words stung. Funny. They wouldn't have bothered her at all a week ago, she thought. Now it hurt that he would ever think of her as so conceited. She hadn't been that awful—she'd only wanted to put order to the chaos and bring a little rationality to the haywire emotions after her mother and sister's awful accident.

"Hey." She turned to find him sitting upright beside her again. "Amelia, I know better now. I know you. I'm not judging you—then or now."

Pricks of miniscule teardrops stung her eyes, the result of extreme embarrassment—and profound relief. She had no idea what to make of the reaction. It was neither logical nor something she ever remembered experiencing.

"I know."

To her horror, the roughness of her emotions shone through her voice, and Gabriel peered at her, his face a study in surprise. "Are you crying? Amelia, I'm sorry—I was just giving you grief, I wasn't—"

"I'm not crying." It wasn't a lie. No water fell from her eyes; it just welled behind the lids. "I'm not upset. I'm... relieved. I...it was nice, what you...said." She clamped her mouth closed before something truly stupid emerged and looked down at the blanket, picking at a pill in the wool's plaid pile.

A touch beneath her chin drew her gaze back up. Gabriel's eyes were mere inches from hers, shining with that beautiful caramel brown that suddenly looked like it could liquefy into pure sweetness and sex. Every masculine pore of his skin caught her attention and made her fingers itch to stroke the texture of his cheek. The scent of wind-blown skin and chocolate tantalized her.

"Don't be anything but what and who you are, Amelia Crockett."

His kiss brushed her mouth with the weightlessness of a monarch on a flower petal. Soft, ethereal, tender, it promised nothing but a taste of pleasure and asked for nothing in return. Yet, as subtle as it was, it drove a punch of desire deep into Mia's core and set her stomach fluttering with anticipation.

He pulled back but his fingers remained on her chin. "I'm sorry. That was uncalled for."

When his fingers slid from her skin she reacted without thinking and grabbed his hand. "No. It's…It was… Gah—" Frustrated by her constant, unfamiliar loss for words, she leaned forward rather than let mortification set in, and pressed a kiss against his lips, this time foregoing light and airy for a chance to taste him fully. Beneath the pressure, his lips curved into a smile. She couldn't help it then, her mouth mimicked his and they clashed in a gentle tangle of lips, teeth and soft, surprised chuckles.

"Crazy," he said in a whisper, as he encircled her shoulders, pulling her closer.

"Yeah," she agreed and opened her mouth to invite his tongue to meet hers.

First kisses in Mia's experience were usually fraught with uncertainty and awkwardness about what should come next, but not this one. Kissing Gabriel seemed as natural and pleasurable as walking along a stunning stream full of rapids and eddies and satisfying things to explore. She explored them all and let him taste and enjoy right back. When at last they let each other go, her head continued to spin with surprise, and every nerve ending sparkled with desire.

"That was unexpected," he said, trailing his thumb down her cheek and alongside the corner of her mouth. "Did you know you have a talent for kissing?"

A grown, professional woman should not turn to hot goo over sophomoric compliments, she knew that. But goo turned her into a puddle while warmth crept up her neck and into her face.

"I've never thought about it," she said, closing her eyes to soak in his touch. "Kissing wasn't on the medical boards."

"Had it been, you'd have aced the section."

"Do you always have such a silver tongue?"

"Always. I've only recently started using it for good, though. It mostly only ever got me into trouble."

She frowned. "I find that hard to believe, I think."

"Oh, believe it. I was not always the suave, debonair, arrogant professional you see before you. I was the class clown, Doc. Voted 'most likely to do a pratfall at a funeral.' It's a true story. I told you I was funny."

"No way. What happened to you?"

"Iraq, I suppose. Not that Mr. Pratfall isn't still in there. I still think they're funny."

She thought a moment and reached for his free hand, contemplating the sinewy fingers, intertwining hers with his. "I guess it explains a few things. Like why you're so tolerant of the men you're working with."

"I understand using ridiculousness to avoid stress. I think I probably made two mistakes with this program—I picked men who seemed to have innate senses of humor, and I shared all my stories of prewar antics. I probably justified the behavior in their minds."

"On the other hand, you told me they didn't start out this way."

"That's right. They started out angry, hurt, defensive. For them to be laughing is, to me, a huge step toward healing. The next step is to channel the behavior and turn it into productivity. A couple of them are already making that change. Brewster is a hard nut. Finney is even harder. But it's in there."

"Have you always fought so hard for the underdogs?"

His only reply at first was a squeeze of her hand. The bright brown of his eyes sparked with deep thought. Finally he shrugged. "I don't know. I don't think so. I was pretty self-centered when I was in school and college—it was all about looking for the laugh because then I knew I wouldn't ever have to walk through life unnoticed. Even when I got to Iraq, hanging out with Jibril and his cousins and friends wasn't about them, not at first. But, I've never wanted anyone to be picked on—my best pranks were always for the bullies."

"And now here you are, pulling out all the stops for a band of misfits you created yourself. And not a prank in sight. You are a mysterious guy."

"I'm not mysterious. I just put one foot in front of the other and try not to be too big a part of the problems. Lately, though, it's been backfiring. Like I said, my bosses don't see these guys as funny, much less improving."

"Let's get them those mustangs."

The words flowed so adamantly from her lips they surprised her. Suddenly it seemed like the most obvious solution in the world, despite the enormous logistic complications. "I'll help you talk them into the idea."

Surprise on his face blossomed into a huge smile and a shake of his head. "I think you're the mysterious person, Amelia. I fully admit, six weeks ago a day like this was beyond my wildest thoughts. Now? I just want to kiss you again."

She released his hand and put both of her palms on his cheeks, allowing herself to explore the skin texture she found so intriguing. Her fingertips slid over the smoothness beside his nose and traveled to the very beginnings of stubble on his jaw. The coarser surface sent tingles through her own skin.

"I told my sisters after the first time you and I met that they needed to fire you and request a new advocate." His eyes rounded in surprise. "But…" She traced his bottom lip. "Now I want you to kiss me, too."

One large hand cupped the back of her head and pulled her to him. His lips claimed hers, and her eyes closed in a rush of sparkler-like chills. The chills intensified when she opened her mouth to meet his tongue. The sigh that emerged almost turned to a groan of pleasure when a loud chirp from her cell phone made her jump and tore them apart. The sound continued—her text notification.

"That's strange," she said, "I'm sorry. There shouldn't even be reception out here. Who'd text me anyway?"

Her pulse sped up in sudden concern. Joely? Her mother?

"You'd better check it," Gabriel said.

The number she saw startled her. "It's from my friend Brooke in New York."

"Is that surprising?"

"Extremely."

Aware of Gabriel's hand at the back of her neck, kneading gently, she opened the text and read:

> Mia, so sorry to bother you. Could you call ASAP?
> I have Rory with me. His mother has taken a turn
> for the worst. He wanted to be with his cat, so I got
> permission to bring him here. He's fine, just scared.
> Will explain when we talk.

She showed it to Gabriel.

"Rory?" he asked.

Once she'd explained the story, she found her pulse pounding even harder. What could be wrong now? Monique had been doing better. Only the worst possible scenarios played through her head. The cancer had metastasized. An infection.

"I—"

He interrupted. "You need to get to cell reception. Absolutely. Let's pack up."

"Raincheck on the—"

He leaned forward, held the back of her head again, and kissed her hard and thoroughly. "There's always time for a kiss," he said. "Come on."

For a moment she sat there, stunned at the sensual assault, wanting only to keep forgetting the real world and let him kiss her again. But he stood, smiled as if everything was going to be all right, and held out his hand.

She took it, believing for the first time in her life she wasn't going to have to face the potentially awful on her own.

Chapter Fourteen

MIA'S CALM RETURNED once the picnic had been packed up, Gabriel was safely mounted again, and they were once more on the trail. Logic kicked back in, and she realized there was nothing she could specifically do for Rory. He was best off right where he was—with his cat. Brooke was a clown for heaven's sake. What better place for a scared little boy than a clown's house?

"So this is a boy you've known a while?" Gabriel asked.

"Three years or so," she replied. "His mother had rotator cuff surgery that was a fiasco. The procedure she had is successful about eighty-five percent of the time, but she was one of the fifteen. She never was able to manage her pain, and the drug addiction happened slowly. I did her second surgery, and it helped some. We became friends. She didn't have any other family. Her own parents were gone. She was doing okay. Then she was diagnosed with breast cancer and after more surgery, the addiction took her over again."

"I see so much prescription addiction in my line of work. I'm sure you do, too."

"The clinic and ER docs and internal med people see much more. I just pray this is only a scare and not really that serious." She took a deep breath. "I'm sorry we didn't get to our mustang spot."

"It's all right," he assured her. "That's not important."

"It is," she said. "Not that I expect to see the horses, but there might be signs that they're still in the area. If we're back to the house in the next three hours, I can call New York before it's too late."

"I don't want you to put something off because of me. I have time to come back sometime."

"I'm torn…"

"Don't be. Let's head back. Believe me, I understand wanting to know what's going on. I had to wait those long hours to dig into what happened with Jibril and his family after the attack in Baghdad. By then, nobody knew anything or they wouldn't talk. Don't wait if you don't have to."

"I can see why you'd make a good therapist or a mentor," she said. "You actually use your experiences."

"Why do you think we have experiences? If we don't learn from them what good are they? That's what I'm trying to get through the guys' heads. They saw and did a lot of shitty things. It's time to put the energy from those experiences, bad and good, into making a future."

"I know you called yourself a foster father in jest the other day, but I can see you'd make a great real dad. In ways that count."

He snorted—scornful-sounding for the first time. "Oh no. No fatherhood for me."

Something unwavering and resolute in his voice sent her stomach plummeting in surprise and disappointment.

"Really? Why would you say that?"

"Bring more children into this world? I don't think so. So much dysfunction, so much loss and abuse. Look at your, what's his name, Rory? A perfect example—"

"Of what? Abuse?"

"I don't know—maybe. But certainly of loss and dysfunction. And his mother might be the most wonderful woman in the world, yet she still abandoned her child because of her choices. Not the cancer, of course, but there are so many kids like him in the world. Take care of them before you add more to the mix."

"But…" She had no idea what to say. In many ways he was absolutely right. Still, something was missing from his argument—something personal and meaningful he was hiding away.

"I'd adopt five kids before I'd have one of my own."

Her heart sank further. She'd always looked forward to having children—to raising them to be good citizens of the world. Good stewards. What had dashed Gabriel's instinct for fathering this thoroughly?

"It's a worthy sentiment," she said.

Her sadness confused her. She wasn't marrying this man. He had no claim on her future. Why did she care what he thought?

"I don't think it's fair to bring a child into this messed up world to try and eke out a place among so many millions of others."

For a man who'd professed to be a class clown, this was such a jaded point of view. All because he'd lost track of one small boy in a country so far away?

"But what about the chance to raise people who can change this messed up world?"

"Influence the ones who are already here."

There was no point in arguing with him. No anger colored his arguments, just that same resoluteness he'd borne from the start. The catalyst for his belief was no longer important. This was now a deep-seated philosophy. She rode beside him in silence, unsettled for the first time since they'd started off that morning with Cole.

Stupid. It's just a conversation. Don't over analyze this.

"This bothers you," he said.

"No," she said, too quickly. "I mean. I get what you're saying. For you. I...I..." She gave up again. Something happened to her brain around the man. "I don't really know what to say, I guess."

"It's okay. I don't expect any response. You aren't required to deal with my crazy rantings."

"I just...the thought of no biological children."

"Look. I like kids, too. They're just a trigger, that's all. I know this about myself."

"Don't deny yourself a future because of an accident from eight years ago. What if Jibril's mother had never wanted children? You'd have lost out on so much."

"So much trauma, you mean. Listen, Jibril was a beautiful mistake, and yes, he's the root of a lot of my crazy. But I understand what happened, and I don't dwell on him most of the time anymore. But it sounds like you've got a Jibril, and I just want you to have the chance to do right by him for your sake. If I get a little off base, just ignore me."

He was a little off base, she thought. But it was in the most sincere kind of way.

"I won't ignore you," she said. "But you should not give up on him. Or on your future."

He didn't say anymore, but his smile relaxed just a little.

GABE PRIDED HIMSELF on being in control—of himself, of his emotions, of those around him. He'd learned the art in Iraq, and it served him well. He didn't let people throw him off course. He didn't let people make him angry. He didn't take shit from anyone, and he knew how to throw it back without pissing anyone off. Amelia Crockett had undone all his careful self-discipline, as if she'd pulled an emotional ripcord and deployed his parachute before the right time.

The kiss had been one thing. That kind of unplanned pleasure he could deal with—especially since she'd clearly enjoyed the surprise as much as he had. The rest of the afternoon, however…that had him reeling.

The child in her life.

The compliments about his potential for greatness as a father.

His bombast about the righteous need to have no more children in a terrible world.

Her stunned reaction.

His babbling idiocy afterward.

She turned him into someone he didn't know. What confused him the most, however, was that he didn't even mind the guy he was around her. But he sure didn't know him very well. He was an idiot who'd told a single female that having children was irresponsible, but if she was self-ish enough to want them, she should stay far away from him. On the crassest level, that was cutting his own throat. On the most intellectual level, it was just hard-assed and maybe a little cruel.

And maybe a faux pas from which there was no recovery.

They reached the barn in a much quieter mood than they'd left it that morning. Gabe flexed his thigh and seat muscles, already knowing he'd be sorer than he'd been in a very long time, probably the moment he dismounted, but the ride had been eye-opening. Paradise Ranch was truly a small kingdom, with land wealth he could barely fathom even after having seen the landscapes that repre-sented a fraction of the whole.

Amelia had been surprisingly proud of her childhood home; not arrogant in the least, but almost reverent, as if she'd been reminded of how impressive it was. He no longer saw anything of the cool, efficient doctor he'd once met. He couldn't for the life of him find the tough, emotionless doctor who'd lost out on her dream job. All he was seeing these days was a warm, caring woman—one who could put any beautiful creature to shame and kissed like she'd been created just to fit with him.

And he'd blown it.

"Four hours, Lieutenant," she said, using the old nickname he'd thought she'd given up. "And we didn't kill you. You did great."

Her smile left him with dazzling hope. She didn't look angry. Or disappointed.

"I'm not trying to walk yet," he said.

"I admit. It'll feel funny."

"I think you're just trying to soften the reality."

"You're the only one who can find out."

She swung her right leg over the saddle in a graceful arc, her sweet butt flexing prettily beneath her jeans, her booted foot landing on the ground with easy lightness. She pulled her left foot out of the stirrup and stood beside her mare, graceful and curved in all the right places, looking nothing like one of New York's best doctors, but like a sexy, wind-kissed cowgirl.

He had no right to be thinking of her that way.

Not after just a few kisses.

"All right, you can't sit up there scared to move all day."

He looked into her teasing eyes and grinned back, feeling like the uncoordinated kid in phys ed who couldn't climb the rope or make the basket. Or get off the horse without damaging something—like his own head.

"Who said I was scared?"

"Maybe you aren't. But you have to prove it before I'll believe it."

This was where they were most comfortable—teasing.

"Watch out then. Here comes proof."

He tried to emulate her effortless dismount and managed to get his right leg over the saddle and halfway to the ground before muscle control abandoned him. For an awkward second he dangled, his left foot shoved as far into the stirrup as the boot heel would allow, and his balance thrown forward onto the saddle horn while his right leg probed the air. Finally he twisted his uncoordinated self backward enough to get his foot on the ground. Hopping like a trapped flamingo, he grasped the stirrup and yanked it off the toe of his boot, getting the second foot to the ground, but barely, before his ass hit it first.

"I think I did it better the first time."

"You did fine. It's just timing now—one more ride and you'll have it."

He groaned and shook out first one leg then the other. "Not too soon."

"Not too soon."

He enjoyed the process of untacking Mitch and rubbing him down, then giving him treats and letting him into the pasture. There was something fulfilling about taking care of an animal that had worked hard for him without complaint or expectation. To be in control of such a massive creature was both powerful and humbling.

"Thank you," he said, as he and Amelia leaned against the pasture fence once both horses were ambling back to their mates.

"For?"

"The tour. The company. The patience. It was…well, fun."

"It was."

In a moment of boldness he faced her and grasped her gently by both upper arms. Turning her in place, he stared at her earnestly. "I'm sorry for the weirdness coming back. I'm pretty sure I ruined something unexpectedly special."

"No!" She faced him with no embarrassment or awkwardness. In fact, a little bit of the efficient, analytical doc was back. "You didn't. I don't begrudge anyone an opinion. We have a little time to spend together, and then I have to be out of here. What you and I have to say to each other should be interesting, not polarizing. We're past that, I hope."

He wanted to kiss her again—to see how pliable he could make her in his arms and test her claim that they were past the animosity that had colored their first encounters.

He didn't.

"When can you call your friend?"

A wisp of apprehension flit through her eyes. "Anytime now that we're here. There's signal strength throughout the ranch yards. We have a tower within a mile."

She was babbling, and for the first time he understood that she'd been procrastinating since first receiving the text message.

"Get it over with," he said. "The longer you wait, the worse the imaginings."

She sighed. "You're right."

"I'll go—"

"No. Please stay. I might need a therapist after this."

She led him past the barn to the yard in front of it, while she scrolled through her contacts for the number she needed. She raised her brows but didn't say anything as she pressed the call button. It didn't take two seconds for someone to answer. Gabe leaned against a support post and watched the ground, listening as unobtrusively as he could.

"Brooke?" Amelia said, the trepidation clear in her voice. "What's going on?"

She listened a long time.

"Oh shit," she said, her voice a near whisper. Gabe's eyes shot up. He'd never heard a single vulgarity from her, and this one made his heart lurch in his chest.

She caught his eyes, her cheeks drained of color, and she shook her head. "What are they doing for her? Does Rory know all of this?"

After another long silence she said a simple "all right," and it was clear when she spoke next it was to the child.

"Hi, sweetheart. Are you and Jack all right?"

He might never have heard her swear, but he was even more taken aback by the softness in her voice now. He'd have given anything to have his parents talk to him the way she greeted the boy she'd only known a few years.

"Rory, honey, they're doing everything they can for your mom. I know you're scared, though...Yes, it's a really stubborn kind of infection, and she's very sick...I know you want me to come back, but, sweetie, the doctors there can take better care of her than I can. I'm not the right kind of doctor for this."

She spoke to him for several more minutes and patiently answered what seemed to be variations on the same question. He guessed it was on the order of "Why can't you come back?" In the end, she made the patience Gabriel felt so smug about look like nothing.

At long last she spoke a final time to her friend, made her swear to call the instant anything changed, and hung up. She sagged in place like a boxer about to go down after the last blow she could absorb. He grabbed her and dragged her into an enormous bear hug.

"I've got you." There wasn't anything else to say. He knew, even from hearing only half the conversation, that nothing was all right, and that promising everything would be in the future was a lie. He had no idea how to help her, but he vowed to try. "You stay right here as long as you need to."

"A staph infection." She murmured into his chest. "At the site of her last lumpectomy. It's just not responding. They're trying some of the last antibiotics possible, and they just don't know."

"I'm so sorry."

"Rory is scared. And he begged me to come back. He thinks I can save her. Why are little kids so blunt? Why is life so simple to them? I can't do anything for her."

"Could you do anything for Rory?"

She leaned back in his arms and stared at him, her eyes pools of liquid brown. "That's an amazing thing to say."

"No." He pulled her to his chest again. "It's just a question. Don't think I want you to leave right now. But if there's something you could do…"

"I think I need to wait. Brooke is keeping him for the rest of the weekend. We'll know more by Monday."

"Good." He kissed the top of her head. "But remember that there's no wrong decision here. Follow your heart—don't try to use your head."

She splayed her palms on his chest and pushed from his embrace. "Stop reading my mind," she said. "I'm never like this, all fluttery and emotional—of course I'm trying to use my head. It's the only place I can make good choices."

"That's because you don't trust your heart. You don't think it's as wise as your head. You're wrong. It has very good instincts."

"Oh, how do you know that?" She turned in frustration and headed for the half-mile trek from the barn back to the house. "Besides. Hearts always make illogical decisions."

"So?"

"How can a bad decision be good?"

"Since when does illogical equal bad? Do you think there's anything logical about the program I set up and am fighting to keep afloat? Logic says to scrap it, it's not working. What's remotely logical about a suggestion to get wild horses for two men who know nothing about any animal bigger than a guinea pig? Sometimes an illogical answer is the only thing in the world that fits."

He could see the thoughts churning behind her eyes when she stopped and looked back at him. "Fine," she said. "Illogic says to run back to Rory and pretend I can rescue him. Logic says that I'm better off waiting to spend money on a ticket until I know I can really help. Pick one."

"I said *sometimes* anti-logic is the only way. In this case, logic wins. Don't go running off. You have time."

She started walking again, but her pace eased, and her spine swayed more easily as she continued up the sweeping driveway.

"It's so foreign for me to act on this concept. But if you're introducing me to it, and I'm not running off to New York, then I have the next thing to do—go talk your men into the horses."

"See?" He fell into step beside her. "Totally illogical. Well done."

She allowed a ghost of a smile. "Just a distraction, Mr. Harrison. Distraction would be good."

"Call it what you want. I'll be right behind."

She touched his arm. "Thank you."

He searched for her hand and twined her delicate fingers through his. She didn't pull away.

Chapter Fifteen

"So you're talking honest-to-God wild horses? As in, don't they kick harder than cows?"

Jason Brewster clearly held back skeptical laughter, but three other pairs of eyes were locked onto Gabriel in serious consideration. The two veterans who had part-time jobs, and the two who had no current work, sat in Gabriel's living room on Monday night, and Mia studied them with interest. She finally had their names down and now worked on their personalities. Brewster, with his constant wagging tongue, was the group goofball. Damien Finney scowled the most and seemed the least impressed by anything, judging from the dark slash his brows made across his forehead. Dan Holt, a tall, wiry, graceful guy had a deceptively quiet voice and intense blue, interested gaze. Pat MacDougal was gregarious and enthusiastic, a short fireplug of an Irishman who'd been nodding his head almost from the moment they'd arrived.

"If Brewster doesn't want in on this, add me to the list," Pat said. "It sounds like fun."

"Hell, I'd give it a try," Dan agreed.

Mia had brought and shown two videos, one an excerpt from a public television special about wild mustangs, and the other a compilation of home recordings chronicling the years she, Harper, and Joely had entered their Makeovers. Aside from the hoots and jibes over her youth, the men had seemed fascinated.

"This isn't a lark," she said, as they snickered at Brewster. "We're talking wild animals that've had nothing more than some gentling done with them. They are halter broken, can be led around, and can load into a trailer. They aren't big dogs. This project would take dedication, consistency, and the willingness to let dumb girls, a kid, and one old Norwegian guy tell you what to do. Your success and even your safety would depend on you giving up your egos."

"Are the dumb girls as pretty as you?" Brewster smiled.

"Shut up, you chauvinist pig," Pat said. "She was kidding. They're all smarter than you are."

"I'd probably have better luck with my own kind—pigs," Brewster said, rubbing his injured leg.

Mia couldn't help but like Jason Brewster. She didn't know why. He and Finney had the roughest mouths and fell back regularly on the most sophomoric humor. But she knew their stories—Brewster had lost his entire squad to an IED and suffered a severe head wound himself. His official diagnosis was traumatic brain injury. Finney had been part of a mission to clear out a neighborhood in

Fallujah. He had discovered later one of the houses had been harboring three families of innocent civilians who hadn't heeded warnings to leave. Mia didn't have any trouble understanding why he suffered from anger.

"I can take out any crap you want to dish out," she said, meeting Brewster's gaze directly without flinching. "But the horses can't. You'll learn a whole new set of very odd skills if you want to try this. I can't tell you whether you'll ever use them again in your lives—but you won't forget the lessons."

"So this is really to teach us assholes all a lesson then." Finney sat back in the armchair in Gabriel's living room and snapped the nicotine gum he chewed like Juicy Fruit.

"Damn right it is." Gabriel hadn't minced a single word with the group from the beginning. Mia approved of how he didn't sugarcoat anything. She was learning to do the same. "You know half of you are in deep shit over all the practical jokes lately. This is a last ditch effort to find you something that will get you out of my hair and out of hot water with the brass."

Rather than piss the men off, the honesty sent a ripple of laughter through the room.

"Fair enough," Dan said. "Even though I'm innocent as the driven snow."

"Driven snow my ass cheeks," Finney snorted. "You're gonna look like a damn giraffe on one of them little horses. We'll see how frickin' happy you stay when one of them gets your number."

Dan turned to Mia with a slightly panicked light in his eyes. "Hey, Doc, *am* I too tall for this project?"

She shook her head, warmed by the first indication that the men were truly considering the crazy plan, and by the first honest concern one had shown. "No. They aren't big horses it's true, but you'd be surprised at how well they take up a man's height and weight. You'd all be fine."

"Even MacDougal the hobbit here?" Brewster grinned and ruffled Pat's red hair.

"Hey, laugh it up, Bicep Brain. At least I've ridden horses."

"You've ridden fillies you mean. I'm sure you're an expert."

"All right, guys." Gabriel reined in the drifting conversation. "Time to get serious. I know this sounds like a game, but it isn't. You know what the deal is, and that this isn't going to be free either in terms of money or in time. We want you to think about it seriously and decide in a few days what you think."

"Hell, I don't have to think," Pat said. "I'd like to try it."

"I would, too," Dan said. "Pat and I have part-time jobs, we don't need to be the ones who work for your family."

"Let Brewster and Finney get their hands dirty." Pat raised a brow in Brewster's direction. "I dare you both."

Finn gave him the finger.

"That would work," Mia said. "But you two don't have to decide tonight. It is a big commitment."

"What the hell?" Brewster said. "If I can start with a gimpy leg, count me in."

"You can," Mia said.

Everyone turned to Finney. He glowered at the carpet, but one finger tapped rhythmically on the arm of the sofa, and his knee bounced up and down like he was prepping to jump to his feet.

"No pressure, man," Gabriel told him. "Despite what I said, you have to do this for you. It's not for me."

"I'll do it," he said.

Mia turned to Gabe in time to see his eyes light with a pleased smile. She allowed one that didn't show too much surprise. She hadn't expected this much enthusiasm from a group of grown men. In truth, she'd been bracing for the disappointment of scrapping the whole idea by the end of the night.

"Well, then," Gabriel said. "The next step is applying for mustang adoption and then finding some horses."

"Two options." Mia scanned the room. "My sister, her fiancé, and I will go pick out the mustangs and bring them home. Or…" She took a breath and nodded to Gabriel.

"Or you can take a field trip to the Bureau of Land Management holding facility in Rock Springs and check out the horses yourselves. Money on the spot. No returns."

"Oh, hell, yeah, a field trip," Brewster said without hesitation.

Dan nodded vigorously. "Damn straight. I want to see these so-called wild horses for myself."

"That's right. Make sure you don't cheat us with some broken-down old trained horses we think we'd be training." Finney crossed his arms, and his knee stopped jiggling.

Mia fixed him with a stare. "You've figured it out, Damien. One broken-down nag for you it is."

He smiled for the first time.

AN HOUR LATER, with four filled-out mustang adoption papers in hand, Mia rested her head against the back of Gabriel's Jeep seat and closed her eyes.

"Tired?" he asked.

"I don't know why. That wasn't as hard or even as crazy as I thought it would be. Which isn't to say they aren't all crazy."

"But you can see they're good guys."

She nodded, affection spreading through her tiredness. His passion for these men's well-being was not just obvious, it was catching. "I can. And you're right. They are every kind of damaged and every level of severity."

"Are you still okay with this plan? We sort of sealed our fate because they're invested now. Two of them are for sure. I have no idea how serious Brewster and Finney are."

"I am sure about the plan, but I'm afraid this is going to come down to how seriously they take the animals and how willing they are to learn. I don't want to see anyone get hurt."

"Yeah."

They rode quietly and without any giveaway extra movement, Gabriel searched for her hand in the dark and wove their fingers together. Her stomach gave a little lurch, and when he squeezed, an electric zip shot up her arm. The goose bumps that followed seemed extreme for an action so simple, but she squeezed back, liking her silly reaction, wanting more of it, marveling at the way their meshed hands made him seem like he was part of her.

"I think having the papers in hand makes it seem all too real," she said. "I'll get these to the holding facility tomorrow. With luck they'll process them and accept the applications this week. Maybe by next weekend, we can go check out the horses."

"And you think everything is okay in New York?"

"For the moment. Monique is not in great condition, but she's stable."

"Rory is hanging in there, you said."

"I'll call him tomorrow. Poor kid. I wish he had some other family. But that was part of the problem. They were always alone, and Monique was so grateful for company."

He squeezed her hand again, replicating the zip, the electricity, the goose bumps. "You do know what I'm hearing here, right? You get just as invested in people as you say I do."

"Bah."

"No 'bah.' You're a softie."

"I want him to be happy, that's all."

"You can tell him that when you talk to him."

"Yeah. I can." She smiled up at him even though it was dim in the car's interior. "You're good at knowing what to say."

"Sometimes it's good just to remind ourselves of the obvious."

The rest of the trip to Paradise passed in easy silence. She couldn't help but search the spot where they'd seen the mustangs, but the full moon no longer illuminated the landscape, and she hadn't seen any sign of the horses since that night. He didn't say anything, but Gabriel slowed down as he negotiated the curve around the turnout. His empathy and his higher than average interest in all things mustang only did more to make him wondrous in her eyes.

"Do you want to come in for a while?" she asked when he'd stopped in the main driveway by the ranch house.

"Yes," he replied. "But you know what? I think I should go back and make sure the guys aren't whipping this plan into something crazy. They'll have questions. Or not. Either way, I want to impress on them again what a big deal this is."

A mixture of disappointment and relief followed his excuse. She was beginning to love having him around, but the one-eighty in her feelings for him confused the heck out of her. "I think that's smart."

"You know I meant it when I said yes. I'd rather stay with you."

"It's all right. It's been a successful night. You really are good with the guys, you know. They respect the heck out of you."

"It's mutual."

She reached for the Jeep's door handle, and he grasped her upper arm to pull her gently around.

"I need to say something."

"Yes?"

A pitter of dread thrummed in her stomach, which was stupid since nothing had happened to give her reason for worry. On the other hand, in her world this was a long time for one man to hang around, and there was that inexplicable one-eighty.

"Our start was a little rocky. I'm glad you gave me another chance, Amelia Crockett."

"I—" She stared at him, her muscles uncoiling from the tension she'd built in the thirty seconds she'd feared he was about to break off a relationship that had barely begun.

"It's okay if you call me Mia," she said for lack of anything more apropos. "Like my family and other friends do."

"I like Mia," he said. "But Amelia is beautiful."

She'd never thought of her name as beautiful. She'd been named for Amelia Earhart, after all. A woman of strength, but also of controversy. A woman who'd gotten lost forever at the moment of what should have been her greatest triumph.

Some role model.

But he thought her name was beautiful.

"I didn't intend to give you another chance, you know." She smiled as her emotions drifted slowly back to her control. "I'll bet you didn't intend to give me one either. But you made it hard not to—give you a chance. I…was wrong about you."

"I was never wrong about you. You fascinated me from day one. I just never knew about this…"

His lips met hers in the dark, soft but firm, chaste and yet trembling with a simmering desire to take the kiss further. Still, he set a languid pace, and Mia forced herself not to change it. She tasted his mint-and-coffee breath. He tested the sensitivity of her lower lip with his teeth and her upper lip with his tongue. She closed her eyes, and all that remained was sensation. Sweet, wet, hot, succulent, their mouths explored and the pace, barely noticed but inexorable, accelerated.

She wanted nothing but to get closer. The bucket seats and the console made it all but impossible. As if he read her mind, however, Gabriel broke the kiss and shoved his seat back as far as it would go, turning to wedge himself sideways between it and the wheel. Mia turned and scrabbled to her knees on her seat, shucking her jacket and then pulling his head toward her and pressing again into the kiss, raking his thick hair with her fingertips. Tilting her head, she covered his mouth with hers.

His hand slipped around her waist and pushed beneath the back of her sweater. Hot sparks led the way up her spine as he traced the skin beside the vertebrae to the back band of her bra. With barely a fumble he squeezed the clasp and it fell loose. She would have laughed and questioned how he'd achieved such prowess if deep shivers hadn't taken her breath away.

"Second chances, second base." He murmured against her lips, and she did laugh, until his fingers skimmed around her ribcage and pushed the bra out of their way. He found her breast and her laughter turned to a small, sweet groan. Fire spread from the nipple that he rolled gently between his fingers to the spot between her legs that liquefied with desire.

"Where is second base on a man?" Her voice was a hoarse whisper, and she was not really serious, she just wanted to touch him. Anywhere.

"Oh, we get to this point, and we don't think with our bases anymore. Just with our baser instincts."

"Oh, well, I know where those are."

At that he laughed, its deep masculine roll generating even more goose flesh across her body.

"Straighten up taller," he said. "My instincts want a taste."

She reluctantly pulled her lips from his and raised higher on her knees. He pushed her sweater up in front and covered her breast with his lips before she could do more than grasp his head for balance and hold it tightly to her, trembling at the suction from his mouth. Whimpering at the intensity she couldn't escape.

When he moved to the second breast, her head fell back, and she didn't even bother to hold in a groan.

Slowly, with great attention and savoring every second, Gabriel finished, replacing his tongue with his thumbs and circling their pads over the moist tips of both breasts.

"I don't think a Jeep is made for more than second base."

"I'm not sure the driveway is either." She felt weak with pleasure. "God forbid my sister sees the car and comes to make sure we're all right."

"We can tell her we are, right?" He pushed her away and grinned.

"I wouldn't know what to tell her. How do you assess the last thing on earth you ever expected to happen?"

"Good point."

He made a show of pushing her farther into her seat and then reaching up her sweater front to stuff her back into her bra. Purposely awkward and forward, his playing only increased the heat in her body. Finally, ready to pull him out of the car right over the shift lever and the console, she batted his hands away and fastened her bra in a flash.

"No more! My body is looking for third base, and I'm so not ready for that."

"Too bad."

"Don't cheapen this." She giggled.

"Uh. Groping in the front seat of a small vehicle might be as cheap as it gets."

"It's so unlike me. I'm never a cheap date."

"Amelia." He said her name like a caress and traced her cheek, suddenly slightly serious. "The cheap tonight is all on me. I didn't plan this, but I'm awfully glad I took a shot."

"I don't know what it means, but I didn't stop it, did I? I'm going in now, and you're going home. And we're going to think about what we've done."

"Yes we are. In a cold shower."

"Hey, don't start that already. We're a long way from a home run, buddy."

He smiled and kissed her quickly. Softly. "Yes. But you sure are fun to tease."

"Who'd have thought?" She kissed him, too. "Good night, Gabriel."

"You could call me Gabe. Like all my family and other friends."

"I'll think about it," she said. "When I know you better."

She didn't let him walk her to the door, afraid that if she got him that far, she'd only start the kissing all over again. And as much as that sounded like the only thing in the world she wanted to do—she definitely needed to think. She'd done long-distance relationships. She didn't want to do another. And yet, she didn't want to push Gabriel away either.

Her brain was great at sorting out hundreds of problems associated with cutting into a human body. Figuring out how to not fall dangerously for Gabe Harrison, however, was a puzzle too difficult to solve.

"How did it go tonight?" Her mother sat in the small, cozy sitting room off the main living room, her right leg propped on an ottoman, knitting on one of her exquisite lacy shawls, working efficiently and surprisingly swiftly despite the cast on her left arm. "Come. Sit for a minute. You look a little flushed."

She did? Her hand rose to her cheek. It didn't feel hot to the touch.

"I'm fine." An old, ingrained protective habit made her tense as she sat because her mother had asked her to. The last thing she wanted was an interrogation. "The talk with the veterans went well."

"That's great. I'm proud of you for taking a chance on this. And I'm so happy you and Harper are working on it together."

Her mother's voice didn't change. Didn't get excited or inquisitive. She simply smiled contentedly and continued her work. Mia hesitated, but then she leaned forward.

"You really think it's okay? It's not too big a risk? I'm not sure what Dad would have said. One mustang was too many for him."

Her mother set her knitting on her lap and captured Mia's gaze. "Your father liked to fuss about things that took extra thought. But he didn't really mind. He was proud of the horsemanship skills you all learned. He knew you were especially talented with the wild horses. He'd be proud, Mia."

The declaration couldn't have surprised her more.

"He never told us that."

"I've been telling all of you girls that there were a lot of things your father didn't do that he should have. I loved him with all my heart. But that doesn't mean I didn't see his shortcomings. And mine. But he's gone now, and you and your sisters have to make your own futures. I'm watching you stretch and grow like a filly let out to pasture just since you've been back. You're trying not to, but you're softening back into the person of your heart. I see it with Harper. I see it with Gabriel."

She didn't want to admit she was any different here than she'd been in New York. But she couldn't deny the changes. And she couldn't be annoyed with her mother for pointing them out. With a heavy sigh, as if letting out the weight of a dozen years, she leaned back in the armchair.

"I kissed him," she said, her voice nearly a whisper.

For a long moment there was no sound from her mother. Mia didn't dare look to see if there was shock, distaste, or censure in her face. Suddenly, a whisper of a kiss fell on her forehead. She opened her eyes. Her mother stood over her, her eyes bright with happiness.

"Praise heaven," she said. "He's perfect for you."

Mia couldn't hold back a burst of laughter. "Good gosh, Mom, we're nowhere near that." It was exactly what she'd told Gabe.

"I know. But even for one day, one week, one month—he's perfect."

She reached for her mother's hand, straightened, and held it with both of hers. "How are *you*, Mom? I have barely asked you that. Do you miss him terribly?"

"Of course. Every minute. But I am fine, honey. I—"

"Mia!" Raquel rushed into the room, holding the house's landline phone. Mia frowned. "I'm so sorry to interrupt, but I thought I'd heard the door. I have a phone call for you. Your little guy in New York? Rory?"

"Rory? On the Paradise line?" She looked back to her mother, torn.

"Take it," she insisted. "We have time to talk later."

Mia took the phone in confusion. She'd given Brooke this number. How had Rory gotten it? Why? He had her private cell number to call…

"Hello? Rory?" She looked from her mother to her sister and shrugged, concerned.

"Dr. Mia?" His little voice trembled. "Dr. Mia, they said my mom isn't ever going to get better." His voice broke then, and only tiny sobs came over the line.

Mia's eyes filled with tears. "Oh, Rory, honey. Where are you?"

"At the Davidsons'. The foster home. She let me call Brooke and then you."

"Tell me what's going on."

"My mom's going to die."

Who would tell a child that? It couldn't be true. Her heart broke—with fury and with despair. Because deep down, of course, she knew it really could be.

Chapter Sixteen

IT TOOK SEVERAL long, hard minutes to settle Rory down, ease his sobbing, and find out that what his newest foster mother had told him was that his mama was very, very sick, and he should be prepared for if she couldn't come back. It wasn't as horrid as telling him out and out his mother was going to die, but it was still pretty horrid. The foster care system was a wonderful resource most of the time. How had this child managed to find his way to the dregs of the program?

"Sweetie," Mia told him, "you know your mom is very sick. You're pretty smart about everything that's happened to her. But you can't ever give up hope. Are you saying your prayers? I'm saying mine. For her. And for you."

"I didn't think doctors had to say prayers. Mama said God just plain guides doctors' hands."

Mia never thought like that. His words shocked her. She'd never relied on anything but her own skill when it came to medicine. Did she thank Heaven for her ability to study and learn? Without question. But asking God to guide her hands? If she couldn't blame Him for the failures, she wasn't going to credit Him with her successes. Still…

"Of course we do," she said. "Saying our prayers can help us through hard times."

"Okay," he said quietly.

"I am coming back in just a couple of weeks," she said. "Until then, you can call me every day if you want to. And I'll call you, too. Have they let you go see your mom?"

"No. They say I can't. She's too far away."

That was ridiculous. "Do you want to see her, Rory?"

"I want to."

"I'll fix it so you can. That much I will promise."

Snuffling filled the line. She could almost see him wipe his nose on a sleeve, and she had the most unfamiliar, gut-deep wish that she could lift him into her lap and let him cry in her arms.

"Rory? I promise. Okay?"

"Yeah." A long, long silence followed. Mia said nothing—letting him think, and being with him the only way she could. "Dr. Mia? Do you like saving people?"

Again his words punched her as solidly as an actual fist. She did her job the best she could, and she was good at it. But as much as she didn't give or take credit from God Himself, neither did she take personal credit. She had no supernatural powers. *She* didn't save people, but her skill sometimes could.

"I like it when I can make something better."

"You're good at it."

"And you're very good at telling me that. But do you know what? You're good at making people feel happy. You are funny and you're smart. So that's making people better, too."

"I'm smart?"

"Very smart. And when you go see your mama, you're going to make her feel better, too."

"I love you, Dr. Mia."

She knew his words stemmed from fear and sadness and loneliness, too, but her eyes filled with tears nonetheless. She had to force herself not to promise she'd fly to him tomorrow.

"I love you, too, Rory. Give Jack a big hug for me. I'll talk to you tomorrow."

"Okay." The word emerged reluctantly in his small voice. "Do you have a cat to hug?"

She laughed. "I don't. Our ranch workers have a lot of dogs, though. I can hug them if I go to the barns."

"Barns sound cool."

"They are. I'll send you some pictures on your phone."

After she'd said her final good-bye to Rory, Mia sat, drained as a marathon runner. Her mother took the chair beside her, but Mia tucked her hands beneath her legs to avoid giving anyone the chance to touch them. What she really wanted to do to was punch somebody—preferably the idiot responsible for keeping Rory from his mother and putting him with another lazy, stupidly cruel foster mother in a row. He hadn't done anything to deserve this.

"Things are not going well," her mother said.

"No." Mia's face felt heated with anger. She'd promised to get Rory to Monique, but helplessness at being so far away swamped her and stripped her momentarily of her normal problem-solving ability. She needed someone like Gabriel at the Department of Corrections in New York and at Social Services. She had Samantha. She had Brooke.

"Is there honestly anything you can do?"

"Oh, I will find something. Somebody isn't allowing the boy to see his mother, and that's not going to stand. Not if I have to make a thousand phone calls."

Despite not having access to Mia's hands, her mother touched her again, cupping a hand over one cheek. "If there's anything I can do to help, you let me know."

"Us, too," added Raquel, still standing in the doorway.

Once more Mia was struck by the difference in atmosphere in the house. Her father had never been loud or abusive, but he also hadn't had time for wild goose chases. Planning a knock-down, drag-out for a child with no family ties two-thousand miles away would have been the epitome of unnecessary energy expenditure. The current all-for-one-one-for-all mentality left her uncertain how to react.

"Thank you," she said, and forced herself to brighten. "If it comes to a letter-writing campaign, you'll be the first to get recruited."

"It won't get that far." Raquel grinned. "You'll have 'em on the run long before we get to that point. I have faith."

Her mother leaned over and kissed her forehead. "That little guy is lucky to have you on his side, Mia. Just know that."

Sitting in the warm, cheery room, surrounded by more support than she could ever remember, Mia almost believed her.

THE NEXT FOUR days were as busy as most of Mia's normal work weeks. A dozen phone calls to New York County social services, Samantha, Brooke, and a rather pointed conversation with Rory's latest foster parent, Karen Davidson, finally resulted in a tentatively planned trip for Rory to visit his mother. Mia also reached one of Monique's attending physicians to find out that her condition was not improving. It only made Mia all the more dogged to get Rory to Monique's side. By the time the plan was made, Mia had made it clear to every person involved that until she had proof from Rory he'd seen his mom, she'd stalk them all like vengeance personified.

She welcomed back her damn-the-torpedoes righteous anger with idiotic adults.

Gabriel welcomed it, too, he said, and proved it by championing her even more heartily than her family. "You have eight veterans who'll write scathing letters if you need them," he said. "A couple of them will travel to New York if you ask them to and wrap somebody's car in cling wrap, I'm sure."

Mia wanted to hug them all.

The best she could do was spend the time not involved with Rory, talking to the director at the Rock Spring mustang holding facility, expediting the men's adoption applications. If the week had to be mostly full of bad news, then she determined there had to be some countering good news. To her relief, the word that finally came down from Rock Springs was that the men could come as early as the weekend to check out the animals.

And the men all hugged her.

SATURDAY MORNING A micro-caravan of two pickup trucks, each bearing Paradise Ranch's sunburst brand and pulling a three-horse stock trailer, made the three-hour trek southeast to Rock Springs. Mia drove one of the rigs with Gabe as her wingman and Brewster and Finney in the back seats. Cole drove the other truck, with Harper at his side, and Pat MacDougal and Dan Holt behind.

"I'm damn impressed," Gabe said once they were underway. "Who knew a little-bitty city doc could haul a trailer full of horses?"

"Well, don't get too complimentary yet." Mia laughed. "My sisters and I pulled rigs all over the state and beyond all through high school, but I haven't driven a loaded trailer since college. You all may be taking your lives in your hands."

She had no such real qualms. It felt amazing to be behind the wheel of a big truck again, and the big goose-neck trailer behind her pulled like a cloud.

"Great. Crazy woman driver," Brewster murmured.

"But what a way to die," Finney replied.

"Pull up your big-boy jock straps." Mia's admonition caused guffaws. "This adventure ain't for wimps."

If she'd expected the drive to drag or be annoying or obnoxious in any way, she was proven happily wrong.

Conversation ranged from books, music, and therapy, to a few war stories. The two toughest guys in Gabe's group participated like genteel Ivy Leaguers and left behind the crude "pass-the-effing-salt" boys she'd met the two previous times. By the time they reached the holding facility, the pair had asked enough questions about the months to come and the horses that Mia had lost her last reservations about taking on this project. The men were not brainless clowns with no common sense. They were simply lost and still aimless. If they needed a challenge to focus them—Mia was more convinced than ever this mustang gig would give it to them.

The director of the facility, a bubbly woman who introduced herself as Claire, shook everyone's hands and gathered the group of eight around her like chicks.

"As I understand it," she began, "none of the adopters has experience with mustangs, but you'll be housing your horses in a place where experts are always available."

"That's right," Mia said. "We have three people who've participated in official BLM Mustang Makeover Challenges. We have a foreman who's trained multiple breeds of horses for ranch work, and we have several talented youth trainers. The horses and the owners will be very well supervised."

"Excellent! We're excited to find a perfect home for four horses. Let's take a tour of the facility first, and I'll show you the groups that have horses available for adoption. Remember, it's coming onto winter now, so their coats are getting long and shaggy. Don't expect to see the glossy herds of snorting stallions and mares you've seen in movies."

The men all looked at each other, fidgeting now that this cool-sounding adventure had turned into stark reality. Mia's agitation manifested as butterflies of excitement.

"Having said that," Claire continued, "you won't have any problem seeing one or two or ten that stand out because of color or some other physical trait you like. I want to caution you—listen to your experts. There's so much more to this process than picking a pretty-colored animal."

Mia exchanged looks with Cole and Harper this time. Her sister nodded knowingly. Cole smiled in wry amusement. He'd never been a horse trainer, but he'd ridden countless horses in his life, and he knew how much more there was to a cow pony than just met the eye.

The men were in high spirits as they started their trek around the twenty-four acre holding ranch. Claire pointed out pens containing horses that had only recently arrived after federal gatherings. They learned about the problems of increasing herd sizes and dwindling land availability. They grew quieter as it began to dawn on them that they were actually part of a very large program and could be considered horse rescuers.

Only Finney showed no emotions and kept a steeled expression throughout the tour.

At last Claire set the group free to wander alongside the corrals she considered to have the best selection. Mia instructed them to note the numbers of any horses they wanted to know more about and find her, Harper, or Cole.

Then she followed Gabe to a six-foot high gate where he rested his arms on one of the bars and peered through.

"How do you even start?" he asked. "It's so overwhelming you kind of want to throw up your hands and leave, and yet you want to take them all."

"I know." She scanned the herd, her memory working hard to bring back everything she'd learned about horses during her younger life. "I wish it made sense to let them all run free, but it doesn't. Horses get tangled in fencing or hit by cars or even starve. So they control numbers and try to find homes for the extras. Here, at least, they get any needed vet work, they're dewormed and checked for disease, and they have plenty of food. It's not perfect, but the staff here cares a lot."

"So many colors," Gabe said. "I like that one."

He pointed out a striking gray with a wide white blaze down its face. Mia nodded and watched its movements as it grazed through the hay. It wasn't big, maybe fourteen hands, and it had a mustang's typical low-set tail and sturdy legs. She wasn't crazy about something in its eyes, however. They were small and close-together. She liked a wider forehead and a more intelligent light in the gaze.

"There." She pointed out a second gray, closer to a charcoal, with one white star and two hind stockings. "He's slightly bigger. Look at his head—a little finer, big, luminous eyes. And his back is straighter. I like the set of his neck better, too."

Gabe bit his lip. "Really? You can see all that?"

She grinned. "I can. But here, let me show you it's a learned skill."

She waved at Harper who stood at the other end of the corral. Her sister trotted to them.

"Whatcha find?"

"Compare the two grays for us. See if you come up with the same things I did."

"Hmmm." She looked them over for several minutes and nodded. "The darker one with the stockings has more height—maybe fourteen-three? He's shorter coupled, and his back is nice and straight. The lighter one is a little swayed. A little sickle-hocked, too. And I like the nice, gentle eye on the charcoal."

Gabe laughed. "All right. You've convinced me. Can I show that one to one of the guys?"

Mia looked at Harper and bit her lip with a wishful heft of one eyebrow. "Tell me to say yes."

"Oh, jeez." Harper tilted her head skeptically. "You're not serious."

"No. But, he sure is gorgeous."

"Serious about what?" Gabe asked.

"Nothing," Mia said quickly.

"She likes the horse." Harper laughed. "And she has a very good eye." Mia waved off the compliment, but Harper leaned on the fence and cupped her chin, deep in thought. Finally she stood. "I think you should get him."

"What? No! That's not what I told you to say!" Mia's laugh escaped, strangled and shocked. But her heart thrummed with impulsive, unexpected excitement. "I'm leaving in a couple of weeks. Getting a horse is not a possibility."

"It'll bring you back to visit. We can work on him together. And Gabe can keep an eye on him while you're gone."

"I...what?" Gabe's eyes went wide as the mustang's.

"Sure!" Harper clearly found the idea suddenly irresistible. "The perfect partnership."

"But I didn't apply," Mia protested. "And four untitled mustangs is the limit."

"For one person," Harper said. "We'll be five separate owners. And we have the perfect facility. Plus we've adopted mustangs successfully in the past. There won't be a problem."

Mia fixed her gaze on the little horse munching hay, completely unaware of the discussion it had incited. The whole idea of her taking home a horse was insane on the face of it. She couldn't come back and forth to Wyoming often enough to train a wild horse. She had work and now Rory...

Rory.

He worshipped his cat. What would he think of horses, animals who couldn't be less catlike if they tried? Would they excite or terrify him? She wished she could find out. For a moment more her mind drifted, knowing Rory would be midvisit with his mother. She wished, too, she could be with him to try and allay his fears.

"So?" Harper pressed.

"Seriously, what's going down here? Are we really getting a horse?" Gabe's eyes were bright, not with uncertainty, but with the hopeful delight of a kid who'd always wanted a pony for Christmas. Which he had not. Until Harper had planted the idea five minutes ago.

Mia shook her head firmly. "I don't know. This is crazy talk. Harper."

"Crazy, and yet totally sane. I think this is the best thing you could do for yourself, Mia."

The gray horse lifted its head as if it suddenly sensed the strange human vibes bombarding it from beyond its fence. Mia lifted her head as well and gazed back. When she met the animal's huge brown eyes, her heart turned to mush.

"What makes you think I need some 'best thing'? I don't need more complications."

"This isn't complicated. This is your heritage."

The words tumbled and slammed into her brain, her heart, her soul. Her heritage? Was it? She'd grown up on a *cattle* ranch. Horses had been frivolous…

That thought screeched to a halt. No. Horses hadn't been frivolous anythings. They'd been challenges, companions, working partners. They'd taught her everything she'd learned about patience in adversity, about learning to think outside the norm and problem solve when you couldn't ask what the trouble was. She was a better doctor because of…her heritage.

"More than the cattle," she murmured.

"For us girls, yes. Far more than the cattle."

Mia found Gabe's eyes again and studied them. "Would you help me?"

"Doubt I could." He grinned. "But I know I'd learn from you."

Her shoulders sagged in acquiescence even as her heart raced. Gabe wrapped his arms around her, shoring her up, and Mia's face heated, knowing everyone watched the physical exchange. There'd be no end to Harper's teasing later, but Mia didn't let that stop her from hugging Gabe in return and burying her face in his jacket in a last bout of uncertainty.

"Please talk me out of this," she said.

Instead, he kissed her on the top of the head. "No. I want a pony."

"Aw, dang." Mia freed herself from his hold, but not before catching the gleeful gleam in her sister's eyes. Mia made a face at her. "Fine. Let go talk to Claire and see how he moves."

Brewster chose a striking dun gelding with a beautiful, floating trot.

Pat found a dark bay with four bright socks and an unusual but attractive half-white face.

Dan's skewbald pinto was on the large side for a mustang, a little over fifteen hands, a fact that pleased him no end.

And finally, Damien Finney set his heart on a fourteen-three hand grulla mare—an arresting light mouse-gray horse with a nearly black face, black dorsal stripe, and zebra striping on her legs. Claire tried vainly to talk him out of the choice—the only horse over which she'd shown any concern.

"Mares are notoriously more difficult than geldings," she said. "And this girl is very much an alpha female— a lead mare. For someone with no horse experience, she could be more than tough; she could be dangerous."

But Finney wasn't a man to back down. Mia led him away from the group and put on her best tough-doc face, meeting his stony implacability without fear, but also with hope that quickly faded.

"You're basing this on her looks, Damien. You know that's the worst deciding factor."

"You don't understand," he said. "That isn't it at all."

"Then what is it? I might be a doctor, but I don't want to be picking your dumbass off the ground with a front loader because you made an emotional choice."

"That's exactly what this is. It's in her eyes."

Mia had to stop, taken aback. "Okay. Tell me about her eyes."

"She looked at me and I could see—she doesn't want to be hurt. I told her I didn't want to be either. We're both scared. We'll take care of each other."

For a moment she couldn't say a word. She fixed Finney with a look he couldn't turn from. "Are you making that up?"

"I wish. I sound like an idiot."

She swallowed, remembering the loss of her heart to the gray gelding she'd chosen. "All right, Damien. She's yours. Come on."

Five hours after arriving, five written checks, and five safely loaded horses later, Cole and Mia pulled their stock trailers out of the holding facility and started home. In Mia's truck, Jason and Finney sat quietly in seeming states of shock.

"You two all right back there?" Gabe asked.

Finney craned his neck to peer out the back of the extended cab and try to see into the side of the trailer. "They gonna be safe all the way home?"

Mia smiled at his worry. "They'll be fine, Damien. Three hours and then they'll have a big, open pasture to run in."

"How'll we catch them?"

"We can partition the pasture. It was built for exactly this purpose."

He nodded.

"Brewster, how's the leg after being on it all afternoon?" she asked.

"Haven't even thought about it," he replied.

"Good. You guys know the next step is coming up with names, right?"

"She has a name," Finney said.

"What!" Mia stole a surprised look back at him. "Already?"

"Pan," he said calmly. "Short for Panacea."

Mia's tongue caught on words of surprise. "Uhh... cool?"

"She's the Greek goddess of healing."

Of course. She'd forgotten the origin of the word that today meant a cure-all. She met Gabe's eyes with true astonishment.

"What can I say?" He gave a smile and a shrug. "I told you. They're deeper than they look."

Chapter Seventeen

GABRIEL FOLDED HIS arms on the top rail of what Amelia called the round pen and let his eyes feast on the woman in the center who fascinated him more than any mystery he'd ever had to solve. Her shapely, jean-clad legs were as long as Brewster's, who stood beside her, but she stood out beside him like a gazelle next to a warthog.

She wore her chocolate-brown cowboy hat so naturally it was hard to imagine her as a New York woman who ever went without it. A double leather band held a simple silver concho at the front of the hat, an understated ornament for her beautiful, high-cheeked features and the flowing sable hair that hung in gentle waves past her shoulders. He itched to sift the waves through his fingers and appease his body's desire to take all of her to him in more than a kiss.

She'd bewitched him. He'd now experienced Amelia Crockett in so many fascinating guises, and he was a goner. He'd seen her fighting mad, laughed at her cool-and-funny snarkiness, and definitely felt her melt into warm sexiness over a kiss in his arms—which wasn't helping him control his baser urges now. But he'd not seen her like this until the past week—tough, firm, kind, and patient all rolled into one amazing teacher. It added a whole new dimension to his attraction.

She'd guided the men into a routine during the first few days with the horses. It was Thanksgiving week, and Pat and Dan came every day, fitting in trips to Paradise Ranch whenever their part-time jobs allowed. Brewster and Finney arrived each morning at seven and, right off the bat, experience everything from fence mending to four-wheeler repair to fixing outdoor automatic waterers.

Then, when Cole, Leif, and Bjorn had finished directing ranch work for the day, Amelia took over. They worked with the mustangs, and they started riding lessons on broke ranch horses so that when it came time to ride, they'd have a few minimal skills. Gabe freely admitted he hadn't had the smallest understanding what a gigantic undertaking this was going to be. The men would be lucky if they didn't all kill themselves.

Mia only laughed at him. "Too late for that worry now," she'd told him. "You guys have to survive like cowboys or die trying."

He waited in certainty for the first of the men to throw in his towel. He had no doubt at least one of them would, but three days into the project nobody seemed inclined to throw in anything yet.

"That's good, that's really good!" Amelia's sweet, calm voice carried from the middle of the ten-foot diameter, circular corral. "Now turn and let him come to you."

Brewster had named his mustard-colored dun Ollie, after one of his friends who'd died in combat. Rather than remind him of horrors, Ollie filled Jason with what seemed to be a cleansing fire. Gabe had never known the man to joke so little yet smile so much.

Ollie lowered his head and walked from a spot next to the fence to where Jason stood, his back to the horse, in the center of the pen.

"Turn," Amelia said. "And reward him."

The reward was a thorough rubbing around the shoulders, neck, ears, and forehead. This was something called natural horsemanship. Amelia, and Harper, had preached the gospel of patient groundwork and gentling through earning trust and using the horse's own language to form a bond. It hadn't made a lick's worth of sense to him at first, but watching the guys learn more every day and become more comfortable around animals they'd had no previous experience with, was convincing him the slow process was worth every minute.

She hadn't left him out, either. Every day he forced himself through the end of his workday. If he was very lucky, she was visiting Joely, and he got to drive her back to Paradise. Otherwise, he kept a bag with jeans and outdoor clothing with him and hightailed it out to the ranch as soon as he was free for the day.

Even though he hadn't picked out a horse of his own, Mia's little gray, whom she'd named London because he looked like London fog, had already wormed his way into Gabe's heart. The gelding had a quick brain and a naturally trusting nature, and he was further along in the socialization process than the other four mustangs. Mia got Gabe to help, telling him he had to keep up the work once she went back to New York. That was the only part of the deal he hated—thinking about the day, planned for the beginning of December, she'd fly away.

He watched her and pushed the thought away. Technically, he supposed, he'd known her for two months, but the first didn't count. They'd been in their resident expert versus visiting expert power struggle. So they'd had a month together, and really just the past two weeks. In that short time, however, she'd brought something alive in him he'd thought had been dead since he'd left Iraq and lost Jibril.

He touched the left front breast of his jacket and felt the soft rustle of an envelope in the shirt pocket beneath it. It contained the letter he'd slaved over the night before. Something nobody had been able to make him face in eight years. Until Amelia.

How could he let her slip back out of his life now? She'd be home for Christmas, she'd said. But he knew that once she returned to her job and set new goals for the future, New York would work its spell on her again, and the Wyoming Wild West would be nothing more than a novelty. Exactly the same thing he'd be.

He didn't know why that should bother him. He'd told Amelia straight out and honestly that domestic bliss, with children and white picket fences, wasn't for him. And yet, the fascination for wide-open ranch land and pastures full of wild horses was spreading through him like fever. More than once the past few days, while desperately trying to think of arguments that would keep her here, he thought he'd be willing to offer marriage and horses if she'd stay.

She caught sight of him, and an unreserved smile blossomed on her lips. He made a silly face—something else from his past that was coming more naturally to him again—and she laughed. He loved making her laugh.

"Hey," she called.

"Looking good," he replied.

"I know—he's got Ollie coming right along, doesn't he?"

He didn't correct her misperception. He hadn't remotely been talking about Brewster or the horse.

Amelia patted Jason on the arm. "Slip Ollie's halter on him and lead him around the pen several times; then take it off and repeat the whole exercise. I'll watch from outside. You're doing a great job. He'll be ready to hop on sooner than you think."

She headed toward Gabe, mesmerizing him with the gentle sway in her walk, so different from the veterans and patients who surrounded him most of the time. She checked over her shoulder as she reached his spot on the fence. Brewster was focused on his horse. Grinning, she turned back to Gabe and popped a quick kiss onto his mouth. The spontaneity delighted him and fueled his hopes.

"Nice," he said.

"Yeah. Kinda nice," she agreed.

"What's nice about it for you?" he asked.

She looked over her shoulder again and two little furrows formed between her brows. "You want to talk about that now? Here?"

He placed his hands on her forearms, clamping them to the top fence rail, and leaned forward. "It's been two weeks, and we haven't had one single argument since you arrived. I'm falling in deep like with you, which seems cosmically improbable, and yet you just gave me a kiss. The improbability is what's nice—more than nice—for me. So, yeah, I'd like to know what's nice for you."

"That I was wrong about you."

The words fell easily from her lips, with no hesitation, no long contemplation. He'd expected her to say something much less significant, and warmth spread through his chest. He climbed up one fence rail and reached over the top to take her in a hug. Her hat slipped back and off her head. Without a pause he delved into her exposed brunette waves, sweeping his fingers through the silk just the way he'd imagined doing moments before. When his hands cupped her ears he tugged her head forward inches to meet his kiss. He made one short, heated foray into her mouth and felt the shock and shiver to his core. When he released her and looked to the center of the arena, Jason was still concentrating on Ollie.

"We're living proof that first impressions don't always count."

"Wrong." She stretched up to whisper in his ear. "I never told you what my first impression was."

"Oh?"

"I came to *think* you were an arrogant know-it-all, but my thought the very first time I saw you was that I'd pay a lot of money to find out if you could kiss to match your looks."

"So I was nothing more than a piece of meat." He tried to hide his grin, but right at that moment she was too cute, too funny, too amazing.

She laughed. "Absolutely true. Pure animal phero-mones. Believe it or not, I'm usually much more restrained when it comes to kissing men, but suddenly I can't help myself. Even weirder, I kind of like you even when I'm not kissing you."

"So, I didn't blow that *first* kiss, obviously."

"It seems pheromones don't lie."

"You won't believe me when I tell you what my first impression of you was."

She checked on Jason again before turning back to Gabe. "Tell me."

"I thought you were the smartest person I'd ever met. I liked the way your voice sounded, and I liked the way you cut to the heart of all the problems without dwelling on maudlin emotions."

"So I *wasn't* a piece of meat? A simple object for plea-sure?" She almost looked disappointed.

"You were not. Until you decided you didn't like me and I found out how beautiful you were when you were frustrated and furious. Then, all I wanted was to fluster you. I would have kissed you back then, but that would have been highly inappropriate."

"It definitely would have been that."

"Come to dinner with me tonight," he said, out of the blue. "After we work with London. After the guys head home. Leave your family."

"A date?"

They hadn't really had an official one. Everything had been wrapped up in work, or Joely, or the horses. He'd eaten here at Paradise often, but he'd never officially asked her out.

"A date," he confirmed.

"I might like that—" A shrill melody cut her off. Her frown returned as she stepped back from the fence and dug for her phone in her pocket. "Sorry," she said. "It's Brooke."

A shiver of dread crawled down his spine as he waved for her to take the call. When she'd listened several moments, she put a hand to her mouth.

"Oh, Brooke, no!"

Dread landed in his gut and slowly solidified into rock hard certainty of disaster.

"Is he all right?" Amelia asked, a tear streaking her dusty cheek. "Did he get to see her before she was gone?"

Rory's mother had died. Amelia hadn't shared a lot of detail about the child, but enough that Gabe knew she took her friendship with the boy and his mother seriously. He left her momentarily, broke into a trot around the perimeter of the round pen and found the gate. As he entered the pen, Brewster watched, his hand frozen on the rope beneath Ollie's chin.

"What's wrong? He asked.

"Something in New York."

Gabe encircled Amelia's shoulders without interrupting her call, and led her out of the pen to a long, low bench normally used as a mounting block. He urged her to sit and, with great effort, left her alone to finish the conversation. She needed to say whatever was in her heart. As much as he wanted with every fiber of his being to stay and help her fix the problem, she didn't need him there stymying her emotions. They were sometimes hard enough for her to show.

He explained the situation to Jason, who left with Ollie, promising to check in later and find out how Mia was doing. By the time she came to Gabe and slipped her arms around his neck, they were alone.

"I'm so sorry," he said. "Really, really sorry. I know you expected her to get better."

"Rory got to see her two days ago. She passed away early this afternoon."

Her voice held no tears, no choked words, just a flat disbelief, as if she was trying to pull together her calm, impartial doctor's demeanor.

"That's good. You helped that happen. Now don't try so hard to keep it together."

"Oh, I have no choice now but to do exactly that." Despite her words, tears dripped from the side corner of each eye. Gabe brushed them away with his thumb. "Rory doesn't have anyone else to keep things together for him."

"You'll see him when you get back. You can be strong then. He's got people to look after him right now."

At that her voice finally broke.

"There's something you don't know. Something I…" She sniffed and wiped her nose and mouth with jacket sleeves pulled over her hands. "Something I neglected to tell you."

"Okay. Tell me now," he said gently.

"Monique named me Rory's legal guardian. And now, they're sending Rory here to me."

THE LOOK ON his face couldn't have been more clichéd: eyes gone immediately wide, jaw slackened just enough so words couldn't be formed, head thrust forward as if he wasn't sure he'd heard her correctly. Mia would have laughed—in understanding if not humor—if she hadn't been numb and so utterly sad.

"I know," she said, before he regained his speech. "I found out only a week or so before I left. I told them I didn't believe it. I told them I was the totally wrong person. I was, am, a friend, nothing more."

"Apparently the mother didn't think so."

She railed at his generic labeling of Monique, but she couldn't muster any extra emotion to call him on it. "Monique," she said dully.

"Sorry. Of course, Monique." Another pause. "They're sending the…Rory here?"

"He has nowhere else to go. The foster parents he'd been with have adopted a child, and they don't have room any longer. He's been at a halfway-type house for the past four days and he's begging to stay with me, I guess. He's coming on Sunday. They're not even having a funeral or service for his mom."

"There are no relatives?"

"Monique has a stepbrother in Florida, I think. But they were estranged. Her parents are gone. She was pretty much an orphan she used to say. Except for Rory."

Telling the heartbreaking story brought tears welling up again in her eyes. She hated the weakness. Hated the system and fate for leaving a traumatized little boy without a safe, real home. And she detested the emotions that clouded her ability to make sense of the situation. She had no idea what to do or what to think.

And then a long, strong arm pulled her into a harbor that stopped her emotional sea from roiling, that protected her from the November chill, and that smelled of wind and pine spice. She breathed in and held Gabe's scent in her lungs like curative vapor. Tears trickled down her cheeks, but they relieved her.

"Why are they sending him all the way here?" he asked. "If they think you're coming back in two weeks?"

The stark question filled her with despair. Not because Rory was coming, but because the thought of returning to New York put a hole in her stomach that reached all the way to her heart. An inelegant sob disguised as a hiccup escaped, and Gabriel pulled her tighter to his body.

"Don't get me wrong," he said. "Even though this is insensitive given the circumstances, I don't want you to go back. Not yet, child or no child. I want to explore this, whatever it is we've started, but it's selfish, I know. So, why go to the expense of flying the boy to Wyoming?"

He didn't want her to go. The knowledge astounded her.

He'd seemed so cavalier about the fling they were having. Easy, breezy, fun, and funny. He'd watch the horse, he'd watch the men, he'd wait for her to visit.

Or maybe that was her self-protective projection of his attitude. They'd never talked at all about the day she would leave. How would she know what he wanted?

"If I'm going to take care of him, Social Services needs to be able to close out his file by saying they believed Rory was going to a safe environment. Since he'll presumably be traveling here with me regularly, they might as well check it out. My friend Samantha can already vouch for my situation in New York."

"And they'll turn him over to you just like that?"

"That's the system for you. They'll be lucky, space- and funding-wise, to have him off their hands. No other relatives are contesting the will. If I say yes, he's one less problem for them."

"Do you *want* to say yes?"

She pulled loose from his arms and met his eyes, hot-chocolate brown and just as comforting. "That's the million-dollar question, isn't it?"

She half expected him to continue with practical questions and even more practical reasons she shouldn't be thinking hard about letting Rory come, and she found herself steeling for the onslaught of reason. The truth was, she wanted nothing more than to have Rory come. Where better to see how they could get along than during the last of her vacation, when she didn't have to shuttle him off to school, or day care.

School.

She covered her eyes again as an avalanche of practical difficulties slammed into her. Day care. Health insurance. Sleeping arrangements. The cat. Buying clothing. Living with a child and knowing nothing even remotely about how to deal with one. Dealing with his grief. Dealing with...

"Hey," Gabriel said. "You're shaking like ghosts are chasing you with ice water."

His voice, filled with gentle humor, slowed her involuntary quaking and pulled a laugh from her.

"Only one ghost—saying she expects me to take care of her son and not screw it up. Oh, Gabe, Rory is an amazing kid, and I have to honor Monique's wishes. But I don't know how to raise a partially grown boy. I can't even deal with people I work with. I was told so unequivocally. How am I going to keep my patience with someone day after day?"

"First of all, you don't *have* to do anything. Your job is to do what's best for Rory. And if that's letting him stay with you, then you don't have to be perfect. No parent is."

"How are you such an expert?"

"I have parents. My friends have parents. You have one. I've already heard how imperfect your father was—yet, look at you."

He pushed her back from his embrace and cupped her face in his hands. His cheeks held a slight burn from the wind, his nose was just starting to tip with red, and his hair had been mussed by the breeze. She leaned into his touch.

"Look at me," she scoffed. "A mess and a half. Nothing in my training prepared me for this."

"No. But that's not a bad thing. You stay in your safe career track because you don't trust that you can handle things outside of the hospital and your relationships with your patients. But you're so wrong, Amelia. You're a great teacher, a caring sister, a loving daughter, a hell of a kisser…"

"Swell." She laughed in spite of herself.

"This is my point. Your father didn't mess you up. Your parents together raised a brilliant girl who became a special woman. They didn't know any more when they started than you do now."

"They started from scratch, though."

"Not a requirement."

"So you think I should do this?"

"I can't answer that for you. But I think you should welcome Rory for now. He needs you, and I can tell you need to do this. This doesn't have to be permanent. This isn't about doing something because you owe it to a woman who passed away. It's about doing what's best. You can't know what that is until you give the situation a try."

She covered his hands on her cheeks with her fingers. "How do you do this whole sensitive guy thing so well?"

"It's what I do all day at work—solve problems, use logic, pretend I'm a therapist." He laughed.

"You make it sound so easy."

"Oh, no. Babe, this is most definitely not easy. This is life-changing. But." He brushed her lips with his. A thrill zipped through her body. "You are a tigress. You can do this."

For an instant the power of his words filled her, and she believed him. After that, she stared into his eyes, dumbstruck. How had this happened? This man, in just over two weeks, had turned her life into a screenplay by Nora Ephron—or Nora Roberts. She couldn't believe she'd won such a fantastic leading lady role. Couldn't believe she was watching the plot unfold as if it were real. But it wasn't really real. The movie was going to end sooner or later.

And she'd have to go home.

Chapter Eighteen

THEY DIDN'T CANCEL their date, and to Mia's surprise, they laughed all through dinner. Instead of the fancier Basecamp Grill steakhouse in Wolf Paw Pass, Mia opted for Dottie's Bistro, the homespun diner owned by Dottie French, whose family had been in the Jackson area almost as long as the Crocketts. Mia hadn't been into the restaurant yet this visit, and Dottie greeted her with squeals, hugs, and kisses in a familiar ritual that usually left Mia tolerating it the way a kid tolerated an overly touchy-feely relative. This time the small-town greeting left her warm and glowing. It seemed, having a community around her when she was hurting felt far better than toughing it out alone.

She and Gabriel ate comfort food to go along with the comfort of Dottie's welcome. Gabe, who Dottie claimed was one of her favorite people in the world, ordered meatloaf with a huge side of mashed potatoes and gravy. Mia ordered beef pot pie—full of locally raised beef, vegetables, thick creamy gravy, and delicious calories she didn't even want to estimate.

After regaling her with stories of getting into regular scrapes with his older brother George—and making her stomach ache from laughter on top of stuffing it with dinner, Gabriel ordered bread pudding for dessert. Despite her protests, not a single drop of rich praline topping remained on her plate when she dropped her fork drunkenly onto the table.

"I can't believe this," she said. "I've been eating like a mustang since I got to Wyoming."

"It's a night for overindulging. Not that I haven't been eating like a horse myself since I started coming around Paradise Ranch for dinners. Are there nothing but gourmet cooks in your family?"

"Just the triplets, with their bakery-slash-organic-foods restaurants in Denver. They learned most of their mad culinary skills from my mother. Harper cooks, too. Grandma Sadie and I are the only ones who don't do much in the kitchen. The triplets usually cook mean and lean, but it's been a calorie-fest the past two weeks. And now I've eaten as many tonight as in the past ten days combined."

"We can walk a few off before I take you home. Let's see who's jumping the gun on Christmas decorations."

"Ugh. Christmas. How will I handle Christmas if I have a small person living with me? What do I know about kids and Santa? Does a ten-year-old still believe in Santa?"

He laughed. "Some do. What about you? Do you believe in Santa?"

She scoffed. "Sure. Why not?"

"I'm serious. Do you have a magical spirit or a totally realistic spirit?"

"Totally realistic. How could you not know that even after the little time you've known me?"

"I think I *do* know. I just don't think you know."

She pushed her chair back and stood with a groan. Gabriel picked up the bill, which got paid the old-fashioned way by bringing it to a cashier at the front of the restaurant. "Let me help with that."

"Absolutely not. This is a strictly old-fashioned date. And here's a perfect example. You think you're practical and realistic, but deep down inside, I know you'd love to just let Prince Charming whirl you away for a while." He winked and grabbed his coat from the back of his chair.

"Oh, I would." She closed her eyes momentarily and sighed. "Do you know him? Prince Charming? Can you set me up?"

"Oh, nice, Amelia." He got to her jacket before she did and held it open for her. "As if I'd introduce you to any other Prince Charming."

"You worried about your competition?"

"Hell yeah."

She wrapped her arms around his bicep and leaned into him. "You probably don't have to. Worry."

He snorted his laughter. "Great. Then I *probably* won't."

He led her to the cash register between the restaurant section and the mountain lodge–themed bar area. It was Friday-night busy, laughter and voices carrying from the solid pine bar and the high-top tables scattered through the space. On the far wall, a large TV screen carried the local news.

"It's so good having you back for a while, Mia." Dottie finished ringing up the check and Gabriel signed the slip.

"It's been interesting," Mia said. "Different without Dad."

"He's sorely missed, I'll tell you that."

"I'm sure. He loved this place."

"Friday breakfasts. Almost without fail. I'm so sorry."

Mia was, too. Especially now in light of what Rory must be going through, she was acutely aware of how much she'd taken her father's omnipresence for granted. Tough, gritty, no-holds-barred Sam Crockett should have been indestructible. Maybe if she'd come back more often, or if she'd spoken to him a little more intimately after she'd gone to school—

She halted her thoughts abruptly. She knew better than to go there. She saw too much guilt in her job, too many "if only I'd dones" to let herself fall into the trap. Everyone had regrets. And, her father hadn't come to her either.

"Everything all right?" Dottie asked. "Sorry to bring up sad memories."

"Oh. No, no, everything's fine. It's good to think about Dad. Don't stop bringing up memories, Dottie. Truly."

The older woman smiled, a hint of shine in her eyes. "Sam was a lucky man. He raised a beautiful family. And now," she scanned Mia's hold on Gabriel's arm, "you're meeting the locals. Can I hope that means you might be staying on with us a while?"

Mia felt the blood rise to her cheeks, and she looked up at Gabriel, surprised to find him unaware of her conversation with Dottie, his eyes focused on something in the bar.

"I'm afraid not," Mia said. "Gabriel and I are just friends. I have to return to New York in a couple of weeks."

"Such a shame." Dottie frowned. "You two look very pretty together."

Small-town mother hens. Mia shook her finger at Dottie, knowing all too well how gossip in the little town flew. She looked again for Gabriel's reaction, but this time she could see immediately he was frozen in place, staring at the television.

She peered at the flat screen and made out the closed-caption crawl across the bottom. As she realized what the story was about, she squeezed Gabe's arm tighter. Footage of soldiers dodging through an Iraqi city was alternated with a video of a family of six. The text told of a reunion—four family members reunited with a grandmother and an uncle after five years of each thinking the others dead.

She stared, waiting for any sign of names. It couldn't be such a coincidence as to be Gabriel's missing family...

The story ended. She hadn't seen most of it, just enough to understand why Gabriel looked shell-shocked.

"Hey," she said softly. "Tell me you didn't just see a ghost."

"Oh, I saw plenty of ghosts." His voice held a touch of grim resignation. "Come on. Let's go."

She followed without questioning him further, letting his tension and his silence settle around them as they left the cozy bistro for the cold November night. The wind had picked up, and Mia buried her face against Gabe's coat sleeve. He pulled free of her grasp and wrapped his arm fully around her shoulders. "Maybe it's a little chilly for a walk," he said.

"For a long walk," she agreed. "But we do need a short one, I think."

"I'm sorry about that, back in the Bistro."

"Don't apologize. For a moment I thought maybe you'd seen something about Jibril."

"No."

"But you think something like that family's separation happened to Jibril's family. I'm sorry. Seems like tonight is one for unpleasant memories."

He didn't say anything but squeezed her more tightly. "I do wish I knew where he was."

"I know. Despite what you've always said."

"I have something to show you. Then when you heard about Rory, I decided not to. Now I've changed my mind again. That report was a little freaky."

He stopped in the middle of the sidewalk, let her go, and reached inside his coat. He pulled out an unaddressed, white, number ten envelope.

"When you told me two weeks ago, the first day you arrived and learned about Jibril, that I shouldn't give up trying to find him, it annoyed the crap out of me.

Who were you to tell me what to do about something so personal?"

"I'm sorry. I didn't know I'd annoyed you."

"Because I didn't tell you. Deep inside, I knew there was truth to what you'd said. Still, I came up with a hundred reasons I wouldn't, couldn't, shouldn't try anymore. But then…" He handed her the envelope but wrapped her with his arm and started walking again so she couldn't open it. "I started watching how you solve problems—one after the other. You don't question, you just do. Things like driving eight people across the state to adopt five wild horses would seem Herculean to most people. You planned it and executed it like it was a church picnic. And it's working."

"Of course it is."

"You told me about the boy *you'd* met several years ago, and how when he came back into your life you searched out a homeless man and a cat in the heart of New York City and then brought the cat back to your house. Who does that?"

"You do. You did the same thing with a squad of injured men—rescued them from homelessness and helplessness. Gabriel stop talking about me. What's this really about?" She waggled the envelope.

"I contacted the US Embassy in Baghdad. Believe it or not, I know somebody who works there—a friend from the VA in Montana. He actually found the name of someone who appears to be Jibril's great-uncle. If I send him some information and pictures, he will try to contact the man. It took me a long time to decide I wanted to do it."

"Gabe, that's fantastic!" She stopped him and tugged on his jacket front to get him turned toward her.

"But then you got the news about Rory and his mother. I didn't want to throw all my potential emotional shit at you when you're dealing with something this big in your life. It was one kid too many, you know?"

"That's ridiculous. One isn't any more important than the other."

He pulled her into a full bear hug. "See? You just go for it, whatever it is that needs going for. I'm acting like the damn girl here."

"Oh, shut up, you chauvinist." She drew back enough to cup his cheeks, now cold from the breeze, as they'd been that afternoon by the round pen at the ranch. "You don't 'go for it' because you survey all the angles first. Then you go into battle mode and fight for the people under your care. I rush in headlong. There's a time and place for both methods. Damn girl, my butt. I'm the damn girl."

With that she dragged him to her and kissed him, long, hard, sweet and hot. His breath warmed her, and her fingers warmed his face.

"Oh yes, you are definitely the girl."

"Let's forget about window shopping and go back to the house. Maybe we can commandeer the family room fireplace for ourselves."

"I dunno." His eyes shone with relief in the glow of the street lamps and his breath hung in frosty smoke between them. "There are five other women there. I don't see us being alone much."

"They'd stay away if I asked them to." She smiled.

"But still, we'd never know when they'd accidently come down the stairs, would we?"

"It would keep us honest."

"That's what you want? Us to stay honest?"

The question was meant to tease, but she couldn't find a quick retort. What *did* she want? Her life was whirling further out of its normal orbit every minute. Wouldn't a night with Gabe fit right into the craziness? The idea of keeping him with her for an entire night was far from objectionable. In fact, it sounded warm. And safe.

"Yeah," she said finally. "Isn't honesty the best policy?"

"How about we go home and find out?"

"What about this?" She lifted the envelope again. "It's a letter, right? To your friend?"

"I wanted you to read it before I sent it. I'd almost decided to wait. Then I saw that story on the news and it was eerie—cosmic."

"My grandma Sadie would say the Lord works in mysterious ways."

"Well something or someone sure does. What are the odds of seeing that exact story right now?"

"Don't question it. Come on. I'll read the letter in the car."

She opened the letter before Gabriel had even pulled away from the curb and read silently by the map light above her, painfully aware of his steel-straight and anxious form behind the wheel.

Dear Paul,

Thank you for your offer to help locate Malik al Hamal. I am enclosing information about the boy, Jibril al Raahim, whom I hope we discover is Malik's great-nephew...

The letter continued with a very clear timeline of Gabriel's tour in Baghdad and the years spent with Jibril. Gabe had given all his contact information and made certain his friend Paul knew to reassure the man that he wanted nothing from the family. He only wanted information about the boy's fate the day the city square had been shelled.

"So?" Gabe asked once she'd folded the letter carefully. "Should I send it?"

She set the envelope on her lap and placed her hand on Gabe's tensed thigh muscle, stroking along its length hoping to comfort. "Of course you should. Why are you nervous to try? Finding this potential relative was such a lucky break."

"Because not knowing might be better than knowing."

"That's never true," she said firmly. "We hear that all the time—people didn't come to the doctor soon enough because they didn't want bad news. But how can you move ahead if you don't know the truth?"

"You just keep moving," he replied. "That's what I did."

"But did you?" She stilled her hand on his thigh for a moment, but then began to knead gently. "You know that part of your life isn't healed. You fight so hard for everything just to make up for what you think was a mistake. You need to find out one way or another."

"This man could be no relation at all."

"And then you're no worse off than you are now."

"Unless Jibril is dead." The tiniest hint of bitterness crept into the words.

"Unless he's dead," she agreed. "And then you'll grieve, and you'll go to a counselor just the way you send your men to therapy, and you'll heal."

"I won't need a counselor if I have you." He covered her hand with his, and she flipped her palm upward so it nestled into his grip.

"No, I'll be your letter-writing consultant, but that's it. Unless you need your appendix taken out."

"Uh, not today thanks."

She grinned. "I have one suggestion for you, but you don't have to take it."

"Hey, a pretty woman is holding my hand. I'll do whatever she says." He squeezed her fingers, and his voice regained its natural humor.

"I think you should make what you have here a cover letter to your friend—it's perfect. But also add a very short letter for the man you're trying to reach. I'm sure someone there can translate it. Assume he's the uncle. Tell him something personal about your relationship with Jibril. Send him a picture. Tell him you've worried about him and would love to hear from any relative—something like that. A personal touch will get you a lot further than simply something official from a government embassy."

He contemplated her suggestion for several moments.

"That's not too much? If it's not a relative?"

"Then it doesn't matter at all. If it is the uncle, then it's absolutely not too much. With luck he'll think of you less as a soldier and more as a friend."

"All right," he said quietly. "I'll think about doing that."

"Don't think too much, you'll think yourself out of it. Just do it."

"If this turns out to be a cluster, I'm blaming you." He lifted their clasped hands and brushed a kiss across her knuckles.

"That's okay. I'm a big girl; I can take it."

MIA FULLY EXPECTED the house to be calm and quiet. Preparations would be started for Thanksgiving in two days. Grandma Sadie would be in bed. Her mother would be knitting or reading. Her sisters would be in their rooms. She had it planned perfectly in her head that she and Gabe would be able to sneak off by themselves. The house was plenty big enough for everyone to have a space.

What greeted them was just the opposite: frenetic excitement and planning that couldn't have been more involved if her sisters, mother, and grandmother had been prepping for a presidential visit.

"Oh, I'm so glad you're back," her mother said, hugging her tightly and then unashamedly offering the same to Gabe. "Are you all right? Are you feeling a little less overwhelmed?"

She'd told her family about Rory. "I'm all right, Mom."

She braced for further parental solicitousness but it didn't come. Instead, Grace tugged her without ceremony toward the stairs.

"You have to see what we've done!" she said. "It's so great."

"What's going on?" Mia exchanged a mystified look with Gabe.

"First of all," her mother said, "since Rory won't be here in time for the real Thanksgiving, we're postponing our celebration until next week. We concentrated instead on a place for him to stay."

"Harper had a fantastic idea," Grace said. "Look!"

She opened the door to the room next to Mia's. In the three hours Mia and Gabe had been gone, Rory had gained a bedroom in what had been the sewing room. It was now decked out with a twin bed, a bookcase, and a desk. Grandma Sadie bent over the bed, straightening a log cabin quilt in deep red, blue, and green. A huge painting of Wolf Paw Peak, which stood on Paradise property near the middle of the ranch's land, hung on one wall. Harper's exquisite work.

Mia marveled at the room. "This is above and beyond. Who moved all the furniture?"

"Cole and Bjorne helped us," Harper said. "We moved the sewing machine and fabric into the guest room downstairs next to Grandma."

"But you were staying there." Mia looked at her mother.

"I decided I wanted to go back up into my own room. I can manage the stairs now. It's good for me to make the effort."

"This is pretty cool." Gabe gazed in from the doorway and nodded.

"We left the shelves and other walls for you to decide about," Raquel said. "You might know some things Rory likes we can put up."

Mia moved slowly around the room, hugging her grandmother, staring at the painting, her mind numb to ideas—blown away by the effort her family had put into creating this spot.

"I…I have no idea," she said. "I'm so grateful. But he'll be here such a short time. You didn't need to disrupt the whole house—"

"Of course we did!" Her mother hugged her again. "This is sad, but exciting. We want Rory to know that whenever he comes to visit with you, he's part of the family now."

Mia's throat tightened and she grabbed for Gabe's hand. Part of the family? Three weeks ago, *she'd* barely felt like part of the family. She didn't even know if Rory was going to stay in her life. A request in a will was important, but not binding. Just as Gabe had said.

But as she took in the eager faces of the women in her life who'd moved a holiday and two rooms, who'd done this huge thing for her, something deep inside shifted. Maybe, she thought, it was to make room for a sad, orphaned little boy. And a cat named Jack.

MIA MET THE plane alone on Sunday afternoon. Rory had no idea of the reception he was in for, and she'd begged her excited family to forego any kind of welcome party. For all she knew, Rory—who was arguably one of the biggest lovers of a party she'd ever met—might want nothing more this time than to curl up and hide.

Nerves like insidious drops of acid assailed her stomach as she waited by baggage claim for a first glimpse of Rory. Half-embarrassed at her anxiousness over a child, she used every yoga breathing technique she could remember, and every head-to-toe relaxation method she'd ever read about to calm herself.

They didn't help. She caught sight of the social worker who'd accompanied him first. It wasn't her friend Samantha—who'd had an emergency to attend to—but Samantha's colleague Hannah White. And then she saw the beautiful head of curls she recognized beyond any doubt. She'd envisioned every manner of greeting from tears and a hug to a stoic high five. She wasn't prepared for what she got.

"Mia!" Rory pulled away from his chaperone with a twist and burst simultaneously into tears and a dead run.

She barely had time to brace herself. From five feet away, Rory, with his backpack flapping, launched himself into her arms and clung like a little spider monkey.

Chapter Nineteen

GABE HAD PROMISED to be at the house when Amelia returned with her new charge, and as he watched her car pull slowly down the driveway, excitement mixed with apprehension. The idea of meeting the boy in his first moments at Paradise Ranch seemed suddenly, enormously important, as if this was a do-or-die test. Ridiculous. It was a child.

He'd once loved kids. Funny guys always liked small people who were suckers for clowning around. Now that he was much less the clown, however, he'd lost his effortless ability to relate immediately on their level.

He hadn't admitted to Amelia—he'd barely admitted it to himself—that Rory's appearance in her life worried him. He wasn't stupid. He knew his nerves stemmed from emotional garbage that had to do with Jibril. He'd followed every wrong instinct in the world with the boy who'd become his little shadow in Baghdad. He'd thought he was being so

smart, so kind, and so righteous befriending a local child
and showing him the wonderful ways of American life.

Instead, he'd been selfish. Nice maybe, but deep down
he'd been making himself feel powerful. And it had cost
a family dearly. Until Amelia, he had preferred to wear
his guilt like a martyr—doing more work with adults and
depriving himself of children. Then she'd started hound-
ing him about not giving up. About closure. About all the
things he'd planned never to face. And for the first time
he'd been willing to search one more time for the truth,
not so he could help himself, but so he could be a little bit
more whole for her.

So he'd put together a note and some pictures for
Jibril's maybe-uncle and sent the whole package off to the
American Embassy yesterday morning before he could
lose his nerve.

But he was losing it. He was glad Amelia was doing
just what he advocated: making a home for a child who
needed one. He just didn't want to blow it. He'd thought
it was just his own biological children he didn't want to
bring into the world and mess up. The truth was, he didn't
want to mess up any kid.

The front door opened slowly, and Gabe stole glances at
Bella and Grace, the other two designated welcome committee members, seated on the couches in the living room
with him. His stomach rolled in queasy anticipation.

He was a grown man, for God's sake.

Amelia stepped through the door, a quiet smile on her
lips as she caught everyone's eyes and then glanced down
at the boy plastered to her side.

"Hi, everyone," she said. "I found the man I went looking for."

Gabe followed her gaze, and his heart punched against his ribcage. Rory held a pet carrier in front of him that took up almost his entire wingspan. Behind the lines of effort on his face, the boy was beautiful. He also could have been Jibril's brother.

His skin glowed like it was bronzed from the sun, and a halo of black curls framed his face. Jibril's hair had been coarse and straight, but his skin tone and dark eyes had been similar.

Amelia spoke quietly to Rory, and he set the carrier down. She squatted with him in front of the little door and helped him open it. She looked like a natural with the boy, peering alongside him, one graceful hand resting on his shoulder, her shapely, jean-clad legs folded easily into the crouch, and her red boots punctuating the picture. Sweet and sexy—a woman who could rescue a child and rock a pair of hot boots.

When she stood, Rory stood with her, holding one of the prettiest cats Gabe had ever seen—a beige-colored mass of fur that squirmed only to get comfortable in the boy's arms. It stared around with eyes as big as its master's.

"I'd like you all to meet Rory Michael Beltane and his buddy, Jack." Amelia put her arm briefly around Rory's shoulders. "Rory, this is my mom, my sister Grace, and my good friend, Gabriel."

"The one who's kind of your new boyfriend?" he asked, assessing Gabe with a gaze that spoke purely of fact-finding.

Amelia's face flushed an attractive light pink, and Gabe smiled, his heart rate calming for the first time in hours. This is why kids were so great—they never minced words, and you couldn't tell them any secrets. As Rory had just made clear. If he hadn't been standing right there, Gabe would have loved ribbing Amelia about this one. "Kind of a boyfriend" was a designation he never would have hoped for. One day he'd thank young Rory.

"I, uh…yeah, that's Gabe."

"Hey, Rory." Gabe didn't make the mistake of trying to offer a grown-up handshake. The cat, Jack, took up both Rory's hands. "Glad you made it safely to Wyoming. How did you and Jack do on that long flight?"

"It was okay." He looked down at his pet. "I was afraid for him in the bottom of the plane. But I guess he's all right."

"He is one handsome dude of a cat. Calmest cat I think I've ever seen." The words started to come more easily.

A little light of pride blossomed in Rory's eyes. Amelia smiled gratefully. Gabe raised his brows suggestively and winked.

"Hi, Rory." Bella approached, gave Amelia a kiss on the cheek, then bent to Rory's level. "I'm Mia's mom. Call me Bella. We're so glad to have you with us, but I want you to know that we understand it's a pretty sad time for you. Right?"

Rory gave a nearly imperceptible nod. This was where Amelia had gotten her ease around kids. Professional mothers were wonders to behold.

"When you're all settled in and feel comfortable, you can tell us anytime you want to talk about your mom. Or you don't have to at all. We'd like to learn all about her if you want to share her with us."

He bit his little lip, but his eyes remained dry, and he nodded again.

Grace greeted him, too. She was the one to tease him into a first pale smile by warning him that he was about to be one of only two men in the house with a whole lot of girls. And he should just run for Cole or hope that Gabe hung around a lot so he could have safe places from all the talking.

Rory buried his face in Jack's fur to hide the grin. Gabe thought he detected a hint of impishness beneath the sober mien. The hug bestowed on his cat was one squeeze too many, however, and Jack wriggled free, plopping to the floor with a plaintive meow and heading for the living room with a confident cat swagger.

"He'll be okay," Amelia said. "Let him explore."

"Didn't Rory fly here with one of the social workers?" asked Bella.

"She's staying at a hotel in Jackson," Amelia said. "I invited her to stay here, but she wanted to get some work done and come tomorrow morning to visit the ranch. It was nice of her to give us some bonding time. So, Rory, that means we'd better start getting you settled so we look good tomorrow, right?"

He nodded.

"Now that you've met part of the family, we can go back to the car and get your suitcase and the things we bought for Jack. I have a special spot for his litter box all picked out. And you can put his new bed in your new room."

"Okay."

There wasn't much luggage for a child who'd been thoroughly uprooted and moved across country. Gabe grabbed the one large suitcase, and Grace easily hauled a box of cat litter. Amelia handed Rory a plastic bag with a pet store logo on it, and she took the new litter box. They paraded back into the house where Jack met them, getting Rory to smile for the second time.

They set up the litter box in an accessible corner of the back hall, and Jack obediently checked it out. Then it was Rory's turn to scope out his room. The first hint of deer-in-the-headlights shock started to appear in his face as he followed Amelia up the grand wooden staircase to the upper floor. When she nudged him gently ahead of her into the newly created bedroom, he halted as if he'd hit a force field.

Amelia had finished off the room by filling the shelves with classic old books found in her mother's stash of things saved from the girls' youth. She'd also made a trip to Jackson the day before and picked up a few toys Bjorn had suggested might be appropriate—a couple of Lego building sets, a Transformer she'd been promised was classic, and a set of Matchbox cars just because. She'd found a bright red bean bag chair that looked inviting next to one wall. But the crowning splurge was a new laptop over which she'd debated long and hard. It wasn't super powerful, Gabe knew, but it could run video games, allow him to do research for school, and she'd had all the parental controls set up and activated so she felt relatively confident he couldn't get into trouble on it.

"He needs something to feel cool and special," she'd said. "This is a tool and a toy. Right?"

He'd kissed her in the middle of the electronics store and whole-heartedly agreed. Rory would not hurt for attention or caring while he was with Amelia.

"What do you think?" she asked Rory as he continued to gape. "Will this be okay while we're here?"

"This is for me?"

"It is. You need a place to make your own. When we get back to New York, we'll figure out a room there, too."

"So…" He looked over his shoulder, desperate hope in his eyes. "I really do get to stay with you?"

"Yes," she said, her voice nearly a whisper. "I'd like that."

Gabe didn't know what caused the more forceful sock to his gut, the reminder that she was leaving soon or the fact that she seemed to have made a decision about Rory's future already.

"I thought I could sleep with you." He looked at the floor.

She knelt beside him and offered a hug. "Sweetie, you can sleep wherever you'd like. Wherever you feel safest. If you want to sleep with me, of course you can."

Rory relaxed as he hugged her. When he let go he turned back to the room, the deer-in-the-headlights replaced by growing excitement. He walked to the desk and touched the laptop in awe.

"I get to use this?"

"It's yours," Amelia said. "You'll need it for school. And for looking things up and getting even smarter than you are."

He whirled around again. "Mine?" He questioned everyone in the doorway with his incredulous eyes.

"I was with her when she picked it out," Gabe said. "She said it was for you."

Rory threw his arms around Amelia again. "I never had nothing so nice as a computer."

"Never had anything," she said, and poked his side softly. "Get used to that. I correct grammar. And I know your mom had a computer she let you use sometimes."

"Yeah, but it wasn't *mine*."

"I'm really glad you like it. There'll be some rules, but only a few," she said. "We can talk about that kind of stuff later. Want to see the rest of the house so you know where everything is?"

He clearly wanted to check out the computer, but he nodded and followed them out of the room.

Rory's excitement had faded back into overwhelmed silence by the time the house tour was finished and he stood in the kitchen, where the rest of the family finally waited to meet him. He shook Cole's hand somberly and responded to Harper like he had to Grace, with a small smile at her compliments of his cat and the admission that she'd already sneaked him a little bit of tuna as a welcome treat.

"You must be ready to eat, too," Harper said. "We'll have dinner in about three hours, but how about something now?"

"I'm not so hungry," he said, moving closer to Amelia and looking up at her as if for permission to say such a thing.

"You don't have to eat," she said.

"Oh, that's just pishposh." The admonition came from Grandma Sadie, who joined the crowd, her black-and-red flowered cane tapping ahead of her lively steps. "Everyone in this kitchen is hungry for cookies. So, sit down, all of you, and I've got my famous old oatmeal chocolate chippers. Hello, Mr. Beltane. I'm Grandma Sadie." She put her wrinkled hand out. "You can call me Grandma Sadie."

To Gabe's astonishment, Rory gave her the biggest smile he'd offered up yet. He held out his own hand. "Are you like a great-grandma?"

"I'm a very great grandma." She winked. "Every house needs one, don't you think?"

"And you still make cookies?"

That garnered a round of laughter.

"It's about all I like to cook anymore, and only for special occasions. I thought this qualified."

The exchange sealed the deal both of cookies and Rory's acceptance of his new home away from home. Cookies, milk, and coffee flowed after that and the atmosphere relaxed. Gabe relaxed, too, less worried about the child now that he knew there were so many women willing to act as aunties and grandmothers.

On the other hand, he didn't want to get in the way of the new, fragile family bonding. He was still an outsider. Maybe he was a "kind of boyfriend," but that and, as the clichéd saying went, a buck-fifty would get him coffee at the nearest gas station. He might be unofficially attached to Amelia, but he wasn't really part of the Crockett clan.

So he settled for quietly watching the ten-year-old try to absorb his new surroundings. Poor kid—this had to be overwhelming. People laughing and joking when he'd just lost his mother and home. He'd certainly be more comfortable once he was back in New York.

A wave of melancholy hit Gabe like a Wyoming thunderstorm. He needed to think hard about what he was doing with Amelia Crockett. This was her life now. Like a boulder thrown into a gentle, quiet pond, the arrival of Rory had tsunami-caliber repercussions. He honestly wasn't resentful or jealous. But he didn't want to hurt someone or be hurt either. His time to pursue Amelia before she left him had run out.

And yet he wanted more of her. Watching her laugh with her family, a woman who'd changed by a hundred and eighty degrees from the cool, stiff, unapproachable doctor he'd met three months before, only increased his desire. So what the hell did he do with this dilemma?

"Time for Rory to choose what we do next." Amelia propped her chin in her hand and raised her brows. "You can rest here in the house, or you can come down to the barns and see some of the animals. I think a couple of the guys are here working with the mustangs."

He didn't hesitate. "Mustangs!" It was the most animation he'd shown since meeting Sadie.

At the mention of horses all the women jumped into motion as if they'd been told Johnny Depp was in the house. One put the milk away, another the cookies, another swept crumbs from the table into her hand and tossed them in the sink. Cole, Gabe, and Rory sat at the table staring at each other in amusement—and a little more astonishment on Rory's part.

"That's how girls act when horses and cowboys are involved," Cole said, leaning toward Rory conspiratorially. "You might want to consider becoming a cowboy, just so you get any attention."

"Are you a cowboy?" Rory asked.

"I guess I am. I raise cows and I got a cowgirl to say she'd marry me—so I speak from a little experience."

"Are *you* a cowboy?" Rory turned to Gabe.

He'd lost count of the number of hits his heart had taken today. With one innocent question, a boy of ten had isolated Gabe's problem. Of course he wasn't a cowboy. He was a city boy who'd moved to a cowboy state.

"I'm pretty much not," he said. "I do like horses, though. Do you?"

Rory shrugged. "I rode in a carriage once, and I petted a policeman's horse. I never saw a mustang. Dr. Mia told me about them when we were driving here."

"Then you should see the mustangs," Gabe said. "Don't you think so, Cole?"

"No question about it."

Gabe smiled encouragement, but he knew he was going to let Cole take the lead on this outing. After Amelia sent Rory out the door with Cole and Harper, she reached for Gabe's hand, and he halted her, spinning her into his arms.

"Thanks for being so patient," she said. "This is completely crazy."

"He's a cute kid."

"He's amazing, too. He's not saying much here yet, but he's smart."

"What would you think if I let you have the rest of the afternoon with him alone?"

"Whoa. Wait? You want to leave?"

"No, it's not that. I thought it would be easier for Rory to have one less body around."

"Easier for Rory? First of all, it wouldn't be. Second, what about me?"

"I just want you to have all the time you need with him." He meant it.

For an instant he thought she was going to let him have it—like the old Dr. Mia. Instead, she pressed her lips to his. When she pulled back from the kiss she grabbed a fistful of his sweatshirt.

"Listen, Lieutenant. No way are you leaving. I need you. I've used up nearly all my expertise on him already, and I'm scared to death."

Her declaration, or her admission if that's what it was, jarred him. She'd looked so calm, so expert with him. How could she be scared?

Finally a familiar rush of his normal confidence flooded back. Here she was embracing this enormous change in her life with fear she refused to show, and he'd threatened to abandon her. In one flash of insight he manned up. This wasn't Iraq. The child wasn't Jibril. He knew how to do this. He grabbed her into a hug.

"Aw, Mia. Of course I'll stay. I just didn't want to hurt or frighten him."

She looked up at him. "You've never called me Mia."

He hadn't. But some little dam had broken inside and a sense of intimacy he'd never known filled him with joy.

"Mia, Mia," he crooned. "I'm sorry. You are so much braver than I am."

"I am not brave."

"As brave as anyone I've ever known. I let myself fear getting to know Rory only to lose him when he leaves. But he's a perfect example of the kind of child I *do* want to know. To help. There are too many Rorys in the world. You didn't run from that."

"Believe me, I want to." For the first time she sounded miserable.

"Okay. For now let's *not run* together. How about I grow a pair and have your back?" She sagged into his hold like a sack of sand, and the first sound of crying emerged—a tiny hiccup of a sob. "Hey," he said. "It's okay."

"It is now," she said. "It is now."

They joined the others already on the way down the long sloping drive toward the ranch yard and the barns. Gabe breathed in the familiar earthy outdoor scents with new appreciation. With Mia's—using her nickname had breached the wall between him and feeling like family—hand in his, he watched Rory bravely facing his own unknown between Cole and Harper, glancing back once or twice to make sure Mia was there. In those moments he knew that for however long he could make this new romance last, he'd do it right.

The universe, fate, God, who- or whatever, certainly did kick people in the shorts in mysterious ways.

The tranquility was interrupted by sudden wild yelling, and the slight figure of a teenaged girl charged toward them. Beside her raced a loose-limbed but graceful Border Collie pup.

"Harper! Cole! Come. Hurry! That grulla mare got loose. She bulldozed over Mr. Finney and broke through a half-open gate. Grandpa is with him, and Dad went after the horse."

"Oh, God, no." Mia stiffened beside him and dropped his hand. She pushed forward in a run and reached Harper. Gabe followed.

"Skylar, is Finney all right?" Mia asked.

Bjorn's daughter, even at fourteen, knew more about horses than a lot of cowboys. She'd been helping with the mustangs, and the guys responded to her with surprising respect. She stood before them now, breathing hard, her eyes as wide as Halloween moons.

"I don't know," she said. "I didn't wait to see. But he wasn't moving much."

Chapter Twenty

MIA TOOK THE deepest breath she could manage and pushed back the gruesome thoughts of a broken, trampled Damien Finney, along with the knowledge that this was all her fault. What a foolish, impulsive, dangerous idea this whole mustang thing had been. She looked to Gabe who was ready to bolt along with Harper and Cole.

"Go," she said. "Rory and I will be right there."

What a terrible introduction to ranch life this would be for him. Fear and dread hung in her chest like stone weights. She turned to Rory and squatted. He stared at the sprinting trio of adults with a mix of fascination and alarm. That's when she realized Skylar had also stayed behind. She offered the girl a weak smile.

"Rory," she said. "Look at me, sweetie." He did. "I'm sorry you're having to see this your first thing at the ranch. We don't have to go down there."

"I…I want to," he said.

"We'll have to stay far back from the accident."

"Did somebody die?" His voice wavered slightly but didn't break, and he set his little mouth firmly—a true tough kid from New York, although he'd hardly been raised on the streets.

"I don't think so," Skylar said.

"Really?" Mia couldn't stop the hopeful question.

"I don't think there was any blood," she said in continued teenage candor.

Mia knew that didn't matter. And for the first time, she remembered that she should be the one at the scene. When had the medical instinct that was her heart and soul abandoned her?

"Rory, this is Skylar. Skylar, meet Rory. Would you both be okay if I did go down there? Maybe I'll be able to tell if Mr. Finney is hurt badly or not."

"She saves people," Rory told her, a hint of pride in his voice. In light of his mother's death only days earlier, it was an amazing thing for him to say.

"And cats." She stroked his cheek. "You're needing to be brave all over the place today, kiddo. I'm really proud of you."

"I'll bring him down, Miss Mia," Skylar said. "Don't worry."

The teen had grown close to Harper in the months since their father had died. Sky had grown into a smart, sassy, highly artistic and insightful young woman in the years all the sisters had been away from Paradise. She was proving right now that her reputation for poise was justified.

"Thanks, Skylar. I'll see you in a few minutes."

By the time she reached the scene, back in doctor mode and steeled for the worst, she found to her immeasurable relief a pissed-off Finney, seated in the dirt of the round pen, arguing with Gabe about getting up.

"Here she is." Gabe caught her eyes. "Let her look you over, and she gets to make the call."

"Back everyone," Mia ordered to the knot of family pressed around Finney's agitated form.

Leif Thorson, the laconic, kind, and mustached original ranch foreman who'd always been like a grandfather to the Crockett sisters, nodded at her arrival. "I think he's just a little shaken up," he said, stepping back, pronouncing it "yoost a little" in his easy Norwegian accent.

"Thanks, Leif. Damien?" She knelt beside him. "Tell me what happened."

"I scared her," he said adamantly. "You've got to let me help catch her."

"Not until I know what happened."

"I forgot to take down the plastic bags we had tied to the rails for desensitizing Pat's horse. He's ready for that. Pan isn't. She spooked even before I got the gate closed. She reared and made this crazy run around the pen and then just galloped right passed me. Her head and shoulder shoved me over so I couldn't grab her halter. I hit the ground hard, got the wind knocked out of me, but I didn't get hurt."

"Did you hit your head?"

"Just on the ground."

"Lose consciousness?"

"No!"

"Do you remember the whole incident?"

"Every second. She was scared to death. I feel awful. About her," he added quickly.

Mia stared at him. She couldn't remember ever hearing Damien Finney say he was sorry for or about anything. Mr. Tough Guy never blamed or took blame. He just got angry. But he wasn't angry at the horse at all. Amazing.

"Any dizziness now? Follow my finger."

"Really?" he asked. "You guys do that?" He followed the motion of her fingertip perfectly.

"Yes. Did Pan's hooves touch you?"

"Not at all."

Finally Mia allowed her breath to release and her pulse to calm. She ran a hand over the back of Finney's head and felt no lumps yet. "Okay," she said. "Let's get you up. Slowly."

Gabe and Leif each grabbed one of Finney's arms and hoisted him to his feet.

"Any dizziness now?" Mia asked.

"Nope. Let me go. She knows me best."

"We need to talk about her, Damien," Mia said. "She's a hot-headed little girl. We've discovered that all week. This was just a warning—you could get seriously hurt. It's possible, in fact it's likely, she just isn't going to make a good project horse. Some never do."

"She is a good horse," he said, his voice tightening. "She's fine. This wasn't her fault."

"But she hasn't learned enough self-control to stay out of your space. She has to do that even when she's scared."

"She'll learn." Anger crept slowly into his words.

Mia looked helplessly at Gabe, but to her dismay he shook his head. "It's his horse," he said.

"Leif?" She tried her old friend. "When I thought he'd been injured, I was beside myself. This whole project is on me."

"No, it's on me," Gabe said, taking her hand. "I gave the okay and got the permission. And now that it is underway, that point about who started it is moot. Stuff happens."

"The point is, the project is only worthwhile if it's safe. That's not a safe horse for a beginner."

"Sweetheart." Leif took her other hand and smiled. "You've been away from this life for too long. You're talkin' like a city slicker. Since when have you been afraid of horses? How many times were you and your sisters knocked down or stepped on or dumped off?"

Mia let out a frustrated growl. This was all beside the point—moot or not. She started to protest but at that moment, Skylar and Rory reached the fence and Sky boosted her temporary charge onto the bottom rail so he could see over the top. Mia's heart skipped in fear. What if it had been him?

She pulled her hands from both men. "You'll be crawling back to me in apology if someone gets hurt."

"He didn't die?" Rory called.

The men broke into laughter. Mia scowled. "Oh, come on, you guys. That's just wrong," she said. "No, kiddo, he's just fine."

Leif patted her on the head as if she were five and walked away chuckling. "Time to go rope us a mustang. C'mon tenderfoot, let's get your pretty little horsie."

He slapped Finney on the back and Damien looked at Mia. "Go," she said. "If she runs at you, next time, dodge."

Two long, strong arms wrapped her from behind. Gabe's familiar, heady scent sent her blood zinging through her veins.

"Thanks for sticking up for me," she said sarcastically.

"Did you see the look in Finney's eyes?" he asked. "I haven't ever seen that kind of passion in him. Taking that mare away from him now would kill it for good. He'd never stop believing that the whole world was against him. You'd be no different to him than the people running the benefits departments. No different than the brass in the army. But let him fight this out, win this battle, and you might save a guy from himself."

She closed her eyes, grabbed his wrists with her hands and leaned backward. "You see the good in everything."

"I see the changes. Finney's change is seismic—in just a week. Don't give up on him."

"I'm not. I've just learned to care about the big jerk."

"Show him, by letting him follow his instincts."

She opened her eyes and spun in his arms. "What are you? Everyone's safety net?"

"I'd be happy to be yours." He nuzzled her nose with his, and she laughed, letting her irritation and worry go. "But there are new and small people here now."

"New and small people go to bed early." She arched an eyebrow at him, her stomach dancing.

"Don't you tease about something like that."

"It would hardly be 'us' if I didn't."

"Hey, newlyweds. Get a room!" Harper's laughter carried from across the round pen. "Or come help find the mare."

"Newlyweds?" Gabe frowned in confusion.

"Any new couple. It's just stupid."

"I vote for the room," he said.

"I'm shocked. And a little flattered." She kissed him on the cheek, afraid his lips would entice her to linger.

"SHE'S REALLY BEAUTIFUL."

Rory stood beside Skylar on the middle rail of a section of six-foot pasture fence, staring at the five mustangs, including Pan, who was now safely contained. Mia stood on the ground beside Gabe and Finney one section to Rory's right, looking between rails. Cole, Harper, and Leif stood two sections to Rory's left. Pan the troublemaker grazed peacefully inside the fence with the others, swishing her tail at the giant, downy snowflakes that had started falling as the search team had brought her home. The mare gave no indication she'd just led half a dozen people on a two-hour chase through Paradise's lower pastures.

Mia lifted her head and let the flakes drift onto her cheeks. Their damp little kisses cooled her adrenaline-fueled flush from the chase, as well as the electric heat from the little circles Gabe massaged into her neck.

"I agree," he said. "She's an awfully pretty horse. You should have seen her running."

"The little siren," Mia said. "She's got the whole place under her spell now, and she knows it. I've changed my mind. She's not mean. She's just vain."

"I've always been a sucker for gorgeous, narcissistic women," Finney said.

"Well you found a doozy," Mia said. "But I have to admit. She does know you. Whether she wants to admit it or not, she has a thing for you, too. You did a wonderful job with her once we had her lassoed. Sorry it came to that."

Finney shrugged. "It was fun seeing you swing a rope."

"Fun?" Gabe repeated. "I've never seen anything so sexy in my life."

"Hush!" Mia cuffed him on the chest. "Small ears."

"Aw, I know what sexy means." Rory gave a perfect and appropriate ten-year-old's sneer of disgust. "I just can't believe Dr. Mia knows how to rope a horse."

"A running horse," Gabe clarified.

"Bah," said Mia. "If Joely had been there she wouldn't have missed even once, and she'd have had her in a fourth of the time I did. I never could beat her. She does rope tricks, too."

"I don't care. You were pretty frickin' awesome, Dr. Cowgirl."

"Can I see you rope sometime?" Rory asked.

"Sure. I'll teach you how. Or Skylar can. She's a good roper, too. Her grandpa Leif taught all of us."

"He did," Skylar agreed.

"How about me?" Gabe whispered. "Can I learn, too?"

"I have other things I'd like to show you how to do with a rope." She snuggled into his side, smiling secretly at the shocked stiffening in his body.

"Oh. My. G— You did not just put that thought in my head."

"Down boy. I'm not that kind of girl. A lariat is far too long for that sort of thing anyway."

With a suddenness that robbed her of breath, Gabe tugged her around a quarter turn and hauled her into his arms. Then he backed her against the fence and pressed his chest, his belly, and thighs to her, rolling hot sparks slowly, subtly down her body.

If no one spared more than passing attention they probably wouldn't see anything but an impending kiss, but still, Mia stole a furtive glance at the others, especially Rory. All eyes were on the horses. Then Gabe obliterated all thoughts of anyone else by rocking his pelvis forward and sending shockwaves to every nerve fiber. Hard and unmistakable, his arousal pressed against her. Heat filled her limbs, chills chased up her spine and spilled across her shoulders. Liquid rushed to her core.

"I've been fighting this all afternoon because of you," he whispered. "And you just lassoed and hog-tied every stitch of my self-control."

He pulled away, leaving her hot and cold but most of all bereft. He shifted and leaned sideways against the fence, facing away from the others. She stroked his cheek because she couldn't stand not touching him. She grinned because she should have been sorry to cause him discomfort—but she wasn't.

"I'm going to leave you here in the snow to cool off. Then I'm going to bring Rory back to the house to get ready for dinner. The sooner he eats," she lowered her voice further, "the sooner he's ready for bed."

He closed his eyes and shook his head. "You're tough on a guy, you know that?"

"I'll try to be nicer next time."

FOR RORY'S FIRST dinner, Grace, Raquel, and their mom had opted for a full-on traditional Sunday supper—a big beef roast with mounds of creamy mashed potatoes, thick gravy, carrots and peas. They plied the boy with fresh rolls and homemade raspberry jam. And for dessert they let him fill his own bowl with Belgian chocolate ice cream. He ate like a starving child, which delighted the latent grandmother in Bella and brought out the "this isn't going to happen like this every night" gene in Mia.

In one short afternoon, Rory had tightened his hold on her heart. Logic told her she hadn't faced anything difficult with him yet. He was still grieving, so he clung to Mia. She hadn't ticked him off yet, or enforced many rules, so he didn't yet look at her as a parental figure. Here in Wyoming she didn't have to get him ready for school or fight about classroom-appropriate slogans on T-shirts. When all that hit the fan, the novelty of imposed guardianship would likely wear off, and then where would she be?

The night went like clockwork after that. No disastrous phone calls came in. Nobody got sick. No dishes broke. No animals were harmed doing anything. Except for the rush of pleasure that washed over her every time she looked at Gabe, the whole atmosphere was mundane, calm, almost boring. And pretty wonderful.

Mia helped Rory unpack his suitcase into dresser drawers. Gabe helped him set up his computer so he could play for a while. But even with the lure of a popular game, he started yawning in front of the screen by seven thirty.

Gabe sat beside him at the desk in the new room, pointing out details of the game they were learning together. Mia stood to the side letting her astonishment mix with the low pulse of desire that hadn't diminished since their episode at the pasture fence. Gabe's warmth of demeanor awed her and made him irresistible. She'd always thought it a made-up trope that women were turned on by men who were good with children. She'd been wrong.

Vibrations that still hummed through her body left her with un-guardian-like wishes that Rory's long trip would conk him out sooner—much sooner—rather than later. She picked a book off one of the shelves and turned it over in her hands. *The Phantom Tollbooth*—a classic. Did modern-day kids, spoiled by the shiny and spectacular entertainment offered by video car races and realistic battles, read anymore? Of course they did. Harry Potter... What else? She cringed inwardly. She knew nothing about what a ten-year-old like Rory liked.

With a sigh she carried the book to where the two men sat and tucked it under her arm so she could rest her hands on Gabe's shoulders. Tentatively she kneaded through his sweatshirt, exploring his shoulders, spreading her fingers and sliding them down to find the taut muscle around his shoulder blades.

A groan of satisfaction floated to her and she smiled. Surprisingly, the little storm he'd started brewing in her by the pasture, he now calmed simply by existing beneath her fingertips. Her insides no longer felt like they'd been shot full of adrenaline. Her impatience disappeared. It was enough that he was here—for her and for Rory. Whatever came later would be sweet, sweet icing on the cake.

When Rory yawned and rubbed an eye, Mia took her cue. "Hey, newest Wyoming Man, I was thinking. My mom read out loud to me and my sisters our whole lives—almost until we left home. How would you like to start a chapter book while we're here?

He turned slightly in his chair, his look quizzical. "What chapter book?" She held up her choice and he frowned. "I've never heard of it."

"This one has been around a long time," she said. "It's a classic."

"That usually means boring."

"Oh, you couldn't be more wrong, champ," Gabe said. "Books don't get to be classics if they aren't totally awesome. I loved that book when I was a kid."

Rory yawned again and shrugged. "Okay."

"Where do you want to go to sleep tonight?" she asked. "Here or in my room?"

He contemplated the choices. "Are you going to sleep, too?"

"Not yet," she said. "But later. My room is right next to my mother's, and she goes to bed pretty early, so she'll be there if you need her. And Grace sleeps right next to this room. So there are lots of people if you get scared."

"I won't get scared." His voice didn't carry a lot of punch, but he was sincere.

"That's really good. Because there's nothing to be scared of. You know, my daddy built this house just the way he and my mom wanted it. So it's strong and safe. But, still, sometimes we need something at night. And anyone here can help you anytime."

"I want to stay in your room."

"Come on, then." She smiled. "I think it's time to tuck you in and start a book."

"Can I listen, too?" Gabe asked.

"If the bed is big enough," Rory replied, and shrugged again.

The steam in Gabriel's look made Mia's mouth go dry.

"Well, let's go and check it out right now." His eyes never left hers. "I'm pretty interested in knowing that myself."

"He made it through about ninety-five percent of the chapter," Gabe said. "Pretty good considering how often his eyes closed."

Mia pulled the sheet and blanket over Rory's gently curled form, and stroked the thick, creamy fur of Jack, who'd found his little master and now nestled into the curve of his body, purring like a feline lawnmower.

Warmth from Gabe's hand on her back spread down her spine. She straightened, and the sense of domesticity, the image of this man as a husband and a father, flashed so strongly through her mind it scared her. She pushed away the thought, but not before the question popped out.

"You really wouldn't want one of these of your own?" She asked. His hand stilled momentarily. "Sorry. I don't know where that came from."

The circles started up again. "He's a perfect example of why."

"I know. So many like him who need help." She understood Gabe's conviction intellectually, but sadness welled up nonetheless. The urge to picture her own child in a bed like this was hard to ignore. "Well, I'm glad he's here," she said. "I feel like maybe this will be good for him—to know a place like Wyoming exists."

She left a lamp on for him and kissed his forehead.

She led the way out of the room, and the moment they were in the hallway and she'd closed the door halfway, Gabe whirled her into his arms and placed his forehead against hers.

"It's good for him to have you in his life. You're going to get him through this sad, hard time. He thinks the world of you."

"What happens, though, the first time I have to say no, or have to get after him?"

"That's too far in the future right now. One day at a time."

Standing there in his arms, the very place she'd been anticipating for the past two hours, a wave of melancholy swept unexpectedly over her. Reality, in the form of the child sleeping behind the door next to her, dampened all the excitement she'd felt just moments before.

"What is this?" she asked.

"What is what?"

"This thing we're doing? We're a walking, talking, kissing cliché, Gabe. Like two kids meeting at summer camp and having a fling. All I wanted five minutes ago was for the kid to go to sleep so I could be alone with you."

"You don't want that anymore?" He raised his head and placed a forefinger beneath her chin.

"Now all I can think about is that we have to leave camp too soon and go back to reality."

"I don't know. This has been feeling very real to me lately. Would you like me to tell you all the ways you've changed my life in three weeks? I didn't think I had a tragic backstory that left me damaged. You made me see the things I've never faced. You're bringing back my inner clown—that part of me that actually forgot to find funny things in the world."

"I hate clowns," she said dully.

He laughed. "Well that's fairly unbelievable, since you understand them so well. At least this one."

"How can you possibly say I understand you? It's been three weeks." She tried to avoid his eyes, but he lifted her chin and gave her no choice but to stare into them. They mesmerized, like looking into the numbing depths of rich, aged whisky.

"It's really been over two months. Tell me you didn't think about me while you were in New York after we butt heads over your sister's care. I thought about you so often you wound up in dreams."

"I did? Like, nightmares?" She smiled.

"No." He drew out the word. "Nice dreams. Unlike you, who hated me, I never felt that way about you."

"Hey! I never hated you."

"Aha! I got you to admit it. You were in deep annoyance with me and I with you, but I spent a lot of time trying to figure out how to thaw your feelings. I knew this warm person you really are existed behind the façade. You wouldn't have fought so hard for your mother and sister if there hadn't been. I knew you were focused, busy, angry, and worried."

"And I didn't know you were Mr. Psychology."

"I'm not. Sweetheart, I just try and understand people. We might all have different stories, but we're all in the same boat, and we all have wounds."

"Yours is Jibril."

"Maybe."

"What's mine?"

"Your father. Your family."

"I love my family!"

"You do. But you also think they have some kind of expectation of you. You need to change your focus. It's you who has the high expectations. Of yourself. But what's amazing is that when I've seen you stop being so hard on yourself and just enjoy, as well as use your God-given gifts, you are unstoppable. And I'm falling in love with the unstoppable Mia Crockett. You know that's the difference between Amelia and Mia right? Amelia wants it. Mia gets it."

"That's a pun, right?"

"See? Mia *understands* it."

A welling of emotion clogged her throat and burned at her eyes. He saw this in her? She sure didn't. To her

Mia was the weaker persona. If Mia understood anything it was that she had to stay strong or fail. Amelia was the strong, sure, take-no-prisoners success.

"Come on." He took her hand and led her down the hall.

She stopped him on the landing halfway down the stairs. "We both know what's coming now, right? We both expect this?"

"What?" He looked at her warily.

"It's been a while, since I…" Discomfiture rang in her ears like bad static. "Well, you need to know that. But I do remember enough to recognize what you were telling me outside earlier."

"Look. You turn me on, Mia Crockett. Beyond that I'm not going to *tell* you anything. We do things together. Especially when it comes to sex. And don't shy away from saying it out loud. You're a doctor. I work with foul-mouthed vets. We don't need to hint around like middle schoolers."

She blushed at the gentle admonishment.

"You're right. Having a child around is suddenly turning me into one. That or there are just too many people in this house."

"I'll agree with that. One of them is sleeping on the only bed that's big enough." He nuzzled her neck and gave a quick nibble to her earlobe.

She sputtered out a laugh and buried her face in his shoulder, letting shivers and goose bumps battle it out across her skin.

"We can't keep doing this here," she said quietly. "The rest of the people aren't sleeping, and that's problematic in other ways."

He straightened. "Listen to me, and believe me. I have no expectations. Not of you. Not of us. Not for tonight. I'm a big boy, and I can control my urges if not my body. And my body is not your problem."

"What if I want it to be?"

She didn't honestly know if she wanted it to be. Two hours earlier she'd told herself she wanted nothing more than to make love to him. Then she'd panicked. But once again Gabe had removed all the pressure she'd let build.

"Oh, sweetheart, then I think we need to find a place with fewer people and have a little talk."

Chapter Twenty-One

GABE FOUND PARADISE totally transformed in the snow. And along with it, so was Mia.

Somewhere between capturing Pan and putting Rory to bed, snow had crept up on Paradise Ranch and fallen in such thick, fleecy luxury that it left no speck of autumnal brown visible. In the moonlight, the world shimmered under a million flakes of diamond dust.

Mia skipped through the unblemished expanse of white in front of the barn, creating serpentine paths, her red cowboy boots flashing against the pristine canvas. Stopping, stooping, and shoveling huge armfuls of snow from the ground so she could toss it in the air, she couldn't have looked more different from the woman who'd stood beside Rory's sleeping form than she did. Gabe shook his head, marveling at the change, hoping it wasn't some kind of manic reaction.

But she looked too relieved and relaxed to be suffering from a breakdown. She stopped at the edge of an unblemished expanse of snow.

"Let's fill this with snow angels," she said.

"We're supposed to be checking on the horses."

"We will definitely check on the horses."

She took his hand and stepped carefully into the white. Without a plan or instruction, she fell backward and pulled him along. Immediately she fanned her arms and legs. Along with the snow had come a fifteen-degree drop in temperature, but Mia didn't seem to care about twenty-degrees of cold.

Laughing, Cole swished out his own angel. He wore an old pair of Cole's boots, and a borrowed hat and mittens for which he was grateful. Harper had agreed to watch and listen for Rory while they checked the mustangs. He could come up with nothing to dissuade Mia from falling into angel and after angel.

"I think you've got issues," he said when he'd added his fifth to the array.

"I'm working them all out." She laughed.

He stood and stalked to where she was preparing to make her seventh angel. The instant she fell backward, he pitched forward and landed atop her.

"Hey! You can't be lewd with angels!"

"I think I'm proving right this moment that I sure can be."

He grasped her pink-and-purple stocking cap—the one that clashed with her red boots, not to mention her blue-and-teal winter jacket—and held it tightly to her head as he pressed a hard kiss to her lips. Her long, thick hair, wet from the snow, hung below the edge of the hat, and the beautiful, high cheekbones of her face drew his lips to her skin.

"You're distracting me."

"Good," he replied. "A dozen angels is plenty."

"No, you can't have too many angels."

She grabbed a fistful of snow and shook it over his head. Most of it slid down his collar in an icy race. He bellowed in surprise.

"Cheat!" he cried.

"Guilty as charged."

Then they were rolling through the white as Mia tried to grab more snow and smash it into his neck, his jacket front, and even his face. He fought off her attacks even though she was lithe and quick and, finally, barely able to breathe from laughing, he pinned her on her back a last time, cuffed her hands together with one of his, and held them above her head. She twisted her lower body, laughing as hard as he was, but he straddled her and ground his pelvis tightly against her.

"Surrender," he said.

She squirmed beneath him and bucked a couple of times to try and dislodge him. Fire raced through his belly, and his body swiftly betrayed him. When she stopped struggling she groaned beneath him and reached up to pull his head to hers.

"I thought cold had the opposite effect on a man," she said, and didn't wait for a reply before invading his mouth with her hot, searching tongue.

He wanted to laugh and let it blow away the pulsing desire but the sound came out a long, hard moan instead, which she captured in her kiss and turned into deep, thrusting passion. He grew harder, and she pushed her hips up to meet the long, captive length of him.

"I think I just made your body my problem," she said.

"Lord above, will you quit saying those things?" He cradled her head between his gloved hands and kissed away snowflakes as they landed on her cheeks and long, dark eyelashes. "You think you're funny, but this is deadly serious."

"Oh, really? Deadly?"

"Yes. We will be found frozen together in a very compromising position come morning if you don't behave."

He kissed the corners of her eyes and sucked her top lip when a flake glided onto its perfect curve.

"Why do I have to behave if you don't?"

"Because I'm on top."

Before she could sputter her protest, he kissed her fully, a little carelessly, sloppily even, for long minutes while the snow covered his back and seeped into his collar and under the wrists of his gloves. The knees of his jeans soaked up the snow, and he was vaguely aware of the cold, but he didn't stop. She arched into him, reaching to the kiss then pulling back, searching for a deeper fit with a tilt of her head and a tug of her hands to bring him closer. He stopped trying to figure out where goose bumps from the cold ended and those from the heat of their mouths began.

Finally he slid his lips from hers, but she continued kissing his neck.

"The barn." He caught his breath and lost it again as desire flared, harder and stronger. "It's a little warmer."

"It's a misrepresentation that a barn is a good place for this," she said. "Shavings and manure balls—"

He put a finger over her lips. "Stop. I believe you. Can you find us a *usable* warm place?"

"I can."

Her quick answer surprised him, and he laughed. "In that case, you've won a temporary release." He pushed himself up and off of her, got to his feet and stood, one leg on either side of her hips. She grabbed the hand he reached out for her and popped up before him. "Show me the heat," he said, wishing he was still on the ground where things had been a lot more comfortable.

"Heat?" She grinned. "I think you requested warm. As in, warmer than out here. We'll have to create the actual heat ourselves." She took his hand. "Follow me."

THE LITTLE CABIN stood across the work yard from the barn, hunkering in place like an old man among his younger, stronger children.

"This was the original cabin my great-grandfather Eli built in 1916," Mia said. "He lived in it as a bachelor for a while, then married my great-grandmother Brigitta, and their only son Sebastian was born here. After that he built a bigger house, which was lost in a fire before my father was born. Sebastian married Grandma Sadie."

"Your Sadie? The love of my life?"

"One and the same. She's seen a lot on this place. Somehow this little cabin has survived storm and pestilence and time. Now it's an office, but not an official one. Nothing too important is kept here—there's a computer and a lot of breeding and heredity info on the cattle. At least that's what it used to be. And, if nothing's changed…"

She ran her fingers along the bottom log next to the door and straightened with a key. Seconds later she swung the heavy oak door open. Ancient door, modern lock. He liked it.

Mia walked unhesitatingly through the blackness and, after a gentle click, warm, yellow light from a desk lamp made out of horseshoes transformed the deep darkness into soft shadows. The room was smaller than Rory's bedroom at the house, maybe nine by ten, and it was dominated by the large, wooden desk. A green couch and a blue overstuffed chair sat on a thick, multicolored braid rug, which covered a worn wood floor rubbed to a rich patina.

The walls were unfinished wood logs also aged to glossy nutmeg.

"Nice," Gabe said.

"It's the family's attempt at historical appreciation. Otherwise, the Crockett patriarchs have been pretty progressive as a whole. My dad was probably the most staunchly traditional—it was kind of his way or no way. Good thing his way was effective—until the end of his life when the finances got away from him. Harper and Cole took on a huge rescue project with this place."

"They seem happy, though."

"I think they are," she said. "Cole grew up ranching, too, as you know. And Harper has found the freedom to not only be on the land she loves, but spread her artistic wings. It wasn't what any of us planned, but sometimes fate is funny. I'm looking forward to their wedding and lots of good times for them."

"And what about you?" He wrapped his arms around her and pulled her close. "Where's the land you love?"

"Right this moment it's this floor in this cabin."

It wasn't an answer to his question. He thought about pushing it and forcing her to face the future right then and there. Where *did* she want to stay? Put down her roots? But that desire lasted only fleeting seconds. She pulled down the zipper of his jacket, tossed her gloves on the chair, and snaked her arms around his torso, rising onto her toes to plant a kiss on his lips.

"Yup," she said against his mouth. "Right here."

"Okay," he replied. "Good choice."

He found her jacket zipper between them as they kissed, and divested her of its bulk. She pushed and pulled his off as well. Next came their hats, and Gabe toed off his boots, all while they laughed and tried not to break the kiss. Silly, fun, slightly immature stuff.

"There's a fireplace in here," she whispered, sucking on his bottom lip.

"It still works?"

"It does."

"Can we build a fire without stopping?" He sucked her tongue into his mouth, briefly but hard enough to make her laugh.

"If you kept up that suction we probably could."

He kissed her cold nose and forehead and stepped away. "Let's build one. Why start being logical now? Nobody will care?"

"They may or may not notice over the next few days. They use this place a lot more in the spring and summer."

She didn't make setting a fire easy. He was proud of his camping skills, but he'd never had to contend with soft hands on his back every time he bent over, and eagerly stolen kisses every time he straightened.

"Are you trying to tell me something?" he asked, when he had the first match ready to strike, and she wrapped her arms around him from behind.

"I don't want you to forget I'm here."

He almost choked on the laughter that bubbled up within him. "I could prove to you in several different ways that it would be impossible to forget you're here."

"Good."

"Snow definitely has an interesting effect on you." He squatted, and she released him, sitting beside his leg as he lit the tinder beneath the logs.

"It's not the snow," she said.

"Is that right?"

Together they watched the fire catch and eat up the paper and smaller branches that would light the larger fuel logs. Mia stretched her long legs toward the fireplace and leaned sideways against him, running her hand along his thigh, kneading through the wet denim to the muscle that strained to hold him in his squat. She skimmed the angle over his knee and shimmied down the front of his shin.

"Nice legs," she said.

"Yeah?" He shuddered in a breath. "Takes a pair to know a pair."

She blushed prettily. "That was a well done compliment, I have to admit. C'mon. Help me pull these boots off. I probably shouldn't have worn the good ones in the snow like that. On the other hand, looks like they're lucky once again."

"Oh, you think you're going to get lucky, huh?"

"I hope so. I know you are."

He snorted. "That was pretty well done yourself."

He sat flat on the floor facing her and took one of her feet in his hands. It took a solid tug to remove the red boot. The second one was even tighter. When they'd been set aside she wriggled her toes into his hands. "Ahhhh," she moaned. "Your hands are so nice and warm."

"I think it's your toes that are so very cold," he said.

He kneaded through her wool socks until she closed her eyes and leaned back on her elbows. "Okay, every single thing I've ever said you were good at? Forget them. You are a born masseur."

"Sure, whatever you say."

He swung her feet off his lap and pushed her all the way back until she lay stretched out beside the hearth. He picked up her hand and kneaded it as he had her foot. He moved to the other hand, and this time worked his way slowly up her arm, kneading turning to caressing and caressing to exploring the soft lines of her shoulder, her neck, and down the center of her chest. He stopped at her navel and pressed in gently with his palms.

"Oh, jiminy Christmas," she whispered. "That fire must be roaring—it's warmed up plenty in here."

"It's not the fire," he whispered back.

It took him less time than it should have, if he'd wanted to continue showing off his slow and sensual side, to pop the snap of her jeans, rasp down the zipper, and expose the soft skin of her stomach. She moaned before he'd even touched her, and when he bent forward to kiss the sweet indentation of her belly button, a strangled sound part laugh and part repeat of the moan lanced straight into his groin and made his jeans uncomfortably tight as well as wet from the snow.

"The floor is a little hard for this," he said.

"Is it?" She opened her eyes to smile.

"It is."

He kissed her skin again and then kissed each breast through her sweater. Her eyes closed and she arched upward ever so slightly. When he moved off of her, she whimpered.

"Patience," he said, and scooped her into his arms. "This is a nice, big sofa. I think it'll do."

"Smart man."

He set her on the cushions but she swung up and stood before him, fingers grasping for his belt, freeing it, unsnapping his fly, and sliding the zipper down so it matched hers. He breathed a sigh of first relief, and she smiled, stroking him through the fabric.

"That's not going to work." He choked on the words.

"Oh?"

"Things are going to have to come off, or the body *is* going to be your problem."

"Then by all means things are coming off."

Slow and careful ended right there. He shucked off her sweater first, and she grasped the hem of his sweatshirt to yank it carelessly up and over his head. He reached for her open waistband, but she got to him first. Delving fingers first into the top of his jeans, she pushed down and peeled them off of him as easily as a banana skin. He stepped out of them, and she made to toss them out of the way.

"Whoa, don't let them get too far," he said. "There's an important piece of equipment in the pocket."

She giggled and stroked him again, this time with only the loose cotton of his boxers between his hot skin and her long, slender, clever fingers. "This is the piece of equipment I'm interested in."

"Yeah, well, you'd better be careful with that. I'm not guaranteeing it will function the way you want it to if you keep working with it that way."

He closed his eyes as waves of pleasure flowed from her hands to his body.

"Oh, it'll function exactly the way it's supposed to. I'll see to that."

He gained control back long enough to see her slick her jeans down and off her legs. He'd never seen anything cuter, hotter, and downright sexier than the picture of her in her plunging bra, purple panties and thick wool socks. Her hair fell over his hands as he slipped one bra strap and then the other down her arms, and it curtained his face as he bent to kiss the swell of her breasts while she arched over him, pulling his head closer.

The bra was the next to go, his boxers after that, and finally the only thing each wore was socks.

"How are your toes doing?" he asked.

"Tingling, like everything else on my body."

"You're warm enough?"

"Want me to take my socks off?" She giggled again.

"If you do, you'll be completely naked," he warned.

"I'll do it if you will."

They fell onto the couch seconds later, sockless and naked and exploring with hands that couldn't touch enough skin with enough speed. He swore she had extra fingers as the sensation built all over his body. She stroked his back, kissed his face and neck. She kneaded his glutes and his forearms and his shoulders, and he had no idea how she got to all the places so quickly.

He lay beneath her, letting her skin slide over his, trying to match her touch but certain the soft skin of her breasts, the feathering of her hair against his chest, and the soft heat between her legs that teased his thigh as she moved against him brought him far more pleasure than he could ever give her.

And then she stopped. She pushed herself up until she could look him in the eyes. A long moment later, without warning, she lowered her head and claimed his mouth in a dizzying, delving kiss. Heat and dangerous sparks headed southward, and a wave of desire made him impossibly harder than he'd been. She suckled his lip, tugged on it with gentle teeth and kissed him as intimately as making love.

And then she left him again, sitting up, smiling like a wild-haired wood sprite and running her hands up his chest, spreading her fingers through his chest hair and licking her lips unconsciously as she sighed. Reaching behind her, she found his erection and closed around it with a velvet touch. He arched in pleasure and let every muscle in his body share the sensation as she began a long, slow stroke like a master musician would make love to a cherished violin with his bow.

The pleasure lasted longer than he could ever remember it lasting until a surge of fiery need warned him he'd nearly waited too long. He sat up to meet her and pulled her hand desperately from him before he stood and took her with him. She wrapped her legs around his hips, only releasing him when he laid her on the sofa and stretched out over her.

"My turn," he said.

MIA SANK INTO euphoria as Gabe's weight pressed her into the cushions. He didn't need to do anything to make her more ready than she was, but as much as her body sang with every touch and begged for him to be with her, inside her, she didn't rush.

He was beautiful—his body fit against her without being hard, his chest was perfectly sprinkled with dark hair, his hands were strong without being harsh. His lips moved down her body, and she let herself fly into shivers and chills and heat as he suckled first one breast, then the other, then moved to her neck, her ear, her lips.

He moved down again, to her ticklish stomach and then to the edge of the curls at the juncture of her thighs. He lingered there, finding sensitive skin to play on and drive her longing through the roof. She dug into his hair, praying he'd wait but panting for him to search just a little lower.

When his tongue found the spot, she cried out in relief and melted into that most intimate swirling kiss two people could share. But it wasn't what she wanted.

"Gabe. Gabe, stop."

She tugged and bucked until he pulled away, kissed her inner thigh, and came back up to her. He grinned. "Lady, why are you bothering me?"

"I don't want it like that the first time. Please? I want all of you." She bit her lip and tried not to blush even though she could feel her face heating. "I want you to come inside and play."

His laughter should have killed the mood, but it didn't. It rolled hot and sexy across her cheeks and made him shake as he twisted to grab his jeans from the floor. Desire sluiced through her anew.

"What did I tell you?" He held up the foil packet.

"Brilliant man. Get dressed and come on over to my place."

"You were right," he said. "It's not the snow."

Silliness vanished when he came to her at last. It might have been a long time, but it didn't matter. He entered her and moved so sweetly, so easily that she felt the buildup immediately. It was just how she wanted it, close, slow, rocking, timeless. Stroke after stroke they rose together, and when Gabe made small warning moans, she answered.

"Yes," he whispered. "Mia, come with me. It's time."

With one aching, erotic blast they hit the peak of hot pleasure and just kept on going, shattering together far above their bodies, coupled in the dark, warm cabin.

The descent was slow and peaceful. Mia tried to wipe the tears of pleasure from her eyes before Gabe saw them, but he hooted at her gently.

"From laughter to tears. Do I have talent or what?"

"Told you you'd get lucky." She smeared the tears away with a palm and snuggled sideways on the sofa with him.

"And you were absolutely right. I doubt you were that lucky yourself."

"You were lucky, but I won the night. Sorry."

He kissed her and grabbed a woolen blanket from the back of the sofa. Deftly he managed to cover them and snuggle in more deeply.

"We can't stay long," she said. "They will eventually come looking for us."

"I have a plan," he said. "We'll warm up, we'll go back, we'll move Rory. I'll sneak into your bed, and then I'll leave before anyone finds us in the morning."

She laughed. "You've thought about it far more than I have. We'll go with your plan. Just don't let me fall asleep."

"Trust me. We aren't going to sleep."

Chapter Twenty-Two

SHE SLEPT.

Until insistent pounding pulled her out of her dreamless haven. "Mia! Mia, get up!"

She lifted her head groggily and looked around her room. "Harper?"

Fireplace, cabin, moving Rory, Gabe...awareness rolled each memory up and out and back into its proper place, and she flipped over with a start embarrassed, that her sister had found them together.

Gabe was gone. She gasped and sat up. "What's wrong, Harpo?" she called.

The door burst open then, and Rory launched himself into the room, tears streaming down his cheeks. "He's gone. Dr. Mia, Jack's gone."

"Gone?" She swung her legs out of bed, grateful she'd put her nightgown back on. "Calm down, sweetie. What do you mean?"

"He's not in the house."

"I'm sure he's here somewhere." Her heart beat up into her throat despite her words. She caught Harper's eyes, and her sister shrugged and shook her head. "He's probably nervous and hiding in a new place."

Jack didn't get nervous. He was the most unfazed-able cat she'd ever known.

"You have to come. He's gone." Rory was sobbing now.

"Hey, what's all this?"

Gabe stood in the doorway like a guardian angel come to life. He was dressed for work, in black dress pants, a striped blue, button-down shirt, and a sharp gray sport coat. In spite of the crisis, Mia's mouth went dry, and memories of the night before threatened to undo her emotions. And where, she wondered out of the blue, had he gotten fresh clothing?

"Well, hello there." Harper, too, forgot the immediate calamity and swept a knowing gaze between Gabe and Mia. "Didn't know you were still here."

"Yup." He answered with his big smile and not a shred of discomfiture. As always, his calm bolstered hers. "We talked until too late to drive home in the snow, so I bunked over. Would have invited you to the slumber party, but you all were asleep."

Slumber party. She almost let her laughter escape. The best one she'd ever had; that was for sure. She wanted him to bunk over every night now, and nobody else, ever, was going to be invited.

"Mmm hmm." Harper didn't hide her smile. "Those horses must have needed a *lot* of help last night."

"They did," he said. "We needed to make sure there were no ill-effects from the day."

"I'm sure they were extremely well tended." Harper sent Mia a smug, happy smile.

"Now, what's this about Jack?" Gabe asked.

Rory's sobs brought them all back to attention. "We've looked everywhere."

"All right." Gabe strode into the room and squatted next to the boy. "Let's let Mia get dressed. We'll go over all the evidence. He was here last night when we got back from the barn, so I'm sure if he's missing he isn't far away. Come on."

He took Rory's hand and led him to the hall. The boy gave a sniff and looked over his shoulder once at Mia. "I'll be right there," she said. "How about I look everywhere up here again?"

He nodded.

"Crap," she said to Harper, when the pair had disappeared. "That cat is his anchor. He has to be okay."

"We'll find him."

"I'm sorry I overslept."

"It's only a little after eight. You're fine."

"But you've had to watch Rory."

"That's what family is for. Mia, you don't have to be strong every second. You don't have to get it all right all the time—we can help. We want to help. And look at you—you're letting Gabriel in, too. I'm so happy. He's such a wonderful guy. He's good for you."

The old familiar prickling of resentment sprouted in Mia's chest. Her family with their expectations and their assessments of her life...and then she stopped short. Harper hadn't told her what to do, or asked her to do anything, or criticized. Why did she always hear criticism in other peoples' words? Her sister was right. Gabriel was very good for her. And the family was slowly coming together—coalescing back into a cohesive whole, where they'd once been fractured.

She sagged back onto the bed. "I like him. It's too soon, but I do. I'm loath to leave in eight days."

The thought blazed through her brain like pain. Eight days? What had she been thinking last night? She wasn't a casual sex kind of woman. She'd never been. It was supposed to mean something—something permanent, something committed.

"You know," Harper said thoughtfully. "It wouldn't be impossible for you to stay. This is a very big house. A very big ranch. And part of it is yours."

Mia scrubbed her face with her fingers, trying to wipe the fog of sleep fully from her eyes and her brain.

"I know. But it's impossible. I've made commitments in New York. I love my job."

The thought of going back to her job sent ribbons of steel jamming down her spine. She could almost feel the tension of the OR reaching its fingers out for her. Intense. Important.

Harper only smiled. "Get dressed. Let's find Rory's cat."

JACK WAS NOWHERE in the house. Gabe called his office and postponed two meetings, and after his help with fifteen minutes of concentrated search efforts, Jack's disappearance was confirmed. Rory was inconsolable. At the height of his distress over the cat's very probable escape to the outdoors, the front doorbell rang. Mia answered it, hoping maybe Leif or Bjorn had found Jack, and was shocked when Hannah, the social worker who'd accompanied Rory, smiled in greeting.

"Hi, there!" she said in a voice a chipper as a spring robin's. "How's it going this morning?"

She looked past Mia's shoulders as Rory shuffled into the living room wearing his snow boots, pulling on his jacket and weeping for the fifth time that morning—something that spoke volumes about his distress since he was normally such a stoic kid.

"I'm going," he said, his nose stuffed, his voice full of tears.

"Goodness, is everything all right, Rory?" Hannah asked.

"No."

Of course this is the scene she walked in on. Mia sighed in frustration. "It looks like Jack escaped out one of the doors this morning. Rory and Gabe are going to look for him."

"Gabe?"

"Mia's boyfriend," he said miserably.

The cheerful robin disappeared. Hannah took in Rory's unhappy demeanor with obvious skepticism, and then Gabe poked his head into the room.

"Hello," he said. "Sorry to run—have an escapee to hunt down. Come on, cat whisperer. I have your hat. Out the back door."

Rory gazed at the two women, looking far too much like a whipped puppy.

"Mia? Is everything all right?"

"Oh, Hannah, come in. Take your coat off. It's been great. We had a wonderful night last night—playing computer, reading books. This just looks bad."

"Should we go with them?"

"We can if you like. Or I can show you the house and introduce you to my family."

"You trust Rory with this...boyfriend?"

Again the urge to rail at stupid questions from people who weren't listening almost overwhelmed her. The retort was on her tongue: *I wouldn't send him with Gabe if I didn't trust him.* She pulled herself together instead, drawing calm from the warmth of her house, the knowledge that her mother was just beyond the door, her sister had her back. And—Hannah was just doing her job.

"You saw how good he is with Rory," she said. "Yeah, he'll take good care of him."

She knew it as well as she knew he'd take good care of her. If she let him.

Hannah smiled. "Okay. If they don't come back soon—we'll go after them."

Her slightly teasing tone surprised Mia. No backlash. No more skepticism. Just belief that Mia cared, not just on a professional level, but a personal one.

Had Mia really always expected people to question her? Had she been equally suspicious of her colleagues? Her head hurt as if someone had swung with a baseball bat and connected. Such a simple lesson. Dr. Thomas had been right.

HANNAH MARVELED AT the house, as everyone did when they saw it for the first time. With its vaulted cathedral ceiling in the living room, the enormous dining table built by Sebastian Crockett to fit all his family at once, the nine bedrooms, five bathrooms, and bright welcoming pine everywhere, it really was a dream home.

And it was made all the more charming by Mia's mother and grandmother, who sang Rory's praises, without making it look like they were trying, and plied Hannah with cinnamon rolls and coffee while they waited. It was all rather silly, Mia thought, worrying about Hannah's reaction. She wasn't going to take Rory back with her unless she saw evidence of totally inappropriate care and facilities. But what she would take back were stories and impressions. Brooke, Samantha, everyone who knew her would hear. About a crying Rory and a lost cat.

The sound of the door in the back hallway interrupted Hannah's description of her job back in New York. There was no waiting before the clomp of boots resounded, growing louder as they neared the kitchen. Rory burst in, his arms filled with buff-colored cat. Mia cheered and jumped from her chair, much more crazily relieved than she'd ever imagined being.

"Now you saved him *and* Gabe saved him. He was in the barn making friends with the barn cats."

"I'm so happy he's safe. Silly boy. He knew where to find some kitty friends."

Gabe appeared in his stocking feet and smiled at the group. "He made us work for it, but we tracked him."

"Like hunting party scouts," Rory said, and handed the cat to Mia. "We were quiet and careful and we followed his tracks."

"He actually left tracks?" She looked to Gabe.

"He kind of did. A lot of hopping and swishing through the snow, but it was unusual enough that we thought it was him. He made quite a trek. And made good time."

Rory turned then and threw himself at Gabe, hugging him. "Thank you for saving Jack."

"Well you're welcome. But you saved him, too. And you said thank you. So we'll just say we make a great detective team."

He held out his hand and Rory slapped him a loud high five. Now *that*, Mia thought, would make a great story for back in New York.

IT PRETTY MUCH amazed Mia that Rory followed her and Raquel, without protest or apparent distressing memories, down the hospital corridor on their way to see Joely. They'd planned a trip into Wolf Paw Pass for afterward, to see the town, have ice cream at Ina's Ice Cream Emporium, which did a brisk business even in the winter, and visit the pet store where they were going to get a new masculine collar and a nametag for Jack. "To tell him from the barn cats," according to Rory. That all was worth a trip to meet Dr. Mia's other sister, he'd said, because then he'd only have one left. The one in Denver named Kelly.

When Mia asked him outright if going to the hospital would make him sadder about his mom he shook his head. "Do I have to wear a mask?" he asked.

"No. Not at all."

"Then she's not like my mom. She was in a kind of dark room that was really quiet and we couldn't bring in any germs because of her bad infection."

The nurses and the social workers back in New York had pegged him perfectly—when he wasn't being a normal ten-year-old, he was scarily perceptive.

Joely was in fairly good spirits this visit. Mia worried about her—she'd lost more than the use of a leg in the accident, she'd lost a lot of hope, too. She smiled and conversed by rote most of the time. She didn't push herself in physical therapy and didn't ever ask about coming home. Because of that, her progress was slow and very uneven. In nine weeks, going from intensive care, to a medical surgical floor, to now making plans for moving her to a rehab care facility, she'd suffered bouts of depression, a case of pneumonia, three surgeries, and no real improvement in her crushed leg. If anyone tried to talk to her about the scar on her cheek and chin from the accident, she nearly curled up in a ball.

Mia hated to miss a day visiting, although she was never sure it helped her sister.

Today, however, Joely smiled when Rory entered the room between Mia and Raquel, and she answered all his intrusive questions about her accident without a flinch. Mia wanted to hug the daylights out of her. Her family was going so far above and beyond for this child—she was still trying to wrap her mind around it. Because of them, Hannah had flown off happy with Rory's new arrangements saying only that she looked forward to seeing them when they got back to New York.

Rory was absorbed in showing Joely a game on Raquel's cell phone when a white-coated figure appeared at the door and rapped softly. "Am I intruding?" Perry Landon stepped into the room.

"Hi, Perry!" she said. "It's been a while since I've been here when you're making rounds. How have you been? How's our sis doing? Behaving herself?"

"Mia." His greeting was warm, and the corners of his eyes crinkled behind his glasses. Geeky and yet quite handsome. "I'm so glad to see you." Then his gaze slid slowly across the room. "And Raquel. It's really good to see you, too."

If she hadn't been used to having everyone goof up the triplets' identities or stammer to try and figure out which one was which, Mia might not have studied Perry the way she did and certainly wouldn't have seen the very faint shuffle of nervousness in his stance or the tic of uncertainty in his features. But he didn't even hesitate when saying Raquel's name—something infinitely more impressive because she was there alone with no other sib to compare her to.

He could tell them apart.

Or at least tell Raquel from the others.

"Hi, doc," she said cheerily, and Mia studied her reaction.

Raquel smiled the way she always did—with an air of casual confidence. She wouldn't notice fidgeting or nuanced changes in a human. If Perry had been a ledger or a business detail, she'd have been on him like a bee to a rose had there been anything different. Or if he'd been a baseball stat or an opponent on the soccer field, she'd have studied him like an ACT test. But he was a normal person, a nice guy, and it didn't dawn on Rocky Raquel to look for more than friendship.

Perry shuffled one more time back in Mia's direction, although nobody else would have identified it as a shuffle. "You asked about Miss Joely here. She's doing great. We all wish there were faster progress in that leg, but we haven't given up. The nerves are still healing. Meanwhile, I've come with some news. We've got a spot in the rehab facility for you, Joely. A month there and you should be well on your way to getting home. In fact, how would like to go home for your family's postponed Thanksgiving?"

Neither Mia nor Raquel gave her any chance to react. They pounced on the announcement like kids on birthday presents.

"Jo-Jo, that's fantastic!" Raquel jumped to hug her.

"I think it'll be so good, for you and for us," Mia added. "And for Mom, to see you getting better. She's so worried."

"I…would love that." Joely took in the hugs and the congratulations, but she was far less excited than her sisters.

"I promise you're ready for the visit," Perry said. "But you'll get tired. We'll work on some occupational therapy that'll prepare you for getting around in the car and at home. Then, you can go right to the new facility after that and that's where the real work will start."

"I haven't been doing real work?" Joely joked.

"Prep work," he winked. "For the hard core."

"Great. Looking forward to it."

Rory listened to the exchange carefully and then, surprisingly, picked up Joely's hand. "You'll get to meet Jack," he said.

That simple promise brought the first true smile to Joely's face since being told she could go home. "You know what? I think I'm most excited about that."

Raquel caught Mia's eye and gave a thumbs-up. Mia understood. Whatever brought light to Joely's eyes was a great thing.

"Mia?" Perry turned to her while Rory went back to the game with Joely. "I actually did come up here for another reason. I asked the desk to page me if you showed up to visit. I'd like to ask for a date."

"Excuse me?" she exclaimed.

Everyone's head popped up. Perry laughed, an easygoing chuckle that diffused Mia's confusion. "Sorry," he said. "I couldn't resist. I just wondered if you'd come and have coffee with me right now for just a few minutes. I'd like to talk to you about a couple of things."

"Woo hoo." Raquel raised her brows at both of them.

Perry's grin turned self-conscious, but he mostly ignored her. "Maybe your young charge could stay here, and I'll have you back in half an hour."

"Would you mind, watching Rory?" Mia asked.

"Nah, we'll have a blast," Raquel said.

Mia nodded, curious now about what this could possibly mean. "Okay, then. You've got a date."

He nodded, pleased. "Excellent. Ladies, we'll be back shortly.

SHE SAT ACROSS from Perry in the cafeteria restaurant that served all buildings and sections of the VA campus. It was a modern, trendy place with California kitchen organic food and a decent grill. She sipped her latte and waited for him to pour two packets of sugar into his black coffee.

"I'm sure this seems pretty odd," he said.

"No. Two colleagues meeting for coffee." She smiled. "Happens all the time." He cocked a brow and she laughed. "Okay, yeah. Unexpected. Not unpleasant."

"I have two reasons for asking you to meet with me. The first concerns you. The second, your sister."

Her nape hair prickled in a first mild note of alarm. "Okay."

"The first is this." He pulled a neatly folded sheet of paper out of his lab coat pocket and handed it to her. This is brand new. It was posted today. I had to sit on my hands to keep from telling you about it early, since I knew the position was opening."

She unfolded the letter and read the job posting. When she finished she looked at him, stunned.

"Board certified, general surgeon? Seriously? Did you make this up?"

"I didn't, but if I'd thought I could ever get someone like you, I would have. The truth is, this is my department once Dr. Swenson, the man retiring from here, leaves. From the moment I read your credentials, I've known we could use someone with your drive and your expertise."

She didn't know what to think. It was flattering, but the thought of moving back here to a tiny, relatively closed community and leaving New York, the place that had made her the doctor she was...The idea sat in her mind as ludicrous. And her heart pumped like it was running a marathon.

Gabriel.

Rory.

Joely.

The horses.

"I am so honored that you're thinking of me," she began. "I don't have some of the other qualifications—orthopedic experience. Trauma."

"Those are plusses, not requirements. If you had any interest in those fields you'd go after them in a flash. I have no doubt."

The flush of excitement that came with a new possibility swept through her. The same flush she got when considering her next career path. Or the anticipation of a challenging case. The only thing that dampened it was the fear that this was just a little too good to be true.

"That's kind of you to say. I just don't know."

"I don't expect you to know. I certainly didn't expect you to jump in excitement over something you'd never considered. But, when this came up, I thought of all that's going on with your family and that you might be considering coming back here at some point. It's just information."

"This is very, very nice of you." Her hand shook a little as she handed the paper back to him.

"No, keep it just for reference. If you do want to know more about it just give the number a call. Or call me."

"No hard sell?"

"If you call for information, then I'll give you my sales pitch. What I will tell you, and don't repeat this, is that I'll have a lot to say about the person who's chosen. If you were to apply I think it's safe to say I could influence the other members of the selection committee."

Flustered, and pleased despite herself, she shook her finger at him. "Why, Dr. Landon. That almost sounds like job fixing."

"Not in the least. It's the closest you'll get to a hard sell today. I won't deny for a second that I would love to work with you. If you were interested, believe me, I'd do everything in my power to see that I got that chance."

She let herself bask in the stunning joy of being so wanted. Such a completely different sensation than the one she'd had after losing the job in New York. Finally she shook her head and smiled.

"Okay, you'll have to let me be overwhelmed and think on this for a while. I truly am flattered. So. Let's go on to topic two. What about Joely?"

"Joely? Oh! It's not about Joely."

"Really?"

At that his face did flush ever so slightly. "It's about Raquel."

"What!" She grinned at him. "What about her?"

"I hope it's not presumptuous to say that I felt comfortable asking you this. Do you think she would ever consider dating an older man?"

"Hah!" Mia jumped to her feet, reached across the table, and gave him a light punch in the arm. "I knew it!"

"Does that mean you mind, or you don't mind?" He looked relaxed now that he'd spilled his secret, all traces of embarrassment had vanished.

"Perry, my new friend, if you can get Raquel the tomboy interested in anything besides her job, we'll throw you a party. How much older do you think you are?"

"I know for a fact because I'm shameless at sleuthing. She's twenty-four, I'm thirty-six." He grimaced. "Sounds a little worse when you say it out loud."

"Nonsense—Grandma Sadie was twenty years younger than Papa Sebastian. Believe me, you're fine. Just go in armed with patience—Raquel is a confirmed tomboy and numbers geek. When she dates it's to get into some sporting event. You'll have to convince her you're not out to be her pal."

"I consider myself forewarned. Thank you, Mia. I should have gone right to her, but I didn't want to make it awkward for her to come around. Now that Joely will be leaving the hospital we won't be in such close quarters." He pushed his chair back and checked his watch. "I have surgery in forty minutes, so I should go. He stood, circled the table, and held out his hand. "Thanks again. For not thinking this is absolutely ridiculous on my part. I promise you my next step is not a note with check boxes: 'Do you like me, yes or no?' "

She waved off his handshake and surprised herself by offering him a friendly hug. "I wish you luck. It's a long distance relationship, you know—even though we're all coming back more often lately."

"I, uh, have family in Denver. I figure in a best case I might make trips that direction, too."

"Then I definitely wish you success. This is how much fun all dates should be."

"Oh really? Should I be taking notes?" Mia jumped at the sound of Gabe's voice.

She pulled away, laughing, from Perry's embrace. Gabe's movie-star features were frozen in bland friendliness, one brow arched, the corners of his mouth tilted upward in a meaningless smile.

"Hello, Lieutenant Handsome," she said. "Guess I was caught red-handed."

Perry offered a handshake, and Gabe took it, his features not warming. Mia's stomach flipped happily at the obvious jealousy.

"I'm off," Perry said. "Good to see you, Gabe. Mia, you think hard about that offer. I want you."

She almost lost it and let her laughter spill. The line couldn't have been more perfectly timed for misunderstanding. Just like Rory and the social worker that morning. Only suddenly, the day sparkled like a sunny Florida summer beach.

She giggled when Perry was gone. "Sit down. Stop looking like he kicked your puppy."

"He was touching my girl."

"No. Really, your girl—wait, is that what I am?"

"After last night?"

"Oh, yeah. *That*." She closed her eyes and sighed. "I never got a chance this morning to tell you that last night was pretty cool. Anyway, I was the one who hugged him."

"That's so much better." He relaxed into the joking, and she reached across the table to take his hands.

"I like the jealousy," she said.

"I don't have to be, though, do I?" He looked at their hands, a smile with a sheepish tinge playing at his mouth.

"You do not. Because…One, he offered me a job. Two? He likes Raquel."

She loved how he could blush and laugh at the same time. All these things she was learning about him.

"I couldn't be happier to look like an idiot," he said, and he kissed her.

Chapter Twenty-Three

"YOU REALLY ARE not adept when it comes to sports, are you?" Gabe nearly tripped over Rory as he led the way through the back door, stomping snow off his boots. A little irony, he supposed, considering he'd just been ragging mercilessly on Mia for being uncoordinated.

"Give me a break. I played chess," she said.

"I can play chess," Rory added.

"I know. You're not bad either, for a football player." Mia tugged his stocking cap over his eyes and Rory flailed his hands, laughing.

"I am a football player," he said.

"Well, I really, really like Mia," Gabe said. "But I can't lie. She is *not* a football player."

"When you both bust your butts playing touch football next time, it's me you'll be coming to see. So I wouldn't be too mean to the doctor."

"Bust your butts." Rory's undulating, Elmer Fudd–like giggle spilled out like a rushing brook. "Bust your *butts!*"

He hung his jacket up on a hook and threw his wet mittens and hat in a basket as he'd been taught and scampered away, still chortling. Gabe was glad to see the little bit of silliness. Three days since arriving, Rory was settling in. He could charm the socks off any of the women in the house. He liked Skylar Thorson who'd come to play video games after school a couple of times, and who was teaching him to be comfortable around horses by letting him help her with horse chores. She also gave him little mini lessons that Rory talked about incessantly. He liked Cole and was enamored with Grandma Sadie, but the person he adored was Mia. And Gabe was in clear second place.

He liked the boy. A lot. Most of the time he forgot how much he could remind him of Jibril. The Jibril of the past, of course, since he would be seventeen or eighteen now, nothing at all like Rory. Gabe consciously refused to think about the letter he'd sent to Iraq. He seriously didn't expect it to bear fruit, so he concentrated on this child, growing ever more grateful for the chance to reconnect with a young person. He'd missed it.

He studied Mia as she removed her hat, jacket, and snow boots. She had the fluid beauty of a woman in total control of her body. Another gorgeous irony, since she couldn't catch a football unless tossed from fewer than twenty feet. He didn't care. She didn't need football on her resume. She straightened, looking like a ski bunny in her purple snow pants and thick white sweater. He wrapped his arms around her and pinned her to the wall with his body.

"Maybe after the *Phantom Tollbooth* tonight we can check on those mustangs again."

Twice now they'd managed their tryst. He doubted anyone was fooled about mustangs or any other excuse, but the sneaking was a little bit fun. He kissed her, lingering over her sweetness, the scent of outdoors clinging to her.

In the main house the landline rang. He ignored it, and she delved deeper into his mouth with her agile tongue, rendering him all but indifferent to the rest of the world. He let himself grow drunk on her sweet wine taste and the little sounds of pleasure she couldn't keep to herself.

"Sorry to walk in on your, ahem, private love suite, but there's a phone call for you, Mia." Harper grinned at them from the kitchen door, not sorry at all.

Gabe liked Harper, too. The dynamics blossoming within the family of sisters fascinated him. Harper was quickly becoming the heart of Paradise Ranch, with her mother's help and her grandmother's towering wisdom. The other sisters, Mia included, looked up to her now. Things were much different than when Gabe had first met them all two-and-a-half months before.

"I'll take it in the office." Mia smiled, and he reluctantly gave her room to duck out from his hold. "I think you're the mustang I'll have to check on tonight." she whispered into his ear as she left, her hair swinging around her shoulders.

"You've been good for my big sister." Harper relaxed against the side of the door. "And I don't mean just a little bit good. I've never seen her like this."

"Like what?"

"Happy and nice. Not nice to us so much as nice to herself. And happy. Did I mention that?"

"You did."

"I don't know where you two will end up. Long term, I mean. I kind of know where you'll end up tonight."

He squinted in embarrassment and scratched at his head, fluffing out the hat hair. "That obvious, huh?"

"I'm still in that stage myself—sneaking away with the guy I love. Be patient with Mia. On the other hand. If you aren't sure for any reason? She's crazy about you. And she's almost as crazy about Rory. Sometimes these things happen overnight—don't doubt it."

"You've all accepted me pretty easily. I appreciate it."

"Hah. That *was* easy. We liked you before she did."

He hugged her on his way through the door and kissed her on the top of the head, feeling, finally, like he belonged.

He headed for the stairs and the guest room where he'd left his dry clothes so he could change out of winter long underwear and wet jeans. Rory was nowhere to be seen, so Gabe planned to head first for his room to make sure he was there. Such a domestic chore. He wondered for the first time what it would be like, checking on his own flesh and blood son or daughter. He didn't need one; he believed that. Rory was the perfect kind of child to make a family with—one who would have to go through The System otherwise. But the thought of biological kids no longer seemed unthinkable. A little girl like Mia. A little brother for Rory...

Whoa!

That was getting so far ahead of himself, or the times. But rather than make him recoil as it maybe should have, the thought of being with Mia forever, come what may, made him smile. Made him excited for the future.

His path took him through the living room and past the open door to Mia's father's old study—a dark navy and burgundy masculine space that hadn't been changed since Sam's death.

"This is very much a dream come true."

He heard Mia's voice, breathless and charged with disbelief. He stopped, frowning. Gabe dealt every moment of his work days with privacy issues and handling peoples' sensitive personal information. He didn't hold with eavesdropping or spying. But some gremlin, fueled by the fantasies that had just been engulfing him, rooted him in place.

"Of course, I would love to talk with you. You know how I feel about that position."

That position.

There was only one "That Position." The pediatric job at New York General. His heart began to race.

"I'm planning to return Friday of next week. Wouldn't that be soon enough?...I see. Wednesday at three o'clock...Can I call you back within the hour, Mason? I have some complications to smooth out here...No, no, just plans to reschedule...Thank you. I'll do that. I'll talk to you soon. Thank you again, so much."

Gabe stood by the open door, his heart in his socks, watching her stare at the cordless phone in its cradle. He shoved down the desire to rush in, grab her into his arms, and beg her to stay. Instead, he turned from the doorway, pressed himself into the corner outside the office, and let his head fall back against the wall. Swallowing, he closed his eyes. Resentment, anger, and hurt burned through him like acid. He'd done it. He'd jumped in all the way, ignoring the inner voices that had cautioned him for the past month. He'd let himself believe that overcoming his fear of openness and commitment was the healthy way to move ahead.

He'd fallen for her. He'd fallen for the kid. He'd fallen for the whole damn family. But when it came down to the truth, it turned out the falling was one-sided. New York and big goals were, just as Gabe had always known deep inside, Amelia Crockett's true lovers. If that weren't the case, she'd be jumping at the new job she'd been handed, and choosing him over a career most of a country away.

His eyes stung, both with grief and anger. Pressing hard into their corners with his thumb and forefinger, he was working to control the emotions when he heard her gasp. He opened his eyes to find her beside him.

"Gabe?"

"Good news, I hear," he said, as evenly as he could.

Her face fell. She bit her lip. "The pediatric surgery chief resident's position," she said. "The person they hired was released from his contract today. Some cheating scandal in his recent school past. I…" She met his eyes. "The job is mine if I go in and pass an interview with the selection committee."

"Well, that's terrific, Amelia. I'm happy for you." His tone was unfair, and her eyes filled with confusion.

"What's wrong?" she asked.

"Nothing. It sounds like your luck has changed. It's wonderful."

She stared as if registering his annoyance for the first time. "My. That was convincing."

"Honestly? I can't say I'm not a little shocked. You'll be heading out almost right away if I correctly understood the end of the conversation I stumbled upon."

"If it's what I decide, I'll fly to New York for the interview tomorrow and be back before our Thanksgiving dinner on Thursday. That's all it is—the interview. They just need it done before December first."

"Friday. And when do you start?"

"Gabe!" She touched his arm. "I haven't taken the job."

"Don't be ridiculous. Of course you have, or you will. It's your dream."

"It is," she said. "So why are you angry?"

He started to deny it, but she was so secure in herself, so single-minded about her dream that his resentment wouldn't let him wimp out.

"I'm angry at myself for thinking you might have considered this something that affected both of us. I realize now that I was presumptuous."

"That is not fair."

"No. It isn't."

"Are you asking me not to go?" She firmed her lips.

"Of course not."

"It sure sounds like it."

He sighed. She was right. He didn't want her to go. He wanted to be more important to her than some job. She was also right that it wasn't fair of him at all.

"I'm sorry. You're right." He tried to soften his voice. "I'm basing my feelings on a very short amount of time spent with you. I don't expect you to change your life for someone you've known a matter of weeks. That would be foolish."

He couldn't read anything on her face. She stared at the floor, her hands in loose fists, her mouth still in a tight line of control.

"How can you talk like the past weeks don't matter? That I'm not considering everything we've gone through?"

"I know you care."

"Then trust me. Let me see what they're offering."

His anger deflated. His resentment dissipated. But the hurt remained, stinging like hell. He pulled her very gently toward him by one arm and kissed her on the brow.

"You're absolutely right," he said. "Go. Follow your dream."

EIGHT YEARS OF living in New York had given Mia a healthy respect and a reluctant love for the city. Truth to tell, she didn't spend that much time walking its iconic paths—most of her time was spent in the hospital or at the homes of her friends. Still, she'd never hated it. Until today.

Admittedly, it had been a little comforting to step back into her condo with all its familiar furnishings and the decorating she'd chosen. But it had also seemed empty and a little sterile, like a pretty museum room. She longed for a touch of warm knotty pine somewhere. And she'd slept fitfully after calling home. She'd talked to Rory and was assured he was fine, having a blast with Skylar's Border Collie, Asta, who didn't even mind Jack although she chased the barn cats. But she hadn't been able to reach Gabe. He never answered his phone, and Mia didn't know whether to be crushed or furious. Part of her knew just how he felt—he didn't want her to leave Wyoming. The other part of her wanted only his support in whatever she chose.

After the restless night, she'd braved the little coffee shop on her building's corner, standing in a cranky New York line and jostling for her turn to be served and fighting her way back out onto the street. Longing for one of Grace's gooey caramel rolls, she'd made her way to the hospital and visited with Brooke and Sam. They fussed over her and feted her with lunch and stories from the past month, but when she'd gone back to her office and greeted her colleagues, there were no hugs or back slaps. Then again, there never had been. She didn't roll that way in her professional life. Why in God's name would she notice it now?

She took an hour before her meeting with the committee to find some kitschy souvenirs for her family. She bought Rory an I Heart NY T-shirt to remind him of home, but the whole time she found herself hating the streets, the crowds, even the Christmas tree sellers taking up space on the sidewalks. She'd always thought the city way of selling trees to hold its own kind of charm. Now she wanted the real pines of Wyoming.

By the time she returned to New York General a familiar headache jackhammered in her temples. As she dug for her ibuprofen, it occurred to her she hadn't taken a single pill in nearly a month. But then she reentered her domain, this time not as a visitor but as a professional. Being back in her element eased her headache and relaxed her knotted shoulders. Familiar and safe, as her apartment had been, the hospital was one of her two havens in the hurricane that was New York. Finally, a tiny flutter of excitement swooped through her stomach. This was her part of the city.

Mason Thomas met her in the conference room and did, actually, offer a welcome embrace. Professional and appropriate. "Hello, Mia. We've definitely missed you around here. There's a little zing and spirit lacking when you're gone."

"You've no idea how nice that is to hear. And I want to thank you for this second chance. I'll do my best to live up to your vote of confidence."

"What is that I hear in your voice? A little softness?" He smiled. "I think your time off did you a world of good."

The tension as she thought about the job she'd be doing, was curling back into her body like it, too, was back from vacation. But it was familiar and good for her. It was what kept her sharp. And ready for anything.

"I haven't changed my philosophy on what makes good doctor, patient, colleague relationships," she said. "But I have done some thinking about how people react to it."

"That's just what I want to hear," he said. "Let's get this show on the road, shall we, Doctor?"

The committee wasn't brutal, but they did grill her. And the session ran for nearly two hours—as if they hadn't already put her through the process during her original interview. What would she do if...? What was the most important aspect of...? Where would she like to be in one, five, fifteen years? What was her philosophy on...everything?

By the time she was finished, she'd kept her cool, explained herself until her answers felt rote, and knew without a doubt she'd gotten what she came for. And when she walked out of the conference room, she had to escape to her office, lock her door, and hide her face in her hands while she shook with excitement and absolute dread. But despite the fearful and gleeful emotion, all she could really think about what how she was going to tell Gabe.

THE THANKSGIVING GUEST list at Paradise Ranch was impressive. When Mia finally set her bag in the front foyer at a little after noon Thanksgiving Day, Rory had to push his way through a lot of tall people in order to reach her. She hugged him as if they'd been apart for weeks.

"I've been riding five times on Bungu. He wasn't crazy at all. And I taught Asta how to roll over." He bubbled over with his news.

Bungu, evidently a Shoshone word meaning horse, was Skylar's pinto gelding. He was young at age four, but Mia had never heard rumors that he was crazy. She took it to mean Rory's nervousness about riding had abated.

"Sounds like you're becoming an official animal trainer. Do you like the horses?"

"I love them."

She squeezed him one last time and marveled at the tenderness welling in her heart. He'd made so many strides in just a handful of days. There'd be ups and downs. She couldn't fool herself into thinking Rory had processed all his grief. Right now he was on a high from all the new experiences. Still, she hoped she'd made the right decision for him.

She waded through the hugs and welcomes.

"Hi, sis!" Kelly, newly arrived herself, offered a Rory-worthy hug.

"Kel!" Mia rocked her with joy. "My triplets are a full set. Welcome back! Are you staying a while now?"

"A couple of weeks. I'm sending Grace back. Raquel will probably follow in a week. I have to stay, though, and catch up on my big sister's news. That big, strong hunk of a Gabe. And that amazing little hunk of a Rory. My gosh, your life is…"

"Out of control? Crazy? A little wonderful?"

"Beautiful. You sound so happy."

"We'll talk. But…yeah."

"Hi, Mia."

She spun to the front drawing room door and, sitting like a princess in her wheelchair, was Joely. Mia ran the few steps and grabbed her.

"You are absolutely the most beautiful sight in the world," Mia said. "I am so glad you're here."

"I am, too."

Pale but lovely, with her honey-wheat hair and her wide hazel eyes, Joely spoke quietly, almost but not quite without conviction.

"Are you exhausted already?" Mia asked. "Are you hurting anywhere?"

"I am tired. But I feel okay."

"You do look beautiful."

"Let's don't go there." She said it without rancor, but her tone was firm. There'd be no discussion of beauty. The decision was irrevocable.

"Okay we won't. But I for one have found what I'm grateful for this year. My *beautiful* sister safely here with us. I love you."

"I couldn't have survived without you, Mia." Joely held open her arms again.

Mia fell into them. "You certainly would have. But I'm glad I could be with you."

To her surprise, the guests included Brewster, Finney, and Pat who, because they had no other family close, all were there to raise glasses of beer in a welcome home salute. Then she found Leif, Bjorn, and their family, which filled the living room and kitchen. But the one person she really wanted to see, hadn't come to the door to greet her.

She forgave him the instant she found him in the kitchen, helping Cole pull two of the biggest turkeys Mia had ever seen from the double-decker oven.

"Hey, you," she called.

His head popped up and for an instant, his eyes lit with a combination of passion, joy, and lust she hoped only she could read. Then he smiled, and shutters of reserve, still warm but unmistakable, darkened his honey-colored eyes. "Hey, Doc. Welcome home."

Home. She liked that he'd said it.

"Give me two minutes," he added, hoisting his turkey roaster from its oven rack and following Cole to the massive island counter.

"To the master of the bird, I'll give all the time he wants."

When the roasters were safely on the counter, Gabe and Cole worked in tandem with two heavy duty spatulas each to move the golden brown birds to platters. The aroma was exquisite. And when the guys shook hands to congratulate each other, Mia slipped behind Gabe and snaked her arms around his torso. "That was male skill at its finest."

He loosened her hands so that he could turn and face her. "You have very low standards," he said. "Easy to live up to."

"I try not to make it too difficult."

"How'd it go?" His question held a hint of wariness. Or maybe she was projecting out of nervousness.

"It went really well. I got what I wanted."

He kissed her on the top of the head and pushed her away again. "I'm really glad. It's good to have you back."

He said the words, but he certainly didn't show them. Slightly wounded, she kissed him once on the mouth. "It's good to be back. New York showed me her most crowded and feisty, noisy side this trip. Kind of an obnoxious lady."

"It's Christmas season. I expect a place like New York would be insane."

She sighed. He was still annoyed. In fact, he was dull, almost uninterested. She missed his spark and the underlying comic bursting to come out.

"Everything all right?" She probed for him to open up and, in fact, he shook himself slightly out of his lifelessness.

"Yeah, sure. Everything's great." He finally kissed her properly, but he wasn't really back.

Dinner was jovial and loud, filled with the laughter and chatter of twenty people. Grandpa Sebastian had known what he was doing when he'd made a table that could seat nine on a side. But the family boisterousness didn't infect Gabe either. At the end of the meal, when two turkeys had been thoroughly decimated, the sweet potatoes, roasted vegetables, stuffing, and cranberries were memory, and nobody had room for pumpkin pie but clamored for it anyway, Mia rose with her sisters. Gathering around Joely's chair, they lifted half-finished glasses of wine in a pre-arranged toast.

"Something a little different from a year ago," Harper said, wrangling everyone's attention with her sweet voice. "A salute—to new family members. Damien, Jason, and Pat, whom we've adopted."

"To Cole!" Kelly said. "He's not new, but now he's officially part of the family."

"Gabe," Mia said with a flush of pride. "He's wormed his way in. And, of course, a very special new member, the newest guy in my life, Rory."

"Now everyone fill up your glass again," Harper said. "Just like these guys fill up our lives."

The schmaltzy show was a huge success. Cheers rang out and glasses were filled with wine, water, and juice. When the hubbub died down again, Leif took a turn calling for attention.

"We haven't had a new young person around her for a long time," he said. "And he's been pretty quick to adopt us all. One thing Skylar has discovered is that Rory here has been bitten by the horse flu. He likes his rides. So, we have an early Christmas present out front. Rory, you want to come and see?"

When Rory saw the black-and-white pony tied to one of the huge old pin oaks on the front lawn, his mouth hung in a silent O.

"One of our neighbors has been keeping this guy since his own kids got too big to ride him. He wanted a good home where someone could really use him again. Rory, that's you. Think you want to learn to get along with a pony named Panda?"

Mia had more tears in her eyes than Rory did when he took Skylar's hand and followed her with hesitant disbelief. He looked quickly back at Mia and she nodded. When he reached Panda, he stared a minute, then threw his arms around the pony's neck.

"Really?" he asked. "Really?"

"Yup, really," Skylar said. "He's here for you whenever you come and visit."

"I'm not coming to visit. I'm staying right here with him."

She felt Gabe's presence without a single touch from him. He stood behind her and, finally, put a hand on her shoulder. She leaned against his chest and tilted her head back to gaze at the underside of his chin. Stiff, sexy stubble shadowed his skin.

"Is this a good idea?" he asked.

Surprised, she frowned. "Look at him. It's a wonderful idea."

"You're rooting him to this place. Isn't it going to be hard on him to leave?"

She smiled secretively. "About that."

"Now's not the time to talk about it."

A tiny bubble of frustration rose in her chest and threatened to blossom into anger. "What's wrong with you?"

"Not a thing."

"I might not be a therapist, but I know bullshit when I hear it."

It was his turn to look stunned. "That was rude."

"You're being a little bit rude yourself. Care to explain, or do you want me to tell you what I think?"

"Mia…" He spun her around and shook his head. "I'm sorry. I…"

"You're wrong." She cut him off. "This is a perfect time to end this."

"End…?"

She'd been purposely obtuse, but he deserved the look of utter destruction in his eyes. Mia whispered to Harper that she had something else for Rory and she and Gabe were going to the barn to get it. A blatant lie, but desperate times…

She grabbed Gabriel's hand and pulled him after her, headed for the barn.

"Mia, what—"

"No talking yet."

She led him all the way to the door of the cabin and finally stopped. With a deep breath she faced him. "Now," she said. "Talk."

"I'm trying to reconcile you leaving with all the sugar-coated family stuff everyone is gobbling up back there. A pony, for God's sake."

"What do you want me to say?"

"Nothing. Nothing, Mia. I just want to know why you're making you and Rory slipping back out of my life so damn painful. It's like promising him Santa is real when he's not."

"Have you ever thought that maybe Santa is real?"

"What the hell is that supposed to mean?"

"It means, Gabriel, that this could work, you and me. If you want it to."

"Long distance doesn't work. Not over the long haul. You can't have someone two thousand miles away asking you to divide your passions."

"That's it? That's what you have to offer me?"

"I'm not standing in the way of your dream. I refuse."

"I don't believe it. Where are the balls you said you grew that day Rory arrived? What about having my back?"

He shuffled on his feet, the fierce light of anger flaring in his eyes, reddening his cheeks even more than the cold air. Mia found the door key and let them into the cabin.

"I have your back," he said. "I want your dreams for you—they're a lot older than the little attraction we've

THE BRIDE WORE RED BOOTS 379

started here. I'm not going to make another mistake by letting you make a mistake."

She'd come down here to surprise him. To let him be depressed until she made it all better. But this? This was a decision carefully thought through and planned. The idiot was breaking up with her before even discussing the matter. It stunned her how painful the wound was.

"I don't believe it. Ever since I met you you've been fighting for something. You're like this Energizer Bunny Warrior for every underdog you meet. My sister, my mother, your squad of misfits who nearly got you fired before they figured it out. You don't care—you're a safety net for everyone. But here I come, with problems that aren't even problems and you pack it in without lifting a finger much less a sword to rescue us. Where's the fight for us? Where's my safety net?"

"You have more safety nets than I could ever provide," he said, anger still flashing. "Your job, a child who needs you, a city full of sophisticated prospects. I belong here— with the misfits. You have a world there. You belong to it. Go grab the future."

She almost let tears fall, but she held resolutely firm. Her decisions and all the plans she'd been so excited to tell him about suddenly felt very unsteady, but her anger remained true.

"My father used to tell me what I should do and where I belonged, Gabriel. Don't you dare go there. How about *I* finally get to decide where I belong?"

"Fine."

She scoffed in retort. "Fine. You talk about grabbing the future. What about yours? When are you going to grab it by fixing the past? When are you going to send those letters you're so afraid of? Don't make all these plans for me when you're—"

"I sent them two weeks ago."

His voice had quieted. His words weren't strong or even proud. He just told her.

"You...you did?"

"The day before Rory arrived."

"Have you heard anything?" She held her breath.

"No."

"Oh! Oh, I'm sorry."

Dead silence filled the cabin. She could hear him breathing. Almost hear their hearts beating.

"Why do you want to push me back to New York?"

"I don't."

"You must; you never asked me to stay. Do you even *want* me to stay?"

He grabbed her with all his old forcefulness. With a deep-diving thrill from her heart to her stomach, she watched his eyes blaze to life, and with it came a little bit of hope. His mouth crushed hers with heat and passion and the hot, angry taste of him. She poured her feelings back to him, delving, fighting, pleading, until at last he gentled. He cupped her face and worked his jaw, his tongue, his body into the kiss. She groaned when one hand dropped to her breast and kneaded through all the layers—more erotic than if he'd mined through the fabric to find her skin. She pushed into his touch. She sent her own hand slipping around to his seat and pulled him to her, thrusting forward to meet him. He moaned and pulled away.

"You said I didn't fight for us. You're wrong, Amelia. I fought harder than anything I've fought for in my life. The trouble is, I fought myself. I've tried to be everything I'm not—selfish, superficial, wounded, sorry, unsure. I didn't want you to think I'm any of those things. But guess what? I'm all of them."

"That couldn't be further from the truth."

"Stop. It is the truth, and I'm done blowing smoke up everyone's ass. I'm superficial, Mia. I want it all. I want stuff. Things like a home, and bikes in the yard, and messes in the kitchen, and fences, and mortgages to pay for it all.

"And I'm wounded. I'm angry that I lost Jibril. I haven't forgiven myself, and I'm tired of pretending I haven't. I'm not stoic and happy and healed. Damn it, I'm not. But I will be. Someday. You're the only one who's ever made me take even two steps in that direction.

"And finally? I am selfish, Mia. I'm damn selfish. You asked if I want you here. You bet your kids, dogs, and stupid new ponies I do. More than anything. I can't tell you how pissed off I was that you wanted to go back to New York more than you wanted to stay with me. Hell, I'm still pissed off. And I'm not sorry. Because it's honest—the first honest thing I've felt since falling in love with you. So go and get your dream. But I'm no longer going to even pretend to be happy about it."

Mia sucked her lower lip between her teeth and bit down to keep tears and laughter from giving her away too quickly. She looked deeply into Gabe's face without saying a word. He didn't flinch. No defiance shone in his eyes. Clear, unapologetic, uncensored Gabriel Harrison looked back at her, and all she saw was truth and love.

"So ask me."

He didn't hesitate. "Stay here. I don't want you to go back. I don't want Rory to go back. I want you to live here where your home is."

"That's good to know," she said quietly. "Because I turned down the job."

Epilogue

"LOOK! THERE'S GRAND Teton!" Mia laughed as Rory popped out of his half-slumber in the back seat of the new Silverado, Gabe's pride and joy, and pressed his nose against the window. He'd learned his Wyoming geography well.

"Not far, now," Gabe said. "Ready to be home?"

After three weeks in New York and five days each way on the road, they were all ready to be home. Pulling the loaded U-Haul trailer, filled with the contents of Mia's condo, across country, had thoroughly broken in the Chevy, the newest addition to the fleet of Paradise Ranch work vehicles.

"I'm ready to see Jack. And Panda. And Buster."

Buster. The fuzz ball of a black lab-slash-something-something-and-maybe-a-little shepherd mutt Rory had begged to bring home when a school mate's dog had birthed surprise puppies. He was named for the New York

Buster, who now had a full-time job in Queens and an address where Rory could send mail.

"Do you think Harper has taught him not to chew since we've been gone?" Mia asked.

The dog was almost two months old. He wouldn't be done chewing for another two years.

"Doubt it," Rory said, and Mia laughed.

She reached for Gabe's hand and gestured out the window to the wild, rolling hills between the highway and the national park. A sheen of pale green graced the undulating landscape and the mountains in the distance wore caps of snow that had shrunk considerably since Gabe and Mia had left with Rory the first week of March. "Look how gorgeous Wyoming is in April. It actually looks like spring."

"There was a reason I moved out here," he said and squeezed her fingers. "What do you think, Rory? Still don't regret moving away from New York?"

"Not for a New York minute." He repeated the phrase he'd learned during their whirlwind trip.

The landscape wound past, and Mia's contentment, which she wouldn't have guessed could get any higher, rose with every familiar landmark. The job at the VA with Perry Landon was hers starting in May, the hours far less than what she'd endured—because now she looked at her old life as an endurance run she'd mistaken for success— in New York; Harper and Cole had set a wedding date for mid-May, six weeks away; and Joely was finally making progress in rehab. Mia loved being home to witness all of it.

She didn't immediately notice when Gabe pulled off the highway and swung the truck and trailer easily onto a flat overlook out of sight of the road.

"Recognize this?" Gabe asked.

"Of course." She smiled. "Where we watched those mustangs that night back in November. The ones that started it all. But, why?"

"We need to have a few things understood by the time we get home," he said. "I have a couple things to ask you."

"What?" Rory asked. "Do you want to finally get a horse, too?"

"Yeah!" Mia laughed. Gabe had stubbornly refused to get his own horse until, as he put it, he knew it was the right moment—whatever that meant. "You want to ask Santa for a pony."

"In April?" Gabe asked. "That makes no sense. I'll tell you what makes sense. Come on. Out of the truck. Stretch the legs a sec."

"We're almost home—"

He cut her short with a finger to her lips. "Just get out."

They made their way around a grassy hillock, and Mia gazed out across the rolling hills. Closing her eyes, she remembered the tiny band of mustangs that truly had led to everything.

"The guys asked me to make a proposal," he began.

Her heart lurched. "Proposal?"

"Sorry, their kind of proposal. They want to start another program at the ranch—one where more injured vets can come and work with horses—either temporarily or to try and adopt a mustang like they did. They've got it all planned—a private enterprise, not funded by the VA. I promised I'd plant the seed of the idea. What do you think?"

She laughed.

"I think it's got great potential. It's a wonderful idea, and I'd like to hear their details. And," she kissed him, "I think you could have asked me that in the truck."

"That, yes. But not this. This is *my* new proposal."

She stared, her heart leaped again, higher this time, and pounded harder as Gabe dug into his jacket pocket, produced a small white box, and sank to one knee in front of her. Rory's mouth popped open, and he flew to Gabe's side, peering into the box as he flipped it open.

"Yay! Yay! Yay! Yay!" Rory hopped in place with each exclamation and then vaulted onto Gabe's back, hugging him around the neck.

"Amelia Crockett, will you marry me?" Gabe made a choking sound and grinned.

She burst into tears.

"Mia?" Rory asked, turning worried eyes on her. She nodded at him and, grinning and snuffling, held up a hand to show she was okay. She couldn't remember ever being so stereotypically female as to actually erupt into crying, but Gabe had shattered the last walls that existed in her heart. "What's wrong with her?" Rory swiveled his head and beseeched Gabe.

"She's happy. I think."

"Wow. That's the dumbest thing I've ever seen." He grinned with relief.

"Yes." She managed the word at last. "It might be dumb, but yes."

"Yes what?" Gabe asked, teasing.

"Yes, I'm happy. Yes, yes, yes, I'll marry you."

With a whoop only a ten-year-old boy could produce, Rory released his neck hold on Gabe and spread his arms, preparing to zoom off like a plane. Gabe snared his hand and stopped him midtakeoff. "Wait. I'm not done with you, kid."

He stood and then squatted directly in front of him. "I have a question for you, too. Rory Beltane, I'd like to know if, when I marry Mia, who I know is your favorite person in the world, you would also let me be your dad."

Rory stood still as the rocks and mountains surrounding them, his zooming wings temporarily grounded. He nodded somberly, and then he burst into tears.

"See?" Mia squatted beside him, too, and reached for Gabe, capturing Rory in their embrace. "This crying thing? It's not so dumb after all, is it?"

"I…I'll have a dad."

"The best one." It was an easy promise.

"If Gabe is my dad…Will you be my mom?"

Tears welled anew and Mia swallowed, gaining time to find her composure. "I'll never be the same as your real mom," she said. "You'll always remember her, and she'll be your guardian angel up in heaven until you see her again. But, yes, I would like to be your mom here on Earth. If you want that, too."

Rory's tears were gone by the time his hug confirmed that he definitely wanted it, too.

They let him loose then, and he revved his happily screechy engine and zoomed off toward the open grasslands, a little wild mustang, finally free and safe.

"What a way to start," Gabe said, sliding his arms around Mia and pulling her close. "I might be crazy. We're probably all crazy. But instant family feels pretty right to me."

"Incredibly right," she agreed, holding up her hand and inspecting the glittering circlet on her finger with awe.

"Can you handle one more piece of news?"

She drew back. "Good or bad?"

"Bad?" he asked. "Really? You think I'd follow all this with bad news?"

She laughed. "This all seems like it could be puffed away like dandelion seeds if I'm not careful to stay asleep. I'm sure something's going to start blowing on my good dream any second."

"You're not dreaming."

Stepping back, he pulled a square-folded paper from his back jeans pocket. He bit a lip and stood a moment. "Harper texted me that an envelope came from the embassy in Iraq four days ago. I asked her to open it."

"Oh, Gabe." Her breath caught in her throat.

"Then I asked her to e-mail me what she found. I printed it at the hotel we were at night before last. She sent me these three sheets."

He handed her the papers and she unfolded them carefully. The top was a brief, one line letter on US Embassy letterhead.

"Dear Gabe," Mia read. "Success can be sweet. Paul."

She looked up, her breathing coming with even more difficulty. Gabe nodded, urging her to keep going. She turned to the second sheet, a much longer typed page.

"Dear Gabriel Harrison. Today has been one of the best days of my life. I heard that you are alive and living in Wyoming in the United States of America. I hope you remember me. I am Jibril al…"

Her hand dropped to her side and, for the third time in twenty minutes, tears made it impossible to speak. She covered her mouth and lifted her eyes to Gabe's. He took the papers and turned the letter from Jibril over. From the back, the photo of a bright, brown-eyed young man with thick black hair and a confident smile, stared out at her.

"That's…?"

"Jibril. His parents and aunts and uncles swept him and his cousins away that day before the chaos ended. They told the children all the soldiers were killed, and then they escaped as a family from the city. They didn't want any more contact with us because we were too dangerous. And they didn't let anyone know who could tell us the truth. This uncle just happened to move back to Baghdad a couple of years ago."

There were no words to say that matched the feeling in Mia's heart or the look on Gabriel's face.

"You didn't tell me." She kissed him.

"I had this planned." He looked around them and lifted her hand with the ring to his lips. "This was more important, and finding Jibril had nothing to do with it.

If you said yes, I knew I had the best engagement present ever."

"Wait. If I said yes? You had doubts?"

"A class clown never knows if people really like him, or just like his silly clown nose."

"I hate clown noses."

"Nah, you don't. You just say that. I know for a fact now, because you said yes."

"I did. But tell me about Jibril."

"I guess there are more pictures at home. We can learn more when we get there. But he's eighteen. He's going to school in Canada, because he couldn't get into the United States back when he applied. He's since gotten a visitor's visa, and he hopes to parlay that into a student visa. He wants to go to Northwestern in Chicago and study journalism."

"Oh, Gabe, you could maybe meet him sometime."

Gabe nodded. "Maybe."

She hugged him, the warmth in her chest spreading until she thought it might explode like fireworks. She'd never had to deal with so much emotional bursting in her life.

"Maybe he can be here for the wedding, although there might not be time." Gabe gave her one more crooked, secretive smile.

"Ummm, not time?"

"Read the last page."

It was a handwritten note from Harper, scanned and sent along with the rest of the e-mail.

Dear Mia and Gabe,

Now that your family is complete (for the moment), I have a very personal wish. You and I have had our sibling moments, Mia, but I love you second only to Cole. You are the big sister I've always cherished. I want to spend the rest of my life with you, too. Please, consider sharing our wedding day. I want us to be brides together. The start of a new Paradise dynasty. Of course it's up to Gabe, as well. But I pray with all my heart you'll twist his arm until he says yes.

I love you both. Congrats on Rory and Jibril.

Harpo

She didn't cry this time. She couldn't for the disbelief that blew every other emotion out of the water.

"That's only six weeks away," she said. "Wait. How did she even know?"

"I asked her permission, along with your mother and your grandmother. They all stood in for your dad. You don't have to decide right now. She knows it's our wedding."

"Yes," she said again. "If you want to."

"I want to tomorrow." He grinned. "I'll marry you here and now."

"Do it. Marry me now. Just us and God's mysterious ways."

He looked down at her feet. "Only if you go get those lucky red boots out of your suitcase. This isn't something a guy wants to leave to chance."

"You are a clown, you clown." She laughed. "There's no chance involved. This is love. Perfect, fast-acting, forever love."

His lips devoured hers and lightning drove through her, hot, fast-acting, forever. Perfect.

"I do," she murmured.

Keep reading for a look at the first book in
Lizbeth Selvig's
Seven Brides for Seven Cowboys series,

THE BRIDE WORE DENIM

When Harper Lee Crockett returns home to Paradise
Ranch, Wyoming, the last thing she expects is to fall
head-over-heels in lust for Cole, childhood neighbor and
her older sister's former longtime boyfriend. The spirited
and artistic Crockett sister has finally learned to resist
her craziest impulses, but this latest trip home and Cole's
rough and tough appeal might be too much for her fading
self-control.

Cole Wainwright has long been fascinated by the sister
who has always stood out from the crowd. His relationship with Amelia, the eldest Crockett sister, wasn't as perfect as it seemed, and with Harper back in town, he sees
everything he'd been missing. Cole knows they have no
future together—he's tied to the land and she's created
a successful life in the big city—but neither of them can
escape their growing attraction or inconvenient feelings.

As Harper struggles to come to grips with new family
responsibilities and her forbidden feelings for Cole, she
must decide whether to listen to her head or to give her
heart what it wants.

Now Available from Avon Impulse!

An Excerpt from

THE BRIDE WORE DENIM

THANK GOD FOR the chickens. *They* knew how to liven up a funeral.

Harper Crockett crouched against the rain-soaked wall of her father's extravagant chicken coop and laughed until she cried. This time, however, the tears weren't for the man who'd built the Henhouse Hilton—as she and her sisters had christened the porch-fronted coop that rivaled most human homes—they were for the eight multicolored, escaped fowl that careened around the yard like over-caffeinated bees.

The very idea of a chicken stampede on one of Wyoming's largest cattle ranches was enough to ease her sorrow, even today.

She glanced toward the back porch of her parents' huge log home several hundred yards away to make sure she was still alone, and she wiped the tears and the rain from her eyes. "I know you probably aren't liking this, Dad," she said, aiming her words at the sopping chickens. "Chaos instead of order."

Chaos had never been acceptable to Samuel Crockett.

A *bock-bocking* Welsummer rooster, gorgeous with its burnt-orange-and-blue body and iridescent green tail, powered past, close enough for an ambush. Harper sprang, and nabbed the affronted bird around its thick, shiny body. "Gotcha," she said as its feathers soaked her sweater. "Back to the pen for you."

The rest of the chickens squawked in alarm at the apprehension and arrest of one of their own. They scattered again, scolding and flapping.

Yeah, she thought as she deposited the rooster back in the chicken yard, her father had no choice but to glower at the bedlam from heaven. He was the one who'd left the dang birds behind.

As the hens fussed, Harper assessed the little flock made up of her father's favorite breeds—all chosen for their easygoing temperaments: friendly, buff-colored Cochins; smart, docile, black-and-white Plymouth Rocks; and sweet, shy, black Australorps. What a little freedom and gang mentality could do, she mused, plotting her next capture. They'd turned into a band of egg-laying gangsters, helping each other escape the law.

Despite there being seven chickens still left to corral, Harper reveled in sharing their attempted run for freedom with nobody. She brushed ineffectually at the mud on her soggy blue-and-brown broom skirt—hippie clothing in the words of her sisters—and the stains on her favorite, crocheted summer sweater. It would have been much smarter to recruit help. Any number of kids bored with funereal reminiscing would have gladly volunteered. Her sisters—Joely and the triplets, if not Amelia—might have as well. The wrangling would have been done in minutes.

Something about handling this alone, however, fed her need to dredge whatever good memories she could from the day. She'd chased an awful lot of chickens throughout her youth. The memories served her sadness, and she didn't want to share them.

Another lucky grab garnered a little Australorp who was returned, protesting, to the yard. Glancing around once more to check the rainy yard, Harper squatted back under the eaves of the ostentatious yellow chicken mansion and let the half dozen birds settle. These were not her mother's pets. These were her father's "girls"—creatures who'd sometimes received more warmth than the human females he'd raised.

Good memories tried to flee in the wake of her petty thoughts, and she grabbed them back. Of course her father had loved his daughters. He'd just never been good at showing it. There'd been plenty of good times.

Rain pittered in a slow, steady rhythm over the lawn and against the coop's gingerbread scrollwork. It pattered into the genuine, petunia-filled, window boxes on their actual multipaned windows. Inside, the chickens enjoyed oak-trimmed nesting boxes, two flights of ladders, and chicken-themed artwork. Behind their over-the-top manse stretched half an acre of safely fenced running yard, which was trimmed with white picket fencing. Why the idiot birds were shunning such luxury to go AWOL out here in the rain was beyond Harper—even if they had found the gate improperly latched.

Wiping rain from her face again, she concentrated like a cat stalking canaries. Chicken wrangling was rarely about mad chasing and much more about patience. She made three more successful captures and then smiled evilly at the remaining three criminals who eyed her with concern. "Give yourselves up, you dirty birds. Your time on the lam is finished."

She swooped toward a fluffy Cochin, a chicken breed normally known for its lazy friendliness, and the fat creature shocked her by feinting and then dodging. For the first time in the hunt, Harper missed her chicken. A resulting belly flop onto the grass forced a startled grunt from her throat, and she slid four inches through a puddle. Before she could let loose the mild curse that bubbled up to her tongue, the mortifying sound of clapping echoed through the rain.

"I definitely give that a nine-point-five."

A hot flash of awareness blazed through her stomach, leaving behind unwanted flutters, and she closed her eyes, fighting back embarrassment. Her voice was still missing when a large, sinewy male hand appeared in front of her, accompanied by rich, baritone laugher. She groaned and reached for his fingers.

"Hello, Cole," she said, resignation forcing her vocal chords to work as she let him help her gently but unceremoniously to her feet.

Cole Wainwright stood before her, the knot of his tie pulled three inches down his white shirt front, the two buttons above it spread open. That left the tanned, corded skin of his neck at Harper's eye level. She swallowed hard. His brown-black hair was spiked and mussed, as if he'd awoken, and his eyes sparkled in the rain like blue diamonds. She took a step back.

"Hullo, you," he replied.

His pirate's grin, wide and warm and charming, hadn't changed since they'd been kids. It had been dorky when he'd been ten and she eight and they, together with Harper's five sisters, had played at being the only pirates who'd sought treasure on horseback rather than from a ship's deck. Then she'd turned twelve and one day found she would have rather been a captured princess than one of the crew. Because that smile had no longer been dorky. It had been a nice fantasy—but Amelia had always made herself the pirate's princess. The highest Harper could rise was to being the round butterball of a maid servant.

Cole's family had owned Paradise's neighboring ranch the Double Diamond. The Crockett daughters and the Wainwright son had all stayed friends through high school, even though Cole had chosen Amelia for, first, the homecoming dance, then Snow Ball, and finally prom. Once the years of exploring their adjoining land on horseback and hanging out being ranch kids had ended, Cole and Amelia had quickly become The Super Couple—gorgeous on gorgeous. Harper had let her secret Cole fantasies fade away, finished high school, gone off to her wild and failed college years, and kept track of

Cole and Amelia only the rare holidays they all visited Paradise Ranch at the same time—like last Christmas when she'd spoken to Cole one-on-one for the first time in years.

His relationship with Amelia had been complicated. Dating for two years after graduation, staying apart for another three years, getting back together so that the family had for a long time considered Cole and Amelia all but married. Then, unexpectedly three years ago, the Super Couple had broken up—amicably but permanently, they'd insisted, even though some people still believed, even hoped, they'd reunite.

They hadn't. It didn't look as if they would. But everyone was still friends.

Except for the eighteen months after Harper's father had purchased the Double Diamond. Cole and Mia had broken up, and Cole had disappeared without a trace.

Eventually he'd come back, and the past two winters he'd worked for Sam Crockett on Paradise. Everyone said he was fine.

"Earth to Harpo."

His hand waved in front of her face. She shook her head, and suddenly she was staring at him, having missed every word he'd said. And there were flutters, deep and unmistakably caused by his proximity.

She blinked. "Oh! I'm sorry. What were you saying?"

He laughed again. "Are you all right?"

No. No, no, no. This was unacceptable. As happy as she was to see him, these were not the memories she'd been after. This was not a reaction she wanted—this electric anticipation that had been thrumming through her body ever since he'd walked into the church that morning almost late for the service.

"I'm fine."

"You still do it." He peered at her, grinning again.

"Do what?"

"Go off into that little artist's daze. I always wondered what you were seeing while you were in those trances. Usually you'd disappear after one of them, and we'd find you in some corner painting or drawing. But you weren't big on showing me your work. I was left thinking you'd gotten some great vision or prophecy. Like now."

She nearly choked on her laughter. "I do not do that! And believe me, I was having no visions of any kind. I was seeing three chickens laughing at me, so I was plotting revenge."

That was a lie, but he didn't need to know it.

"Well, you *did* go into trances, but who am I to argue? If this was only revenge plotting, I think you're justified. You are kind of a mud ball, aren't you?"

His familiar, mischievous voice finally calmed her, sent her gaze downward to survey the damage to her only dressy clothes, and, most importantly, made her think the whole episode including the wet clothing, was funny. She lifted her eyes.

"I dunno. I think mud is the new chic."

"Aw, Harpo, if mud is in, then you look fantastic." He hesitated and studied her, his bright blue eyes as warm as his smile. "You look pretty fantastic even if mud isn't a fashion statement."

She lifted her face to the sky, letting the rain that was starting to slow into huge drops burst like little water balloons on her cheeks, keeping the heat in them from showing.

"Yeah? Well, thank you, my old silver-tongued friend. But you know you're going to look equally fantastic if you stay out here much longer."

Without thinking, she brushed raindrops off the shoulders of his shirt, skimming their broad expanse twice with cupped fingers. Then she flicked drops from his hair. The tousled, just-out-of-bed look was beginning to flatten like the chickens' wet feathers.

He stared at her, and she jerked her hand away, dismayed by her bold touches.

"You should get back inside," she said. "I was on my way to the barn to find Joely, but the chickens' gate got unlatched. I had to side track. I'll get these last three chickens and join you."

"I'll help. It'll go faster."

"That's silly. You'll only get muddy, too."

"No, just wet. Because unlike you, I'm good at this."

"Oh, wow. There was a gauntlet hitting the lawn with a giant, rippling splash."

He grinned. She returned it.

"He who returns the most remaining chickens to the yard, gets to…" Cole made a show of thinking up the prize. "Put anything he wants on a piece of Melanie's lefse and make the loser eat it."

"Oh my gosh, what are you? Ten?" She sputtered with more laughter.

Melanie Thorson, the Southern belle wife of Paradise Ranch's foreman who was, in contrast, a first generation Norwegian-American through and through, had learned to make the best lefse this side of Oslo. The trouble was, a mean person could stuff it with anything from cinnamon sugar to pickled herring.

"Deal or no deal?" Cole asked, his handsome nose now dripping water.

"Oh, it's a deal. But I warn you, the winner? *She* is going to come up with something really disgusting."

"Dream on. One, two, three, go. Catch one if you can, Harpo."

The three chickens had huddled for safety and shelter beneath a huge linden tree, but the instant Harper and Cole took off, the birds clucked into panic mode and went three different directions like possessed bobblehead dolls. Harper went after the Cochin that had left her in the grass and caught her in seconds.

"Hah!" She held up the chicken in triumph, only to see Cole with a flapping Plymouth Rock hen.

"Lucky," he called.

"You keep thinking that," she replied.

They reincarcerated the two chickens and turned to the last escapee. This hen, Harper knew, was the oldest chicken in the flock, the only Rhode Island Red, a hen that had been around at least five or six years. She was wily and stubborn and laid a lot of eggs.

"Roxie Red," Harper said, in the same tone she might have said "Lizzie Borden."

"They all have names, don't they?" Cole asked.

"He always named them, but I don't know what they are. Who can tell them apart? She stands out, the old, cranky biddy."

"Don't you worry your head," he teased. "Let me take care of her."

"Not on your life."

The ridiculousness of their impromptu game felt a little disrespectful given the reason she and Cole were really here, but Harper couldn't rein in the streak of temporary insanity she'd obviously caught from the chickens. At last she'd found the release—the relief—she'd wanted.

They chased the crafty old hen for five full minutes, cutting each other off, herding her into corners, cooing softly but then charging when she dodged and bobbed like a running back. Harper swore the old girl was having as much fun as they were. At last she managed to streak ahead of Cole and reach Roxie as the hen made it to the rabbit fencing around her mother and grandmother's huge vegetable garden behind the coop.

"Gotcha!" She sprang forward, but she tripped and landed on Cole's arm. His hand covered hers as both of them grasped simultaneously for the scolding Roxie.

"Get away from my bird!" Harper shot Cole a withering look.

"Hands off *my* chicken." His voice was high-pitched with mirth.

Roxie flapped easily away, and Harper dissolved into laughter, splayed once again face down on the ground. She lifted her head to find Cole flat on his back gasping for air. He reached across her back, grabbed her arm, and rolled her over, until she, too, lay on her back, her head cradled on his shoulder.

Her first shivering instinct was to leap away, but his laughter held her in place—rumbly and comforting beneath her.

"Remember when we used to do shit like this all the time?" he asked.

"Again," she said, firming her voice so it didn't match her wayward, quivering insides, "when we were ten."

"It's really good to see you, Harpo."

"Yeah." She closed her eyes while the rain splashed her face again, definitely feeling closer to ten than her sometimes ancient-seeming thirty.

They lay a moment longer, letting their laughter ebb, but then, with her heart pounding, Harper came to her senses and scrambled to her feet. It had to be the raw, seesaw emotions of the day causing this unwarranted reaction to him. Her friendship with Cole went back too far for her to allow some rogue attraction to take root. He and Amelia might be ex-lovers, but there was a code between sisters you didn't break.

She held out her hand this time, and he took it. Once he was standing, she dropped the contact.

"I declare this a tie," she said. "I propose we work together to get the chicken and neither of us has to eat lefse."

"We call it a tie. I'll help you catch the chicken. We both eat lefse," he said, making a counteroffer.

"Oh, fine."

Once they weren't sabotaging each other, they cornered Roxie and had her in custody within two minutes.

Since Harper was the dirtiest—and she was extremely dirty—she carried the ticked-off chicken to the coop. Once she'd double-checked the gate, she sagged against it, wet to the skin and slightly chilled from the breeze, despite it being August.

"Thank you," she said, as her adrenaline drained away and took her energy with it. "I'm sorry you got caught up in the rodeo."

"Don't be. The company inside was…frankly, not this much fun."

"I never asked why you came out here in the first place."

He gave a quick frown, an attractive wrinkle forming between his brows. He'd changed over the past decade. All signs of the cute-faced boy and young man he'd been had disappeared beneath the angles and planes of a stunning adult-male face.

"Oh yeah, I guess I did have an official mission," he said. "Joely got back from the barn fifteen minutes ago, and we wondered where you ended up. Your grandmother has called an all-hands meeting."

"Grandma Sadie?" She shouldn't have been surprised. Sadie Crockett had to be the only nonagenarian who could still command her family like a naval admiral. "What's our matriarch got under her bonnet now? Another private prayer meeting? A final eulogy? Can't be about the will; that isn't a secret."

"I don't know," Cole said. "The only thing she told me was that attendance isn't optional."

"Crazy old lady," Harper said fondly, feeling the mood start to slide.

Grandma Sadie wasn't even a little crazy. She was still sharp as a pinprick, and if she wanted a meeting, she had all the moral authority in the world. At ninety-four she had buried a son.

As Harper and her sisters had buried a father.

As their mother had buried a husband.

And not one of them understood how Samuel Crockett could be dead. In the space of a finger snap, the hurricane that had been his big, intense life had gone aground and dissipated long before any expert had predicted or expected.

She tried to cling to the silliness of the chicken chase, but it was fully gone. A tear escaped, and she swiped it away before it could traverse her cheek. They'd all cried plenty in the past days. Wasn't that enough of a tribute to the man who'd inspired awe, respect, sometimes even adulation, but never warm, schmaltzy emotion?

Cole's arm came around her, and he pulled her close. She felt his kiss on the top of her head.

"Look." He pointed across the yard, past the working heart of Paradise Ranch with its barns, sheds, and cattle pens, to the view of Grand Teton National Park sixty-five miles away. In the deep purple sky over the mountains, one fat sunbeam had beaten back the rain clouds to create a brilliant rainbow. "I think that came out for you," he said. "You've always known how to pull hope out of a rain cloud."

How did he know to say something that would soothe her so perfectly?

"If only my father had shown me a fraction of that kind of insight. After all these years—that was really nice of you to say."

"You weren't big on letting us see your work when we were younger, but I still caught wisps of your talent. We all did. I know you still have it."

She wanted to tell him then. She'd promised herself not to say anything to anyone about her news until after the funeral. This was not about her and her dreams—this was about her father and the end of his. She stared at the sky and, in her mind, mixed the oil colors that would approximate its vivid beauty on canvas.

Her fingers itched for her brushes. Her head and heart longed for a secluded room and an easel. But she hadn't brought any supplies with her from Chicago. She'd contented herself with a sketchbook and case of pencils. This trip was not about escape, and a good daughter wouldn't keep wishing for it. Then again, when had she ever been the good daughter?

The rainbow intensified. Cole held her more tightly. The rain slowed further, and after a few more moments, she realized it had stopped altogether.

"I guess we should go in. I volunteered to find Joely for purely selfish reasons—I wanted to get away."

"There's nothing wrong with that."

"I should be in with the rest of the family. It seems better if I don't spend too much time with Mia, and I was one step from having to organize food with her. Not a good plan."

"Your Mia? Dr. Amelia Crockett, the very one who keeps all order and makes all peace? Why would you need to keep your distance from your sister?"

"Amelia moved out a dozen years ago and has never looked back. We haven't lived together in all that time. But to her, I'm still the hippie screw-up, the sister who couldn't be organized if her life depended on it. She's a lot like Dad. I get tired of her telling me what to do as if I don't understand the world." She laughed humorlessly. "She was always the border collie, and I was the sheep she couldn't get into the pen."

"I miss the border collies," he said. "Loved the ones we had. But Mia is no border collie, Harpo. She doesn't care where the sheep go—she's only worried about her own destination. She's more like a bloodhound."

"I disagree. Mia could organize squirrels to line dance if she wanted to. Sorry. I'm speaking ill of your ex."

Harper hoped no old bitterness bled through the words. Childhood pettiness had no place in their lives anymore, especially at a time like this.

"I love Mia," he said, "and I'm sorry things are strained between you. But 'ex' is the operative word here, so I'm not necessarily on her side. I think this is a hard time, and you sisters haven't been around each other enough to smooth things over. Give it time."

"Okay, enough of the sensitive cowboy."

That was another thing she was remembering about Cole. For a ranch-loving cowboy, he'd always been accused of having a streak of insight and chivalry in him that most macho guys lacked. The soul of a cowboy poet. It was why he'd once juxtaposed so well with the straight-shooting, ultra-efficient Amelia.

"Hey, I'm no cowboy anymore. At least not most of the time."

"Oh yeah," she said, glad to leave talk and thoughts of Mia behind. "You have some sort of mechanic's job now."

"I work for a company that contracts out big-machinery mechanics to anyone who needs them. It's not a bad fit for me during the summer. I always liked working on the equipment around here and home. I'm staying on here through the winter now, though. I left the other job early when I heard about your dad. Leif and Bjorn will need all the help they can get, and I was coming back in three weeks at the beginning of September anyhow."

Her heart squeezed at the mention of Leif and Bjorn Thorson. Leif had been her father's right-hand man for forty years. His son, Bjorn, was now the best foreman any ranch owner could ask for. They were devastated by the loss of their tough, savvy boss. Harper felt worse for them than she did for herself.

"You're a good guy, Cole. It can't be easy for you to come back since the Double Diamond was sold."

He shook his head. "I was really angry at first. But not at your father like you might think. He did my dad a favor by buying him out so we didn't have to sell to developers. But I was furious at my father for giving up. For selling off our legacy."

"And still, you came back to work for the enemy."

"I got over it. I understand what happened to the Double Diamond, and my father made the only choice he could. But I won't lie. I'm not letting it out of my sight, and I'll stick around until I can get it back. I'm damn close, Harpo. I'd almost convinced Sam he didn't really want to keep that little piece of property."

"It is a gorgeous hunk of land."

"The Double Di was in my family as long as Paradise has been in yours. I'd like to be the one to restore the legacy."

"Ironic."

"What is?"

"Out of four tries and six children, my dad didn't get a son—or even a daughter—who wants this place as much as your father's one child wants his. You lost yours to our passel of ingrates."

"I wasn't going to say it."

"Hey." She frowned. "You're not supposed to agree with me."

"Hey." He echoed her. "This is an astounding legacy you girls walked away from."

She felt the slight, sudden tension. "C'mon, Cole. You know how he was. It was impossible to fall in love with a place that was run like a cross between boarding school and a tough-love boot camp for delinquents."

"I do admit, your father was the nicest asshole I've ever known."

The accurate oxymoron drew rueful laughter from Harper, and the tension dissipated. "Yeah. And nobody said that out loud at the service did they?"

"Funerals aren't for honesty. You know that. And Sam was a good man. He wasn't cruel."

"Just obsessed," she said.

"Exacting. Demanding." He nodded.

"Arrogant." Harper sighed. "He chose Amelia to take over, but in truth I think he had his best chance at an heir with Raquel. He lost her when the other two triplets left. She wasn't about to stay here alone. Besides, my father's hired workers always did better dealing with his rigidness than we did."

"If you did your job around him, showed a little initiative, based on his standards, of course, he left you alone," Cole said. "On the other hand, look what he built because of those standards. This place is spectacular. The man was brilliant."

"He was that."

She looked up, surprised to see they'd left the chicken coop and nearly reached the long, triple-level back deck of the big log ranch house, surrounded by its trellises of stunning blue and lavender morning glories—her mother's favorite flowers. The chickens might have the Hilton because of her father, but the family had this warm, wonderful place, Rosecroft, because of their mother. Bella Crockett had designed and decorated the big house, planning its charm from the ground up, including the name because she'd fallen in love with the tradition of naming homes during a trip to Scotland in her youth. It was the one place on Paradise Ranch Harper always missed.

To her surprise, Cole picked up her hand and squeezed it between both of his. He'd held it plenty of times in their lives—after she'd been teased on the school bus, the first time she'd been bucked off a horse—but the strong, long-fingered, broad-nailed hand engulfing hers caused as much trembling as it did comfort. "The bottom line is Sam Crockett left us too soon."

"Not that long ago, sixty-eight would have been *old*," she murmured.

"He might have been an ass once in a while, but your father was not old."

She nodded and sighed. "I figured he'd live forever."

They both hesitated, as if heading up to the back door was something neither of them wanted.

"I hear you're not staying long," he said. "That's too bad. Are you sure you don't want to hang around another week or so? Take some rides around the old place, for the heck of it?"

She debated only a moment before lifting her eyes to his, a slow burn of excitement taking the place of heavy sadness. "Can I swear you to secrecy?"

"Ah, intrigue. Sure." He crossed his heart, eyes sparkling.

"Tristan, you remember me talking about him? He booked me a gallery showing."

The genuine pleasure in Cole's eyes thrilled her. "Seriously?"

She nodded, and before she could elaborate he crushed her into a bear hug and twirled her in place hard enough to swirl her wet skirt in a dripping circle.

"Tristan. He was that hippie-assed boyfriend of yours, right? The one who promised to make you famous?"

Tristan Carmichael was her de facto manager—a fellow artist with far more connections than Harper would ever have. He'd been a…What? A lover for a while. But a boyfriend? She laughed. "He's definitely not my boyfriend."

"Not what I heard."

She frowned at his teasing and finger-flicked him on the shoulder. He laughed and set her down. "The point is, Tristan found a small, classy private gallery and gave them three of my paintings. The owner loved them, sold one the day he put it on display, and he agreed to host a full show. It's scheduled to open a week from tomorrow." Her words came in a rush now. "The gallery is called Crucible—it's on the lakefront in Chicago—and I have a million things to do to get ready…"

He bent. To the shock of her entire body, he slipped a kiss onto her mouth, and she froze. Wrong. This was very wrong. But the kiss fit as if it had been custom made for her lips. Sparklers zipped to life deep inside her belly, and she closed her eyes when she should have pulled away. Whatever scent or aftershave it was that made him smell like a spicy movie star turned her knees to rubber, and she couldn't stop drinking it in.

As kisses went, it was simple. No tongue, no sound. He opened and closed his mouth so lightly on her bottom lip she should barely have felt the butterfly touch, yet shivers rolled down her neck and across her shoulders like explosions.

This was insane.

She gasped and pulled away, avoiding his eyes. "Cole, no. We can't…"

"I'm sorry," he said.

"Mia is—"

"No longer anything except a friend." He turned her face gently with one finger, so she had to meet his smiling eyes. "But still, I know that was too quick. I didn't mean to make you uncomfortable. Especially if there's anyone else—I didn't even ask. I honestly just got excited for you."

Mia was more than his friend. She was and always would be his ex-girlfriend, lover, almost fiancée. No matter how strained her relationship with her sister might be, Harper would never do the stealing thing. The comparison thing.

"There's no one else."

She stared, dumbstruck at herself. That wasn't what she'd intended to say.

"Well, then. That's good." He let her go. "And for the record? It was a good kiss."

It definitely had been that.

"And congratulations on the art showing. I know this is your dream."

"Uh…" She scrambled to regain her composure. "It is. But don't tell anyone."

"Why would you keep it a secret?"

"I didn't feel right celebrating it before Dad's funeral. Tomorrow is soon enough."

"Okay. But then you're shouting it from the rooftop."

Her composure wouldn't quite cooperate by fully returning, but Cole looked down at their clothing and made a face that at least dispelled her awkwardness.

"We'd better go in. I've pushed the limits of your grandmother's timeline. I was supposed to have you back ten minutes ago. She didn't seem much inclined to be patient."

"Grandma gets what she wants, that's for sure. But I'm sure it's something simple like what to do with all the flowers. It has to be."

She looked to him for confirmation, but a surprising shadow of concern crossed his eyes. "I don't know," he said. "In all honesty I got out of the house to procrastinate, too. I had the weird feeling this meeting might be something we all wish it weren't."

About the Author

LIZBETH SELVIG lives in Minnesota with her best friend (aka her husband) and a gray Arabian gelding named Jedi. After working as a newspaper journalist and magazine editor, and raising an equine veterinarian daughter and a talented musician son, Lizbeth won RWA's prestigious Golden Heart Contest® in 2010 with her contemporary romance, *The Rancher and the Rock Star*, and was a 2014 nominee for RWA's RITA® Award with her second published novel, *Rescued by a Stranger*. In her spare time, she loves to hike, quilt, read, horseback ride, and spend time with her new granddaughter. She also has many four-legged grandchildren—more than twenty—including a wallaby, two alpacas, a donkey, a pig, a sugar glider, and many dogs, cats, and horses (pics of all appear on her website www.lizbethselvig.com). She loves connecting with readers—contact her any time!

Discover great authors, exclusive offers, and more at hc.com.

Give in to your Impulses . . .
Continue reading for excerpts from
our newest Avon Impulse books.
Available now wherever e-books are sold.

RIGHT WRONG GUY

A BRIGHTWATER NOVEL

By Lia Riley

DESIRE ME MORE

By Tiffany Clare

MAKE ME

A BROKE AND BEAUTIFUL NOVEL

By Tessa Bailey

An Excerpt from

RIGHT WRONG GUY
A Brightwater Novel
by Lia Riley

Bad boy wrangler Archer Kane lives fast and
loose. Words like *responsibility* and *commitment*
send him running in the opposite direction. Until
a wild Vegas weekend puts him on a collision
course with Eden Bankcroft-Kew, a New York
heiress running away from her blackmailing
fiancé . . . the morning of her wedding.

"Archer?" Eden stared in the motel bathroom mirror, her reflection a study in horror. "Please tell me this is a practical joke."

"We're in the middle of Nevada, sweetheart. There's no Madison Avenue swank in these parts." Archer didn't bother to keep amusement from his answering yell through the closed door. "The gas station only sold a few things. Trust me, those clothes were the best of the bunch."

After he got out of the shower, a very long shower which afforded her far too much time for contemplating him in a cloud of thick steam, running a bar of soap over cut v-lines, he announced that he would find her something suitable to wear. She couldn't cross state lines wearing nothing but his old t-shirt, and while the wedding dress worked in a pinch, it was still damp. Besides, her stomach lurched at the idea of sliding back into satin and lace.

She'd never be able to don a wedding dress and not think of the Reggie debacle. She couldn't even entirely blame him, her subconscious had been sending out warning flares for months. She'd once been considered a smart woman, graduated from NYU with a 4.0 in Art History. So how could she have been so dumb?

Truth be told, it wasn't even due to her mother's dying wish that led her to accepting him, although that certainly bore some influence. No, it was the idea of being alone. The notion didn't feel liberating or "I am woman, hear me roar." More terrified house mouse squeaking alone in a dark cellar.

She clenched her jaw, shooing away the mouse. What was the big deal with being alone? She might wish for more friends, or a love affair, but she'd also never minded her own company. This unexpected turn of events was an opportunity, a time for self-growth, getting to know herself, and figuring out exactly what she wanted. Yes, she'd get empowered all right, roar so loud those California mountains would tremble.

Right after they finished laughing at this outfit.

Seriously, did Archer have to select pink terrycloth booty shorts that spelled *Q & T* in rhinestones, one on each butt cheek? And the low-cut top scooped so even her small rack sported serious cleavage. *Get Lucky* emblazoned across the chest, the tank top was an XS so the letters stretched to the point of embarrassment. If she raised her hands over her head, her belly button winked out.

As soon as she arrived in Brightwater, she'd invest in proper clothes and send for her belongings back home. Until then . . . time to face the music. She stepped from the bathroom, chewing the corner of her lip. Archer didn't burst into snickers. All he did was stare. His playful gaze vanished, replaced by a startling intensity.

"Well, go on then. Get it over with and make fun of me." She gathered her hair into a messy bun, securing it with a hair elastic from her wrist she found in her purse.

"Laughing's not the first thing that jumps to mind, sweetheart."

Her stomach sank. "Horror then?"

"Stop." He rubbed the back of his neck, that wicked sensual mouth curving into a bold smile. "You're hot as hell."

Reggie had never remarked on her appearance. She sucked in a ragged breath at the memory of his text. *Bored me to fucking tears.*

"Hey, Freckles," he said softly. "You okay?"

She snapped back, unsure what her face revealed. "Tiny shorts and boob shirts do it for you?" She fought for an airy tone, waving her hand over the hot pink "QT" abomination and praying he wouldn't notice her tremble.

He gave a one-shouldered shrug. "Short shorts do it for all warm-blooded men."

"I'll keep that in mind," she said, thumbing her ear. He probably wasn't checking *her* out, just her as the closest female specimen in the immediate vicinity.

He wiggled out of his tan Carhart jacket and held it out. "You'll want this. Temperatures are going to top out in the mid-forties today. I've stuck a wool blanket in the passenger seat and will keep the heat cranking."

Strange. He might be a natural flirt, but for all his easy confidence, there was an uncertainty in how he regarded her. A hesitation that on anyone else could be described as vulnerability, the type of look that caused her to volunteer at no-kill rescue shelters and cry during cheesy life insurance commercials. A guy like this, what did he know about insecurity or self-doubt? But that expression went straight to her heart. "Archer . . ."

He startled at the sound of his real name, instead of the Cowboy moniker she'd used the last twenty-four hours.

His jacket slipped, baring her shoulders as she reached to take one of his big hands in hers. "Thank you." Impulsively, she rose on tiptoe to kiss his cheek, but he jerked with surprise and she grazed the appealing no-man's land between his dimple and lips.

This was meant to be a polite gesture, an acknowledgment he'd been a nice guy, stepped up and helped her—a stranger—out when she'd barreled in and given him no choice.

He smelled good. Too good. Felt good too. She should move—now—but his free hand, the one she wasn't clutching, skimmed her lower back. Was this a kiss?

No.

Well . . . almost.

Never had an actual kiss sent goose bumps prickling down her spine even as her stomach heated, the cold and hot reaction as confused as her thoughts. Imagine what the real thing would do.

An Excerpt from

DESIRE ME MORE
by Tiffany Clare

From the moment Amelia Grant accepted the position of secretary to Nicholas Riley, London's most notorious businessman, she knew her life would be changed forever. For Nick didn't want just her secretarial skills . . . he wanted her complete surrender. And she was more than willing to give it to him, spending night after night in delicious sin. As the devastatingly insatiable Nick teaches her the ways of forbidden desire, Amelia begins to dream of a future together . . .

Why hadn't she just stayed in bed? Instead, she'd set herself on an unknown path. One without Nick. Why? She hated this feeling that was ripping her apart from the inside out. It hurt so much and so deeply that the wounds couldn't be healed.

Biting her bottom lip on a half-escaped sob, she violently wiped her tears away with the back of her hand. Nick caught her as she fumbled with the lock on the study door, spinning her around and wrapping his arms tightly around her, crushing her against his solid body.

She wanted to break down. To just let the tears overtake her. But she held strong.

"I have already told you I can't let you go. Stay, Amelia." His voice was so calm, just above a whisper. "Please, I couldn't bear it if you left me. I can't let you leave. I won't."

Hearing him beg tugged at her heart painfully. Amelia's fists clenched where they were trapped between their bodies. There was only one thing she could do.

She pushed him away, hating that she was seconds away from breaking down. Hating that she knew that she had to hold it together when every second in his arms chipped away at her control.

"You are breaking my will every day. Making me lose myself in you. Don't ask this of me. Please. Nick. Let me go."

If she stayed, they would only end up back where they were. And she needed more than his physical comfort. He held her tighter against his chest, crushing her between him and the door like he would *never* let her go.

"I told you I couldn't let you go. Don't try to leave. I warned you that you were mine the night I took your virginity."

Tilting her head back, she stared at him, eyes awash with tears she was helpless to stop from flowing over her cheeks. "Why are you doing this to me?"

The gray of his eyes were stormy, as though waiting to unleash a fury she'd never seen the likes of. "Because I can't let you go. Because I love you."

His tone brooked no argument, so she said nothing to contradict him, just stared at him for another moment before pushing at his immovable body again. Nick's hand gently cradled her throat, his thumb forcing her head to lean against the door.

"I've already told you that I wouldn't let you walk away. You belong to me."

Her lips parted on a half exasperated groan at his declaration of ownership over her.

"How could I belong to you when you close yourself off to me? I will not be controlled by you, no matter what I feel—"

Before she could get out the rest of her sentence, Nick's mouth took hers in an all-consuming kiss, his tongue robbing her of breath as it pushed past the barrier of her lips and tangled with her tongue in wordless need.

Hunger rose in her, whether it was for physical desire or a need to draw as much of him into her as possible was hard to say. And she hated herself a little for not pushing him away again and again until she won this argument. Not now that she had a small piece of him all to herself. Even if it wouldn't be enough in the end.

Without a doubt in her mind, she'd never crave anything as badly as she craved Nick: his essence, his strength, *him*.

Her hands fisted around his shirtsleeves, holding him close. She didn't want to let go . . . of him or the moment.

His touch was like a branding iron as he tugged the hemline of her dress from her shoulders, pulling down the front of the dress. The pull rent the delicate satin material, leaving one breast on display for Nick to fondle. His hand squeezed her, the tips of his short nails digging into her flesh.

Their mouths didn't part once, almost as if Nick wanted to distract her from her original purpose. Keep her thinking of their kiss. The way their tongues slid knowingly against the other. The way he tasted like coffee and danger. Forbidden. Like the apple from the tree he was a temptation she could not refuse.

His distraction was working.

And his hands were everywhere.

An Excerpt from

MAKE ME
A Broke and Beautiful Novel
by *Tessa Bailey*

In the final Broke and Beautiful novel from
bestselling author Tessa Bailey, a blue collar
construction worker and a quiet uptown virgin
are about to discover that the friend zone
can sometimes be excellent foreplay . . .

Day one hundred and forty-two of being friend-zoned. Send rations.

Russell Hart stifled a groan when Abby twisted on his lap to call out a drink order to the passing waiter, adding a smile that would no doubt earn her a martini on the house. Every time their six-person "super group" hung out, which was starting to become a nightly affair, Russell advanced into a newer, more vicious circle of hell. Tonight, however, he was pretty sure he'd meet the devil himself.

They were at the Longshoreman, celebrating the Fourth of July, which presented more than one precious little clusterfuck. One, the holiday meant the bar was packed full of tipsy Manhattanites, creating a shortage of chairs, hence Abby parking herself right on top of his dick. Two, it put the usually conservative Abby in ass-hugging shorts and one of those tops that tied at the back of her neck. Six months ago, he would have called it a *shirt*, but his two best friends had fallen down the relationship rabbit hole, putting him in the vicinity of excessive chick talk. So, now it was a halter top. What he wouldn't *give* to erase that knowledge.

During their first round of drinks, he'd become a believer in breathing exercises. Until he'd noticed these tiny, blond curls at Abby's nape, curls he'd never seen before. And some-fucking-how, those sun-kissed curls were what had nudged him from semierect to full-scale Washington-monument status. The hair on the rest of her head was like a . . . a warm milk-chocolate color, so where did those little curls come from? *Those* detrimental musings had led to Russell question-ing what else he didn't know about Abby. What color was everything else? Did she have freckles? Where?

Russell would not be finding out—ever—and not just be-cause he was sitting in the friend zone with his dick wedged against his stomach—*not* an easy maneuver—so she wouldn't feel it. No, there was more to it. His friends, Ben and Louis, were well aware of those reasons, which accounted for the half-sympathetic, half-needling looks they were sending him from across the table, respective girlfriends perched on their laps. The jerks.

Abby was off-limits. Not because she was taken—thank Christ—or because someone had verbally forbidden him from pursuing her. That wasn't it. Russell had taken a long time trying to find a suitable explanation for why he didn't just get the girl alone one night and make his move. Explain to her that men like him weren't suitable friends for wide-eyed debutantes and give her a demonstration of the alternative.

It went like this. Abby was like an expensive package that had been delivered to him by mistake. Someone at the post office had screwed the pooch and dropped off the shiniest, most beautiful creation on his Queens doorstep and driven away, laughing manically. Russell wasn't falling for the trick, though. Someone would claim the package, eventually. They would chuckle over the obvious mistake and take Abby away from him because, really, he had no business being the one whose lap she chose to sit on. No business whatsoever.

But while he was in possession of the package—as much as he'd *allow* himself to be in possession, anyway—he would guard her with his life. He would make sure that when someone realized the cosmic error that had occurred—the one that had made him Abby's friend and confidant—she would be sweet and undamaged, just as she'd been on arrival.

Unfortunately, the package didn't seem content to let him stand guard from a distance. She innocently beckoned him back every time he managed to put an inch of space between them. Russell had lost count of the times Abby had fallen asleep on him while the super group watched a movie, drank margaritas on the girls' building's rooftop, driven home in cabs. She was entirely too comfortable around him, considering he saluted against his fly every time they were in the same room.

"Why so quiet, Russell?" Louis asked, his grin turning to a wince as his actress girlfriend, Roxy, elbowed him in the ribs. Yeah. Everyone at the damn table knew he had a major thing for the beautiful, unassuming number whiz on his lap. Everyone but Abby. And that's how he planned to keep it.